Richa... ....
May 2... .... won the Bram Stoker .... .ard for
Best Hor.. .r ..Tovel, a prize for which Laymon had previously been
shortlisted with *Flesh, Funland, A Good, Secret Place* (Best Anthology)
and *A Writer's Tale* (Best Non-fiction). Laymon's works include the
books of the Beast House Chronicles: *The Cellar, The Beast House* and
The Midnight Tour. Some of his recent novels have been *Night in the
Lonesome October, No Sanctuary* and *Amara.*

A native of Chicago, Laymon attended Willamette University in
Salem, Oregon, and took an MA in English Literature from Loyola
University, Los Angeles. In 2000, he was elected President of the Horror
Writers Association. He died in February 2001.

Laymon's fiction is published in the United Kingdom by Headline,
and in the United States by Leisure Books and Cemetery Dance
Publications. To learn more, visit the Laymon website at: http://
rlk.cjb.net

'A gut-crunching writer' *Time Out*

'Incapable of writing a disappointing book' *New York Review of Science
Fiction*

'No one writes like Laymon and you're going to have a good time with
anything he writes' Dean Koontz

'One of the best, and most underrated, writers working in the genre
today' *Cemetery Dance*

'This author knows how to sock it to the reader' *The Times*

'This is an author that does not pull his punches . . . A gripping, and at
times genuinely shocking, read' *SFX Magazine*

'A brilliant writer' *Sunday Express*

Beware!

and

Dark Mountain

headline

BEWARE! first published in Great Britain in 1985
by New English Library

DARK MOUNTAIN first published in Great Britain in 1987
by New English Library

First published in this omnibus edition in 2006
by HEADLINE BOOK PUBLISHING

A HEADLINE paperback

5

ISBN 978 0 7553 3171 0

Typeset in Janson by Avon DataSet Ltd, Bidford on Avon, Warwickshire

Printed and bound in Great Britain by
CPI Group (UK) Ltd, Croydon, CR0 4YY

Headline's policy is to use papers that are natural, renewable and recyclable
products and made from wood grown in sustainable forests. The logging and
manufacturing processes are expected to conform to the environmental
regulations of the country of origin.

HEADLINE BOOK PUBLISHING
A division of Hodder Headline
338 Euston Road
London NW1 3BH

www.headline.co.uk
www.hodderheadline.com

Beware!

Chapter One

On the night it began, Frank and Joan Bessler left the stifling heat of their home and walked four blocks to Hoffman's Market. Frank wanted a six-pack.

'Doesn't look open,' Joan said.

'It has to be.' Frank checked his wristwatch. 'I've got nine-fifteen.'

'Why aren't the lights on?'

'Maybe she's saving on electricity,' he said. He hoped he was right, but didn't believe it. For as far back as he could remember – and he'd spent all of his twenty-nine years in Oasis – the market had remained brightly lighted until closing time.

Closing time was ten o'clock to keep an edge on the Safeway that shut at nine. When Elsie Hoffman's husband died, three years ago, there'd been talk she might sell out, or at least close down earlier. But she'd held onto the tiny market and kept it open till the usual hour.

'I do think it's closed,' Joan said as they stopped by its deserted parking lot.

The store sign was dark. The only light in the windows was a dim glow from the bulb Elsie always left on overnight.

'I can't believe it,' Frank muttered

'She must've had a reason.'

'Maybe she changed hours on us.'

Joan waited on the sidewalk, and Frank stepped up to the wooden door. Crouching, he squinted at the window sticker. Not enough light for him to read the times.

He tried the knob

No go.

He peered through the window, and saw no one. 'Damn,' he muttered. He knocked on the glass. Couldn't hurt. Maybe Elsie was in the back someplace, out of sight.

'Come on, Frank. She's closed.'

'I'm *thirsty*.' He rapped harder on the window.

'We'll go over to the Golden Oasis. I'd rather have a margarita, anyway.'

'Yeah, well, okay.'

He took a final look into the dimly lighted store, then turned away. Behind him, the door banged and shook.

Frank jumped. Whirling around, he stared at the door, at its four glass panes.

'What was that?' Joan asked in a whisper.

'I don't know.'

'Come on, let's go.'

He backed away, staring at the windows, and decided he would have a heart attack, then and there, if a face should suddenly appear. He turned away fast before it could happen.

'Who's minding the mint?' Red asked.

Elsie sipped her whisky sour. It was sweet and tart. Nobody could make whisky sours like Red. 'I closed up a little early,' she said.

'Must get lonely in there.'

'I tell you, Red, I'm not as young as I used to be, not by a long shot, but I've still got my senses. I haven't gone mush-brained. Not yet. Wouldn't you say so?'

'You're sharp as a tack, Elsie. Always have been.'

'Now, I went through pure hell when Herb passed on. Miserable old skinflint that he was, I did love the man. But that was three years ago, come October. I've perked up pretty well since then. Even at my worst, though – right after I lost him – I never cracked up.'

'You were solid as a rock, Elsie.' He glanced down the bar. 'Right back,' he said, and went away to serve a new customer.

Elsie sipped her drink. She looked both ways. To her left was Beck Ramsey, his arm around the Walters girl. A pity on her, Elsie thought. Beck would bring her nothing but trouble. To her right, separated from Elsie by an empty stool, sat the newspaper gal, Lacey Allen. A pretty thing. The men say she's a cold fish, but they'll say that about any gal who won't drop her pants first time you smile at her. She always seemed pleasant enough in the store. A pity to see her sitting all alone at the bar like she didn't have a friend in the world.

'You're an educated lady.'

Lacey looked over at her. 'Me?'

'Sure. Went to Stanford and all. You're a doctor of something.'

'English lit.'

'Right. Probably one of the best educated folks in town. So you tell me something, if you don't mind my asking.'

She shrugged. 'All right. I'd be happy to try.'

'Is there such a thing as ghosts?'

'Ghosts?'

'You know. Ghosts, spirits of dead folks, haunts.'

Lacey shook her head. 'You've got me. I've never seen one. All through history, though, people have claimed they exist.' She looked away from Elsie, picked up her wine glass, and raised it to her lips. But she didn't drink. Her eyes suddenly opened wide. She gazed at Elsie, and set down her glass. 'Did *you* see one?'

'Don't know what I saw. Not sure I saw anything.'

'Mind if I . . . ?' Lacey looked at the empty stool between them.

'Help yourself.'

She slid off her stool and climbed onto the one beside Elsie.

'This is just between us. I don't want to be written up in the *Trib*, everyone in town saying Elsie's got cards gone.'

'I promise.'

'Okay then.'

A hand from behind patted her shoulder. She jumped, splashing her dress.

'Jeez, I'm sorry!'

'Lord!' She looked around. 'Frank, you scared the daylights outa me!'

'I'm really sorry. Gosh, I . . .'

'Well, that's all right.'

'Let me get you another drink.'

'I won't argue with that.'

He nodded a greeting to Lacey, then smiled at Elsie. 'I guess I owed you a scare, though, after the one I just got at your store.'

'What do you mean?'

'Have you got a watchdog in there, or something?'

'What happened?'

'We were over at your place a few minutes ago. I looked in the door, you know, to see if you were in, and something gave it a bash you wouldn't believe. Scared the socks off me.'

'Did you see what it was?' Lacey asked.

'I didn't see anything. It sure gave me a start, though. Did you get yourself a dog, Elsie?'

'I don't keep animals. All they do is die on you.'

'What was it, then?'

'I wish I knew,' Elsie said. 'Heard something, myself, around nine. Sounded like someone walking. I looked everywhere – up and down the aisles, back in the storage room. I even checked the meat locker. No one in the store but yours truly. Then the cash register opened on its own accord, and that did it. I closed up.'

'Maybe you've got a ghost,' Frank said, half grinning.

'That's what I wonder,' Elsie said. 'What do you think, Lacey?'

'I think we should drive over to your store and take a look.'

* * *

Lacey swung her car into the parking lot of Hoffman's Market.

'Why don't you wait here,' Frank told his wife.

'And miss the fun?' She flung open a rear door, climbed out, and smiled at Lacey. 'You think we'll make the paper?'

'That depends on what's inside,' she said, and followed Elsie to the door.

'We'll make the paper for sure,' said Frank, 'if we all get slaughtered in there.'

Elsie frowned over her shoulder. 'You do talk, Frank.'

'If you're so nervous,' Joan told him, 'maybe *you* should wait in the car.'

'And let you get slaughtered without me? How would that look?'

Elsie peered through a window. 'I don't see anything. Course, I didn't before.'

'Let's go in,' Lacey whispered. She rubbed her arms. In spite of the night's heat, she had goosebumps. Maybe this wasn't such a great idea, she decided as Elsie pushed the key into the lock. But it had been *her* idea. She could hardly back out now. Besides, she did want to find out what had caused the trouble.

Elsie pushed open the door and entered. Lacey followed her in. The hardwood floor creaked under their footsteps. They stopped near the counter. Except for the light from a ceiling fixture near the door, the store was dark. Lacey could see only a short distance up the aisles.

'Maybe you could turn on some . . .'

'Holy shit!'

She swung around. Frank's hand was still on the door. He'd stopped in the midst of shutting it. He and Joan stood motionless, staring.

'I'll be . . .' said Elsie.

Lacey walked to the door and crouched. 'Wicked looking thing,' she said. The meat cleaver was buried deep in the wood only inches beneath the lower windows.

'A little higher . . .' Frank muttered.

'That's what hit the door!' Joan cried.

'That's right.'

'God, you could've been killed!'

Lacey stood up. 'I think we'd better get out of here.'

'Yeah,' Frank said. 'And quick. Whoever threw that sucker isn't fooling around.'

'Shouldn't we call the police?' Elsie asked.

'From the bar. Come on.'

Oasis Tribune
Saturday, July 12

BURGLAR ATTACKS LOCAL MAN

Frank Bessler, local TV repairman, narrowly escaped injury last night when he interrupted a burglary in progress at Hoffman's Market.

Bessler and his wife, Joan, arrived at the market shortly after it was closed for the night by its proprietor, Elsie Hoffman. As Bessler peered inside, the front door was shaken by a cleaver thrown by an unseen assailant.

Police were summoned after Bessler notified Mrs Hoffman of the occurrence. The responding patrolman, Ralph Lewis, searched the market and determined that the assailant had fled.

No signs of forced entry were found. According to Mrs Hoffman, no money was taken. The empty wrappers of two T-bone steaks were discovered behind the meat counter, along with an empty bottle of wine.

Elsie Hoffman, who has operated the market alone since the demise of her husband, admits she is troubled by the burglary and the assault on Bessler, but has no plans to change the store's hours of operation. 'Fear can run your life if you let it,' she states. 'I won't let it run mine.

Says Bessler, 'I went in for a beer and almost bought a farm.'

Oasis Tribune
Tuesday, July 15

MARKET HIT AGAIN

Hoffman's Market, over the weekend, was again the target of an unknown vandal. Opening her store for business, Monday morning, proprietor Elsie Hoffman found the empty wrappings of beef, potato chips, and other edibles scattered about the floor.

'Looks like someone had another feast,' commented Mrs Hoffman, whose store was the scene of a similar invasion on Friday night. On that occasion, local TV repairman Frank Bessler barely escaped serious injury when the surprised vandal hurled a meat cleaver at his head.

Police believe that both incidents are the work of the same individual. To date, nobody has seen the perpetrator. Nor is it known how he gains entry to the store.

Red Peterson, bartender at the Golden Oasis and a long-standing friend of Mrs Hoffman, has offered his German Shepherd, Rusty, to guard the market's premises. 'I'll put Rusty up against any ten hooligans, and we'll just see who takes a bite out of what,' says Red.

Mrs Hoffman has agreed to use the dog in hopes of preventing further losses.

Chapter Two

Dusk settled over Bayou Lafourche, and the participants began to arrive. They came in dinghies and skiffs and canoes, silently paddling or poling their way around the bend, landing on the high ground and dragging their vessels ashore.

The man's black, sweaty face looked grim in the telescopic sight of Matthew Dukane's rifle. 'Smile,' Dukane said. Though his whisper seemed loud, he doubted anyone would hear him. He was sitting astraddle a branch high in the tree. Even in total silence, those below would be unlikely to catch his whisper; in all this din, they didn't stand a chance.

A Chicago boy, Dukane didn't know what the hell was causing such a racket. The place sounded like the Brookfield Zoo gone manic. Or the jungles of Vietnam.

He sighted in an old, white crone. A teenaged girl with corn-rows. A fat white man who looked like a good ol' boy. A bony red-haired gal. A strikingly beautiful mulatto woman. A black fellow with the build of a Sumo wrestler.

Quite a congregation, Dukane thought. But then, Laveda was quite a woman. Hard to imagine anyone so beautiful could be so damned evil.

She hadn't shown herself yet. That was her style, though. Like most ladies who thought too highly of themselves, she had a fondness for dramatic entrances.

The drums began. Dukane glanced at the three drummers. They were all black men, naked to the waist, squatting at the edge of the clearing with their drums between their legs. They thumped the skins with their open hands.

Dukane looked away, and saw another skiff land. Its lone occupant climbed out. A white girl in cut-offs and a T-shirt. Quite attractive. He found her in the scope. The girl was

8

Alice Donovan, no doubt about it. Though her hair was longer now, she still bore a striking resemblance to the graduation photo given to Dukane by her parents when they hired him.

Even as she walked towards the clearing, she began to sway with the low throb of the drumbeats.

The ceremonial fire was lighted.

The drumbeats quickened, and the dancing began.

Resting the weapon across his lap, he watched. The tempo was picking up, the drummers pounding out a frenzied beat. The dancers twirled and leapt in the firelight. Several were already naked. As he watched, Alice skinned off her T-shirt. She whirled, waving it like a banner while her other hand opened her cut-offs. She didn't pull the shorts down. She danced as if forgetting them. They hung in place, at first, then slowly slipped lower and lower until they were halfway down her bare rump. They suddenly dropped. Dukane thought they might hobble the girl and trip her, but she jumped gracefully free. He turned his gaze to the mulatto woman with skin the color of tea. She was glossy with sweat, writhing as she rubbed her breasts.

Plenty of guys, Dukane thought, would pay through the nose for a show like this. He was slightly aroused, himself, but frightened. He'd heard people say fear is an aphrodisiac. Maybe it was, for them. In Dukane's experience, he'd found fear to be a great shrinker of erections.

Erections. Plenty of them down there. No coupling, though. Not yet. Nobody was even touching – not each other, anyway. They danced alone, jerking to the wild race of the drums, stroking themselves as if no one else existed.

Suddenly, the drums stopped. The dancers dropped to their knees.

A single, low voice said, 'Laveda.' Other voices joined it in a slow chant. 'Laveda, Laveda, Laveda . . .'

Dukane flinched as something dropped onto his head. It moved in his hair, scurried down his forehead. He brushed it away. Probably a goddamn spider. The swamp was full of them.

The group kneeling around the fire continued to chant.

Out of the darkness behind the drummers stepped Laveda. Dukane had kept her under surveillance for two weeks in New Orleans hoping she would lead him to Alice – but he'd never seen her like this. He stared.

She wore a sheathed dagger at her side, suspended from a belt of gold chain. She wore a gold band on each upper arm. She wore a necklace of claws. And nothing else.

Her thick, blond hair hung past her shoulders. Her skin glistened as if rubbed with oil. Dukane couldn't take his eyes off her. She was six-foot-one of the most stunning woman he had ever seen.

The chanting stopped as she walked among her congregation.

'The river flows,' she said.

In unison, the others chanted, 'The river is red.'

'The river flows.'

'Flows from the heart.'

'The river flows.'

'All powerful is the river.'

'Its water is the water of life,' she said.

'All powerful is he who drinks at its shore.'

'Who, among us, would be all powerful?'

'I,' answered the chorus.

Dukane spotted Alice. She looked ecstatic.

Laveda drew out her dagger. Standing near the fire, she raised it high and slowly turned in a circle. 'Who, among us, would drink at the river?'

'*I.*'

'For he who partakes of the flowing river shall inherit all powers.'

'The power of life, the power of death ...'

'... shall vanquish all enemies ...'

'The strong and the weak shall perish at his command!'

'. . . shall do what he will!'

'What thou wilt shall be the law!'

'Who shall drink at the river?'

'*I!*' they roared.

The drums rumbled. The congregation, still kneeling, swayed to the rhythm.

'The river flows!' Laveda yelled, wandering among her people. 'It flows and winds. We shall drink from its shores, this night. We shall drink its all powerful waters and take its power into ourselves. The river is endless. Its waters flow forever. Eternal power shall be ours!'

She stopped and placed her open hand on the head of the beautiful young mulatto. The woman rose to her feet.

'We shall drink at the river!'

Dukane winced as Laveda jerked the woman's head back by the hair and flicked her knife across the throat. She pressed her mouth to the spouting wound.

Two men held the convulsing mulatto from behind, and Laveda stepped back. Her face was smeared with blood. It streamed down her body.

'Drink, all of you, at the river!'

As the drums roared, the whole mob rushed forward. Including Alice. They caught the blood in their mouths and hurried off, smearing their bodies, dancing with sudden fury as if they'd all gone mad. Laveda, herself, leapt and spun like the others, her golden hair flying, flesh shimmering in the firelight, breasts slick with blood. A huge, black man fell to the ground at her feet. She dropped onto him, impaling herself. As she rode him, she took a man into her mouth.

Everywhere Dukane looked, bodies were falling upon each other, mounting and thrusting to the thunder of the drums.

Alice, on her back near the center of the group, was barely visible under the pale body of a middle-aged man.

Slinging the rifle across his back, Dukane climbed down from the tree. He propped his rifle against its trunk. He tried to ignore the lump of fear in his belly as he disrobed.

11

A piece of cake, he told himself.

Cakes get eaten.

Screw that analogy, he thought, and managed a smile.

When he was naked, he mussed up his hair until it hung over his eyes. Then he slipped his Buck knife from its sheath.

The things I'll do for money.

Even as he cut into his forearm, though, he knew this wasn't just for money. Now that he'd located the girl, he could think of several less hazardous ways to snatch her from the cult. But none were this daring, this exciting. None would give him the same thrill.

Gonna get myself killed one of these days.

With a trembling hand, he smeared blood over his cheeks and mouth and chin.

He stabbed his knife into the trunk of the Cypress, then made his way towards the clearing. His heart pounded with the thudding drums. His mouth was parched. Licking his lips, he tasted his own blood.

From behind a bush, he studied the fire-lit congregation. No one was standing, no one keeping watch. All were busy writhing in groups of two or more, or crawling off to join new partners.

Six feet from where he stood, two women were entwined, faces buried between wide-spread thighs. The one on top was a lean, white woman with a strawberry birthmark on her rump. Dukane crawled forward and nipped it. Her buttocks clenched and she yelped with surprise. Twisting her head around, she gazed at him with wild eyes. Dukane leered. He threw himself onto her sweaty back. Together, they rolled off to the side. She squirmed on top of him, moaning as he nibbled the side of her neck and fondled her breasts. The other woman scurried to join in. She pried apart their legs and knelt between them, her mouth going to the girl, her hand groping Dukane.

It squeezed him, massaged him, stroked him. He grew

hard, his erection rising and pressing against the groin of the girl on top of him. He felt a tongue.

Then the woman tumbled away, sprawling as a burly black man fell upon her and rammed in.

Dukane threw himself over, rolling onto the girl who'd been on top of him. She clawed at the grass as he wedged her legs apart. Kneeling behind her, he stroked her wet opening. Then he clutched her hips and thrust into her. His quick, hard lunges soon brought her to a quaking orgasm. He withdrew, rigid and aching, concentrating to prevent his own body from finding its release. With a pat on her rump, he crawled away from the girl.

He spotted Alice. She was several yards away, on her back, her heels embedded in the rump of a fat man, pressing him down deeper. As Dukane crawled toward her, a hand darted from behind and gripped his erection. Lowering his head, he looked between his legs.

A chill swept up his spine.

Lying on her back, one hand clutching him, was Laveda. She licked her lips. Her eyes looked dull and glazed.

Maybe she's too far gone, Dukane thought, to realize I don't belong.

He started to crawl backwards as Laveda pulled him.

There are thirty others here, he told himself. At least thirty. She couldn't know them all on sight.

Could she?

No. The New Orleans group was only one of a hundred. She had followers all over the country. Several thousand. New members all the time. She couldn't possibly keep track.

Her face appeared between his legs. Lifting her head, she sucked him into her mouth. He felt her tight lips, her pressing tongue, the edges of her teeth.

If she knows, Dukane thought, she'll bite. Or ram that dagger . . .

But she didn't. Her mouth held him tightly, sucking.

At least she can't see my face, he thought.

And then he was lost in the growing ache of need. Images flashed through his mind of Laveda writing in the firelight, her skin glossy, her firm breasts tipped with rigid nipples.

Her hands spread his buttocks. She pushed a finger in, and he burst with release. She sucked hard as he pumped inside the tight wetness of her mouth. After he was done, she continued to tug at him for a few moments.

Then her head lowered. Her eyes were shut. She licked her lips.

Dukane crawled forward. Looking back, he saw her curl onto her side and reach out for the foot of a nearby girl. The girl, astraddle an older man, freed herself from his embraces and scurried toward Laveda.

He looked for Alice, and found her in the same place, still gasping under the fat man. He hurried to them. The fat man was grunting and pumping, his rump shaking like jello.

Dukane pinched his carotid artery, felt him go rigid for a moment, then limp. He rolled the man off Alice, and took his place.

She smiled languidly. Her hands stroked his back. Her heels caressed his rump. She was hot and slick beneath him. She shivered as Dukane gnawed the side of her neck.

He pushed himself to his hands and knees. Alice clung to his neck, at first, when he started to crawl forward. Then her grip loosened. She fell to the ground and he kept crawling. Her hands trailed down his belly as he passed over her. They fondled his penis.

Dukane lowered his head to look at her. 'Ride me,' he said.

Alice made a husky laugh. Then she rolled over and climbed onto Dukane. She straddled him, thighs hugging his hips, breasts against his back, arms wrapping his chest. 'Giddyap,' she whispered.

He crawled past several squirming piles of bodies. Once, Alice reached out to squeeze a looming breast and fell from Dukane's back. She quickly remounted.

Dukane continued forward.

'My turn,' Alice whispered in his ear.

'Huh?'

'You ride me.'

Dukane dropped to his elbows. She slid forward. Dukane climbed onto her back, but kept his feet on the ground for support. With one hand, he gripped her hair. He raised her head and pointed her toward the bushes. With his other hand, he slapped her rump. She whinnied and started to move.

Dukane walked, keeping most of his weight off her back while he guided her away from the group. At the edge of the clearing, she halted. She began to chew the leaves of a nearby bush.

Hunching low, Dukane pressed himself to her back. His right arm reached under her and caressed a breast. His left hand pinched her carotid. She started to collapse. He threw her over and they rolled together under the sheltering bushes.

For a long time, Dukane lay motionless on top of the girl. He watched the crowd.

Apparently, the disappearing act had drawn no attention.

He climbed off Alice. Staying low, he dragged her deeper into the undergrowth. When they were well away from the clearing, he hoisted her over his shoulder and ran.

Oasis Tribune
Wednesday, July 16

GUARD DOG SLAIN

The dismembered body of Rusty, bartender Red Peterson's German Shepherd, was found yesterday morning inside Hoffman's Market where the dog had been left, overnight, to guard the store against recurrent vandalism and grocery thefts.

Says proprietor Elsie Hoffman, who found the slain canine, 'I'm just sick about it, just sick. We shouldn't have left that poor dog in here. I just knew he'd come to no good.' In tears, she added, 'That dog was the world to Red.'

Red Peterson, owner of the dog and bartender at the Golden Oasis, was unavailable for comment.

Chapter Three

Lacey climbed onto a bar stool. She tapped a cigarette out of its pack, and pressed it between her lips.

George O'Toole swiveled toward her. His ruddy, broad face crinkled with a smile, and he struck a match.

'Thank you.'

'And what'll it be you're drinking tonight?' he asked, with a lilt Lacey assumed he had picked up from Barry Fitzgerald movies.

'A little red wine.'

'A dainty drink for a dainty lady,' he said. He raised a thick, weathered hand and caught the bartender's eye.

The bartender was Will Glencoe.

'A spot of red for the lady, Will. And another Guinness for himself.' The bartender turned away. 'You did Red a fine turn, writing up your story the way you did. He was almighty ashamed of the way he carried on about Rusty. I can understand a grown man weeping over the loss of a good dog – done it myself more than once. But it's a private thing, and a man doesn't want it blatted about. You did him a fine turn.'

'He's right, there,' said Will, setting down the drinks. 'Take your average reporter, he'd have a field day. Bunch of blood-suckers, that's what they are.'

'But not our Lacey. You did yourself proud, young lady.'

She reached into her purse.

'You put that away.'

'Thank you, George.'

He paid, and Will stepped away to take an order down the bar.

'Where *is* Red tonight?' Lacey asked.

George narrowed one eye. 'Now where would *you* be, if a heartless so-and-so had done your dog that way?'

'Elsie's?'

He turned his wrist over, and peered at his watch. 'She'll be closing up in ten minutes. Red's there with his twelve gauge. He'll be camping there tonight, hoping the filthy beggar shows up again. I offered my services – two guns are twice one – but he's after doing it alone, and I can't say I blame the man.' George lifted his stein. 'To your health,' he toasted.

'And yours, George.'

He winked at her, and drank.

Lacey sipped her wine. 'What's Red planning to do, shoot the man?'

'The beggar cut down his dog, Lacey.'

'I know, I saw it.'

'And was it as bad as they say?'

'My God, George. I've never seen anything like . . .' She gagged. Tears filled her eyes.

'Now, now.' George patted her shoulder.

She wiped the tears away, and took a deep breath. 'I'm sorry.' She managed a smile. 'I don't normally go around gagging in public. Just thinking about that . . .' She did it again.

'Careful there. Say now, do you know how to tell the groom at a Kerryman's wedding?'

She shook her head.

'He's the one in the pinstriped Wellingtons.'

She wiped her eyes, and sighed.

'Feeling better, now? Have another wine, and we'll talk of other things. I've a raft of Kerryman jokes. They're sure to gladden your heart.'

'Thanks, George. I really should be going, though.'

Outside in the warm night air, she felt better. She climbed into her car and rolled down the window. Her hand paused on the ignition. She wanted to go home, take a long bath, and get to bed. But she couldn't. Maybe it was none of her business. Knowing Red's plan, though, she wouldn't feel right if she didn't at least talk to him, warn him of the possible consequences.

You don't blow a man apart with a shotgun because he killed your dog. Not unless you want a prison stretch. Even shooting an intruder, unless the man is armed, could mean more trouble than Red probably bargained for.

She started her car and drove the three blocks to Hoffman's Market. Its sign was brightly lighted; it hadn't closed yet. She pulled into the parking lot, and stopped beside Red's pickup truck. In the past, she'd rarely seen the pickup without Rusty pacing its bed, tail wagging, fur ruffled by the wind. She used to fear for the dog's safety. Suppose it leapt over the low panel as the truck sped along? Once, she'd voiced her fear to Red. 'Would *you* jump off a moving truck?' he'd asked. 'No, but I'm not a dog.' Red grinned at that. 'You can say that again.'

Lacey ran her hand along the tailgate and looked into the empty truck bed, then hurried away.

The door of the market wasn't locked. She pushed it open, and stepped inside. Nobody at the counter.

'Hello,' she called.

Swinging the door shut, she glanced at the pale gash left by the meat cleaver.

'Elsie? Red?'

She looked down a bright aisle. At the far end, just in front of the meat counter, a shotgun lay on the floor. An icy chill washed over Lacey, raising goosebumps. Even the skin of her forehead felt stiff and prickly. She rubbed it as she walked between the grocery shelves, eyes fixed on the shotgun.

The air, she noticed, had the faint but pungent odor she knew from shooting skeet with her father.

Only when she was standing over the shotgun did she lift her gaze to the meat counter and see Elsie's head wrapped in cellophane.

Lacey's mouth jerked open. Her scream came out voiceless, a quiet explosion of breath.

She dropped to a crouch, grabbed the shotgun, and pivoted. Nobody coming up behind her. She worked the pump action. It made a loud metallic *snick-snack*, and a blue shell tumbled to the floor.

Keeping her eyes averted from Elsie, she walked along the meat counter. Just ahead, a display of Diet Rite had been blasted apart. Cans lay in all directions, half of them pierced by shot. The floor was slippery with a thin layer of cola.

Beyond the display, barely hidden by the shelves of the next aisle, she found Red. He lay on his back, alive, reaching across his chest, trying to fit his severed left arm into place.

'Oh boy,' he whispered. 'Oh boy.'

'Red?'

He glanced up at Lacey, then looked back at his arm. 'Oh boy,' he mumbled.

'I'll get help,' she said. Keeping the shotgun ready, she ran for the front. Elsie, she knew, kept a phone on a shelf behind the cash register. Should she go for that, or . . .

She was tackled from behind. She hit the floor flat-out and hard. The wind burst from her lungs. She tried to push herself up, but a weight on her rump and legs held her down. Her collar jerked back, choking her. Then something struck the side of her head.

* * *

She opened her eyes and saw the ceiling. On either side were shelves of groceries: cans of soup and chili on the left, cookies and crackers on the right.

Even without moving, she knew what had been done to her. She could feel the gritty, cool wood under her bare skin. She could feel hot areas where her skin had been mauled. Her nipples burned and itched. So did her vagina. She felt stretched and battered inside. Her eyes filled with tears.

Raising her head, she looked down at herself. Her breasts were red as if they had been wrung. She saw teethmarks on both nipples. Fingernail scratches trailed down her belly. Propping herself up with stiff arms, she felt a slow trickle inside her.

At the end of the aisle lay Red. His severed arm lay across his chest. He was motionless.

With tissues from her handbag, she cleaned herself. She wasn't afraid. She felt dirty and sick and ashamed. When she used her last tissue, she picked all of them up off the floor and stuffed them into her bag.

She started to dress, watching the door, worried that someone might enter before she could finish. Her panties were torn apart; she put them in her bag. Both straps of her bra were broken, the catches in back ripped loose. She pushed it into her bag, and stepped into her jeans. She struggled to pull them up. They encased her, snug and protective. She wished her blouse were as sturdy and tight as her jeans, but she felt bare even after putting it on.

The walk to the checkout counter seemed to take a long time. She moved slowly, carefully, feeling that the slightest jostle might shake something loose inside her body.

Finally, she reached the counter. She picked up the phone.

Chapter Four

'Okay, Lacey. If you remember anything else, though, give me a call.'

'I will.'

Rex Barrett drew a thumb along the handlebar moustache that he'd raised since becoming chief of the Oasis Police Department. To Lacey, it made the lean lawman look like a twin of Wyatt Earp. She often suspected that he'd grown it for that reason.

'You'll be writing this up for the *Trib*?' he asked.

'Yes.'

'I'd appreciate your not mentioning specifics about the way he did Elsie.'

'Fine,' she said, leaning back against the counter. There were other specifics she planned not to mention.

'Now, if I were you, I'd drag my doctor out of bed for a quick once-over. You took some good knocks tonight and you just never know, with a head injury.'

'I'll do that,' she lied.

'I would, if I were you.'

'Is it all right if . . .?' Two men wheeled a stretcher down the aisle. One hurried ahead to open the door. She looked at the body bag. The contours of the black plastic resembled a human. Had they pieced Elsie back together?

Shutting her eyes, she tried to think about something else. Her shoulder was touched. She flinched and snapped open her eyes.

'It's okay,' Barrett said. He squeezed her shoulder.

'Sure.'

'You go on, now. See your doctor. Get a good night's sleep.'

'I will. Thanks.'

Outside, she saw the stretcher being slid into the rear of the coroner's van. She hurried past Red's pickup, and opened her car door. The ceiling light came on. As she started to climb in, goosebumps prickled her skin.

She snapped her head sideways. Nobody in the back seat.

But she couldn't see the rear floor.

Silly, she thought. Like a kid checking under the bed.

Silly or not, she had to make sure nobody was hunched out of sight behind the front seats. Planting a knee on the cushion, she grabbed the head-rest and eased herself forward. Her breast hurt as it pushed against the vinyl upholstery. She peered over the top of the seat. Nobody down there.

Of course not.

But she'd had to make sure.

She twisted around, sat down, and pulled her door shut. She locked it. With a glance to the right, she saw that the passenger door wasn't locked. Stretching across the seat, she jabbed the button down with her forefinger. She checked the rear doors. Their lock buttons looked low and snug.

She sighed. With a slick, sweaty hand, she rubbed the back of her neck. Then she pushed the key into the ignition, and started the car.

A cigarette. She wanted a cigarette. A little treat for herself, an indulgence, a comfort that didn't have to wait till she reached her home on the outskirts of town. The drink and the bath had to wait: not the cigarette.

She opened her handbag. With a glance around the parking lot to be sure no one would see, she pulled out her ruined bra and panties. She tossed them onto the passenger seat. Then she reached into the bag, looking down into its darkness, hoping to find her pack of Tareytons without touching the sodden wads of tissue. Her body jerked as she fingered a cool, slippery ball and gagged. The pack of cigarettes was beneath the mess. She pulled it out, gagging again as her hand came out wet and sticky. She rubbed her hand on her jeans.

'God,' she muttered.

Her whole body ached, as if the pressure of the spasms had burst open all her injuries. She pressed her legs together, and held her breasts gently until the pain subsided.

Then she shook out a cigarette. She held it in her lips and lit it, staring at the glowing red coils of the car's lighter. The smoke was as soothing as she'd hoped. With a sigh of satisfaction, she turned on the headlights and backed her car out of the parking space.

The coroner's van was gone. Three police cars remained, as did Red's pickup. She supposed the pickup would be towed away before morning.

The road was deserted. She turned her radio on, and listened to a country station from Tucson. Ronnie Milsap was singing 'What a Difference You Made in My Life'. When his song ended, Anne Murray came on with 'Can I Have This Dance?' Nice of them to play a couple of her favorites. The songs helped to soothe her shattered nerves.

As she reached her block, she took a final, deep drag on her cigarette. She held the smoke in, stubbed out her cigarette, and let the smoke ease out of her mouth.

From behind her came a muffled cough.

Her eyes snapped to the rearview mirror. A slice of ceiling. The back window. The empty road.

Had it been the radio?

No, the cough had come from behind. She was sure. It sounded like someone in the back seat. Impossible. She'd looked so carefully.

The muffler? A simple backfire? No.

Lacey swerved across the road, shot up her driveway, and hit the brakes. The car lurched to a stop. She shut it off. Grabbing her handbag, she threw open the door and leapt out. She slammed the door.

Fighting an urge to run, she stepped close to the rear window and peered inside. Nobody there. Of course not.

Under the car? Could a man hang on, down there? It

seemed impossible. But now that the idea had entered her mind, she had to check. She dropped to her knees, planted her hands on the cool concrete, and lowered herself until she could see under the carriage. She scanned the dark space.

Nobody.

The trunk? She stood up, brushing off her hands, and stared at the trunk's sloping hood.

How could anyone get in? Pick the lock? Child's play, probably, for someone who knew how. And if he could get in, he could get out just as easily.

What if it's not even latched?

Holding her breath, Lacey stepped softly toward the rear of the car. The edges of the trunk's hood were not perfectly flush with the bordering surfaces. Slightly higher. Less than a quarter of an inch, though. Maybe that was normal.

Maybe not.

Maybe the killer, the slug who raped her, was hunched inside the trunk, holding it shut.

She lunged at the trunk, slapped both hands on its top, shoved down and threw herself forward. The car rocked under her weight. But no *clack* of the trunk's lock. She lay there, thinking. No clack. The trunk had been locked, after all. Probably. But that didn't mean the killer wasn't inside, didn't mean he couldn't get out.

He can't get out if I stay like this, she thought. But she couldn't stay that way, sprawled on the trunk with her face pressing the back window, her legs hanging off. Her belly, on the trunk's rim, took most of her weight so she could hardly breathe. And the pain of lying on her injuries was almost unbearable.

She squirmed backwards until her feet found the driveway, then pushed herself off and ran for her house. She leapt onto the stoop. Sliding her key into the lock, she glanced over her shoulder. Her blue Granada stood in the driveway, looking as it should, as if nothing were wrong. For an instant, Lacey questioned herself. Had she imagined the cough?

No.

He's in there. In the trunk.

She shoved open the front door, shut and bolted it behind her, and rushed across the living room. She dropped her handbag on the dining-room table. Skirting the table, she entered her bedroom and flicked on a light. She rushed to her bed. Jerked open a nightstand drawer. Took out a Smith and Wesson .38 caliber revolver.

Then she ran from the house. She started to leave the front door open in case she needed a quick escape. But the man could've already left the trunk. Not likely – Lacey had been in the house no more than half a minute. That could be time enough, though. He might be out of the trunk, hiding nearby, ready to jump her or sneak inside the house. So she closed the front door and locked it.

She stood on the Welcome mat, holding the pistol close to her belly. Its weight felt good in her hand. She felt safer than before, as if she'd been joined by a powerful trusted friend – a brother who would nail the bastard for her.

Just point and fire.

The only real danger, now, lay in being caught from behind. Like before. That's how he got me before.

Not this time.

He might be in the geraniums.

He's probably still in the trunk.

Lacey sprang from the stoop, past the geranium bushes, and raced into the center of her lawn. She spun around, pistol ready. No one.

Okay.

Still in the trunk.

She ran to her car. Standing behind it, she studied the keys in her left hand. She found the trunk key. Pistol ready, she stabbed the key into the lock and twisted it. The latch clicked.

She jumped back, and aimed. The springs groaned as the trunk began to open. The lid inched upward. Lacey stared at the dark, widening gap. Her finger was tense on the trigger.

The lid gathered speed, stopped abruptly at its apex, and quivered for a moment.

In the darkness of the trunk, nothing moved.

Lacey stepped closer. She saw her spare tire, a pack of road flares, and an old towel she sometimes used for wiping the car windows. There was certainly no man in the trunk.

She sighed. She felt weary, disappointed. She'd been sure she would find the killer there.

The rapist.

The man who tore her and bit her and pumped his foul seed into her.

He would be in the trunk and Lacey would pump him full of a different kind of seed – the kind that grows death – the lead kind. He would never hurt anyone again.

'Damn,' she muttered.

Reaching up with her left hand, she slammed the trunk shut. The car rocked slightly with its impact.

She remembered her torn undergarments on the front seat. Better pick them up.

Stepping around the end of the car, she saw that the rear door jutted out an inch. Its lock button stood high.

'My God,' Lacey said. She covered her mouth, and staggered backwards.

Chapter Five

She refused to run. Back in the market, she had run and he'd taken her down from behind. It was a mistake she would not repeat.

Cautiously, turning to check every side, she made her way to the front door. She stood against its cool wood, the handle near her hip, and reached behind her with the key. It clicked and skidded against the lockface. Finally, it slid in. She turned it. The lock tongue snapped back.

Through the bushes to her left, she saw a quick pale movement. She jerked her pistol toward it. The shape rushed clear of the bushes and appeared in the open ahead of her, just across the lawn.

A man. Cliff Woodman. Out for a run.

He glanced toward Lacey, waved, and suddenly stopped.

'That you, Lacey?'

'It's me.'

'Is that a gun?'

'Yeah.'

'Trouble?'

'I don't know.'

Lacey stepped away from the door and lowered her revolver as Cliff jogged toward her. She immediately felt better. Cliff, a gym teacher at the high school, was forty years old and an ex-marine. Tonight, in his running shoes, shorts, and a bandanna knotted around his head as a sweatband, he looked almost savage.

'What's the problem?' he asked.

'I think I've got a prowler.'

'Where?' He squinted at the bushes in front of the house.

'I don't know. I think he was in my car.'

'Your car?' Cliff strode toward it, hunched slightly, arms away from his sides like a wrestler about to do battle. Lacey hurried after him. He jerked the handle of the passenger door.

Thank God it's locked, Lacey thought, hoping he wouldn't discover her torn bra and panties.

He tugged open the back door. 'Nobody there now,' he announced, and flung the door shut. 'I'll look around the back.'

Lacey held out the revolver. 'You'd better take this.'

'Couldn't hurt.' He took it, and started up the driveway toward the rear of the house.

Lacey followed. 'I'll go with you.'

He nodded.

She hurried forward until she was beside him. 'You've got to know, Cliff,' she whispered. 'I think he's a murderer.'

'For real?'

'I just came back from Hoffman's Market. Elsie was killed there tonight. So was Red Peterson.'

Cliff's heavy brows lowered. 'Fella that offed Red's dog?'

'I guess so. I think he hid in my car when I left there.'

'Maybe he high-tailed it.'

'I don't know.'

'Well, if he's around here, we'll get him.' Cliff grinned. 'Save the tax payers the expense of a trial.'

They followed the driveway past the back of the house. Cliff stared ahead at the garage.

'It's padlocked,' Lacey said. 'The laundry room's open, though.'

'Let's have a look.'

Walking near the front of the garage, Lacey scanned her yard, the lounge chairs and barbecue, the hedge along the far side.

Cliff took her arm. He pushed her against the wall, close to the laundry-room door. 'Don't move,' he whispered. He knelt in front of her. Reaching up, he slowly turned the knob. He threw open the door and leaned forward to peer in. Then he rose to his feet. He entered the laundry room, crouching. Lacey stepped in after him.

'Do you want the light on?' she asked.

'It'd wreck our night vision.'

He went to the far end, then hurried back. Together, they cut across the yard. They walked single-file through the narrow space between the side of the house and the hedge. Then he led her to the front door.

'Any chance he got inside?'

'No, I don't . . .'

Cliff opened the front door.

'Oh no,' Lacey sighed. 'I unlocked it just as you came along.'

'I'd better have a look.'

'Yeah, please. Damn, that was stupid.'

They entered the house, and she locked the door. Cliff walked ahead of her, glancing behind furniture, lifting draperies. In the lamplight, his back was glossy. The band of his gray shorts was dark with sweat, and Lacey caught herself wondering what – if anything – he wore beneath them. She suddenly became very aware of her own nakedness inside her jeans and flimsy blouse, a body beaten, soiled by another man's filth.

She tried not to think about it.

She followed Cliff around the dining-room table, and into her bedroom. The lamp was still on, the nightstand drawer still open. She stood against the doorframe, watching him. On the far side of the bed, he dropped to his knees and lifted the coverlet. Then he got to his feet again, and came back. His eyes met Lacey's, and he smiled as if to reassure her. When he looked toward the closet, Lacey lowered her gaze. His chest was muscular, his belly flat. His shorts hung low on his hips. They fit snugly. She glimpsed his bulge, and quickly looked away, a warm thickness of revulsion in her stomach.

He opened the closet door and looked inside.

'So far,' he said, 'so good.'

Lacey backed out of the doorway. She followed him into the kitchen. He walked through, glancing to each side, ducking to peer under the heavy wooden table that barely fit into the breakfast nook, opening the utility-closet door and shutting it again after a quick inspection. He checked the back door. Locked.

Glancing at Lacey, he shook his head.

He had, she realized, a dangerous face: deep-set, dark eyes, jutting cheekbones, thin lips, a blocky jaw. A somewhat hand-some face, but not a face to inspire any special feeling of tenderness.

He stepped past her, his arm brushing against her breast. She flinched away from the unwanted contact. Had he done it on purpose? Staying farther away from Cliff, she followed him around the corner and into her study. He walked past its bookshelves, checked behind an easy chair, and looked in the closet.

'I really appreciate your helping me like this,' Lacey said.

'Glad I came by when I did.'

'I guess it's just a wild-goose chase.'

'Not yet,' he said, stepping toward her. She quickly backed out of range. He went past, pulled open the linen-closet door, then entered the bathroom and turned on its light. He walked past the toilet and sink. At the tub, he slid back the frosted glass door. Then he turned to Lacey and smiled. Not an open friendly smile: it was guarded and sardonic. '*Now*,' he said, 'it's a wild-goose chase.'

'Well, thanks an awful lot.'

'I'm just sorry we didn't bag him. For your peace of mind. If you'd like me to stick around for a while, I'd be happy to.'

'Thanks. I think I'll be all right.'

'Suit yourself.'

He handed the revolver to Lacey. 'If you ever have to use this, go for the torso and don't settle for one hit. Put three or four in him, but save a shot or two, just in case.'

Lacey nodded. Strange advice, she thought, but coming from Cliff it sounded perfectly natural.

'And remember I'm just three houses away, if you need me. Let me give you my number.' He wrote it on a pad by the kitchen telephone. 'If you have any trouble, give me a ring. I can get here a lot quicker than the cops.'

'All right.' She walked ahead of him to the door.

'Sure you won't feel better if I hang around for a bit?'

'I'm sure. Thanks anyway.' She opened the front door for him. 'Have a good run.'

He jumped off the stoop, and raced across the lawn.

Lacey shut the door and locked it, relieved that he was gone. Had it been intentional, touching her breast? Probably. He'd been so insistent on staying. More than likely, he'd hoped she would fall into his protective arms and . . .

Hell, he was just being a good neighbor.

She tried to push the revolver into her waistband, but the jeans were too tight. She shoved its barrel down a front pocket. It wouldn't go in past the cylinder, so she pulled it out and carried it into the kitchen and held it while she poured herself a glass of Pinot Noir. She took the revolver and wine into her study and sat at her desk.

Her back felt exposed. Turning her chair, she could see the open door. That was better, though she still felt vulnerable. She placed the revolver on her lap. With a trembling hand, she lighted a cigarette.

Then she sipped her wine and picked up the phone. She dialed.

On the other end, the phone rang twice.

'*Tribune*,' said James, the night editor.

'It's Lacey. I've got a story for you. There were two killings at Hoffman's tonight.'

'Ahhh.' He sounded disgusted. 'Okay, you want to give it to me?'

'*Tribune* reporter Lacey Allen last night discovered the mutilated body of Elsie Hoffman and fatally injured Red Peterson when she entered Hoffman's Market shortly before closing time.'

'*You* found them?'

'Afraid so.'

'Christ!'

'Before she could summon authorities, Miss Allen was herself assaulted and rendered unconscious by an unseen assailant. Paragraph. Police, arriving on the scene, found that

Red Peterson had succumbed to his injuries. A thorough search of the premises revealed that the killer had fled.'

For the next five minutes, she continued to tell her story to James and the *Tribune*'s tape recorder, filling in details, never mentioning her rape or the specifics about the killings or her suspicion that the assailant had escaped in her car, finally recapping the earlier incidents at the market. 'That about does it,' she finished. 'Except for one thing. I'd like some time to recuperate. Tell Carl I won't be in tomorrow, okay?'

'Sure thing. You all right?'

'Just beat up a little. I'll be in Friday.'

'Fine. Great work, Lacey.'

'Just happened to be at the right place at the right time.'

'I detect a note of irony.'

'Only a note?'

'Take care of yourself, kid.'

'I will. Night, James.'

'See ya.'

She hung up. With the revolver and empty wine glass, she returned to the kitchen for a refill. Then she went into the bathroom. She shut the door and thumbed down its lock button. A feeble measure. Any pointed instrument turned in the keyhole, she knew, would pop open the lock. But the little precaution was better than none at all.

She set her pistol and glass on the floor beside the tub, and started the water running. When it felt hot enough, she stoppered the drain.

She turned to the medicine cabinet mirror. The face looking back at her was a bad copy of the one she was used to: slack and pallid, dark under the eyes, the eyes themselves wide and vacant. Turning her head, she fingered back the hair draping her right temple and studied the patch of swollen, red-blue skin. The ear, too, was slightly puffed and discolored.

'A shadow of her former self,' she muttered. It brought a slight smile. Part of the strangeness left her eyes.

She took off her blouse. Then she unfastened her jeans, tugged them down, and kicked them off. She tossed the blouse and jeans into the hamper.

She looked down at herself. Fingers had left red-blue impressions on both her breasts.

Must've grabbed them and squeezed.

The teeth indentations had disappeared, but her nipples were purple. She touched one and winced.

Her body was seamed with fingernail scratches: her shoulders and upper arms, her sides, her belly, her thighs. At least he hadn't raked her breasts, and none of the scratches would show when she was clothed – the silver lining.

She tested the water with a foot. Hot, but not burning. She climbed in and slowly lowered herself, clenching rigid with pain as the water seared the raw lips of her vagina. The pain faded, and she let herself down the rest of the way. She gritted her teeth as the water scorched her torn thighs. But that pain soon faded, like the other. She took a deep breath. Leaning forward, she turned off the faucet.

The house was silent except for the slow plop of water drops near her feet.

Bracing herself against the shock, she splashed water onto her scratches. At first, it felt like lava running down her open flesh. Then it wasn't so bad. After a sip of wine, she lathered herself with soap and rinsed.

She picked up her wine glass again, and lay back. Head propped against the rear of the tub, she sipped the wine. It felt warm and good going down. Holding the glass in one hand, she reached down with the other, down through the hot water between her open legs. Tenderly, she fingered herself.

He must've chewed her there, too.

Filthy bastard!

At least he didn't kill me – another silver lining?

Fuck the silver linings.

Lacey blinked tears away, and reached for the bar of soap. She rubbed herself gently.

And the bathroom lights went out.

She threw herself against the side of the tub. She clawed the rug, trying to find the revolver.

Where *was* it?

Then she touched its cool steel. She picked it up by the barrel, found its handle, and gripped it tight.

She stood up. She lifted one foot out of the water and stepped over the tub's wall. With that foot firm on the rug, she leaned out. In the vague light from the window, she searched the bathroom. She saw no one. The door appeared to be shut.

Must be shut. Still locked. I'd have heard the button pop . . .

Okay, maybe the bulbs in the fixture blew. *Three* bulbs? Fat chance. How about a general power failure? Sure thing. No, it had to be the fuse box.

He's in the house!

Slowly, she raised her other foot out of the water. She stepped clear of the tub and stood aiming at the door.

Naked and wet, she felt more vulnerable than ever before in her life. She backed up, and knelt beside the hamper. Switching the pistol to her left hand, she reached in. She pulled out her jeans, her blouse.

The blouse was easy. She got it on without letting go of the gun. But she needed two hands for the jeans. She set the pistol on the counter by the sink, within easy reach.

Stupid, she thought as she fumbled with her pants. This is just the moment he'll choose to bust the door in. But she heard nothing. Only a car speeding along, somewhere far away. If he'd just hold off for a few seconds, she would be dressed and ready for him. She had to be dressed.

She was bent over, balanced on one leg, her other foot high and pushing into the jeans, when she felt fingers clutch her ankle and jerk it out from under her.

She hit the floor.

Rough hands jerked her pants off. She tried to scramble up, but the weight of a man drove her against the floor, forced her legs apart. Her blouse was ripped off her back. Then he was lying on her, pinning her arms to the floor. She felt his hardness against her rump.

'Scream, cunt, and I'll rip off your head.'

She pressed her face to the rug. She cried, she whimpered with pain, she bit her lips until she tasted their blood, but she didn't scream. At some point, with the man grunting and thrusting in the darkness above her, Lacey passed out.

Chapter Six

Dukane landed his Cessna Bonanza, that night, at Santa Monica airport. He stepped into the passenger cabin.

Alice smiled at him. 'Hello, dead man.'

'Pleasant flight?' he asked.

'Very nice. I spent it thinking about what they'll do to you.'

'Nothing too drastic, I hope.' He bent down and unlocked the cuffs chaining her left wrist to the seat's armrest.

'You messed with Laveda, man. You're good as dead.'

'*Better* than dead, at the moment.'

'Sure, joke. You'll be laughing outa the other side of your face when they catch up with you. And they will. And I'll be with 'em, you can count on it. I'll be the one with the knife, cutting out your eyes.'

'Such talk,' he said.

'You can't hide from us. We're everywhere. We know all. We're all powerful.'

'Yep. Okay, stand up.' He backed away. Alice stepped into

the aisle. She looked good in the yellow sundress – fresh, and even younger than her nineteen years. Dukane had bought it at a Penny's in Houma, leaving Alice drugged in the passenger seat of his rented car. After buying the dress, he drove to a deserted stretch of road. He braced her against the side of the car, stripped off the oversized shirt he'd earlier used to clothe her, and wrestled her limp body into the dress.

'Are we getting outa this plane, or you just gonna stare at me all night?'

'We need to make a decision. I can either take you out of here handcuffed, as a prisoner, or you can agree to cooperate and we'll go to my car like friends. Which do you prefer?'

'You don't need the cuffs.'

'If you try to get away, you'll be hurt.'

'I know, I know. You proved that back in the bayou, didn't you? Well, I'll tell you something. I don't have to get away from you. They'll come for me. Wherever you take me, they'll come. I don't have to lift a finger – just wait and use my powers to call them.'

'Fancy car,' Alice said as Dukane climbed into the Jaguar beside her. 'Kidnapping must pay good.'

'Yep.' The car grumbled to life.

'How much did my folks pay you?'

'Enough.'

'Enough to die for?'

'That's not in my plans.'

'It's in mine. They'll have to die, too. Can't go messing with Laveda.'

'You're a sweetheart,' Dukane said. He backed out of the parking space, and headed for the exit.

'Wouldn't want to be in your shoes, man.'

'I know. You're all powerful. You've drunk at the river.'

'Fuckin' right.'

'Imagine. All that from drinking a gal's blood.'

'The blood is the life.'

'Where've I heard that before,' he said, and switched the radio on. He turned left onto Ocean Park Boulevard.

'This isn't the way home.'

'I'm not taking you home. You've got a date with a certain Dr T. R. Miles. He specializes in deprogramming screwed up kids.'

'Deprogramming?' She made a quiet, nasal laugh. 'What do you think I am, a Moonie?'

'I didn't hire him, your parents did. Far as I'm concerned, you and the rest of Laveda's gang ought to be burnt at the stake.'

Her head jerked towards him.

'That's how the old-timers dealt with witches, I believe.'

'We're not witches,' she muttered.

'Near enough. Laveda's got her own set of rules and rituals, but it boils down to the same thing – you're a bunch of homicidal lunatics on a power trip. You need to be stopped.'

'We can't be stopped,' she said, but the earlier tone of scornful confidence was gone from her voice. 'We're everywhere.'

'Put the torch to Laveda, and the whole gang would fall apart.'

'Shut up.'

A layer of fog hung over the road as they neared the ocean. It swirled in the headlights, rolled off the windshield. Dukane slowed down. He squinted ahead, searching for the dim glow of traffic lights.

In the silence, he thought about Alice's bluster falling away at the mention of fire. She seemed to have an exaggerated fear of burning.

He'd noted the same dread in the man named Walter. The muscular fellow had acted brazen, at first, during Dukane's interrogation three nights before the bayou gathering. Like Alice, he'd claimed to be invulnerable. He'd refused to talk. But he broke down, whimpering and pleading, when Dukane doused him with gasoline. In short order, he told about

Laveda's group, its structure and purposes, the extent of its membership, the time and location of the meeting. What Dukane learned had scared the hell out of him, but it gave him all he needed to know in his search for Alice.

At the blur of a red light just ahead, Dukane eased down on the brake. He hit the arm of the turn signal, hoping this was Main, and turned left when the light changed. He drove slowly, gazing into the fog, seeking a landmark. When he saw the Boulangerie, off to the right, he knew where he was. He continued down Main, glimpsed a cluster of vague figures at the entrance to the Oar House, and kept going until he reached the traffic signal at Rose. A pair of dim lights appeared ahead. He waited for the car to pass, then turned left and parked at the curb.

'Let's go,' he said.

They climbed from the car. Alice followed him up the street, hunched slightly and moving fast, her bare arms crossed against her breasts.

'We're almost there,' Dukane told her, his chin shaking. He clenched his teeth, then made a conscious effort to relax his muscles and stop the shivering. Alice, he knew, must be freezing in her thin sundress. He put an arm across her shoulders, but she whirled away.

'Don't touch me,' she said.

'Just trying to help.'

'I can live without it.'

They crossed a dark street, and hurried up the sidewalk. 'This is it,' he said, nodding toward the lighted porch of a small, wood-frame house. He opened the gate. They rushed up a narrow walkway. Dukane took the porch stairs two at a time, and rang the doorbell.

Alice waited beside him, legs tight together, arms hugging herself, teeth chattering.

The door was opened as far as the guard chain allowed. A black-haired, attractive woman studied them through her wire-rimmed glasses.

'We're here to see Dr Miles,' Dukane said.

'Yes?'

'I'm Dukane.'

The woman nodded. She shut the door briefly, then swung it open. 'Please come in.'

They stepped into the warm house. The woman shut the door, took a sip of coffee from her Snoopy mug, and turned to them. 'You must be Alice,' she said.

Alice curled her nose.

'You both look chilled to the bone. Let's go in by the fire, and I'll get you some coffee.'

They followed her into the living room. It was wood paneled and cozy, with the feel of a summer cottage. Alice crossed toward the fireplace. She stopped two yards from its screen, and held out her hands.

'Cream or sugar?'

Alice didn't respond.

'I'll take mine black,' Dukane said.

'Back in a jiff,' the woman said, and left.

Dukane stepped past Alice. He stood close to the fire, feeling its heat through his trouser legs, then crouching to warm his upper body and face. He turned around, still squatting, and smiled up at Alice. 'Nothing like a nice, crackling fire.'

'Get fucked.'

The woman came back, carrying a coffee mug in each hand. Dukane noticed the way her breasts jiggled slightly under the cashmere of her white turtle-neck. Below the hem of her tweed skirt, her calves looked trim and well defined. Probably, Dukane thought, she jogs on the beach – just like half the other residents of Venice.

He stood, and accepted a hot mug. This one came from the Hearst Castle gift shop. She held out a Big Apple mug to Alice.

Alice swatted it from her hand. The mug flipped away, exploding coffee, and bounced off the rug.

The woman slapped her face.

Alice leaped at her, snarling, hands out like claws. As Dukane set his mug on the mantle, he saw that the woman needed no help. She grabbed Alice's right arm, jerked it toward her, and swiveled around. Her rump caught Alice low. The girl flew over her back and hit the floor with a grunt.

'Sorry about that, but I won't allow intemperate behavior.' Her sweater had pulled up, revealing lightly tanned skin above her belt. She adjusted her sweater, and stared down at Alice. 'Is that understood?'

Alice gazed at the ceiling. 'You're gonna die.'

'Not before I've straightened you out.'

'You're Dr Miles?' Dukane asked.

Her smile caught him off-guard; he'd expected a condescending smirk. 'Don't be embarrassed,' she said. 'A doctor with a name like Teri Miles is begging for erroneous assumptions of gender. You thought I was the good doctor's receptionist?'

'Or wife. I was starting to envy him.'

She smiled, and surprised him again – this time by blushing.

Dukane took a sip of hot coffee. 'I see you can handle yourself well.'

'One has to, in this line of work. I've had patients a lot rougher than Alice.'

'She seems to think she'll get away in short order.'

'I have a locked room for her, grates on the windows. So far, I haven't lost anyone.'

'She thinks she'll have help.'

'You made sure you weren't followed?'

'In that fog, it would've taken Rudolph to follow us.'

Dr Miles grinned. 'Any red noses in the rear-view mirror?'

'Not a one.'

'We should be all right, then. Nobody knows where she is except you and her parents.'

'*They'll* know,' Alice said from the floor.

'She thinks they'll find her through telepathy.'

'I'd say that's remote.'

'Hope so,' Dukane said. 'Laveda's gang believes in all sorts of hogwash, but if they have any special power, I haven't seen it in action. I observed one of their meetings, infiltrated it, even had contact with Laveda herself. If she's some kind of mind-reader, I think she would've known I didn't belong. She acted as if I were just another member of the group. They all did. So I think their magic is a lot of talk, not much else. It's a dangerous bunch, though. They *think* they've got a handle on magical powers, so they act as if they do. They're basically fearless, think they're invulnerable.'

'We are,' Alice said. She sat up, crossed her legs, and looked up at them, smirking.

'They do fear burning.'

'Fire,' said Dr Miles, 'has traditionally been associated with purification. I've dealt with satanists who actually exhibit a phobic response to it.'

'There's something else I should tell you. They practice human sacrifice. I saw a young woman murdered at their meeting. The others drank her blood. Even Alice, here.'

Dr Miles stiffened slightly.

'So it's a blood-thirsty group.'

'You could be in a great deal of danger if they do find out, somehow, that Alice is here.'

'Well . . .'

'It might be wise for me to stick around.'

'I'm sure that won't be necessary.'

'I'd feel easier about it.'

'I don't think you realize – the process could take weeks, depending on the depth of her conditioning. Besides, I really don't imagine there's much cause for concern. Her location's secret. As for telepathy, I agree with you that it's hogwash. I've been involved with these matters for several years, and haven't lost a patient yet.'

'All right,' Dukane said. He felt a bit rebuffed, and realized his offer had been motivated by more than simple concern for her safety. He was attracted to her, wanted to spend more time in her presence. 'Well, I'll check in occasionally.'

'Better that you don't. We wouldn't want to compromise her location.'

'Whatever you say. But be careful, all right?'

'I always am.'

'For all the good it'll do,' said Alice.

Chapter Seven

Lacey woke up, and wished she hadn't. She lay on her back, eyes shut. Her arms, stretched overhead, were numb. Moving slightly, she felt a sheet beneath her. She wasn't covered: a mild breeze stirred against her skin, probably from the window above her bed.

She tried to lower her arms, but a tightness around the wrists held them in place. They were tied.

She moved her feet. They, at least, were free.

She licked her lips. No gag.

But she was blindfolded. She could feel it. She tried to open her eyes, but couldn't raise the lids. From the sticky stiffness against them, she guessed they were taped shut.

Lying motionless, she listened. The only sound in the bedroom was the hum of her electric clock. Through the open window came sounds of birds, a car door banging shut, a power mower somewhere in the distance.

So it's morning.

And I told James I wouldn't be coming in. Neat play. Somebody'd come by to check on me, if I hadn't told him that.

Just as well. This maniac would only kill him.

If he's here!

Lacey realized, with a dizzying sense of relief, that he might very well have departed – tied her up, took her car, and headed for distant places. Why not?

Because, as David Horowitz always says, if it sounds too good to be true, it usually is.

He's still here. Probably watching me right this second. Does he know I'm awake?

Lacey tried to breathe slowly and deeply, feigning sleep.

What does he want? she wondered. Why the hell hasn't he killed me like he did the others? Don't worry, he probably will.

Unless I get him first.

Fat chance.

You can't kill a man you never see.

She hadn't spotted him in the car, though he'd been in the back seat on her way home from Hoffman's. She and Cliff had missed him when they searched the house – unless he sneaked in later.

But how, in God's name, did he get into the bathroom? That door never opened, she was almost positive. And he sure didn't climb in through the window. He was just suddenly there. A magician, a regular Houdini.

How do you kill a guy like that?

Easy, you don't.

But maybe he is gone.

No, he's here. Still here.

But why?

Because he *likes* you.

Scream, cunt, and I'll rip off your head. Sure he likes me.

The doorbell rang.

Footsteps raced toward her.

She opened her mouth to yell, and a hand slapped across it.

'Don't make a sound,' whispered the low, scratchy voice from last night.

The bell rang again, loud in the silent house. Who was there? James or Carl coming by to check on her, after all? Cliff? It rang again. She kicked her legs high, twisting to swing them off the bed, but an arm hooked them behind the knees and stopped them. She bucked and writhed. The powerful arm pressed, curling her back, raising her rump off the bed, forcing her legs down until her knees mashed her breasts.

She shook her head, tried to bite the hand. But it stayed tight on her mouth. Her teeth couldn't find flesh to bite, only scraping it without doing damage.

Mouth covered, compressed as she was, she couldn't bring in enough air through her nostrils. She stopped struggling and tried to breathe. Her lungs burned.

The doorbell rang again.

Go away!

She sucked air in through her nostrils, but couldn't draw it in deeply enough, couldn't seem to get it to her lungs. She felt as if she were drowning. The man seemed to realize this, and pressed his hand slightly upward to block her nose.

No!

A roar filled her head. She sucked against the hand. No air came through. She kicked, but the man pressed her knees harder against her chest. Her heart thundered as if it might explode.

Then the arm stopped pushing at her legs. As she lowered them, the hand left her mouth. She gulped in air.

'I oughta kill you,' the man whispered.

Lacey kept gasping.

He shoved her legs apart, and she felt his mouth. Then he was on top of her, pushing inside her, ramming. Lacey didn't struggle. She lay still, trying to catch her breath, trying not to think, to build a wall in her head that she could hide behind, away from the pain and filth and terror.

'I'll untie your hands,' he said when he was finally through.

Lacey nodded.

'You can't hurt me. You can't get away from me. Don't try.'

'I won't.'

He removed the bonds. Lacey tried to lower her arms. At first, they wouldn't move. They burned and tingled as feeling slowly returned to them. At last, she was able to bring them down. She rubbed the deep indentations on her wrists.

'What do you want?' she asked.

He made a nasty laugh. 'I've got what I want. You. And your house.'

Reaching to her face, she touched the adhesive tape over her eyes. Her hands were slapped away.

'Leave it.'

'Who are you?'

'If I told you that, you'd know.'

What kind of answer was that? 'Do I know you?' she asked.

'Damn right.'

'What did I do? Did I *do* something to you?'

'It's what you didn't do. But we've taken care of that, haven't we?' Lacey flinched as he put a hand on her breast. She didn't try to remove it, didn't dare. 'I've always wanted you. Now I've got you. Want to know what's next?'

She nodded.

'I'm gonna be your guest for a while. For a long, long while. This is a lot better than the market. The market stinks. No bed, no pussy to curl up with. This is just what I want, and I'm gonna stay.'

'Are you . . . hiding out?'

'Oh yes. And they're a sharp pack of bastards. They'll come looking. Might even check here, but we're too smart for 'em. Lacey's gonna answer the phone, Lacey's gonna answer the door, Lacey's even gonna go to work after today, just like everything's normal. But she won't let no one in, and she won't tell our little secret, and she won't try to run away. 'Cause if she does, I'll do horrible disgusting things to her.'

She couldn't believe it! He would actually let her leave the house? 'All right,' she said.

'I know what you're thinking. You're thinking, soon as I let you free, you'll run off to the cops. If the cops don't get me, you'll leave town. Either way, you'll be safe from me. But you're wrong. Wrong wrong wrong. You can't escape.'

The hand went away from her breast, picked at the side of her face, and ripped the tape away. It came off with a sound like tearing cloth, stinging her skin, uprooting brows and lashes. Lacey clutched her eyes until the pain subsided. Then she lowered her hands. She opened her eyes. Squinting against the light, she looked up. Then to the sides.

The man was gone!

She bolted upright, and studied the sunlit room. He was not there! She swung her legs off the bed, knocking the wadded tape to the floor, and stood up. Dizzy. She grabbed the top of the dresser for support. When her head cleared, she lunged for the doorway.

The door slammed shut. She rushed against it, grabbed the knob.

A hand clutched her shoulders and swung her around.

Nobody there.

She felt hands on both her breasts. They squeezed. She saw depressions the fingers made in her flesh, but not the fingers themselves.

'Get the idea?' the man asked.

'Oh my God,' Lacey muttered. 'You're invisible!'

'Fuckin' right.'

Reaching to her breasts, she touched his hands. Their surface stopped her fingers like a layer of hard air – but air with the texture of skin. She shook her head. 'How?'

'A little miracle.'

46

'No, really,' she said, trying to sound eager, as if suddenly overcome with curiosity. She touched his hairy wrists, his thick, heavily muscled forearms: he was standing directly in front of her. 'Who did it to you? How?'

'If I told you that, you'd know.'

'I want to know.'

'Then you'd . . .'

Lacey clenched his forearms and kicked, shooting her leg up high through the space in front of her. Her instep smacked flesh. The man's arms jerked away and he bellowed. Lacey tugged open the door. She dashed out and across the dining room to her kitchen. Grabbing the knob of the back door, she hesitated. What use to run away? How do you hide from an invisible man? You don't. Sooner or later, he'd get her.

She slid a carving knife out of its rack, and dashed toward the breakfast nook. She rushed alongside the table, swinging a chair out behind her to block the narrow passage. Spinning around, she shoved the other chair out. Now she stood behind the table, both sides blocked, knife in front of her, ready.

Almost ready.

She opened a cupboard behind her. She lifted out a heavy bag. Clamping the knife in her teeth, she unrolled its top.

With a skidding rumble, the table scooted toward her. She lurched backwards. The edge of the counter caught her rump. She leapt, throwing herself backwards, drawing up her knees. Her buttocks hit the countertop, and the table crashed against the cupboards.

Lacey dropped her feet to the table. Lunging forward, she flung out the contents of the sack. A cloud of flour filled the air.

The man dived through it, an empty shape in the white powder.

Jerking the knife from her mouth, Lacey plunged it into his back. He shrieked. His head drove into her belly, slamming her backwards. Grabbing his shaggy, powdered hair,

Lacey tugged away his head. She saw the hazy image of a face, and smashed her fist into its nose. Then she kicked and shoved at the writhing figure until it slid to the floor.

She crawled to the table's edge, and looked down. He was on his knees, head to the floor, growling, reaching behind him with dusty white arms, groping for the knife. His back was half-clear where his blood had swept the flour off.

Lacey jumped, landed beyond him, and fell. Scurrying to her feet, she ran from the kitchen. She grabbed her handbag and keys off the dining-room table, and raced into her bedroom. She yanked her bathrobe off the closet hook. Pulling it on, she ran for the front door. Got outside. Sprinted to her car and locked herself inside and shot it backwards out of the driveway. She hit the brakes. Shifted to Drive. And sped up the road away from her house and the man and the horror.

My God, she thought, I did it!

Chapter Eight

Lacey rolled a clean sheet of paper into her typewriter at the *Tribune* office, and rushed through her story:

> *Tribune* reporter Lacey Allen warded off a masked assailant in her home, Thursday morning, and escaped with minor injuries after stabbing him with a kitchen knife.
>
> According to Miss Allen, the attacker likely concealed himself in the trunk of her car the previous night, after

brutally murdering Elsie Hoffman and Red Peterson at Hoffman's Market. 'Some time during the night,' remarks Allen, 'he must have sneaked out of the trunk and broken into my house.'

Awakened in the early morning hours, the young reporter was subdued by the intruder and told that he wished to use her home as a temporary refuge. She was warned of severe consequences if she refused to cooperate.

Later in the morning, while preparing coffee at his request, Miss Allen surprised the suspected killer by flinging flour into his face. Wielding a butcher knife, she attacked and wounded the man, enabling herself to escape.

She sped from the scene in her car. Pulled over by Officer Donald Martin of the Oasis PD, Miss Allen blurted out her story. The officer radioed for back-up units. Minutes later, officers Martin, Grabowski and Lewis rushed the house, only to find it deserted. A thorough search of the premises and surrounding neighborhood proved fruitless.

Though authorities are baffled by the suspect's disappearance, the incident at Miss Allen's home provides the first clues to his identity. Full sets of fingerprints were discovered at the scene, and have been wired to the FBI headquarters in Washington, DC for possible identification. Also, impressions of his bare feet were found on the floury kitchen floor, and photographed for later comparisons.

According to Miss Allen, the suspect was a white male in his late twenties, six feet tall, weighing 180 pounds, with long hair. From bits of conversation, Miss Allen feels certain that he is, or has been, a resident of Oasis.

Citizens are urged to exercise extreme caution until the suspect has been apprehended.

Lacey reread her story, then got up from her desk and took the two typewritten pages to Carl Williams. She handed them to the lanky editor, and hiked up her loose corduroys. The rest of the clothes fit no better. Somebody might've at least asked her sizes before sending Alfred out for a new wardrobe. At the time, she'd been too upset to care.

Carl finished reading the story. He rolled back his chair, and frowned. 'Left something out, didn't you?'

'Do *you* believe the guy was invisible?'

'That's what you told me. And the police.'

'But do you believe it?'

He sighed, and rubbed a hand through his short curly hair. 'Hell no,' he said. 'I don't believe it. Not for a second.'

'You figure I imagined it.'

'Well, Lace, you've gone through a lot of . . .'

'Slipped a cog or two?'

'I'm not saying that. But it's not unusual for someone – in a car accident, say – to lose her memory of what happened. Goes on all the time.'

'I remember everything.'

'I'm not saying you don't. I'm just saying that, under the circumstances, your sense of reality might've taken a beating.'

'Okay, and that's basically what the cops thought. And it's what our readers will think, too. I have to go on living in this town, Carl. If I claim this guy was invisible, I'll be a joke.'

'Word'll get out, anyway.'

'It'll only be rumor, if it does. I can deny it. But I can't deny something in a story I've written for the *Trib*. Besides, it's not really a lie; I'm pretty sure my description is accurate – as far as it goes. I just can't admit he's invisible, though. I can't. Not in public.'

'Yeah.' He rubbed his face. 'Guess it wouldn't do the *Trib*'s credibility any good, either. Can't have a reporter who *sees* things – or doesn't, as the case may be.' He gave her a weary smile. 'We'll run it this way.'

'Thanks.'

'You'll give me a call when you get to Tucson?'

'Right away.'

'Fine. Take care of yourself, Lace. I'll keep you posted on any new developments.'

'Thanks. See you in two weeks. Sooner, if they get him.'

Lacey went out the rear door to the *Tribune*'s small parking lot. After the air conditioning, the heat outside felt like the breath of an oven. Too bad Alfred didn't buy shorts instead of these corduroys. Squinting against the brilliant glare, she stopped at the rear of her car.

Her stomach fluttered a bit as she opened the trunk. She swept a hand through its emptiness, touched her spare tire, her towel, her flares. Then, satisfied, she shut the trunk and went to the driver's door. She unlocked it, opened it, and reached around to flip up the lock button of the back door.

She opened the door. Crawling over the seat, she reached down and ran her hand along the floor. Then she climbed out, locked and shut the door.

She slid in behind the steering wheel, and locked herself in. Leaning sideways across the seat, she raked the floor with her fingertips.

Okay.

No passenger.

She started the car, and drove from the parking lot. Her tank was full. She drove for two hours, and didn't stop until she reached the Desert Wind hotel in Tucson.

Chapter Nine

'Alfred, go on over to Harry's and pick me up some lunch.'

With a nod, Alfred fumbled among half a dozen pens safely clipped inside his plastic pocket shield. He plucked out a Bic, and slipped a note pad from his trousers. 'What'll it be?'

'Pastrami on a sourdough roll, hold the onions. Fries, and a Bud.' Carl waited for the young man to finish scribbling, then gave him a five-dollar bill.

'Want a doughnut or something?'

'Nope.'

'Back in a jiff.'

'No hurry.' Carl followed him outside, watched him start down the sidewalk toward the deli three blocks away, and called after him, 'Don't forget to bring me back some ketchup.'

'Oh, I'll remember.'

He watched Alfred slip the note pad out of his seat pocket. He stepped back inside the office. He shut and locked the door, then hurried through the deserted room to his desk. His hands were sweaty and trembling. He wiped them on his pants legs. He took a deep breath, and picked up the telephone. On the first try, his finger slipped and he had to dial again.

At the other end, the phone rang six times before it was picked up. A woman's pleasant voice said, 'Spiritual Development Foundation, Miss Prince speaking.'

'This is Carl Williams, number 68259385.'

'Just a moment, please.'

He waited for her to punch the code number into her terminal.

'Level?' she asked.

'Red.'

'Very good. What can we do for you, Mr Williams?'

'I have an urgent message for section three.'

'Just a moment, please. I'll put you through to the section three coordinator.'

Carl heard the faint ringing of a phone. Then a strong male voice said, 'Farris, here. What have you got for us?'

'This is Carl Williams, publisher of the *Oasis Tribune*. That's Oasis, Arizona.'

'Right.' He sounded impatient.

'We've had a series of incidents here that I suspect might be related to the SDF – a couple of nasty murders and an assault on one of my reporters, a Miss Lacey Allen.'

'I see. And what makes you think they may be connected to SDF?'

'Oasis is the home town of Samuel Hoffman. Also, Hoffman's mother was one of the murder victims.'

'You think Hoffman may have been the perpetrator?'

'My reporter, Miss Allen, claims that her attacker was invisible.'

'Sounds like our man,' Farris said, sounding pleased. 'Any knowledge of his present whereabouts?'

'Miss Allen wounded him this morning – about four hours ago – at her home here in town. The police couldn't find any trace of him, but I imagine he isn't far from here.'

'Excellent.'

'I may be wrong about this, sir, but I think he's still after the Allen woman. While she was his prisoner, he threatened to hunt her down if she ever escaped.'

'I see. Where is Allen now?'

'She's on her way to Tucson. She took his threat seriously, and plans to hide out there for a while.'

'Her exact location?'

'I don't know. She's promised to give me a call, though, once she's found a room. I suspect she'll check into a hotel.'

'Very good. I'll alert our Tucson personnel. Now. This Allen woman, does she trust you?'

'Yes.'

'As soon as she gives you her location, I want you to do two things. First, inform me immediately. Second, drive to Tucson and meet her. Stay with her, and keep us informed of her movements. If Hoffman goes for her, we want to be there.'

'What if . . . suppose he attacks while I'm there?'

'Any sacrifice you make on our behalf will be rewarded.'

'I mean, do you want me to kill him?'

'Laveda would prefer him alive. It's a moot point, however; you probably couldn't kill him if you tried.'

Chapter Ten

A quiet, rumbling sound entered Dukane's mind. He realized, vaguely, that the sliding glass door to his balcony was being opened. Suddenly alarmed, he tensed and opened his eyes.

It was morning. He stared at the nightstand, thought about jerking open the drawer and grabbing his automatic. Then he remembered bringing a woman home last night from the bar at La Dome. Rolling over, he saw that the other side of the king-size bed was empty.

'Cindy?' he asked.

'Out here.'

He crawled across the bed, climbed off, and saw her standing naked on the sunlit balcony. Her back was toward him, her hands on the railing. He stepped out. The sun felt warm on his bare skin. She looked around and smiled. Kissing her cheek, Dukane pressed himself lightly against her back. He slipped his hands up the smoothness of her sides, and held her breasts.

'It's a lovely day for a swim,' she said.

'If you're planning a dive from here, don't. I tried it once. Broke my ankle.'

'Yuck. I guess I won't.'

'It's farther than it looks, and the concrete is very hard.'

'Were you drunk?'

'When I jumped? Cold sober.'

She sighed as he fingered her rigid nipples. She squirmed, her buttocks rubbing him. Then she turned around. She leaned back against the railings. 'Right here,' she said.

'A bit awkward.'

'Consider it a challenge.'

'I'm always up for a challenge.'

She gripped the railing with both hands and spread her legs. Dukane clutched her hips. Crouching slightly, he found her wet slit. He thrust upward into her. Her head went back and she moaned.

When they were done, they left the balcony. Cindy disappeared into the bathroom. Dukane put on his robe, and went downstairs. He started to prepare coffee. As its thin stream trickled into the pot, Cindy entered the kitchen. She was wearing one of his short-sleeved plaid shirts, and nothing else.

'Okay if I borrow this?' she asked, raising her arms and turning around.

'Wish it looked that good on me.' As he spoke, he remembered Alice wearing one of his spare shirts before he bought the dress for her. He wondered how Dr Teri Miles was faring with her. He didn't envy the woman, spending days alone with the little bitch. Thinking about it, a familiar worry whispered in his mind. He pushed it away. They're all right, he told himself.

'What's your drothers for breakfast?' Cindy asked. 'I make a mean Spanish omelet, if you've got the makings.'

'Hmmm?'

'Spanish omelet. Hello? You tuned in?'

'Yeah. That sounds great. There're chilis in the refrigerator.'

'Cheese, eggs?'

'Them too. You go ahead and get started, I'll bring in the paper.'

'*News*paper?' She wrinkled her nose. 'How dreary.'

'I just read the funnies.'

'Liar liar, pants on fire.'

'Not at the moment.'

With a laugh, she pulled open the refrigerator. She bent over, the tail of the shirt riding up. Dukane glimpsed her pale rump, then turned away.

Outside, he spotted the *Times* halfway up his long driveway. He crossed the lawn, its grass cool and dewy under his feet. The driveway felt pleasantly warm and dry. He picked up the paper. Heading back to the house, he pulled off its plastic ribbon.

The bold letters near the bottom corner of the front page made his heart lurch. 'KABC ANCHORMAN AND WIFE SLAIN.'

He stopped in the wet grass:

KABC news anchorman Ron Donovan and his wife, Ruth, were found brutally murdered last evening in their Hollywood Hills home. The bodies . . .

He didn't read more. He ran to the front door, flung the paper down in the foyer, and raced upstairs. In his bedroom, he grabbed his trousers. He tugged his wallet from the rear pocket, flipped it open, and searched the bill compartment. He pinched out a business card: Dr T. R. Miles, MD. At the telephone beside his bed, he dialed.

The phone rang fifteen times before he hung up.

In less than a minute, he was dressed. He rushed downstairs.

Cindy was on her knees, reaching into a cupboard, when he entered the kitchen. He patted her bare rump. 'Come on.'

'Huh?'

He held out her panties and skirt. 'Put 'em on, quick. I've gotta get somewhere fast.'

'What's wrong?'

'Just hurry.'

Looking puzzled and worried, she started to get dressed. 'Where're we going?'

'Venice. I have to check on someone.'

She zipped the side of her skirt and followed him to the side door. 'My shoes.'

'You can stay in the car.' He rushed into the connecting garage, climbed into his Jaguar, and pressed the remote button to raise the door. Cindy slid onto the passenger seat as he gunned the engine to life.

'Are you going to tell me what's up?' she asked.

'No,' he said, and sped backwards up the driveway.

'That's a hell of a note.'

'It's business. It's dangerous. You're better off not knowing.' He glanced back to make sure the road was clear, then swung onto it, hit the brakes, and shifted to first gear.

'Then why are you taking me with you?'

'Wouldn't be safe to leave you behind.'

'Safe for who?'

'You.'

'Oh wonderful.'

'It'd probably be all right,' he said, 'but I don't want to take the chance, so it's better if you just stick with me for now.'

'God, what've I got myself into?'

'Consider it an adventure.'

'Maybe you could just drop me off at my apartment, huh?'

'No time.' He sped down the wooded hillside, stopped at Laurel Canyon Boulevard to wait for a break in the traffic, then shot out.

'Look, I'm really not up for an adventure.'

'I'm sorry. Believe me, I was looking forward to your Spanish omelet, a day of swimming and lying in the sun, passionate embraces . . .'

'Me too, damn it.'

'Things go wrong.'

'Yeah. How about letting me out?'

'Barefoot and purseless?'

'Just stop down here at Ventura, and I'll hop out.'

'That's a long hike to Hollywood.'

'I've got a girlfriend. She's only a few blocks away. I'll be fine, thank you.'

Dukane thought it over. He didn't like the idea of dumping her out, but he saw no point in dragging her to Venice, possibly into danger. Steering with one hand, he slipped the wallet from his pocket. He gave it to her. 'Keep that until I get your purse back to you. Collateral.'

'Oh, Matt, that's not necessary.'

'There's some cash in it. Use whatever you like.'

She laughed. 'Are you joking?'

'Not at all. Pick up a pair of shoes, treat your friend to lunch, whatever. I'll get your purse and stuff back to you tonight. You'll be home?'

'I'll be there.'

'The address on your driver's license right?'

'Yep.'

The traffic light at the intersection with Ventura Boulevard was red when they reached it. Cindy leaned across the seat, kissed Dukane quickly on the mouth, and sprang from the car.

It took him three freeways and twenty minutes to reach the Lincoln exit in Santa Monica. The traffic on Lincoln was heavy. He finally reached Rose, turned right, and sped up the street for several blocks. He parked on Rose. He ran to the other side, then walked.

Approaching Dr Miles's house, he saw that the gate of its low picket fence stood open. His stomach knotted.

Maybe the mailman had left the gate open.

Wishful thinking.

They got to Alice's parents, found out where she was being kept. No telepathy necessary. No magical powers. Just a check of their records, a visit to the girl's home, an interrogation.

Shit! He'd known, damn it, that something like this could happen. He should've insisted on staying. He'd let the lady talk him out of it, he'd gone against his better judgement, and . . .

The front door stood ajar. Grabbing his automatic, Dukane toed it open. The foyer, the hallway, were deserted. The house was silent.

With his elbow, he eased the door shut. He stepped forward, silent except for the groan of the hardwood floor. At the edge of the living-room entry, he stopped. He listened, but heard nothing. Holding his breath, he peered around the corner.

The naked, headless body of a woman was sprawled on the floor, her flesh carved, a fire poker protruding from between her spread legs.

Alice smiled at him. 'I knew you'd come,' she said. She sat cross-legged near the body, her face and yellow sundress smeared with blood. The head of Teri Miles lay in her lap. She lifted it with both hands. The wire-rimmed glasses were in place, one lens webbed with cracks. The eyes were open, staring. Alice grinned.

From behind the couch and easy chair, three men rose into view.

'These are my friends. I told you they'd find me.'

'Drop your weapon,' said the man behind the chair. He wore a three-piece suit and a confident smile. In his hand was an automatic, probably .25 caliber, small enough to be concealed easily in a pocket. Too small for much accuracy.

Neither of the others held a gun.

The one on the left, a fat bearded man dressed like a biker, climbed over the back of the couch. He stepped down, his belly swinging, and waved a bloody Bowie knife in front of his smile.

The one on the right stepped around an end of the couch. He wore grease-stained coveralls. He held a pipe wrench.

Dukane took a step into the living room.

'I told you to . . .'

'You drop yours,' he said, raising his .45. 'Mine's bigger.'

The man's eyes flicked to the side. Catching the movement, Dukane whirled around, flung up his left arm, and blocked the knife. The woman wielding it hissed and jerked the blade back, tearing open his forearm. Dukane swung his heavy Colt. It slammed across her cheek and she stumbled backwards, grabbing her face.

Dukane started to turn. He heard a quick flat *bam* like a screen door slamming shut. The bullet punched through his jacket sleeve, but he felt no hit. The clean-cut man tried again as Dukane brought up his automatic and fired. The man's chin dissolved in a burst of red.

Even as the gun bucked, the biker chopped down with his knife. He missed Dukane's wrist, but the powerful blow against the barrel knocked his pistol free. Alice grabbed his ankles. He fell backwards as the huge knife slashed at his belly. Hitting the floor, he jerked a foot free. Alice reached for it. His heel smashed her face aside.

He kicked out at the legs of the biker, but the bulky man lunged forward, kicking back, slashing at his shins.

The grease monkey, at the biker's side, hurled the wrench down at Dukane's head. It almost missed. It numbed his ear and brought tears to his eyes. Dukane grabbed the wrench. He sat up, swinging it to keep away the knife. It clanked against the blade. Before the knife could slash back, he leaned far forward and hammered the man's knee. With a cry of pain, the biker hobbled and fell.

The mechanic was bending down, reaching for Dukane's automatic. Dukane threw the wrench. It bounced off his shoulder, knocking him off balance. As he dropped to one knee, Dukane scrambled toward him. He saw the man pick up the gun, swing its barrel toward him. His fist cut upward. Hit the man's hand. The barrel jumped with the impact, tipped high and blasted a hole through the mechanic's upper teeth. The bullet exited the top of his head, splashing gore at the ceiling.

Dukane jerked the pistol from his dead fingers. He stood as the biker limped toward him, snarling, waving the knife like a pirate's cutlass.

He shot the man in the chest.

The woman who'd caught Dukane's barrel with her cheek was on her hands and knees, spitting blood and bits of broken teeth. She was wearing a tennis dress. Across the seat of her panties was printed 'DON'T POACH'.

Alice lay on the floor, curled up, blood spilling out between the fingers holding her face.

Dukane went to her.

He snapped a handcuff around her left wrist and dragged her across the floor. He cuffed her to the tennis player.

Then he searched for a telephone and called the police.

Chapter Eleven

Lacey was awakened by maids giggling and chattering in the hallway. They spoke Spanish, a language she had picked up as a child in Oasis. She grinned as she listened.

Two of the women had gone on a double-date to the drive-in, last night. Infuriated by their drunken boyfriends, they'd insisted on sitting together. The boyfriends climbed out of the car and went stumbling away, at which point the girls grandly drove off.

Lacey wondered who owned the car.

She flung the sheet aside, and groaned as she sat up. All over her body, her muscles ached with stiffness. She felt better than before, though. Waking up in the hotel room yesterday morning, she'd felt like the loser in a scrimmage with the Dallas Cowboys. Today, by comparison, was great.

Getting off the bed, she hobbled into the bathroom. She studied herself in the full-length mirror. Though her hair was a mess, her face had lost its haggard, haunted look. The bruises mottling her body had turned a sickly, greenish yellow. Hard ridges of scab had formed on her scratches.

'Won't be posing for a centerfold,' she muttered. 'But not bad.'

She took a shower in the huge, glass-sided stall, then dried herself and got dressed in the same baggy clothes Alfred had bought on Thursday.

This was Saturday.

Escape day. Thursday and Friday, she'd been afraid to leave her room. She'd sat around reading paperbacks from the hotel gift shop, watching television, smoking, indulging herself in incredibly expensive food and wine from room service. After two days of it, she was ready to get out. More than ready.

She intended to buy several items, but the sun felt wonderful so she left her car in the hotel parking lot and walked. Three blocks away, in a sporting goods store just off Stone, she found most of what she wanted: a web belt to hold up her corduroys, a tank-top and gym shorts, a one-piece bathing suit, suntan oil, a pocket knife, and a sheath knife with a six-inch blade. After purchasing the items, she shut herself into a dressing room and changed into the shorts and top.

She wandered the downtown area, enjoying the feel of the sun, pleased but slightly nervous with the stares of passing men.

Near noon, she entered a hardware store. She bought a spray can of 'aluminum'-colored paint. She ate lunch at a McDonalds, then returned to her hotel.

She put on the swimsuit. With its high neckline, it concealed the worst of her injuries. Scratches and bruises showed on her thighs, her shoulders, her arms. But that couldn't be helped. She was determined to use the pool, no matter how she looked. Turning, she studied her back. The suit left it bare almost to the rump. Her back, at least, looked reasonably unmarred.

She emptied her handbag on the bed, and filled it with what she needed: suntan oil, an Ed McBain paperback, the can of spray paint and her sheath knife. With a bath towel draping her shoulders, she left the room.

The pool, in the hotel's center courtyard, was nearly deserted: a young man was swimming lengths in a steady crawl; a deeply tanned woman lay facedown on a lounge with the top of her black bikini untied; and a middle-aged couple sat beneath an umbrella, sipping Bloody Marys. Lacey spread her towel on a lounge far from the others, and sat down.

She slicked herself with coconut oil, breathing deeply of its aroma, a rich sweet fragrance that reminded her of others, better times.

Of Will Rogers State Park, near Pacific Palisades where she stayed with Tom and his family that week in spring, six years ago. Her senior year at Stanford. They spent every day at the beach, swimming far out, body surfing, walking the shoreline, or just stretching out on their towels. Tom would trickle coconut oil onto her back. His hands would glide over her, sometimes slipping down between her legs.

Brian used to do that, too, but she never loved Brian. Never loved anyone after Tom. But Brian came along at a time when she needed a man, and she'd never had such sex; Brian cared about nothing else.

Lying back, Lacey sighed and remembered those times by his pool when she lay on her back with her eyes shut and the sun on her naked body – the sun, the oil, and Brian's sliding, searching hands.

Now, she wondered if she could ever allow another man to have her. She knew her desire was strong: it always had been. But could she let herself be touched without recoiling, entered without shuddering in revulsion?

Sprawled on the bathroom floor. The rug against her face. Fingers clamping her shoulders. Erection ramming her.

Hurt by the sudden shock of memory, she opened her eyes, groped inside her handbag, and took out the book. She struggled to read, but her mind soon strayed from the words. She saw herself tied to the bed and she heard the scratchy voice – 'I oughta kill you' – and felt him jerk her legs apart, felt his mouth. She shut the book.

The pool was deserted. The man who'd been swimming lengths now lay on the concrete, dripping, hands folded under his head. Lacey took off her sunglasses. She got up from the lounge and stepped to the pool's edge.

She dived in, jerking rigid at the cold blast of water, gliding through its silence and finally curving upward to the surface. She swam to the far end, turned, and swam back with all her might. Then she turned again and raced to the other end and back. She sidestroked two lengths, then breast-stroked two lengths, then climbed exhausted from the pool. She lowered the back of her lounge and flopped on it facedown, gasping.

She heard the slap of footsteps.

'You're quite a swimmer.'

Raising her head, she looked up at the man – the one who'd been in the pool before her. 'Thanks,' she told him.

'I'm Scott.'

'Hi.'

He was slim and muscular and tanned. His tight bikini trunks covered little of him, and concealed less. He sat on the concrete beside Lacey, facing her. 'Do you have a name?' he asked.

'Doesn't everyone?'

'Oooh. Touchy.'

'Sorry. I'm just not in the mood for company.'

'That's the time when you *need* company the most.'

'Wrong.' She lowered her head, and shut her eyes.

'Can't get rid of me that easily. Nothing I enjoy more than a challenge.'

'Climb a mountain.'

'Too rough. I prefer smoother terrain.'

'Leave me alone, all right?'

'Your back will burn. Would you like me to apply a dab of oil?'

'I wouldn't. I'd like to be left alone. Why don't you go try someone else?'

'Because you're beautiful and lonely.'

Lacey sighed. 'I really don't need this. If you won't leave, I will.'

'Ah, say no more. I can take a hint.'

She opened one eye enough to see him stand. Scott smiled and waved as he backed away.

Resting her head on her crossed arms, Lacey tried to sleep. Her mind replayed the encounter. The guy had been arrogant and pushy. But, damn it, she could've at least been polite. She'd acted like a bitch. She felt herself blushing at the memory.

Well, what's done is done.

She tried not to think about it.

She lay motionless, concentrating on the hot pressure of the sun.

'A libation for the lady.'

Lifting her head, she saw Scott above her, a Bloody Mary in each hand. 'You don't give up, do you?'

'That's why I seldom fail.'

Lacey turned over, stared at the grinning man, and finally sat up. 'I'm Lacey,' she said. 'And I apologize for acting creepy.'

'Creepy is a fair first-line of defense,' he said, sitting down on the concrete. 'Only fair, though. Total complacency works better. It reduces the woman's guilt factor. Much more difficult to penetrate.'

'You've studied the subject.'

'Women fascinate me.' He took the dripping celery stalk from his drink and licked it.

Intentional symbolism? More than likely. Holding back a smile, Lacey removed her own stalk and tapped off its drops on the rim of her glass. She set it down beside her lounge. Scott placed his beside it.

'To our fortunate encounter,' he said.

'Okay.'

He clinked his glass against hers, and they both drank. Her Bloody Mary was hot with tabasco. It made her eyes water, her nose start to run. She sniffed.

'So tell me, Lacey, what is a lovely young lady doing alone at this fashionable resort hotel?'

'What makes you think I'm alone?'

'I have an unerring nose for such things.'

'Unerring?' she asked, somewhat surprised that he had used the correct pronunciation – err as in purr.

'*Seldom* erring. But it's hit the mark this time, hasn't it?'

'Isn't "mark" a conman term for a sucker?'

'Do you see yourself as a sucker?'

'Do you see yourself as a conman?'

He grinned – a boyish, disarming grin. Lacey wondered how much time he spent at mirrors, practicing it. 'A confidence man? Of course. Here I am, trying to win your confidence.'

'When's the pitch?'

'Later. I haven't won yet, have I?'

'Far from it.'

'Are you always this distrustful?'

'Only of strangers who approach me uninvited.'

'Ah. You assume I have mischief on my mind.'

'Do you?'

'That would be telling.'

If I told you that, you'd know. The low, rough voice. She suddenly trembled as if a cloud had smothered the sun, an icy wind blown across her.

'What's wrong?'

'Nothing.'

'Hey, I was only joking about the mischief.'

'I know.'

'Are you all right?'

'I just . . . what you said, it reminded me of something.'

'Must've been something unpleasant.'

'It was.'

'Want to talk about it?'

'No.'

'A chance like this doesn't come along every day, you know: a friendly, willing ear, the sunlight beating down, a Bloody Mary in your hand. Besides, I might be able to help.'

'How could you help?'

'How will I know unless you tell me your problem? Let me guess, though: it involves a man.'

She took a drink, and stared at the glistening pool.

'He did something to you.'

The bantering tone was gone from Scott's voice. Lacey glanced at him. He was staring at his drink, his face solemn.

'Yes,' she said.

'He didn't jilt you, nothing like that. Whatever he did, you're frightened of him. He hurt you, didn't he? Beat you up.'

'You're very observant,' Lacey muttered, glancing down at her bruises and scratches.

'You came here to get away from him. You're hiding out, probably even registered under a fake name in case he comes looking for you.'

'I couldn't,' she said. 'I had to use a credit card to get the room.'

'But the rest is right?'

'Close enough.' Lacey sipped her drink and set the glass on her belly. Its cold wetness soaked through her damp swimsuit. It felt good.

'Husband, boyfriend, or stranger?'

'Stranger.'

'Did you go to the police?'

'He got away.'

'And you're afraid he'll come after you?'

'He'll kill me, if he can.'

'We won't let him.'

'We?'

He winked. 'You and me, kid.'

'Thanks for the offer, but I don't want anyone else involved in this. Besides, I don't think he'll find me here.'

'It doesn't take a genius to find someone hiding out at a major hotel – particularly if she's using her real name.'

'Thanks.'

'How long have you been here?'

'This is the third day. I got in Thursday afternoon.'

'Then you've been here much too long. You're lucky he hasn't already shown up.'

'He doesn't even know what city I'm in, Scott.'

'You're not from Tucson?'

'No.'

'But I'll wager this is the nearest large city, and the place he'll look first.'

'I guess so,' she admitted.

'If I were you, I'd get out of here today and check into a different hotel. Better still, head for another town.'

'It's past check-out time. Besides, I don't want to. I like this one.'

Scott shrugged. 'In that case, I think you should allow me to act as your escort.'

'No. Really, Scott . . .'

'I'd be happy to do it. After all, you're a beautiful woman, and we're both alone in the city. How could I spend my time better than by keeping company with a creature like you?'

'A creature?' she asked, smiling.

'A damsel in distress.'

'It might be dangerous.'

'I'm good with my dukes. Besides, I pack heat.'

'A gun?'

'A Colt .45 automatic. Never go anywhere without it. Except, of course, to the swimming pool.'

'What are you, a bank robber?'

'You ever hear of Charlie Dane?'

'*San Francisco Hit, Manhattan Mayhem* . . .?'

'*Tucson Death Squad*. That's to be his latest battle against the forces of evil. The galleys are up in my suite this very moment.'

Lacey stared at him, frowning. 'But those are written by Max Carter.'

'Otherwise known as Scott Bradley.'

'You.'

'Me.'

'That still doesn't explain the gun.'

'Max keeps the rod at his side when he sits at the old typewriter. It puts him in touch with Charlie Dane.'

Lacey grinned. 'Does Max also wear Charlie's trench coat?'

'Too hot. But he does don the battered fedora.'

'Not while he's escorting me, I hope.'

'I'll leave Max in the room, and borrow his piece.'

'He won't mind?'

'He's always eager to please.'

Chapter Twelve

Carl grabbed the phone before its second ring. '*Tribune.*'

'Carl?'

His heart began to hammer. 'How's it going, Lace?'

'So far, so good. He hasn't found me yet. Any activity on your end?'

'Nope. There haven't been any incidents since you left.'

'Damn. I almost wish . . . At least I'd know he's still there.'

'Well, maybe he's just lying low. Or maybe your knife did the trick.'

'Don't I wish.'

'So, how are you feeling?'

'Scared. Other than that, I guess I'm all right. Recuperating.'

'That's good. Look, you'd better let me know where you're staying. If something breaks, up this way, I'll want to let you know.'

'Sure. I'm at the Desert Wind, room three sixty-two.'

Carl wrote it down.

'I meant to call you yesterday, but . . . couldn't get myself to do anything. Felt like crawling under a rock.'

'That's all right, Lace. Perfectly understandable.'

'Anyway, I'm better now.'

'Glad to hear it. Look, is there anything I can do for you?'

'Just keep me posted, is all.'

'Sure thing. Take care of yourself, now.'

'I'll try. So long, Carl.'

He hung up. Across the room, one of his reporters hunched over a typewriter working on the lead story for tomorrow's edition. Otherwise, the office was deserted. 'Jack?'

The reporter looked up, raising his eyebrows.

'See if you can't hunt down Chief Barrett. Try to talk him

into letting us release the details of the Hoffman and Peterson murders.'

'He's already refused, Carl.'

'Try him again. Tell him a blow-by-blow description would be in the public interest, make them more aware of the danger. Maybe he'll go for it.'

'Okay,' Jack said, sounding reluctant. He pushed his chair back, stood up, and stretched. Then he headed for the door.

The moment he was gone, Carl dialed the telephone.

'Spiritual Development Foundation.'

He gave his name, number and level.

'Very good, Mr Williams.'

'Let me talk to Farris. It's urgent.'

Farris's voice came over the phone. 'We've been waiting for your call,' he said.

'Sorry. I just received the information. Miss Allen's at the Desert Wind hotel in Tucson. Room number three six two.'

'Excellent. I'll notify our personnel in the area. Your next step is to join her.'

'Right.'

'Do that at once.'

'I'll leave right away.'

As he hung up, a voice from behind asked, 'What was that all about?'

Carl swiveled around. Alfred, standing in front of the rest-room door, looked at him with suspicion. 'You told where Lacey is. Who'd you tell?'

'Chief Barrett.'

'What'd you want to do that for?'

'She asked me to.' Turning back to his desk, Carl pulled open the top drawer and removed a letter opener. 'Bring me Jack's story,' he said.

Alfred walked toward Jack's desk, his head low and shaking. 'I don't think you should've done that,' he said.

'You're not paid to think.'

'Well . . .' He gathered two pages from the desktop, and walked slowly back toward Carl.

Carl got up from his chair. With the letter opener behind his back, he reached out his left hand for the papers.

'Here they . . .'

Carl grabbed Alfred's wrist, jerked him forward, and plunged the slim blade into his belly.

Chapter Thirteen

A strolling guitarist stopped at their table. 'A song?'

Scott nodded. 'How about "Cielito Lindo"? ' he asked Lacey.

She dipped a tortilla chip into hot sauce. 'Fine.'

With a smile, the white-clothed Mexican began to strum chords and sing. Lacey sat back, munching her chip and sipping her margarita as she watched him. He stood with his back arched, his head thrown back, his dark face writhing as if the song called up unbearable sorrow. His plaintive voice pushed Lacey's mind back to a strolling minstrel in Nogales, only a few days before her break-up with Brian. One of their last good times together. The next week, back in Oasis, he brought a man to the house and insisted the three of them go at each other. Lacey refused, and he beat her. No more Brian. No more men, at all, after that.

For a moment, she felt the void and sank into it. No man, no love, no babies, only empty darkness. She was cut loose and drifting. Starting to panic.

She took a long drink from her margarita, and managed a smile for Scott.

Get off it, kiddo, she told herself. A hell of a time to worry about becoming an old maid. You should live so long.

The singer finished his song, and Scott handed him a dollar.

'*Gracias,*' the man said. With a slight bow, he turned away.

'Are you all right?' Scott asked.

'Just beweeping my outcast state.'

Scott raised an eyebrow. 'Troubling deaf heaven with your bootless cries?'

Lacey grinned. 'Yup.'

The waitress set down plates in front of them. They had both ordered Dinner #6: a chimichanga, refried beans, rice, and a taco. Lacey took a deep breath of the steam rising from her meal. Her mouth watered.

'Plates are hot,' warned the waitress. 'Will there be anything else for you?'

'Want a beer?' Scott asked.

'I'll stick with margaritas.'

'That'll be it for now,' he told the waitress, and she left.

Across the candle-lit room, the singer began 'The Rose of San Antone' for two lean men in business suits. One of them saw Lacey watching. He met her gaze, looked her over, then turned away and spoke to his friend. The other man glanced at her. She looked away, embarrassed, certain they were wondering about her appearance. In her plaid blouse and corduroys, she felt shabby: all right for McDonalds, but barely good enough for a restaurant of Carmen's quality.

She should've found time to buy a dress. When Scott escorted her back to her suite that afternoon, though, he gave her strict orders not to leave it without calling him. She hadn't wanted to drag him around Tucson in search of evening wear, so she'd simply stayed in her room until he picked her up for dinner. Now, she regretted it.

She swallowed a mouthful of rice, and said, 'What's next?'

'Find a good piano bar . . .'

'I mean, tomorrow and the next day and the day after that.'

'Depends on you.'

'Are we just going to *wait*? I mean, I could stay at the hotel for two weeks, as I planned, and nothing happen, and the minute I step into my house back in Oasis, *wham*.'

'You think he's at your house?'

'He could be anywhere: in my house, at the hotel, even here. He might even be dead, but I think that's too good to hope for.'

'So you don't want to wait around? You'd rather go on the offensive? Good. That's just what Charlie Dane would suggest.'

'Are you willing?' she asked.

'I was planning to suggest it myself.'

She cut into the chimichanga with her fork, and scooped a bite into her mouth. The fried tortilla crunched. She chewed slowly, savoring its spicy meat and cheese.

'So tomorrow, we'll go to your house.'

'That'd be great.' Lacey took another bite. Then she picked up her handbag and set it on her lap. She opened it. She took out the can.

'What's that, paint?'

'There's something you have to know. You may decide I'm crazy and call the whole thing off, but I have to tell you the truth. This afternoon, when I explained the whole situation to you, I left something out. It's why I have this paint. I told you the man was wearing a mask. That's my story for public consumption, but it's not quite the truth. I told the truth to the police and my editor, and they didn't believe me. I don't really expect you to believe me, either. But here goes. The man who killed Elsie Hoffman and Red Peterson, the man who attacked me – he's invisible.'

Scott stared at his plate. He forked a huge bite of chimichanga into his mouth, and chewed slowly, frowning.

He swallowed. He finished his margarita and refilled the glass and took another sip. 'Invisible?' he asked, as if he thought he'd misunderstood.

'Not a ghost or apparition or hallucination,' Lacey said. 'It's a man. But you can look right at him and see right through him and never know he's even there. He's invisible.'

'How?' Scott asked.

'He didn't tell me. "A little miracle," he said.'

'A miracle, all right.'

'That's what the paint is for. It'll adhere to him, and he won't be invisible again till he gets it off his skin.'

'Invisible,' Scott said, shaking his head.

'Do you believe me?'

'Let me put it this way: we'll proceed as if I do. Hell, if it's true, I might get a whizz-bang story out of this. Another *Amityville Horror*. Who knows?'

Back at the hotel, Scott drew a Colt .45 automatic from the shoulder holster under his sports coat.

They searched Lacey's suite, walking behind chairs, feeling inside closets and under the beds, stepping into the shower stall. At last, Scott sighed and sat on the couch. 'If the guy's invisible,' he said, 'there's no way we can be sure he isn't here.'

'He hasn't attacked,' Lacey said.

'Maybe he's waiting for me to leave. So I guess I'd better stay.' He patted the couch. 'This'll do fine.'

'You're really going to stay?'

'I can't do much protecting from the end of the hall.'

'Well, I guess it's all right. I won't let you sleep on the couch, though, with two beds in the other room.'

'You sure?'

'It'd be ridiculous.'

Grinning, Scott drawled, 'Mighty grateful, ma'am. I accept your hospitality.'

Lacey went to bed first. Though she usually slept in the

nude, tonight she wore her jogging shorts and tank top in case her sheet should slip off during the night. She lay wide awake. From the other room came quiet TV voices. She listened, but couldn't make out their words.

Had it been a mistake, offering the other bed? It might've sounded like an invitation for something more. Had Scott taken it that way? God, what if he came over to her bed and climbed in?

He would say something cute. 'I'm here to guard your body at close range.'

She rolled onto her belly, and forced her mind away from the possibility. How'll we work it in the morning? Each drive our own cars, I suppose. Meet at my house. We'll park in front. Go in together? Sneak in? And search the place. Spread flour around so we can see footprints? God, what a clean-up job. Would it come out of the carpet?

The television voices stopped.

Lacey heard quiet footsteps. She expected Scott to enter the bathroom just off the hallway, but the steps kept coming. The doorknob rattled a bit. Then the door swung open.

She pressed her face against the pillow and shut her eyes.

Please, let him go straight to his own bed.

I'm here to guard your body at close range.

The footsteps stopped between the beds. She heard the squeak of springs, followed by a whispered 'damn' as if he were angry about the noise. Obviously, he thought she was asleep and didn't want to disturb her. So he had no intention of coming to her bed, after all.

Lacey remained motionless, listening to his breathing, to the quiet sounds the bed made as he shifted to remove his shoes, to the single tink of his belt buckle and the whisper of his zipper. Then the springs squawked.

He's standing up.

Coming here, after all? Lacey's heart began to thunder.

Turning her head slightly, she opened one eye and saw him in the darkness only a yard away. He stepped out of his pants, folded them once, and placed them on the floor beside his bed. He took off his shoulder holster, then his shirt. His tanned skin looked very dark against his white briefs. Crouching, he folded his shirt and set it on top of the pants. Then he turned away to pull down the bed covers. He climbed in without taking off his briefs.

Lacey shut her eye. Her heart was still racing, and she realized that she'd barely been breathing since Scott entered the room.

She was parched. She tried to work up enough saliva to moisten her mouth, but couldn't.

She waited.

I'll die if I don't get a drink of water. Probably those margaritas.

Slipping her sheet aside, she swung her legs off the bed and stood up. She rushed through the darkness to the bathroom, and turned on a light. Squinting against its glare, she ran cold water. She filled a glass and drank. In the mirror, she saw hair clinging to her sweaty forehead. She shook her head at the image. She drank another glassful of cold water, then turned off the faucet and used the toilet. The flush sounded very loud. If Scott heard it . . . No, he's all right. He'll stay in bed. If he'd wanted to try anything tonight, he would've done it by now.

She flicked off the light and opened the door.

Scott clutched her shoulders. He was wearing only his briefs. In his right hand, upraised to his shoulder, he held the pistol. It smelled oily and metallic.

'What . . . ?'

'Shhhh. We've got company.'

Chapter Fourteen

Standing close to Scott in the dark hallway, Lacey heard the quiet rap of knuckles on wood. 'Where's it coming from?' she asked.

'Our door.'

'You sure?'

Scott nodded.

'My God.'

'Come on.' Holding her by the elbow, Scott led her into the main room. They stood motionless. After a moment of silence, the knocking resumed. 'I'll watch from the closet,' Scott whispered. 'You get the door.'

'What if it's *him*?'

'Then we're in luck.'

As Scott hurried to the coat closet, Lacey turned on a lamp. 'Right there,' she called. She scanned the room, and found her handbag on the coffee table. Rushing to it, she took out the can of spray paint and the knife. She pulled off the leather sheath, and slid the knife under the waistband at the back of her shorts. The blade was cool and flat against her rump. She felt the scrape of its edges as she walked to the door.

She peered through the peephole. Though the man in the bright hallway looked shrunken and distorted as if viewed in a distant funhouse mirror, Lacey recognized his lanky build, his haggard face and short, curly hair.

'Carl?'

She flicked off the guard chain, and pulled the door open. Carl gazed at her with grim, red-rimmed eyes. 'Hi, Lace.'

'Carl, what's going on? What're you doing here?'

'I'm sorry. Did I wake you?'

'No. Come on in.'

Lacey stepped aside to let him enter. Then she shut and chained the door. She turned to him. 'Did something happen? What's wrong?'

'Our man paid a visit to the *Trib*. He . . . he killed Alfred.'

'Oh my God!'

'I came back from lunch, and . . . Alfred was on the floor.' Reaching into a pocket of his baggy slacks, Carl pulled out a folded sheet of paper. 'The police have the original. It was pinned to him, to his belly . . . with my letter opener.' He handed the paper to Lacey.

She set the spray can on the coffee table, and unfolded the paper, and stared. The photocopy was stained as if it had been used to mop up a spill of black ink. But the typing was legible. She read it in silence. 'Can't get rid of me that easy. Better come home, bitch, or you editor's next.' With a trembling hand, she gave the note back to Carl.

'I thought I'd call you, but . . . Hell, I remembered what you said about him being invisible. Still not sure I can believe that, but I figured I'd better be careful. If he *is* like you say, he might've been right behind me, watching me dial. If he got the hotel's number . . . Well, I figured I'd drive on out to be on the safe side.'

'He could've been in your car!' Lacey blurted, suddenly alarmed.

'No. I checked it over.'

'Your trunk?'

'Checked that, too.'

'Maybe he followed you.'

'I don't think so. Wasn't much traffic. The only car behind me much had a couple in it – a man driving, a woman passenger.' He made a grim smile. 'Neither one was invisible. So I think we're okay on that score.'

'You saw the man's face?' Lacey asked.

'Not up close, but he had one. It's all right, Lace. Now stop worrying. I wasn't followed.'

'He could've put something on. A mask, make-up . . .'

Carl shook his head. 'We've gotta figure out what to do about this guy. Seems to me, we're both in the same boat, now. I don't think I want to hang around Oasis and just wait for him to slit my gullet. I figure, if we stick together on this . . .'

'What about the woman passenger?' Lacey asked.

'Huh?'

'In the car that followed you.'

'It wasn't *following* me. It was just *behind* me.'

'All the way?'

'I don't know.' He sounded annoyed. 'I didn't keep track. It was just some clown and his wife.'

'How do you know it was his wife?'

''Cause,' Carl said, smiling slightly, 'she was asleep the whole way.'

'*Asleep?*'

'Sure. Slumped over, her head against the side window . . . Oh, for Christsake, Lace, don't turn paranoid on me. Don't start telling me she was dead, and the driver was your invisible man decked out in a Stetson and mask.'

'You think that's not possible?'

'I think you're jumping to some mighty big conclusions.'

'He figured you would know where to get in touch with me. Killing Alfred, leaving the note, he did it so you'd lead him here. For Godsake, he's probably . . .'

'Now don't get all worked up. Calm down. There's nothing to . . .'

Lacey jerked stiff as her knife turned, the blade slicing a white-hot line up her buttock. She clutched the wound and spun around. The suspended knife slashed through the air, barely missing her face, and jerked toward Carl.

'*Scott!*'

The closet door burst open. Scott crouched, pistol forward, but his face was twisted with confusion. '*Where?*'

Even as Lacey pointed, the blade punched into Carl's throat. Blood shot out. It spurted a few inches, then splattered as if hitting a sheet of glass. It sprayed and sheathed the surface – the face and shoulders and chest of a six-foot man.

Scott gazed, his mouth agape.

'Shoot him!'

The figure, vague as a patch of floating red Cellophane, raised Carl off his feet and flung him at Scott. Scott leapt sideways. The body hit the closet door, crashed it shut, and thudded to the floor. The knife, Lacey saw, was still embedded in Carl's throat.

Scott aimed at the film of blood rushing toward him. 'Stop!'

Lacey braced herself for the roar of gunfire. It didn't come.

A yard in front of Scott, the figure halted.

'Fuckin' blood,' muttered a scratchy voice.

The layer of red shifted as if a child were fingerpainting on his face.

'Hands on your head,' Scott ordered.

The top of the head wasn't there, but Lacey saw two hand-shaped images of blood suspended above the concave face – a face like the back of a translucent red Halloween mask.

Lacey grabbed her can of silver paint from the coffee table and tugged off its plastic top. Tossing the cap aside, she shook the can. It rattled as if a marble were trapped inside. She stepped close to the dripping, red veil in front of Scott's automatic.

'Don't do it,' the man muttered.

As her forefinger lowered to the plastic nozzle, the red membrane shifted like a flag struck by wind. Something struck Lacey's hand. The can tumbled away. Then a tightness clenched her wrist and swung her toward Scott. He jumped out of the way, rushed in front of her, and dived. He landed flat on the floor, his hands grabbing only air.

The door flew open, ripping the guard chain from its mounting, and slammed shut.

Scott pushed himself to his knees. His eyes met Lacey's. He shook his head.

Lacey stepped over to Carl's body. She knelt down beside him. Blood no longer pumped from his torn throat. She covered her face with both hands, and started to cry.

Chapter Fifteen

Lacey lay face down on the living-room floor, her shorts around her knees, Scott patting her cut buttock with a cool, damp washcloth. 'Not much bleeding,' he said. 'You don't have bandages or anything, do you?'

'Afraid not.'

'Have any sanitary napkins?'

She felt heat flood her face, and wondered if the blush extended to her rump. 'Not with me.'

'Well, it's not much more than a scratch, but...'

'Oh, I think there *is* a pad in the medicine cabinet. The hotel variety. Right behind some kind of shower cap and shoeshine rag.'

'Advantages of a first-rate hotel,' Scott said, and left her. He returned, seconds later, tearing open the white wrapper. He knelt down, and pressed the soft pad against her wound. 'The tape's on the wrong side,' he muttered.

'Supposed to be. My underwear'll hold it in place.'

'Oh.' He went for her panties, and hurried back.

'Thanks,' Lacey said. 'I can take care of the rest.'

While she pulled on her panties and shorts, Scott went into the hallway. He came back with a blanket.

He used it to cover the body of Carl Williams. Dots of

blood darkened the fuzzy pink blanket, bloomed, and grew together. Lacey turned away.

She got to her feet. Wandering to a far corner of the room, she picked up the can of spray paint. She sat gently on the couch, clutching the can with both hands.

Scott sat beside her. 'I screwed up,' he said. 'I'm sorry. I thought everything was okay until you yelled. Then I couldn't find a target.' Shaking his head, he sighed. 'Christ, what a screw up. I'm sorry about your friend. If I'd just been . . .'

'Don't blame yourself. Nobody could've stopped it, at that point.'

'Charlie Dane could've,' he mumbled.

'Charlie would've shot the bastard when he had the chance,' Lacey said.

'Yeah.'

'The bastard's out there, now. He's had time to get the blood off.'

'Yeah.'

'Why didn't *you* shoot him?'

For a long time, Scott stared at the coffee table.

'Scott?'

'I thought we had him. I figured we'd tie him up. I've got a cassette recorder in my room. I thought . . . well, I'd get his story. You know, before calling in the cops. Interview him, find out how he got that way, what he's been doing, if there are others like him.'

'Others?'

'If one man can be made invisible, why not more? Christ, can you imagine an army of them? Think what they could do. They could turn the world upside down.'

'I suppose so,' Lacey said. 'But there's only one here, and he's probably figuring a way, right now, to get at us. You aren't going to have much luck writing a book about him if we're both killed, so next time . . . My God!' Jumping to her feet, she rushed to the desk and grabbed a straight-backed chair.

'What?'

She ran to the door with it, tipped it backwards and braced it under the knob. 'Maybe that . . .' she muttered. She turned to Scott. 'A passkey. He could get one so easily.'

Scott sighed. 'Damn, I should've thought of that. Afraid I'm not helping much.' He looked at her with despair. 'Sorry. I'm really not good enough for this kind of thing. Living it isn't quite the same as writing it.' He propped his elbows on his knees, and rubbed his face.

Lacey went to him. Crouching, she placed a hand on his back. 'Hey, it's all right. Don't feel bad. If you hadn't been here, he would've had me.'

Scott raised his head and looked at her. 'Thanks.'

'It's the truth. You saved my life.'

He smiled slightly. 'You're right.'

'Of course I am.'

'But I'm right, too,' he said. His face changed, turning hard and determined. 'This is out of my league. I'm not going to let my inexperience jeopardize you any longer.' He touched her cheek, stood up, and walked toward the desk.

'What are you doing?'

'Calling in reinforcements,' he said, and picked up the telephone. He set his automatic on the desk, then dialed with quick, sure strokes of his forefinger. Eleven numbers.

Long distance?

Chapter Sixteen

The bedside telephone woke Dukane, and he saw a naked woman bending over him in the darkness. Her head jerked toward the phone. In the moments between the clamors of the first and second rings, Dukane realized that the woman – a stranger before he brought her home tonight – had been interrupted in the process of tying his left wrist to the headboard.

He yanked both arms. The headboard shook and a cord bit into his right wrist, but his left pulled free.

The woman grabbed it, tried to force it down.

'Thanks,' Dukane said, 'but I'm not into bondage.'

He twisted his arm out of her grip. As the woman reached for it again, he clutched her neck and thrust her forward, ramming her head against the oak of his headboard. She slumped. He shoved her off the bed, rolled to his right, and picked up the phone.

'Hello?'

'Dukane? It's Scott. I'm in deep trouble, pal.'

'What's the problem?'

'There's a killer after me. An invisible killer.'

'Invisible?'

'I know it sounds ridiculous, but believe me, it's true. He just murdered a guy here in the room.'

'Okay. Where are you?'

'The Desert Wind hotel in Tucson. Room three sixty-two.'

'Where's this killer?'

'Probably right outside the door.'

'Okay. Hang tough, kid, I'm on my way. It'll take me about four hours, though. Maybe less, but don't count on it.'

'Hurry.'

'Right.' Dukane hung up. He slid open a drawer of the night stand, took out a switchblade knife, and severed the cord binding his right hand to the headboard. Then he turned on a light. He climbed across the bed and knelt over the unconscious woman.

She lay on her back, breathing deeply as if asleep, her arms and legs outflung. A beautiful, slim, small-breasted blond. Just his type. Too much his type, perhaps. But he'd known a lot of women over the years, and only a handful had turned out to be plants. He should've been a lot more careful, after Friday's disaster. He should've expected something like this.

Confidence kills.

She began to stir, her eyelids squeezing tight with a stab of pain, a hand rising to her head. She pursed her lips and said, 'Oooh.' Then her eyelids fluttered open. She gazed at Dukane with confusion for a moment before her memory apparently returned and she bolted upright.

Dukane clutched her throat and slammed her down. 'Who sent you?'

She sneered. 'No one.'

'I don't have time for games.' He jabbed his knife down. Her body jerked as if jolted by a cattle prod, mouth springing open to scream. He stopped the point of his knife above her bulging right eye. An eighth of an inch above it. She blinked, her lashes flicking over the steel tip. 'Who sent you?'

She said nothing. Slowly, the panic left her face. Her body relaxed. Even the straining tendons and muscles of her neck went slack under Dukane's hand. She smirked up at him. 'Do as you like,' she said. 'Cut out my eye, if that's what pleases you. Take whatever you wish. My breasts?' Her hands moved, stroking them. The dark nipples stood rigid. 'I am all powerful,' she whispered. 'I am immortal.'

'Have you drunk at the river?' Dukane asked.

'Oh yes, oh yes.'

He eased the blade away from her eye.

'Immortal,' she said. 'All powerful.'

He removed his right hand from her throat. 'Okay, get up.' As he inched the knife away, her fingers caught his wrist. Dukane tensed, expecting an upward thrust. But she tugged down. He wasn't ready for that. The blade punched into the pale flesh between her breasts.

Dukane snatched it free.

The woman bucked, clutched the wound, and sat up with a look of sudden terror on her face.

Blood spilled out between her fingers. She glanced at it, then gazed at Dukane with eyes like a hurt child.

'Shit,' Dukane muttered, suddenly feeling sorry for her. 'Don't worry, you missed your heart. I'll call an ambulance.' He rushed around the end of the bed. 'Press down hard on the wound.' He picked up the phone.

As he started to dial, the woman grabbed the bed and pushed herself to her feet.

'Lie down, damn it!'

She suddenly ran.

'Hey!' Dukane dropped the phone and scrambled over the bed, hoping to stop her before she reached the sliding door to the balcony.

She was too quick.

Her forehead rammed the door. The plate glass burst. She lunged through a spray of tumbling shards that slashed her bare skin, and disappeared onto the balcony. Dukane rushed after her. As he ducked through the smashed door, she threw herself headfirst over the railing. Dukane lunged, reached for her foot, and touched its heel with his forefinger. Then all he could do was watch.

She kicked and twisted for a second that seemed like minutes even to Dukane, then threw out her arms to break her fall. The concrete slab of the pool's apron smashed her arms out of the way, and she hit it with her face.

Dukane looked down at her body, and sighed. He knew he

shouldn't feel sorry for her; she'd probably planned to kill him tonight. But Christ, the waste . . . a beautiful girl . . . Why the hell did she ever get mixed up in such . . .

He clutched the railing, frozen by a sudden chill as a huge, black-robed man darted from behind bushes beside the pool. The man crouched at the broken body, flung it over his shoulder, and lumbered away.

Dukane pried his fingers off the railing. His skin was crawly with goosebumps. He stared down at the dark figure and knew he should give chase, but he couldn't move.

Besides, he told himself, Scott has priority. He watched, rubbing his prickly arms and thighs, thinking it strange that he should be so spooked. Whoever the bastard was, Dukane could probably nail him in unarmed combat, even with one hand tied behind his back. Probably. The thought didn't give him much comfort.

He picked bits of glass out of his feet, then hobbled down the long balcony to its guest room entrance. He slid open the door and stared at the pale carpet.

'Shit,' he muttered.

One ruined carpet was enough for one night.

On hands and knees, keeping his feet elevated, he crawled across the carpet. In the guest bathroom, he found iodine, adhesive tape, and gauze. He quickly bandaged his feet.

Ignoring the slight pain, he rushed back to his bedroom. He glanced at the clock. Less than five minutes had passed since Scott's call.

A long time, five minutes.

A long time for that dumb woman. A long time for a guy like Scott, waiting to get bailed out.

It took him under a minute to dress.

Then he ran downstairs, through the dark house, and out to his garage. He jumped into his Jaguar. Thumbed the garage door switch. Keyed the ignition. The engine thundered, shaking the car.

In his rearview mirror, he watched the door rise. The gap widened. He saw the dark-robed man looking in at him, the naked body of the girl still over his shoulder.

Dukane jammed the shift to reverse and floored the gas pedal. He popped the clutch. The car leapt backwards. He gripped the wheel, expecting an impact, but the car shot past the figure. Caught in the headlight, the man turned slowly to face him.

Dukane's foot hovered over the brake. He could easily stop and have another try.

But Scott was waiting.

He'd already wasted too many minutes.

So he sped backwards to the street, leaving the strange man alone in the driveway with the corpse.

Chapter Seventeen

'What was that about?' Lacey had asked as soon as Scott put down the phone.

'Saving our hides.'

'Dukane? Who's he?'

'The real-life Charlie Dane. Excuse me a minute, I want to get dressed.' He left her alone in the room.

Lacey got up and followed him. When she reached the bedroom, Scott was stepping into his pants. 'There really *is* a Charlie Dane?'

Scott fastened his trousers and picked up his shirt. 'Sure is. No trench coat and battered fedora, and he operates now instead of the forties, but the rest is pretty close. A hell of a guy. He'll get us out of here. We just have to stay alive for the next four hours, till he arrives.'

'Maybe we should call the police.'

'What good would they be against an invisible maniac?'

'What good will this Dukane be?'

Scott grinned, for the first time since the attack looking calm and confident. 'Good enough.'

'What time is it?' Lacey asked.

'Eleven-forty.'

'Is that all?' Only twenty minutes had passed since Scott's talk with Dukane. For the past ten, Lacey had been sitting cross-legged beside the barricaded door, her pocket knife open on her lap, the paint can beside her ready to spray if the door should be forced open.

Scott had spent much of the time wandering the suite. He'd looked out the windows and determined that no ledges ran over from adjacent rooms. He'd shoved the couch against a locked, connecting door. Then he'd knelt down to remove the knife from Carl's throat.

'Should you do that?' Lacey had asked. 'What about fingerprints?'

'We need it.'

'But the police. My God, we don't want them thinking *we* killed Carl.'

'Don't worry.'

'Thanks, but I can't help it.'

'The police are the least of our problems right now.'

Lacey had looked away when he pulled out the knife. He arranged the blanket again over Carl's head, then took the knife into the bathroom and cleaned it.

Now Scott was turning over the coffee table.

'What're you doing?'

'Clubs,' he said, and began to unscrew one of the short, tapering legs. When it came free, he tossed it underhand. It thumped the floor near Lacey, and rolled toward her. She picked it up by the narrow end. It felt like a small baseball bat. A thick, inch-long bolt protruded from the top.

As Scott twisted another leg off the table, Lacey heard voices in the hallway.

'Six fifty for a Piña Colada,' said a man. 'You believe it?'

'That's not so bad,' a woman said. 'It included the glass.'

'Sixty cents worth of glass. A nickle worth of booze.'

'They're awfully cute glasses.'

'Maybe we should get a few more.'

'It would be nice to have a complete set.' The woman's sudden yelp made Lacey jump. Her mind flashed an image of the two under attack, and she grabbed the spray can, tensing, ready to unblock the door and rush out to help. But the yelp led into a giggle. A different kind of attack. 'Jimmy, *don't!* Christ, I almost dropped the glasses.'

'Anything but that.'

Lacey heard a key ratchet into a lock. A knob turned. A door swung open with a barely audible squeak, and banged shut.

'Hope they got in alone,' Scott said, starting on a third leg.

'I sure hope so. They sounded nice.'

'The guy's a cheapskate.'

'He was just kidding around.'

'Yeah. On the surface. Underneath, he's a cheapskate.'

'He did buy two of those drinks.'

'At six-fifty a whack. Not only a cheapskate, but he likes to play martyr.'

Lacey looked at Scott, and saw he was smiling.

The door's lock button snapped out. Lacey turned, saw the door lurch, the chair tip forward a fraction. She thrust herself to her knees. The knife fell from her lap. She grabbed it. Scott threw himself against the wall on the other side of the door. He held a table leg in one upraised hand, the knife in the other. The automatic remained tucked in his belt.

The door eased back silently, then rammed the chair again, this time forcing the legs to scoot an inch across the carpet.

'Shoot him through the door,' Lacey whispered.

Scott shook his head. 'Louder,' he mouthed.

'Shoot through the door!'

'Right.' Clamping the club between his legs, he pulled out the automatic. He held it close to the door and worked its slide, jacking a live cartridge out.

The door settled back into place.

Lacey waited, holding her breath, expecting another thrust. Scott picked up his bullet and dropped it into his shirt pocket.

Nothing happened.

'Whatever he is,' Scott whispered, 'he doesn't like bullets.' Tucking away the pistol, he shoved the chair more firmly under the knob. 'I think we're all right for a while . . . till he figures a new way to get at us.'

'What'll he do?'

Scott shrugged.

'What time is it now?'

Scott glanced at his wristwatch. 'Five minutes later than the last time you asked.'

'Encouraging,' she muttered.

'Three and a half hours to go.'

'If your man's on time.'

'Knowing Dukane, he'll be early.'

'I hope so.' Lacey sat down again, feeling a slight pain as her shorts drew taut across her wound. Raising herself for a moment, she tugged the shorts to loosen them. Fortu-nately, the cut was high enough so that she didn't rest on it, sitting upright. It hurt very little, except for a frequent, achy itch. It itched now. She scratched it gently with her fingernails. 'What makes you think this Dukane will do us any good?'

'He's brilliant, innovative, a crack shot . . .'

'Able to leap tall buildings in a single bound?'

'Damn near. Won the Medal of Honor in Vietnam. Dropped in behind the lines, killed God-knows how many gooks, freed two dozen POWs and led them all back. Alone.'

Scott shook his head, looking astonished by the feat. 'He's been a private investigator and bodyguard for nine years. An amazing guy. He's actually lived the Charlie Dane stories. Most of them are based on incidents from Dukane's past.'

'Hope I live long enough to meet him.'

'I keep trying to figure out what he'd do, if he were here instead of me.'

'What would he do?'

Scott shook his head. One corner of his mouth smiled. 'He'd make clubs out of the table legs.'

'Would he shoot through the door?'

'More than likely.'

'I wish you had.'

'Don't tell anyone, but my shooting has been limited to pistol ranges. I've never killed a man.'

'That would've been a good time to start.'

'Well . . .' Scott sighed. 'I'm not against it – morally, I mean. Sort of a big step, though. Besides, I'd still rather take him alive. I mean, can you imagine the *story*? It'd be terrific! Do it up non-fiction. A hardbound sale. Major advertising and promotion. Whammo, a bestseller!'

'Give *me* your gun,' Lacey said, scrambling to her feet. She held out her hand. 'Come on, give it. If you aren't willing to shoot him, I sure am.'

He held onto it. 'Sorry.'

'Sorry won't get us out of a coffin. Now come on! You've missed two big chances to blast this bastard to hell. Let *me* do it.'

'Lacey, don't get . . .'

She lunged, reaching for the automatic. Scott knocked her arm away. He shoved her backwards with the table leg, its bolt biting into her chest. 'Calm down!'

'You'll get us killed!' she blurted, and suddenly started to cry. She turned away. She wanted to run for the bedroom or bathroom, to let out her despair in private, but was afraid to leave him. So she faced the wall, crying into her hands. She heard Scott approach. His arms reached forward and folded lightly across her belly.

'I won't let anything happen to you,' he said, his breath warm through her hair. 'I promise.'

'What about your bestseller?'

'I won't let him get you.'

Lacey turned around. Blinking tears away, she stared up into his serious eyes. 'You could shoot to wound,' she said, and tried to smile.

'That's it.' His fingers brushed the tears off her cheeks.

Lacey put her arms around him and shut her eyes. If she could only keep on holding him, feeling his strong body against her, the easy rise and fall of his chest, the gentle stroke of his hands on her back, then maybe nothing bad would happen.

The handle of his automatic felt flat and hard against Lacey's belly.

She might reach for it. But that would end the closeness, the trust. Better to keep that, to stay with him, than to risk losing it by going for the gun.

She felt another hardness, lower down.

Scott plucked the tails of her tank top from her shorts, and reached up inside it, caressing her back, then easing her away and moving gently to her breasts. He held them in each hand, his palms gliding against her turgid nipples. Lacey moaned. The hands continued to caress her for nearly a full second after she heard the crash of shattering glass.

Scott looked at her, stunned. 'The windows!'

Chapter Eighteen

The noise of the bursting window came from a distance, from the bathroom or bedroom. Lacey broke for the door. Dropping to a crouch, she grabbed her spray can and pocket knife. She glanced back. Scott was at the hallway entrance, pistol out.

'Let's run!' she snapped.

Scott glanced at her, frowning.

She kicked the chair. It dropped backwards to the floor, and she tugged the door open.

'Come on!'

Scott whirled around and ran. He scooped up a table leg and dashed after her through the door. He jerked it shut. 'Get ready. When he comes out, we'll . . .'

Lacey raced up the corridor. When she reached a corner, she looked back. Scott glanced from the door to her. She motioned for him. He muttered something through his teeth, then ran to join her.

'We had a chance . . .'

'We've got a better chance if he can't find us.' She shoved open a fire door.

They entered a dimly lighted stairwell. Scott thrust the door shut and leaned against it.

'Come on,' Lacey said. She started up the concrete stairs. 'He'll expect us to head down.'

'Where we going?'

'I don't know.' She turned at the first landing, and started up the next flight of stairs. Above her, she saw the blue metal door to the fourth floor. She raced up, Scott close behind her, and grabbed the knob. As she pushed the door open, Scott patted her arm. He pressed his forefinger to his lips. They stood motionless, listening.

For a moment, Lacey heard nothing. Then the metallic sound of a springing latch echoed quietly up the stairwell.

Scott shoved the door hard. It flew open, and he pointed to the upper steps. The door banged against the outside wall as they turned away and leapt up the stairs three at a time. In seconds, they reached the landing. Lacey charged up the remaining stairs. Halfway to the top, she heard the lower door clump shut.

Would it fool him? If so, he would only be delayed long enough to leave the stairwell and glance down the fourth floor corridor.

Scott, slightly above her, was first to reach the door. He held it open for Lacey. She raced through. Scott eased it shut, turning the knob to prevent the latch from snapping back into place.

With a few steps, they passed an ice machine and rounded a corner. Scott stopped, looking each way.

To the right, the corridor led past the doors of only half a dozen rooms, then abruptly ended. To the left, it seemed to stretch on forever.

'This way,' Scott muttered. He ran to the left.

Past rooms. Past a fire hose and ax. Past swinging doors of staff rooms.

Lacey, sprinting to stay beside him, saw a bank of elevators ahead. 'Let's try those,' she gasped.

They ran for them. The doors of all four elevators were shut. Scott threw himself against the nearest panel and jammed fingers into both buttons. Double disks of light appeared between each of the door sets: one with an arrow point up, the other down.

Lacey pressed herself to the wall beside him. Craning her neck, she gazed at the dark arrows above the doors. She gasped for air. The spray can and knife were slippery in her hands. She could feel the vibrations of the elevators against her back, hear the distant, quiet bells as they stopped at other floors. She looked up the corridor, squinting as if that might help her see the man's approach, then glanced again at the arrows above her. They stayed dark.

'This is no good,' she whispered.

With a nod of agreement, Scott flung himself away from the wall. They left the elevators behind and dashed down the corridor. Their feet thudded on the carpet. From behind came the quiet ding of an elevator bell. Lacey looked back. They were too far away to return in time. She ran hard to catch up with Scott.

Just ahead, a hallway led off to the left. Scott slowed and turned the corner. He stopped, and Lacey halted beside him. She leaned back against an ice machine, panting for breath.

'What now?' she gasped.

Scott pointed with the club in his left hand. A yard away was a fire door.

'Might as well.'

Across the hall, a door opened. A slight, young man in blue pajamas and a satin robe stepped out backwards. He pulled his door shut gently so it stopped against the frame. Turning around, he smiled a surprised greeting. In his hands, he held a cardboard ice bucket.

'Cheerio,' he said.

Scott lunged across the hall, grabbed the front of his robe, and thrust him into the room. Lacey followed. She shut the door quickly and silently.

'Hey now!' the man said. He seemed more offended than afraid. 'What . . .?'

Scott snarled and raised the club. The man's mouth snapped shut. He looked from Scott to Lacey, eyes narrowing behind his oversized glasses.

'We're Nick and Nora Charles,' Scott said. 'Asta's back in our room.'

'Oh?'

Scott let go of him. The man offered a small, pale hand. 'Hamlin Alexander.'

After shaking hands, they moved away from the door.

One of the double beds was mussed, the other neatly made.

'You alone?' Scott asked.

'I just shooed away a nymphet. I don't expect her to return in the immediate future.' He set the ice bucket on the dresser beside a full bottle of Stolichnaya. 'Room service didn't provide ice. Expected me to fetch it myself, obviously. I don't suppose we might venture out for some, now that we're acquainted?'

'I don't think so,' Scott said.

'If you're indeed Nick and Nora, I doubt you intend to rob or mutilate me. Would you care for a warm drink?'

They nodded, and he opened the bottle.

'I don't suppose you caught my concert tonight? Really first-rate.'

'Sorry,' Scott said.

Hamlin poured vodka into three glasses. 'To a warm and *healthy* relationship,' he toasted.

Lacey sipped her vodka. Its strong taste made her cringe, but it felt warm and pleasant going down.

'Now,' said Hamlin. 'To what do I owe your presence? You're not a pair of lunatic fans, obviously. Am I a hostage of choice or opportunity?'

'Opportunity,' Scott told him. 'You came out your door at the right time.'

'The right time for you, perhaps.'

Though they were talking softly, Lacey worried that their voices might carry through the door. She crossed the room and turned on the television.

'Oh, please,' Hamlin muttered. 'Ah, I see,' he said as Lacey increased the volume. 'Background noise. That's about all the cyclops is good for. Now, what brings you into my august presence?'

'We're being pursued by a killer.'

Hamlin raised his eyebrows, sat on his rumpled bed, and crossed his legs. 'I see you're well armed.'

'He has an Ingram, a small assault weapon capable of firing twenty rounds per second.'

'Nasty.'

'Extremely. So you can see that we'd prefer to avoid a confrontation. If he didn't see us come in, we'll be all right. Even if he knows which floor we're on, I don't think he'll take the chance of barging into every room.'

'I hate to appear simplistic, but have you considered bringing in the gendarmes?'

'A special team is flying in from Washington,' Scott told him. 'We expect it to arrive,' he checked his watch, 'in roughly three, three and a quarter hours.'

'Washington? So we're embroiled in a cloak-and-dagger scheme? I should have guessed; you have that clean-cut, boy-next-door, FBI look about you.' He peered at Lacey as she sat down beside Scott on the other bed. 'Nora, however, is not an agent. No no. Too delicate, feminine, vulnerable. I should think Nora is an innocent bystander cast by mischance into the role of heroine.' He nodded shrewdly. 'Perhaps a witness?'

'Very observant,' Scott said.

'The fellow with the nasty weapon, a Ruskie agent?'

'Can't tell you.'

'The solution to your problem is make-up. I just happen to have, in my possession, an elaborate make-up kit complete with hair, teeth, blood, and Dick Smith's Flex-Flesh. I don't *just happen* to have it – very deliberate. I often travel incognito. For security and privacy, you understand. The kit has many uses, however. The nymphets blush and cream at the chance to be transformed into the monsters they are: zombies, hags with oozing pustules, vampires. The vampire is my specialty. Those sub-moronic sexpots throw themselves into the role with such abandon – snarling, baring their fangs – and it's rarely my neck they insist upon sucking. Quite delightful. I'd be more than happy to transform the two of you. Not into monsters, perhaps, but with a few deft touches and a change of clothes you might walk right past the murderous Ruskie without being recognized.'

'Thanks anyway,' Scott said.

'On the other hand, I might apply a multitude of wounds: bullet holes, slash marks, quantities of artificial blood. I'm superb at corpses. I'll arrange you on the floor. If your maniacal Soviet should burst through the door, he'll assume you've already been dispatched. No need to repeat the process. *Voila!*'

'That's ridiculous,' Scott told him.

'It's genius. A subtle but profound difference.'

'Maybe. But I still think . . .' The deafening clamor of a bell in the corridor stopped his words.

Hamlin jumped, spilling his drink.

The high-pitched ringing went on.

'Fire alarm!' Scott shouted.

'You don't think . . .?'

Grabbing his makeshift club, Scott scurried off the bed and raced toward the door. Lacey picked up her spray can, her knife. Hurrying after him, she saw him touch the knob. 'Not warm,' he said. He looked back. 'Hamlin,' he yelled over the din. 'Get over here!'

The small man rushed to them. His face, so confident before, now looked drawn and pale.

'Look out the door. See if there's smoke.'

They stepped aside so they couldn't be viewed from the hallway, and Hamlin opened the door. 'Appears fine,' he said.

'Check around the corner.'

He stepped out. Scott held the door open a crack. A moment later, Hamlin shoved through it and gazed at them. 'Jesus H. Christ! The other end of the hall – all kinds of smoke. People spilling out of their rooms like . . . Christ, my horn!' He hurried past them. Seconds later, he returned with a black leather case. 'Don't know about you, but I'm getting the fuck out of here!' Flinging open the door, he dashed across the hallway to the fire door.

Lacey stepped out beside Scott. Half a dozen people were now in the short hall, most in night clothes, rushing for the door. Hamlin threw it open. He coughed as dark smoke bellowed into his face. He started to shut it, but the door knocked him backwards and a flaming man stumbled from the stairwell. His fiery arms reached for Hamlin, but the little man smashed them aside with his instrument case and leapt out of the way.

Screams mixed with the blaring alarm bells as the burning man staggered toward the onrushing group of guests. They scattered. Falling among them, he clutched the negligee of a horrified young woman. She lurched away, but flames were already starting to curl up her white gown. A nearby man ripped it from her shoulders. She kicked free of the garment and threw herself into his arms.

Scott grabbed Lacey's wrist. He jerked her after him, around the corner to the long corridor. Hamlin was far ahead of them, dashing through stunned guests, dodging some, stiff-arming others aside, the black case hugged under one arm like a football. Though the far end of the corridor was gray with rolling smoke, Lacey saw no flames.

'This way's blocked,' Scott yelled to an elderly couple heading toward them. The couple stopped, looking at each other with confusion as Scott and Lacey hurried by.

The greatest number of people was gathered in front of the elevator bank, screaming and shoving in a frenzy to get closer to the doors.

As Scott and Lacey reached the edge of the crowd, an elevator arrived. Its double doors slid open, but the small enclosure was already packed. A roar of protest bellowed from those inside as the mob pressed forward. Through a gap in the crowd, Lacey saw one of the men in the elevator jerked out. Amid darting fists, a new man took his place. The doors rolled halfway shut, then slid open again. A tiny, dark-haired man leapt high, clambering over the shoulders and heads of those inside, his right hand clasping a black leather case. A moment later, the doors closed.

'What'll we do?' Lacey asked.

'Forget the elev . . .'

A woman's shriek rose above the tumult. Lacey looked, couldn't see her, then saw the bloody head of a fire ax rise above the figures at the far side of the crowd. It swung down. The mob parted, people stumbling out of the way, yelling and screaming. The ax chopped down, knocking through the upraised arm of a man staggering backwards, and split his head. As he fell, the ax swung sideways, biting into the belly of a naked woman – the one whose nightgown had caught fire earlier.

Lacey gaped as the slaughter continued, the ax chopping from side to side, catching people in the chest and belly and throat. They fought and tripped over each other, trying to get away. For an instant, Lacey glimpsed the length of the weapon. It swung, held by no one – no one she could see. It hacked through a man's neck. His severed head tumbled through the air, spraying blood.

Lacey clutched Scott's arm. 'It's him!' she shouted.

'Come on!'

'Where?'

Side by side, they raced down the corridor. As they neared the corner, Lacey looked back. The ax had finished hacking its way through the mob. Splatters of blood hung suspended in the air behind it. Abruptly, it lurched forward.

Lacey gasped, and rounded the corner after Scott. He threw himself against the door of Hamlin's room – locked.

'Come on!'

They rushed farther down the short hall, leaping past the small fire spreading around the dead man like a pool of strange, burning blood.

The next door, too, was locked.

Only three remained. Scott glanced at them, apparently decided they would offer no more than this one, and drew out his automatic. He blasted a single shot through the area where the lock tongue entered the frame, and kicked the door open.

Lacey looked back.

The ax flew at her, flipping end over end.

Scott jerked her inside and slammed the door. He threw himself against it.

'Get a chair!' he yelled.

Lacey dashed across the room, grabbed a straight-backed chair from beneath the table, and ran with it to Scott. He braced it under the knob.

An instant later, the door thundered. An ax-head burst through it, high up, throwing out a shower of splinters.

'You're mine!' a man's voice cried out. 'Mine, cunt!'

The ax crashed again through the door, this time lower, smashing the chair down from the knob. The door flew open.

Gunfire shocked Lacey's ears, and she gazed at Scott. He was crouched and snarling, the automatic bucking in his grip as he fired shot after shot at the doorway.

Lacey covered her ears against the gun's endless roar.

The ax lunged forward, jerking in midair, and dropped to the floor.

Chapter Nineteen

'Spray him,' Scott snapped as he braced the door shut.

Kneeling, Lacey aimed the paint can toward the ax. She pressed down the nozzle. A fine, silvery cloud sprayed out and drifted down, spreading into a layer half a foot above the carpet. As she moved the can back and forth, the surface took on features. She saw the heavily muscled, jutting slopes of shoulder blades, and realized she must be kneeling at his head. She gave it a quick blast. The paint misted his thick hair and sprayed cool against her own thighs. With a quick sweep to the right, she coated one of his arms. Then she sprayed the other. Its thick hand still gripped the haft of the ax.

Scott crouched and pried the fingers loose. He held the wrist. 'Still has a pulse,' he muttered. 'Hit lower, let's find the wounds.'

Lacey sprayed down the long, tapering expanse of his back. She hesitated at his waist, but only for a moment. Invisibility was his greatest weapon: painting him was like cutting Samson's hair. The hell with modesty. She sprayed his buttocks.

Then she took her finger off the nozzle and stared at his shiny back, at its three gaping, ragged wounds. Looking into them, she saw the green carpet several inches down. Clear, silver-dusted fluid overflowed the holes.

At the shoulder, she saw the crater of a healed gunshot wound. Near the center of his back was a narrow, inch-long ridge. The knife wound from Wednesday night? She touched it, feeling an edge of hardness. A scab? Her finger came away wet with paint. As she wiped it on her shorts, the fire alarm stopped blaring.

She looked at Scott. He shrugged.

In the quiet, she heard distant voices.

'Maybe it's out,' Scott said, his voice sounding odd in the stillness.

His hands moved from wound to wound. 'I missed the heart, thank God. Not much flow. If I didn't hit a major vessel . . .' He took off his shirt, and ripped its sleeves off. Folding one of the sleeves into a thick pad, he pressed it tightly to a wound near the side of the back. 'Hold it there,' he said. 'Hard.'

While Lacey kept the pad in place, he folded his other sleeve and pressed it to a second wound, lower down. Lacey held that one for him. He tore his shirt up the back, and used one of the halves to make another compress. He pushed it against the final wound.

'Right back,' he said. He hurried away and returned seconds later, holding a suitcase. He dropped it to the floor and threw it open. Crouching, he rummaged through it. He flung out a pair of pantie hose, a halfslip, several pairs of briefs. 'Those'll do,' he muttered. He took out a leather case, jerked open its zipper, and upended it. Out fell scissors, a plastic container of rubber bands and safety pins, a tiny sewing kit, a tube of Krazy Glue, a Swiss Army knife, and a roll of adhesive tape. 'Fantastic!' he blurted. He snapped open the metal cannister of tape.

Tearing off a strip, he tried to secure one of the bandages in place. The tape slid on the wet paint. Scott cursed under his breath, then grabbed the torn remnant of his shirt from the floor and swabbed the man's back, clearing off excess paint around the compresses until each was surrounded by no more than a vague, translucent stain. He tested the tape: it held.

Working together, Scott and Lacey quickly secured the pads to his back.

'Let's turn him.'

They rolled him onto his back.

'Don't paint him yet. I'll work by touch.' He picked up a pair of nylon briefs, scowled, and tossed them aside. Then he pulled a cotton blouse from the suitcase and started to tear off its sleeves. As he folded them into pads, Lacey gazed down at the strange, sprawled shape of the man.

He looked like a legless, one-sided sculpture molded of aluminum foil. Circles of carpet were visible around his bandages. The unreality of the sight made Lacey nervous. 'I want to spray him,' she said. 'I'll stay away from the chest.'

Scott nodded. He bent over, a compress in one hand, reaching down with his other hand like a mime pretending to examine a make-believe patient.

Lacey aimed the paint can at the silver half-shell of the man's nearest arm, and sprayed. The paint wrapped over it, and the arm was suddenly human. Crawling past Scott, she sprayed the other arm. Then she scurried alongside the body. Using the concave globes of his rump as a guide, she sprayed the tops of both legs. Then she lifted them at the ankles and coated their undersides.

Scott was busy applying the final compress as Lacey shot spray from hip to hip, spreading a silver layer over the man's groin.

She stared at his penis. It lay to one side. Even flaccid, it looked thick and heavy, much larger than others she'd seen. No wonder it had felt so enormous inside her – ramming painfully, stretching her, making her bleed.

Disgusted, she looked away.

Scott met her eyes. 'Are you okay?' he asked.

'Yeah.'

Down the hall, someone knocked roughly on wood. 'Fire's out,' called a strong voice.

'Quick,' Scott said. 'Get the ax.'

Lacey picked it up. Scott grabbed the man's hands and raised his back off the floor. He dragged him away from the door. He pulled him around a corner of the room, and let him down alongside a wall. Then he took the ax from Lacey. He lifted a corner of the mattress, and hid the ax beneath it.

'Okay,' he said. 'Let's go see.'

'Just . . . leave him here?'

'Come on.' Scott slid his automatic under the bed, and hurried to the door. As they stepped into the smoky corridor, a policeman came out of the first room – Hamlin's room. He pivoted, bringing up his service revolver.

'Thank God you're here,' Scott blurted. 'Some maniac . . .'

'I know.' The cop holstered his pistol.

A fireman with a smudged face stepped out of the room.

'Came after us with a goddam ax,' Scott said. 'We were over by the elevators, and . . . Christ, did you see what he did to those people? He came after us – my wife and I . . .' Scott put an arm around Lacey. 'We barely got away. He tried to bash our door down.'

'What did he look like? Couldn't get a decent description from the others.'

The fireman walked past them, past their broken door, and knocked on the next door down. 'Fire's out,' he called. 'Anybody here?'

'Describe him,' the cop said. Glancing at the fireman, he called, 'Don't go in there without me.'

'Tall, maybe six-two. Long dark hair.'

'Caucasian?' the cop asked, writing on his note pad.

'Yes. Maybe thirty years old. He was wearing pajamas. Striped pajamas. Blue and white. I'm not sure, but I think he went out there.' Scott pointed at the fire door across from Hamlin's room. 'Didn't see him, but the door made a metal sound, you know, like it was closing.'

'ID?'

'Ours?' Scott asked.

'Please.'

Scott slipped a wallet from his hip pocket. He pulled out the driver's license and handed it to the officer.

'Name?'

'Scott Bradley.'

'This is your current address?'

'Yes.'

He copied the information, then returned the license. 'Thank you, Mr Bradley, missus. Now you two go on downstairs, see one of the officers in the lobby.'

'Can we get some things from the room?'

'Go ahead.' The policeman stepped past them.

Scott and Lacey entered the room. Scott shut the door.

'Now what?' Lacey asked.

'I don't know. I've got to think. They're clearing the building. We have to get him out of here, somehow.'

'Why don't we turn him over to the police?'

'Now? Are you joking? I've got to have a few hours alone with him.'

'But . . .'

'We could make a million bucks off the guy. Nobody's going to get a crack at him till I've had a chance to get his story.'

'If he dies . . .'

'Bite your tongue,' Scott said.

They stepped around the corner and Lacey looked down at the man. His chest and face were still unpainted. The chest bandages seemed to hang in space above his silver back.

'Okay,' Scott said. 'Let's leave him. We'll come back and pick him up later.'

Together, they pushed the body under the nearest bed. Scott retrieved his automatic. He shoved it into a front pocket, but the grips protruded. In the suitcase by the door, he found a pink bathrobe. He put it on and belted it. 'How do I look?'

The robe was much too small, his shoulders straining the fabric, the sleeves reaching only halfway down his forearms.

'Pink's your color,' Lacey said.

'We'd better make sure we get back here before the lady,' he muttered, and turned off the lights.

Chapter Twenty

Dukane brought his Cessna Bonanza in for a landing in Tucson, rented an Oldsmobile from Hertz, then sped toward the city.

He pressed a switch to lower the window, and put an arm out to catch the air. The night felt warm and dry.

Tuning in a country music station, he pressed the gas pedal to the floor. A straight, deserted road like this, no reason he shouldn't get it up to eighty. Cut off a few extra minutes. Might mean the difference to Scott.

Up against an invisible man? The more he thought about it, the crazier it sounded.

How the hell do you make a man invisible?

Even better, how do you nail him?

We shall see, Dukane thought, and began to sing along with Tom T. Hall.

When he reached downtown Tucson, he knew there was too much commotion for 3 am. He swung the Olds onto Garfield Street. A block ahead of him, a fire truck and a dozen police cars filled the road. Their spinning domes flung red and blue lights over the crowd of onlookers, splashed their colors against walls and store windows. Most of the crowd's attention was focused on the hotel. The Desert Wind. Peering up through the windshield, Dukane saw no trace of fire or smoke. Except for a few broken windows, the hotel looked fine. Whatever had happened was over.

That explained why there was only a single fire truck. The others had already left. This one remained for the mop-up. Its crew might stay for a few hours, checking around, making sure the fire wasn't still burning secretly inside a wall, ready to blaze up the minute they took off.

But why all the police cars?

Easy. Because more must've happened than a fire.

He hadn't been in time to prevent it. From the look of things, whatever happened must've been an hour ago. At least. No way he could've arrived in time to help. Christ, he just hoped Scott was all right.

He turned the corner, and found an empty stretch of curb. He pulled over, took his attache case from the back seat, and walked back to Garfield Street. Crossing to the left side, he made his way through the crowd. Many of the people were dressed in nightclothes, obviously hotel guests who'd been evacuated.

'What happened here?' he asked a man in a bathrobe.

'*Some* excitement, huh? Fire. And I hear some nut went after folks with an ax. Panicked, I guess. Killed half a dozen folks. I saw 'em cart out the bodies.'

'How long ago?'

'Seems like hours. All over, now. You should've got here sooner. Brought 'em out in body bags, just like in the news. All over, now. Hope they're gonna let us in pretty soon. Got a conference at nine. Can't very well go dressed like this, can I?'

Dukane shook his head, and moved on.

A hand clapped his shoulder from behind. He whirled around and looked into the haggard, boyish face of Scott.

'Glad you made it,' Scott said.

'Glad *you* did.'

'Dukane, this is Lacey Allen.'

She nodded a greeting. Her hair was mussed, her face dirty or bruised, the tail of her tank top half untucked.

'Let's go to my car,' he said. 'We can talk there.'

'So he's still in that room,' Scott finished, 'unless he walked off.'

'Or the police found him,' said Dukane.

'If they did, they haven't brought him out.'

'Not that we saw,' Lacey added, and stubbed out her cigarette in the car's ashtray.

'What'll we do?' Scott asked.

'If you're so determined to get his life story, I suppose we'll have to go up there and bring him out. Lacey, you'd better wait here. They'll have found the editor's body in your room. They'll be looking for you, and we can't have you pulled in for questioning just now. Scott, take off that silly robe.'

'But my Colt . . .'

'Leave it with Lacey.'

In the hotel lobby, Dukane showed a false FBI credential to the officer in charge, explaining he needed to retrieve paperwork from his room. He and Scott were allowed to pass.

As they stepped into an elevator, two men in plain clothes joined them. Dukane pushed a button for the fifth floor.

'Which floor?' he asked the men.

'Same.'

The door closed, and the elevator started upward.

'Are you gentlemen guests of the hotel?' asked the taller of the two. He was about forty, with neatly trimmed black hair and the weary, cynical eyes common to cops. He appeared in better shape than his younger buddy. From the thickness of his neck, Dukane guessed that he worked out with weights.

'We're on official business,' Dukane said.

'ID?'

Dukane showed it.

'FBI, huh? I'm impressed. Aren't we impressed, Arthur?'

'I know I am,' said Arthur.

'What about you?' he asked Scott.

'Me?' Grinning, Scott scratched his bare chest. 'I'm impressed, too.'

The man didn't look amused. 'Got an ID?'

'He's with me,' said Dukane.

The doors opened, and all four left the elevator. A uniformed cop nodded to the other pair. He glanced at Dukane and Scott.

'Let them pass,' said the tall one. 'FBI.' He pointed to a dark pool of blood. 'Try not to step in it.'

'We'll be careful,' Dukane said.

Scott nodded to the left.

'Hope you catch him,' Dukane told the men, and started away.

'We're not the FBI, but we sometimes do get our man.'

'I'm sure you do.'

'Come along, Arthur.' The pair turned to the right and started up the corridor.

Dukane and Scott walked the other way. As they reached the corner, Dukane glanced back. The uniformed cop was still near the elevator bank. The two in plain clothes had nearly arrived at the far end of the corridor.

'Lucky they didn't come with us,' Scott said.

'We're not out of here yet.'

Halfway up the short hall, Dukane spotted the battered door. He entered first, stepping over the strewn contents of a suitcase. Women's clothing.

Scott pointed to the first bed.

They crouched beside it. Dukane lifted the draping edge of the coverlet. In the space below the bed, he saw a naked, silver-skinned man. He grabbed an arm, and dragged the man out.

'Good Christ,' Dukane muttered, staring at the empty face, at the bandages suspended over the hollow chest cavity. He laid a hand on the chest. He felt the texture and warmth of skin where none was visible, felt the slow rise and fall of breathing. 'I'll be damned,' he said. 'I never would've believed it.'

'Thought I was kidding you?'

'Not exactly. Just figured you were mistaken, somehow. But he's invisible, all right.'

'How'll we get him out of here?'

'Won't be easy. Especially the way he looks.' Dukane swiped a finger over the paint. It was dry. 'Got any turpentine?'

Scott made a feeble laugh.

'Too bad he's not completely invisible when it would do us some good. Where's your room?'

'Third floor.'

'You still have the key?'

'Sure.'

'Go downstairs and bring up your luggage. You have extra clothes?'

Scott nodded.

'They'll be a tight fit on this guy, but we can't haul him out of here looking like this.'

'What about his face?'

'I don't know. Go get your stuff, though. Take the stairs. I don't want you running into more cops.'

Scott stood up. He started to turn away, but hesitated. 'You know, Matt . . . those cops. The plain clothes guys? They looked familiar to me. I can't quite place them, but . . .' He chewed his lower lip. 'They worry me.'

'Think about it. In the meantime, get your stuff up here.'

'Right.'

While Scott was gone, Dukane searched the suitcase of the room's occupant. He found no make-up, so he checked the bathroom. There, on a shelf above the sink, was a blue canvas satchel. He unsnapped it, folded it open, and studied the contents neatly arranged inside clear plastic pockets: cue tips, skin moisturizer, fingernail polish and remover, blush-on, mascara, lipstick, an eyebrow pencil, and a tiny tan bottle of make-up base. He took out the bottle of base, dabbed a bit of the fluid onto his fingertip, and tapped it on the mirror. The smudge was opaque, and nearly flesh colored. A bit too dark, with a reddish tinge, but close enough.

He took the bottle into the bedroom. Kneeling down, he poured the beige fluid onto the man's face and spread it evenly. The face took form under his fingers. He saw the broad forehead, the prominent cheekbones, the hollow cheeks, the long narrow nose. As he progressed, he wished he had shaved the man. The make-up clung to his heavy eyebrows, gave his whiskers the look of spiky, mutated skin.

At the sound of footsteps, Dukane drew his automatic from its shoulder holster. Scott came in, swinging his suitcase and attaché case onto the bed.

'Any trouble?' Dukane asked.

'Didn't meet a soul. But I remembered about the cops. I saw them at dinner tonight.'

'Where?'

'At Carmen's, a couple of miles from here. They sat at a table across from us. Maybe it's just a coincidence . . .'

'A surveillance team.'

'Why would cops be watching Lacey and me?'

'Good question.'

Scott opened his suitcase. He tossed a sport coat, shirt, and a pair of trousers to the floor.

'Sunglasses?'

'Yeah.'

'We could use a hat.'

'He'd better not lose it,' Scott said, and removed a battered, tan fedora from his suitcase. He took out a shirt for himself. 'You did a nice job on his face.'

'If those cops were watching you, they might be showing up. Better watch the door. I'll dress our friend.'

Scott left.

Dukane slid the brown trousers up the man's legs, tugging to get them over his buttocks. They were a tight fit, but he managed to hook the waist shut. The bulky, silver privates still hung outside the fly. Dukane hesitated, reluctant to touch them. Holding his breath as if he were handling excrement, he tucked the scrotum into the pants, then pushed the penis inside. As he started to withdraw his hand, silver fingers grabbed it and pressed it to the soft flesh.

Dukane jerked his hand away.

The man chuckled.

Backing off, Dukane drew the automatic from his shoulder holster.

'You don't need that,' said a quiet, raspy voice. 'I'm going with you guys.'

'Explain.'

'I been listening. Don't know who you are, but you're not with The Group. You get me out of here, protect me, I won't give you no trouble. I'll do whatever you want. You name it. Just don't let the others take me.'

'A deal,' he said, but didn't lower the gun. 'How are you feeling?'

'Like I got the shit kicked out of me. I been shot before, only not this bad.'

'Those wounds should've killed you.'

'Not me, man. I'm Sammy Hoffman, Wonder Man. Takes more than a few fuckin' bullets to switch me off.'

'Can you sit up?'

Grimacing, he pushed himself off the floor. He raised his arms in front of his face, and turned them. 'Fuck, man, I look like the Tin Woodsman.'

'Put on this shirt.'

He took it. 'Where's my pal, Lacey?'

'Waiting outside.'

'She going with us?'

'Yes.'

'Oh good.' He drew the shirt taut across his chest and buttoned it. Dukane gave him the sport coat. 'You guys gonna try and walk me out of here?'

'That's the idea.' He found a pair of socks in Scott's suitcase, and tossed them to Hoffman.

'Those bastards from the Group'll give us trouble.'

'We'll handle it.'

'Man, you better. They want my ass.' He finished putting on the socks.

'Put your hands on top of your head.'

'Hey, come on.'

'Do it,' Dukane said, and tugged handcuffs out of his rear pocket. He stepped behind Hoffman, pulled one arm down behind him, cuffed it, then brought down the other arm and snapped the second bracelet around its wrist.

He put the sunglasses on Hoffman's face, concealing the empty eye sockets. Then he placed Scott's old fedora on the man's head. 'Okay, on your feet.'

Hoffman stood up.

Dukane led him to the door, where Scott was crouched and peering through the ax holes.

'Any sign of our friends?'

'Looks clear.' Scott turned, glanced at Hoffman, and wrinkled his nose. 'He doesn't look like much.'

'It's the best I can do. He'll pass, as long as nobody gets a close look.'

'Long as they're a mile off.'

'Better leave your luggage here.'

'Gotta bring my galleys. And recorder.' He hurried away, and returned a few seconds later with his attaché case.

They left the room, Dukane holding Hoffman's right arm, Scott his left. Dukane shoved open the fire door.

Two revolvers pointed at his chest. Two men grinned.

'Greetings,' said the taller one. 'Come in, come in. Don't just stand there.'

They stepped onto the landing.

'Well, Arthur, looks like the FBI got their man – *our* man. Tough rocks, Sammy. That *is* you, I take it.'

'Go fuck yourself, Trankus.'

'You're not an easy guy to catch. I must thank you fellows, and of course Miss Allen, for being of such invaluable assistance.'

'Glad to help,' Dukane said. He glanced at Scott. 'Don't try anything.'

Scott nodded.

Arthur frisked him, taking his knife. Then he took away Dukane's automatic and switchblade.

'Very good,' said Trankus.

'Glad to cooperate with the police.'

'Now, let me lay out our alternatives. Arthur and I are, of course, bona fide members of the Tucson Police Department. As such, we'll be able to walk you three gentlemen out of the hotel, no questions asked. We will then transport you to the destination of our choice.'

'Not the police station, I assume.'

'True. You're a bright fellow, probably not FBI at all.'

'Just a regular guy.'

'Valuable catches, all three of you. Wonderful bonuses for us, if we deliver you intact. On the other hand, Sammy is top priority. You two are quite expendable, whoever you are. Therefore, if you make any attempt to resist us, we shall cheerfully expend you. Right now, if you prefer.'

'We won't resist,' Dukane said.

'Excellent. You two hold onto Sammy, and precede us down the stairs. When we reach the lobby, we'll leave by the main door.'

'Whatever you say.'

Keeping their grips on Hoffman, they started down the stairs.

'You fuckers aren't gonna let these guys have me?' he whispered.

'We don't have much choice.'

'You're nuts. You don't know what they'll do to you. You never been questioned by The Group, man. They'll stick an electric wire up your dick . . .'

'Knock it off,' Trankus said.

'You guys are better off shot dead here on the stairs. I'm telling you . . .'

'Where there's life, there's hope,' said Trankus.

'Not if they get you to the compound.'

'Compound?' asked Dukane. 'What's that?'

'Get me out of here, and I'll take you. A guided fuckin' tour.'

'You always did have stupid ideas,' Trankus said. 'That's what got you into this mess. How could you have *imagined* you'd get away with it?'

'Done all right, till now.'

'Certainly. Our people have been following your progress, Sammy. For an invisible man, you left a wonderfully visible trail. A word of advice, though it's a bit late – always conduct your affairs in such a way as to stay out of the news.'

'Thanks.'

They reached the door to the lobby. 'Stop,' Trankus said. He stepped past them, and pushed open the door.

They drew curious glances as they crossed the lobby. 'Looters,' Trankus explained. That seemed to satisfy the other cops.

In seconds, they were outside.

'What about Lacey?' Dukane asked.

'For Christsake!' Scott snapped.

'Oh, we wouldn't forget Miss Allen.' When they reached the sidestreet, Trankus said, 'This way.' Apparently, he knew just where to find the car.

They walked up the center of the deserted street.

As they neared the car, Dukane saw Lacey watching through a window. He raised a hand as if to scratch his belly, made a fist with his forefinger protruding and worked his thumb up and down.

They reached the car.

'Miss Allen, would you care to join us?' Trankus pressed the muzzle of his revolver against Dukane's ear.

Dukane nodded.

Lacey swung open the driver's door. She held Scott's automatic at her waist.

Dukane threw his arm up, knocking Trankus's pistol back. The blast deafened him, scorched the nape of his neck. A second blast, from the car, caught Trankus in the chest.

Arthur crouched and aimed at Lacey.

Hoffman started to run.

Scott swung his attaché case, smashing aside Arthur's pistol.

Dukane tripped Hoffman. As the man tumbled to the street, Scott drove two fingers into Arthur's eyes, then chopped his throat. Grabbing Trankus's gun off the pavement, Dukane put a bullet into Arthur's head.

They retrieved the other weapons.

Then they dragged Hoffman to the car and flung him into the back seat. Dukane climbed in on top of him. Scott shoved Lacey into the passenger seat, and the car sped away.

Chapter Twenty-one

Lacey sat huddled against the passenger door, shaking as her mind replayed the kick of the pistol, the stunned look on the man's face when her bullet slammed into him, the way he flopped backwards with his hands groping the air. She told herself it was necessary, she *had* to shoot him. That didn't help. She felt cold and sick.

At first, the car hurled up the street, skidded around a corner, then around another corner. Lacey held tightly to the door handle as the momentum tugged at her.

Then the car slowed to a moderate speed.

'Looks all right behind,' Dukane said.

'Where to?'

'The desert?'

'Which way?'

'This way's fine. I'll tell you when to turn.'

Scott nodded, then looked over at Lacey. 'How are you doing?'

'Rotten.'

'You did great.'

'Who . . . who were they?'

'Apparently from some group that's after Hoffman.'

'Hoffman?'

'Our invisible friend,' Scott said. 'His name is Samuel Hoffman.'

'Elsie's son?'

'That's right,' Hoffman muttered.

'My God! He did that . . . butchered her that way? His own mother?'

'She was a cunt,' came the rough voice from the back seat. 'Same as you.'

'Shut up,' snapped Dukane.

Turning, Lacey looked around at the man beside Dukane. The hat was gone. So were the sunglasses. The eyeless blur of face looked grotesque and unfamiliar, more like a death's head than the face of Sammy Hoffman. She quickly turned away.

She hadn't seen Sammy in nearly ten years, not since the day he attacked Miss Jones. But she remembered the way he always stared at her. Sometimes, he even followed her.

Then came the night in her bedroom. She always liked to open the curtains, after getting into her nightgown, so the sun would fill her room in the morning. This time, when she opened them, she found a monster staring up at her, its nose and cheek mashed crooked against the window screen. She screamed. The hideous face lurched back, its features returning to normal, and she recognized Sammy. 'You creep!' she shrieked as he dashed away. 'You goddamn creep!'

Her father phoned Sammy's parents that night. They were furious, said they would make Sammy wish he'd never been born. They must have carried out their threat, too; the next morning, Sammy showed up in class with a black eye and welts on his arms.

That was the day he attacked Miss Jones. Lacey never

heard for sure, but rumor claimed that he raped the young teacher. Afterward, Lacey felt sick when she thought about it. Had she been to blame, somehow? It only made her feel worse to realize how glad she was that Sammy had chosen the teacher to rape, not her.

Well, he'd got her at last. Over and over again. She pressed her thighs tightly together, as if to prevent him from getting between them once more.

Looking out the windshield, she saw that they had left the city behind. The desert road was dark except for a half-moon and the bright tunnel of the headlights. Off to the sides, the terrain looked bleak and rugged. Saguaro cacti stood in the distance like lonely, disfigured men watching them pass. Occasionally, she saw a house. They were few and dark.

She wished she were home and safe, and Sammy Hoffman far away, locked up where he could never get at her again. Locked up or dead.

'Make a left here,' Dukane said.

Slowing the car, Scott turned onto a narrow, two-lane road.

'We'll find a place to hole up, get your friend's story.'

'Gonna write me up?' Hoffman asked.

'Lacey and I,' Scott said, 'want to write a book about you. We want to get your whole story on tape.'

'Don't waste your time. Laveda, she'll see you never live to do it.'

'Laveda?' Dukane asked, sounding shocked. 'She's mixed up in this?'

'Mixed up? Hell, she's it. She's behind the whole fuckin' thing. And you're all on her list, now. They know you've been with me. They've gotta shut you up. Too bad, huh, Lacey? I hate to see good quiff get wasted.'

Lacey heard Hoffman grunt.

'Just pointing out the facts of life.'

Scott glanced at Lacey. 'You'll be okay. We'll take care of you.'

'Is he right, though? Will they try to kill us?'

'They won't get us,' Dukane said.

'What's to stop them?'

'Me and Scott.'

'I'm glad *you're* so confident,' Lacey said.

'If necessary, we'll set ourselves up with new identities.'

'I don't think I'd like that,' she said, and stared out the window. A new identity. No more Lacey Allen, no more Oasis. Life in a strange town, always afraid the truth will be uncovered and the hunters will come. On the other hand, she no longer had strong ties to Oasis. After her parents were killed in a car crash, she'd simply stayed on because the town was familiar and comfortable. Most of her childhood friends had moved on. The job at the *Tribune* was pleasant and secure, but she'd often felt restless, had thought of heading out for a more challenging job in LA, or San Francisco. Only inertia held her back. Why abandon the safe, routine life of Oasis for the unknown? Someday, maybe. Someday, she would just up and leave. Alone, if she had to. But she always imagined a man would come along, one day, and take her hand, and lead her into a new life.

The man, apparently, was Sammy Hoffman. But he didn't lead her into a new life, he dragged her screaming.

She wished for the old security, the peace she'd known before he came along. But it was gone forever. She'd been terrorized, beaten and raped, she'd seen people butchered, she'd killed a man herself, and now she was faced with a life of hiding.

She suddenly realized, with a mixture of regret and excitement, that she had already lost Lacey Allen. Lacey had died, had been reborn into a new and horrible world. No longer the same person, she deserved a new name.

A natural step, when the rest of your identity has changed so completely. Maybe the new Lacey, whatever her name might be, would make a better life for herself. The old one hadn't done so well, not really. This was a chance to abandon her old ways, to seek out what she had missed.

'Might not be so bad,' she said.

'What?' Scott asked.

'Starting over.'

'Better than the alternative,' said Dukane.

'Don't worry about it, Lacey.'

'She better worry about it,' Hoffman said. 'You all better. Only way I stayed alive, this long, is 'cause I'm invisible.'

'There is another solution,' Dukane said.

'Yeah? I'd like to hear it.'

'Kill Laveda.'

Hoffman made a single, husky laugh. 'Sure thing. You saw how easy it is to kill me? All those fuckin' bullets and here I am, like nothing happened? Well, Laveda made me that way. And next to her, I'm nothing. I bet I don't have a tenth of her powers. You're crazy if you think you can kill . . .'

'Damn,' Dukane muttered. 'There's a car behind us. No headlights. About half a mile back.'

'How long's it been there?'

'I just spotted it. The moon caught its windshield, I think. Could've been on our tail since Tucson.'

'I thought you said we were clear.'

'Thought we were.'

Looking over her shoulder, Lacey glanced at the grotesque, eyeless face of Hoffman and felt the back of her neck prickle. She quickly turned her attention to the rear window. She saw the red glow of their own tail lights, the pale moonlit strip of road, but no other car. 'I don't see it,' she said.

'It's there.'

'Police?' Scott asked.

'Cops wouldn't run blind.'

'You guys gotta do something,' Hoffman said. He sounded scared. 'They got us spotted, they'll start coming out of the fuckin' woodwork.'

'Not much woodwork around here,' Dukane said.

'You got no idea, man. No idea. You think we've got guys in the cops, we've got 'em *everywhere*. Every fuckin' corner of the country. Man, I'm top priority. There ain't nothing they won't do to nail my ass. They'll swarm us. We'll be dead meat in an hour.'

'Calm down.'

'You gotta get this *paint* off me!'

'Shut up. Scott, cut the lights as we round this bend, then swing off the road. See if we can't lose 'em.'

As the headlights died, Lacey faced front and grabbed her door handle. The car swerved to the left and sped off the road, lurching over the rough ground, slamming down a cactus that stood in the way like a man with upraised arms, bounding over hillocks and landing hard, finally careening down the steep side of a gully. Lacey threw a hand against the dash as the car slid to a stop.

'Watch Hoffman,' Dukane said, and leapt from the car.

'I ain't going nowhere.'

Lacey saw Dukane scramble to the top of the gully and sprawl flat. She opened the glove compartment. With trembling hands, she took out a cigarette and lit it. She inhaled deeply, held the smoke inside, and slowly blew it out.

Hoffman coughed. 'Bad for your health,' he said. Then he laughed softly. 'Not that it matters. None of us gonna live long enough for cancer.'

'Shut up,' Scott said.

She was nearly down to the filter by the time Dukane returned.

'It went by,' he said through the window.

'It'll be back,' said Hoffman. 'The fuckers are psychic.'

Ignoring him, Dukane stepped to the front of the car and crouched down. 'Oh shit,' he muttered. 'I thought so. Broken axle.'

'What'll we do?' Scott asked.

'Walk.'

Chapter Twenty-two

They traveled parallel to the road, well away from it so they wouldn't be spotted if a car should pass. They only saw the road, themselves, when they sometimes reached higher ground.

Scott carried both attaché cases. Dukane, pistol in hand, walked behind Hoffman. Lacey stayed close to Scott, her eyes on the rough ground.

A long time had passed since Lacey's last hike in the desert. She remembered that time clearly. She was with Brian. They left his car by the road, and walked for nearly an hour in the fresh warmth of early morning. He took photos with his Polaroid: of cacti, of wild flowers, of lizards, of Lacey. They drank wine and ate cheese. The heat and alcohol made her tipsy. When she got tipsy, she got horny. They stripped and took pictures of each other, and that turned her on even more, and finally they spread their clothes on the burning ground and made love.

She looked at Scott, walking slightly ahead and to her right. His shirt clung to his back with sweat. His wallet made a bulge over his left buttock. She remembered the feel of him during those seconds when they embraced in the hotel room. If only they hadn't been interrupted . . .

Three years, now, since she'd taken a man in her arms, into her body.

Except for Hoffman.

He doesn't count.

She felt his hardness plundering her, and her excitement turned into an icy knot of revulsion. She watched him walking beside Dukane, the back of his head silver in the moonlight, his hands cuffed behind him. He looked undamaged. Why hadn't the bullets killed him, damn it? She should've grabbed

Scott's gun, when they had him down, and pumped a few rounds into his head.

Maybe she still could.

But that would end Scott's dream of a bestseller.

Besides, she didn't know if she could kill another person – even Hoffman. The look on that man's face when her bullet hit him . . .

A dead saguaro lay at her feet like a rotting corpse. She stepped over it.

'Ah ha!' Dukane said, and pointed.

On a distant rise of land stood a small house. Its windows were dark, its stone walls pale. A pickup truck stood in front of it.

'The gods are smiling on us,' Scott said.

Lacey guessed the house was half a mile away, and set far back from the road – far enough, she hoped, so that it hadn't been noticed by those in the other car. Of course, they must've seen its entry drive. Maybe they'd already checked the place and moved on.

The house vanished as she made her way down the side of a gully.

Hoffman grunted. He stumbled, fell headlong, and tumbled to the bottom. 'Shit!' he snapped, rolling onto his back. 'Fuckin' handcuffs!'

Dukane pulled him to his feet.

'Get these things off me, 'fore I kill myself.'

'That's hardly likely.'

'Damn it, take 'em off! What do you think I'll do, run for it? Where'll I go? I'm with you guys, now. You're my only chance. I wouldn't break for it if I could, not with The Group on our fuckin' tails. I'm yours. Get me someplace safe. Man, those bastards are gonna roast me. Just let me have my hands so I don't bust my damn neck. That asking too much? I ain't gonna be any good to you guys with a busted neck.'

Dukane took a key from his pocket.

'Don't,' Lacey warned.

'We'll cuff him in front.'

'No! For Christsake, he'll get loose!'

'It's risky,' Scott said. 'He's stronger than you'd think.'

'Okay. I'll lay down. How's that?' Hoffman asked, dropping to his knees. 'Can't run if I'm lying down, right?' He fell forward, landing on his side, and rolled to his belly. 'Just put the cuffs in front. That'll be okay. You oughta try walking in this fuckin' desert with your hands behind your back, see how you like it.'

Dukane crouched over him.

'Wait!' Lacey said. 'Maybe he tripped on purpose. Just so he'd have an excuse for you to take off the cuffs.'

'Shut the fuck up,' Hoffman snapped.

'He didn't have much trouble before. Now, when we're in easy shot of a pickup truck, he suddenly can't stay on his feet.'

'Stupid cunt.'

'Lacey's right,' Scott said.

'Yeah. Okay, up.'

'Up *yours*. I'm not taking one more step till you change the cuffs. You want to drag me? Go ahead. Have fun.'

'What happened to your spirit of cooperation?' Dukane asked.

'You can fuckin' carry me.'

'Is that your last word on the subject?'

'Damn right.'

'Sorry to hear that.' Dukane stepped close to Hoffman's head.

'Are we gonna carry him?' Scott asked.

'I think he'll decide to walk.'

'Think again, asshole.'

Dukane stomped on his head, smashing his face into the gravel floor of the gully. Lacey cringed, shocked by the sudden violence. As she turned away, Scott took her into his arms. She pressed her face to his chest. Behind her, Hoffman's yell of pain became hysterical gasping.

'You . . . you . . . oh you bastard! I'll kill you, I'll kill you!'

'You'll walk with us,' Dukane said, his voice quiet and calm.

'I'll tear out your heart, you motherfuckin' . . .'

Lacey heard a thud, a grunt.

'You . . .!'

'Time to go,' Dukane said. 'You won't like it, if I lose my patience.'

'It's all right,' Scott whispered. He eased Lacey away, and she saw Dukane jerking the man to his feet.

'My *face*!'

'Not much loss, Hoffman. Nobody can see it, anyway.'

Hoffman turned to Lacey. She stared at his moonlit face, its eyeless sockets, its snarling mouth, gaps in its forehead and left cheek where the make-up or skin had been scraped off, a few patches of tinted flesh hanging like torn cloth. 'Your fault,' he told her. 'I'll get you for this.'

'You'll get no one,' Dukane said, and shoved him toward the slope.

They climbed out of the gully. The house seemed no closer than before. Lacey wondered if its occupants had heard Hoffman's outcries. Noise carries far in the desert, just as it does over water. But the windows were still dark. Perhaps the walls of the gully had contained most of the sound. Or maybe those in the house were heavy sleepers.

Lacey hoped the house was deserted. That seemed unlikely, though, with a pickup parked in front.

Along the way, Hoffman fell several more times as if to prove his point. Each time, he cursed the handcuffs that stopped him from catching himself. But he didn't stay long on the ground. He struggled quickly to his feet, looking around at Dukane.

Finally, they made their way up the low hill to the house. They took a path through the cactus garden at its side.

'Give me your shirt, Scott.'

Without hesitation, Scott took off his shirt and handed it

over. Dukane draped it over Hoffman's head and used his own belt to cinch it around the neck.

'Want me to go around back?' Scott asked.

Dukane shook his head. 'Let's play it straight.' Holstering his pistol, he took Hoffman's elbow and led the way to the front door. He pressed the doorbell. From inside the house came a quiet ring of chimes.

They waited.

He rang again.

A light came on above the door.

'State your business,' called a voice from inside – the voice of a young woman.

'Our car broke down,' Dukane said. 'We'd like to use your phone.'

'I don't have one. Go on, get out of here.'

'We're worn out,' Lacey said. 'At least let us have some water. We've been walking a long time.'

'Use the tap by the garden,' she called. 'You're not getting in here. I saw you coming. You've got guns.'

'We're FBI, ma'am,' Dukane told her.

'Sure. And I'm John Edgar Hoover.'

'She hasn't got a phone anyway,' Lacey whispered.

'Okay, Scott. Get over there and hotwire the pickup.'

With a nod, Scott turned away.

'All right, lady,' Dukane said. 'We'll leave.'

'That's just fine.'

Lacey turned to follow Scott, and grabbed his arm as a woman with a double barreled shotgun lurched upright in the pickup's bed.

'No you *don't*!' yelled the woman.

Chapter Twenty-three

The front door swung open. A woman stepped out with a revolver. She was slim, no older than twenty, with black hair cropped short. Though she must have had plenty of time to dress, she wore only a short pink nightgown. Apparently, thought Lacey, she'd been determined to keep them out.

'Put down your guns,' she said.

Dukane nodded to Scott. They set a total of four pistols on the ground: two of their own, plus the two they'd taken from Trankus and his partner.

'They were planning to make off with the truck,' said the other woman, climbing down. 'Otherwise, I would've let them go.' She was larger than the one in the doorway, with broad hips, and breasts that swung loosely inside her T-shirt.

'What'll we do?' asked the smaller one.

'Let's get them inside and call the police.'

'You *do* have a phone,' Dukane said.

'Of course.'

'Okay, inside.'

The small one backed into the house, waving her revolver. The one with the shotgun took up the rear. When they were all inside, she shut the door.

'Okay, Nancy, call the cops.'

'Don't do that,' Dukane said. 'Here, look at my credentials.' He handed his wallet to the girl with the pistol.

She slipped it open and stared. 'Says he's FBI, Jan.'

'Anybody can get a fake ID.'

'We were escorting our prisoner to Tucson when our car broke down.'

'What's he doing with a shirt on his head?' Jan asked.

'He's deformed,' Dukane explained. 'We put the shirt over him to spare you the sight.'

'Bullshit,' Jan said.

'It's true,' Lacey told her.

'They covered my head 'cause they kidnapped me and don't want you seeing who they've got. They snatched me this morning. I'm Watson Jones, vice president for Wells Fargo . . .'

'Can it, Hoffman.'

'Let him talk,' said Jan.

'They're holding me for two million bucks. The three of 'em, they're in it together. Look, get these cuffs off me, huh? Dukane, he's got a key.'

'Heard about a kidnapping?' Jan asked Nancy.

'No.'

'They ain't released it to the news.'

With relief, Lacey saw a wry smile on Jan's face.

'For the vice president of a bank, buster, you ain't got such good grammar.'

'He's a rapist and murderer,' Dukane said.

'That's a con! Get his fuckin' key before he grabs your guns.'

'Nobody's going to grab your guns,' Dukane said. 'This is your house. Fine with us if you want to hold the artillery. As I said before, we just want the use of your telephone. I need to call headquarters so they can pick us up.'

'We'd better call the cops. Nancy?'

'You don't want to do that,' Dukane said.

'Yes, I think we do.'

Nancy walked backwards across the red ceramic tile of the living room, and lowered herself onto a couch. She reached out for a telephone on the lamp table.

'Where'd she go?' Hoffman blurted. 'What's she doing? Don't let her call!'

'If you make that call,' Dukane said, 'it's quite possible we'll all be dead by morning.'

Nancy looked at Jan.

'Explain yourself,' Jan said.

'Our friend here belongs to a certain organization – a cult

that wants him back. They have connections inside the Tucson police.'

'Suppose we call the Highway Patrol?'

'They may or may not be infiltrated. I don't know about that. But I do know this: if you phone in, they'll dispatch a car to this location by radio. Any joker with a Bearcat scanner will know right where to find us.'

'We'll be dead meat,' Hoffman said.

'What do you think?' Jan asked her friend.

Nancy shook her head, looking confused.

'It's all too damned fishy for me. Go ahead and call the Highway Patrol.'

'Don't,' Dukane warned.

Nancy lifted the receiver and dialed for the operator. 'Hello? I'd like the number . . .'

'Please,' Lacey said, starting forward. 'Put it down.'

Jan swung the shotgun toward her. At that instant, Dukane leapt. He caught Jan around the hips, throwing her backwards. The shotgun fired.

As its roar stunned Lacey's ears, she saw the base of the phone jump from the table, exploding, crashing into the lamp behind it. Phone and lamp flew against the blasted wall. Dukane and Jan hit the floor.

Scott rushed Nancy. The girl, frozen by the blast that barely missed her, offered no resistance. She sat on the couch, phone receiver still in her right hand, gazing at the splintered table surface as Scott freed the pistol from her left hand.

'What happened?' Hoffman yelled. 'Somebody take this fuckin' shirt off my head! Who got shot?'

Dukane, on top of Jan, shoved the shotgun across the floor. She stopped struggling. As he pinned her arms, they both gazed toward Nancy.

'She's okay,' Dukane said.

'Get off me,' Jan muttered.

He climbed off, and went for the shotgun. Jan hurried to the couch. She sat down and put an arm around the girl. 'I'm sorry,' she said. 'I almost . . .' She began to cry. The daze left Nancy's face. Her chin trembled, and she lay her head against Jan's breast.

'Why don't you all just get out of here,' Jan blurted. 'Get the hell out. Take the pickup. Just get out of here.'

'Where are the keys?' Dukane asked, his voice gentle.

'My purse. In the kitchen.'

He went for them, and returned a moment later. 'I'll see that the truck's returned to you,' he said.

'Just get out.'

'Come on,' he said.

They went outside, leaving the two women on the couch. Dukane lowered the tailgate. He and Scott lifted Hoffman onto the truck bed. 'I'll ride in the back with him,' he said, climbing aboard with the shotgun.

They closed the tailgate. Scott lifted the two attaché cases over the side panel. He took the pistols off the ground, and gave two of them to Dukane.

'You take this,' he said, handing Nancy's revolver to Lacey.

They climbed into the cab.

As Scott started the truck, Lacey saw Jan gazing out one of the front windows of the house.

'They'll be all right,' Scott said.

'Now that we're gone.'

'Yeah.' He pulled the truck away from the house, with the headlights off, and sped up the long, narrow road. The deep blue of the sky was lighter in the east. Lacey wondered at it, for a moment, then realized the night was nearly over.

She leaned back and shut her eyes. She felt weary and sick, but not sleepy. Taking a deep breath, she was nearly overcome by nausea. Her mind whirled with images of Nancy's shocked face, the face of the man she had shot, the screams as Hoffman chopped through the crowd at the elevators, little Hamlin Alexander leaping into the packed elevator, the knife plunging into Carl's throat. She snapped open her eyes. 'Oh God,' she muttered.

'It'll soon be over.' Scott patted her leg.

'All this death . . .'

'I know.'

And then she saw a dark car ahead of them on the road, its doors open, men crouched behind the doors with guns.

'Down!' Scott yelled, and hit the brakes.

Chapter Twenty-four

Lacey flung herself sideways as the night exploded. Scott dropped in front of her, his back striking her nose, shoving at her breasts. Dazed, she wondered if he'd been hit. But she felt him moving. Then the truck lurched backwards. It gained speed. The rear end swerved and she felt the truck bound off the smoothness of the road. It rose. It pounded down. Through the gunfire and roar of the engine, she heard rapid thunks like a dozen hammers pounding metal. The tail of the truck swung back. She felt the smoothness again.

Raising her head, she saw the blasted windshield and Scott's hand gripping the side of the steering wheel. As she looked, a bullet blasted through the top of the wheel. She ducked again.

The truck sped wildly, bumped off the other side of the road, swerved back, stayed on the pavement for a while, then lurched off again.

The shooting stopped. She felt Scott raise himself slightly, perhaps enough to peer out. Then he moved higher. He sat up. Lacey lifted her head. The road had turned. The other car was out of sight.

Scott floored the gas pedal.

'You okay?' he asked.

'Yeah.' Sitting up, she realized her nose was bleeding. She licked the blood from her upper lip, wiped it with the back of her hand.

The truck skidded to a stop. They were in front of the house again. Looking down the road, Lacey saw no sign of the car. She jumped from the cab and followed Scott to the house. He unlocked the door. Stepping inside, she scanned the living room. Deserted.

She returned to the truck and grabbed the attaché cases while Scott and Dukane hustled Hoffman to the ground. He fell. As Dukane stood over him, Scott climbed into the pickup. Lacey watched him drive the smoking vehicle along the front of the house and through the cactus garden. At the edge of the slope, he jumped clear. The pickup plunged down. She heard it bang and slam. She expected it to explode, but it didn't.

'Why'd he do that?' she asked Dukane.

'The truck's no good. Too shot up. No point giving the bastards any extra cover.'

'At least we don't have the ladies to contend with,' Scott said as he returned. 'They high-tailed it. I saw 'em out there, running like a couple of jack rabbits.'

'They're best out of it,' Dukane said.

He and Dukane grabbed Hoffman and dragged him into the house. Lacey shut the door, locked it.

'Get the lights,' Dukane said.

Lacey switched off the outside light, then stepped to the near end of the couch and turned off the remaining lamp. Darkness filled the room.

'Watch out the window, Lacey. Scott, give me a hand. We'd better secure our friend.'

They pulled Hoffman to his feet and led him out of the living room.

Moving a rocker away, Lacey knelt at a front window. The road was deserted. In the east, the sky was a pale blue. She took a deep, shaky breath, and touched the skin beneath her nostrils. The bleeding had stopped. She folded her arms on the window sill, and rested her chin on her hands.

She thought of Jan and Nancy running through the desert, and wished she were with them. Running. Leaving all this behind. But she couldn't leave Scott. She would stick this out with him, see it through to the end.

She thought of the old movie, *Bonnie and Clyde* – the ambush, bullets ripping into Warren Beattie and Faye Dunaway, making their bodies dance and writhe as if in a horrible orgasm.

Maybe it wouldn't hurt so much. You must go into shock right away. And then it's over.

The glow of the sun reached over the horizon, casting gold across the desert. She lay her forehead down on her folded hands, and wept.

'It's all right,' said a voice behind her. Scott's voice. His hands slipped under her armpits, and he lifted her. He turned her around to face him. 'It's all right,' he said, more softly. His fingertips brushed tears from her cheeks.

'I don't want us to die.'

'"We owe God a death," as Falstaff says.' He kissed her. 'But it's not due yet.'

She put her arms around him, and held him tightly. She pressed her face to the warm curve of his neck. He rubbed her back, her shoulders. Then he eased her away and led her past Dukane.

'I'll tuck her in,' he said.

Dukane nodded.

Scott guided her to a bed of cushions and blankets prepared in a short hallway. The nearby doors were closed.

'Where's Hoffman?' Lacey whispered.

'The bathroom. We cuffed him to the base of the sink. He can't get loose.'

'Can we use the bedroom?'

'Safer here. No windows.'

He lay down beside her, and held her gently.

Closing her eyes, Lacey felt his mouth on her open lips. His hand stroked her belly and slowly, so slowly, inched upward. Fingers glided over her breast as if seeking out its shape and texture through the fabric of her shirt. She lifted the shirt, and moaned as he touched her bare skin. His fingertips moved lightly, teasing like feathers, making her squirm with pleasure as they brushed circles around one nipple, then the other.

His mouth went away briefly. Then it took a breast sucking gently, the tongue probing and flicking.

This is how it should be, she thought. Gentle and slow and loving, the desire almost painful, wanting him so badly that nothing else matters. For an instant, she thought of Hoffman cuffed inside the bathroom, only a few yards away, but the image was washed away with a thrilled tremor as Scott's hand slipped under the waistband of her shorts. A finger traced her panties' elastic strip, moving slowly from side to side, lightly scraping her skin, toying with the band.

Lacey pushed a trembling hand down the front of his pants. Sliding it inside his shorts, she felt his hot erection. As she curled her fingers around it, she felt Scott's hand slip into her panties. She gasped as he found her opening. While she stroked his thick shaft, his fingers glided against her, slipped into her, probing and pushing. Her own hand explored Scott, wanting his penis inside her. He eased away. Kneeling beside her, he tugged her pants down. She kicked them off, reached out for him, and opened his trousers. She pulled them down, freed his erection, fondled it, held its burning flesh as he climbed onto her, then guided it between her spread legs.

It sunk into her, filling her, gently pushing deeper and deeper.

'Oh dear God,' she sighed. 'Dear Scott.'

Chapter Twenty-five

Dukane knelt alone at the window, staring through its open louvers at the area in front of the house. The low, morning sun made his eyes burn. An effect of going too long without sleep. He closed them. The lids shut out the sunlight, felt soothing on the raw tissue.

He saw Nancy. She winked at him, and lifted her pink nightgown. He expected bare skin, a thatch of pubic hair, perky breasts with upthrust nipples. But no. Not yet. Under the nightgown were red gym shorts and a tank-top. She pulled the top over her head, and there they were, her breasts, firm creamy mounds with nipples erect. She began to dance, whirling, waving the shirt like a flag as her other hand lowered to her gym shorts. But now they were faded blue cut-off jeans. She opened them, continuing to dance, and they slowly slid down her legs. She skipped out of them.

She lay on her back, knees up, thighs apart, rubbing herself with both hands, then beckoning him. But as he approached, he saw jagged shards of glass embedded in her skin. They protruded from her breasts, belly, thighs – glistening, clear blades waiting to rip him up. With a grin, she opened her mouth. Her tongue slid out, weighted with a jagged triangle of glass. Reaching between her legs, she spread her flesh. Powdered glass spilled like salt from her vagina.

'Fuck me,' she said.

'Not till you take the glass out,' he told her.

She spat the chunk from her mouth. It shot out like shrapnel, flipping and twisting toward him. He flinched away. His forehead struck the window sill.

He awoke with a gasp.

'*Christ*,' he muttered, angry at himself for dozing off, and shaken by the dream.

He scanned the area in front of the house. Still no sign of the car or any people. Getting to his feet, he crossed the room. He knelt on the couch and parted the curtains behind it. Fifty feet away stood a garage of white stone. Nobody at its corners or visible on its roof. But off to the left, a hundred yards away, a figure was lying prone on a rise among balls of cacti. Dukane saw a rifle in his arms. He ducked away, and hurried into the kitchen. From its window he saw another distant sniper.

He filled a glass with water. As he sipped it, he entered the hallway. Scott and Lacey were asleep on the floor, holding each other. He carefully stepped around them, and entered the bedroom. From its window, he spotted another man with a rifle.

At least they're not assaulting the place, he thought. Containing us. Maybe waiting for reinforcements. That would explain why the car hadn't shown up again. One of them must've taken it to alert others.

If the girls got away all right, they'd go for the authorities. An army of cops might descend on the place any time.

Interesting to see which army arrives first.

Setting down his empty glass, he went into the hallway and shook Scott's foot. The man woke with a start. Lacey moaned, but didn't awaken. Scott gently untangled himself from her, and followed Dukane into the living room.

'I want you to take over the watch. They've got snipers stationed on both sides and the rear. Maybe one in front, but I haven't spotted him.'

'All right.'

'I don't think they'll rush us, but we can't rule it out.'

He left Scott by the front window, and went into the kitchen. He searched a utility closet, a cupboard under the sink, and wasn't surprised at not finding what he wanted. People don't usually store combustibles in the house.

He returned to the living room.

'I'm going out for a second,' he said, unholstering his automatic.

Scott frowned.

'We've gotta get the paint off Hoffman.'

'What for?'

'Have to make him disappear in case the cops show up. That's assuming you're still hot to get his story for yourself.'

'I am. But I don't like the idea of you going outside.'

Dukane slapped his shoulder. 'Buck up, boyo, I'll be back.'

He led Scott to the window over the couch, and pointed out the rifleman. 'I don't expect you to hit him at this range, but put a few rounds close enough to worry him if he starts tracking me.'

With a nod, Scott opened the louvered window.

'You have the keys?'

Scott fished Jan's key case out of his pocket. Dukane took it. He went to the front window.

Scanning the area in front of the house, he saw no one. He pushed open the door and stepped out. Back against the wall, he searched the barren terrain. Odd if nobody was covering the front. If there were only four, though, and one had to drive for help . . . Well, the two at the sides could easily pick off anyone trying to break from the front.

He stepped off the edge of the stoop. Pressing his back to the wall, he made his way toward the corner. Prickles stung his legs, and he looked down to see cactus spines clinging to his trousers. The girls had apparently planted 'jumping cactus' along the wall, a variety that seems to shoot its quills into anyone venturing too close.

Nice of them, he thought.

At the corner, he blinked sweat from his eyes and crouched down. The spines dug into his calves. Ignoring the pain, he peered around the wall's edge. He glimpsed the sniper, saw the rifle aimed his way. Two shots blasted at once. As a bullet whined off the wall inches from his face, he sprang up and dashed for the garage. Gunfire erupted from both the house and sniper, a roar that seemed to jolt the air around him as he ran.

A bullet tugged his sleeve near the shoulder.

Abruptly, there was silence. He threw himself against the side door of the garage, and shoved a key at the lock face.

Didn't fit.

He tried another. This one slid in. He turned it, threw open the door, and burst into the stifling heat of the garage.

There were no windows.

Feeling along the wall, his fingertips found a light switch. He flicked it. A single bulb came on.

No car.

But he smiled as he saw what he wanted.

Lacey, shocked awake by the shooting, grabbed her revolver, scrambled off the makeshift bed, and rushed into the living room. She saw Scott kneeling on the couch, aiming through the open slats of a window.

He glanced around at her.

'Come here,' he said.

She hurried to the window.

'See that guy out there? Dukane's in the garage. He'll be coming out in a minute, and the guy'll try to nail him. Take my place here. I'll go to the front. When Dukane comes out, start shooting.'

'It's too far.'

'Doesn't matter. With fire coming from two angles, he won't know whether to . . .'

'Shit or go blind?'

'Exactly.'

Lacey nodded, and Scott ran out the front door. She cocked the revolver. She lined up the distant man in the sights, glanced away at the garage door, then back to the man. From his location, it looked as if the garage would give Dukane shelter for the first two or three yards. Then he would be in the open.

Her hand was sweaty on the walnut grips.

Too bad the man's so far away, she thought. If he was half

that distance, she'd stand a much better chance of hitting him.

Just as well, maybe. She didn't need another killing on her conscience.

The garage door opened. She sighted on the man and held her breath. Then she glanced again at the door. Dukane stepped out, a large metal container in each hand. But he didn't run. Instead, he set them outside the door and vanished into the garage. Moments later, he reappeared. With a ladder!

He spread the ladder's legs, climbed it, and boosted himself onto the roof of the garage.

He was gone.

Seconds passed. Lacey licked her parched lips.

Then a single gunshot roared in the stillness.

The distant figure of the rifleman lurched as if kicked, and dropped flat.

Dukane climbed down the ladder. He made a thumbs-up gesture toward Lacey, then carried the ladder back into the garage. He picked up the two containers, and strolled across the open area.

He and Scott came into the house, beaming like boys who'd just won a no-hitter.

'Nice play,' Scott said.

'The bastard came too close, first time across. I chickened out of the return run.'

'Wonder if we can get his rifle?'

'Not worth the risk. The rear man would pick us off. But I got what I wanted.' He raised the cans: a two-gallon tin of gasoline and a gallon container of turpentine.

Lacey frowned. 'Turpentine? You're going to take the paint off Hoffman?'

'Right.'

'Don't.'

'Could come in very handy. Lacey, you stay out here and keep an eye on the situation. Scott, get your recorder. No time like the present to get his story.'

Chapter Twenty-six

Statement of Samuel Hoffman
July 20

Okay. You want me to talk, I'll talk. Give you everything you need to know for your fuckin' book that's gonna get you killed.

I'm Sammy Hoffman. You guys know that, right? Okay. So I'll start with something you don't know. How about this? I banged my English teacher way back in high school. She was a cunt. That's what you do to cunts, bang 'em.

The one I really wanted, it was Lacey. Used to spend all my time looking at her, thinking how she'd look naked, thinking how her tits'd feel, and her ass and her puss. Now I know, now I know. Only wish I'd got her then. She was just sixteen. Should've took her someplace and kept her. But I was chicken shit. She was too damn beautiful. Scared me off. Yeah, well, got her at last. Well worth the wait, I tell you that. You guys oughta have a sample, if you haven't already.

Okay, so I had this hard-on for Lacey but I was scared to touch her and this English teacher bitch pissed me off so I did her instead. Right on top of her desk after school. It was a kick.

I was dumb, then. If I was smart, I'd of turned the bitch's switch off so she couldn't put her mouth on me. But I didn't, and she did.

Adios, Oasis.

So I'm on the road, here and there and everywhere, doing people every chance I get, always on the move. Shit, I've probably got kids from one end of the country to the next, 'less all the hons got themselves scraped. Yeah, well, plenty were probably on the pill.

Left lots of graves, too. Dead men don't yap. Learned my lesson from the English teacher. See, she taught me something, after all. Thought I was stupid.

Stupid, all right. I should've stayed on my own. That was my big mistake.

Klein. Harold Klein. Met him in LA. A bar on La Cienaga. Tiny's Place. We tipped a few, and he saw my piece and we started jabbing and he figures I'm up for some action. Says he needs a driver and he'll pay me a thousand. That sounded good, only he didn't level. Told me he was hitting a Wells Fargo. I park in front of the bank, only he goes in next door to this TV station and blows the face off this anchor gal, Theresa Chung. Remember her?

Okay. We get the fuck out of there and he has me drive up in this canyon and stop. Only instead of pulling out the bucks he owes me, he pulls a Colt automatic. Dead men don't yap, right? Only he didn't figure on Sammy Hoffman, and guess who winds up in the ditch?

Next thing I know, I wake up in the middle of the night with a muzzle up my mouth. Friends of Harold, right? Wrong. Co-workers. They figure, if I'm good enough to put the dark on Harry, I'm good enough for them. Smart fellas.

Too bad I wasn't that smart. I'd of kissed them off.

But I went along, and pretty soon I'm a hot-shot assassin for The Group. They don't want people snooping into their business, you know? Blowing the whistle on them? Snatching off some of their converts for deprogramming? That sort of shit. They set up the hits real good and paid me through the nose and took good care of me. I was living like a fuckin' tycoon.

Who'd I hit? Senator Cramer, for one. Guy was calling for an official investigation. Seems his son got mixed up in the SDF. That's The Group, you know. The Spiritual Development Foundation. Anyway, that's what got me into this piss soup, that bastard from *People* catching a shot of me in the crowd.

Before Cramer was that nigger mayor in Detroit. Jackson? The LA city council explosion, that was me. The New York police commissioner, Barnes. This ain't necessarily in order, you understand. I can give you guys all the details later, when you get me out of this rat trap and take me someplace safe. Give you something to shoot for. If I tell you everything now, you might just let those bastards have me, right? I'm no fool. I'll just whet your appetites a bit, okay?

Remember Dickinson? Heart attack in his office while he was dickin' his secretary? That was me. Tricked up his rubbers. Chavez, the *investigative* reporter? He put his nose into the SDF. The o.d. that put him away, it wasn't self-inflicted: it was Sammy inflicted.

That's just scratching the surface. There's plenty more. Shit, I worked six years for The Group.

Anyhow, it was that *People* shot that put me away. They figure I can't show my face around, so I'm the perfect sucker for their experiment. They're gonna make me invisible, they say. Sure. Invisible. And shit smells like Chanel, right?

Only they do.

Lacey knocked on the door.

'Come on in,' Dukane said.

Lacey opened it, and stepped into the bathroom. The air was pungent with the smell of turpentine. Scott and Dukane, kneeling over Hoffman, were scouring him with washcloths. The small cassette recorder from Scott's attaché case rested on the toilet seat.

Scott smiled up at her. His face was sweaty, damp hair clinging to his forehead. 'How's it going?' he asked.

'One of the men changed positions. He went over to the body. He's still near it.'

'They had to correct their field of fire,' Dukane said. Tipping the turpentine can, he dampened his washcloth and started working on Hoffman's shoulder. Most of the back was clear, now. The arms, still painted, remained cuffed behind him. One leg was gone, as if it had been amputated below the rump. Scott was busy cleaning the other.

'How about joining the party?' Hoffman asked. 'I been entertaining these guys with my exploits. Great stuff, I hate you to miss it.'

She ignored him. 'There's plenty of food,' she said. 'Shall I make some breakfast?'

'I'm starving,' Scott said.

'Bacon and eggs all right?'

'Can't eat that shit,' said Hoffman. 'Get me some beef, and don't cook it.'

'What about you, Matt?'

'Bacon and eggs sound fine. I could use some coffee, too.'

'Gonna get me that meat?'

'It's frozen,' she said.

'So unfreeze it.'

She left the bathroom, never mentioning why she had come in. She couldn't ask them to move out, and she certainly had no intention of using the toilet in front of them. In a kitchen cupboard, she found a plastic pitcher. She lowered her pants and squatted over it. When she finished, she flung its contents out the front door. Then she washed her hands, and set about preparing breakfast.

Guess she didn't want to hear, huh? I get the feeling she don't like me.

Anyway, The Group's got this lab. It's out in Iowa, looks just like a farm. Even grow stuff there. The lab's underground, all kinds of security. Make up all their shit there: potions, amulets, stuff like that. Witchin' shit.

Okay, they take me to the lab. I figure I'm in for it. I mean, how they gonna make a guy invisible, you know? I figure I'm in for shots, at least. God only knows. You don't make a guy invisible with food coloring.

But they don't put me in a cell or a dissection room or nothing, they put me up in a nice room above ground. I've even got my own little enclosed garden right outside my door. This isn't so bad after all, I figure.

And it gets even better. These two gals come in, and they're both fantastic knock-outs. One of them, the gal in charge of the project, she's . . . you'd have to see her. Give you wet dreams. But man, I know right off I'd be in deep shit if I crossed her. It's her eyes. She has this look like she wouldn't mind eating your heart. Well, that wasn't what I wanted eaten so I figured I'd keep off her.

The other, her assistant, wasn't any slouch but she didn't have that wicked look so I was hoping to get a piece of her.

Okay, they're in charge. They're witches, and the gorgeous one turns out to be the leader of the whole ball of wax. Laveda herself. I'd worked six years for her, never seen her. Keeps herself a low profile.

They come in one morning before dawn, it's a Wednesday, with a sack. Laveda tells me to open it. I do, and inside is this guy's head. Nothing else, just his head. A fresh one.

'What am I supposed to do?' I say. 'Eat it?' They don't even crack smiles. Instead, Laveda hands me these black beans and tells me what to do.

I'm not a squeamish guy, you know? I was okay, sticking the beans in his mouth and ears and nose. Then it came to the eyes. You oughta try it sometime. I've gouged a few eyes in my time, but I never stuck around to inspect the damage. Anyway, okay, I popped this guy's eyes and stuck the beans in and shut the lids. Made my skin crawl.

Then they give me a shovel and we go out in my little garden and I have to dig a hole. It only has to be a foot deep. When I'm done, we all get naked. I figure, this is getting better and better. Maybe next is an orgy, who knows? I'd heard plenty about Laveda and her orgies.

Okay, the three of us are standing there bare-ass in the dark, with Coral hanging onto the head. Laveda's wearing this gold chain belt with a dagger at one side and a gold flask on the other. She takes out the dagger. Coral gets on her knees and holds out the head.

What Laveda does then, she starts carving a design on the guy's forehead. Looks like a figure-eight with x's in the middle.

Okay. After she's done with the cutting, she takes the flask off her belt and opens it and holds it up at the sky. 'The river flows,' she says. 'Its water is the water of life. All powerful is he who drinks at its shore.' She takes two drinks out of the flask, and some of it runs off her chin and I see it ain't Scotch, it's blood. Then she takes a mouthful of the stuff and gets the guy's head from Coral and spits it right into his mouth.

Coral does the same thing. Two gulps for her, one for the goddamn head. Then it's my turn. I've done a lot of shit, but I'm no fuckin' vampire. You oughta try a swig of blood, sometime. Put you off your appetite for a week. But that wasn't the worst, the worst was putting my mouth up to this guy's mouth. I didn't want to shut my eyes, you know, and have the gals think I couldn't take it. So I stare the poor dead bastard right in the face and hold his mouth open and try to spit in the blood without touching his lips. But I touched them, all right. And his mouth couldn't hold all this blood, you know, so it came slopping back like he was puking.

Shit. Enough of that. So much for my goddamn orgy. We plant the head face-up, and that's it. The gals slip into their clothes again. *Adios*, see you tomorrow.

I brushed my teeth so hard my gums bled and I figured it was more of *his* blood, and the harder I brushed the more blood came out. I figured the only way to get all the blood out was to upchuck. Didn't do that. It might break the spell, or whatever, and we'd have to go through the whole thing again. So I finally quit brushing, and gargled a lot with Irish, and spent the rest of the day killing the bottle.

The next morning, Coral comes in alone. She's got a bottle under one arm, and I'm hoping it isn't blood. It's Remy Martin. Not for me, though. It's for our pal in the garden.

She has me water the fuckin' head with it. A whole fifth of cognac. I suggest we save some for ourselves – I mean, is *he* gonna miss a couple of shots? But she doesn't go for it. Doesn't go for me, either, when I try out a few moves on her.

Okay, we keep this up for a week. Every morning, she wakes me up and we go out with a fresh bottle to dump on the ground.

I keep putting moves on her, and she's getting more bitchy all the time. But I figure I'll get her, sooner or later. One way or the other.

The eighth day, Laveda's with her. She tells me to keep my hands off Coral, and I figure it out. They're a couple of dykes, right? Says she'll cut off my cock . . . Yeah, well, she hasn't yet. The cunt.

Anyway, after she lays this on me we go out to the garden and get naked, and Laveda starts this chanting shit, holding up a fifth of Remy. I was cold sober. I never do drugs. Maybe she had me hypnotized or something, who knows? But anyway, pretty soon I hear this other voice – a man's voice. Coming out of nowhere. It says, 'What are you doing?'

Laveda hands me the bottle. 'Say, "I'm watering my head."'

So I say it.

'Let me water the head,' the voice says.

'Tell him "no."'

So I tell him no.

Then the dirt over the head starts to move, like a finger's drawing in it. It draws the same design, that figure-eight with the x's, like Laveda cut in the guy's forehead.

'Now he may water your head,' Laveda tells me.

'Go ahead,' I say.

Something snatches the bottle out of my hand and it falls to the ground and the cognac spills out. That's it. We get dressed, and the gals take off.

I spent a while out there looking for a speaker. Figured there might be one hidden around somewhere. But if there was, I didn't find it.

The next morning, Laveda and Coral come back. First we strip down, then I have to dig up the head. What a fuckin' sight it was. They made me take out the beans, dig 'em right out of his ears and nostrils and mouth and . . . and out of his eye holes. The beans'd sprouted a little, by then. Laveda held up this mirror and told me to put one of the beans in my mouth. 'Don't swallow it,' she told me. She didn't have to tell me that.

I put one in my mouth, like she said, and held it in my cheek like a wad of chewing tobacco. Only it didn't taste like tobacco. It tasted like a rotten fuckin' corpse.

Anyway, I look at the mirror and *bango*, I'm gone.

Lacey knocked on the bathroom door and entered. 'Breakfast is . . .'

On the floor where Hoffman had been, she saw six bandages: three hovering several inches above the tile, the others pressed against it. And she saw his silver penis and scrotum. He lay on his back, one handcuff around a leg of the sink.

'Just in time,' Hoffman said.

Dukane poured turpentine onto a washcloth. The cloth left his hand, moved through the air, and began to stroke the penis.

'He's *free*?'

'Just one hand,' Scott told her.

'All I need,' said Hoffman, rubbing himself to an erection. 'Squeamish guys. Don't want to touch my dick. How about you?' He flung the cloth at Lacey. It slapped her upraised arm, and she knocked it away. 'Rather lick me? Wouldn't get the paint off, but it'd get *me* off.'

'Shut up!' Scott yelled.

'Touchy touchy. This guy's got a hard-on for you, hon. Don't we all?'

Dukane pounded down, his fist hammering the emptiness near the bandages.

Hoffman grunted.

Lacey hurried from the bathroom. 'Breakfast is on the table,' she called back.

She rushed into the kitchen, breathing deeply, fighting her revulsion. Afraid she might vomit, she bent over the kitchen sink.

'That guy's an animal,' Scott said, stepping up behind her.

'Stop maligning animals.'

He laughed softly, and kissed her bare shoulder.

Chapter Twenty-seven

Okay, where was I? Oh yeah, just popped a bean in my mouth. Just like that, I'm gone. I look down and can't see nothing – no legs, no dick, no nothing. I feel myself. I'm all there, just like normal, only I can't see myself. I give Coral's tits a squeeze and watch 'em bunch up, and Laveda stabs me in the back with a fuckin' dagger.

Hurts like shit. I go down, wondering why they went to all the trouble making me invisible if they're gonna kill me.

Laveda says, 'I warned you not to touch her.' Then she tells me I'll be okay, I can't be killed 'less I'm hit in a vital place like my heart or a big artery or I'm burnt, or something; I've drunk at the river and I'm all powerful and I'll heal up in no time flat. She tells me to get up, and I do. I can feel myself bleeding for a while, but pretty soon it stops.

She tells me to take the bean out of my mouth. I do, and *presto* I'm there again.

Long as I've got one of the beans in my mouth, she says, I'll be invisible. When I spit it out, you can see me again. But if I swallow one, it's so long Sammy for weeks, maybe months. It'll digest, see, and some of it'll get in my system. Long as any's in my system, I stay invisible.

Then Laveda lets me know what it's all about. She's got big plans for me. Tomorrow, I'm supposed to head off for DC and do a job on the President, the VP, the Speaker of the House. Presto, instant chaos. That's just the thing for Laveda and her bunch. They'll be free to do whatever they want. And it'll be a cinch for me, right? I can go anywhere, do anything. I can't be stopped. I pretend it's a great idea.

Well, that night, I get a few ideas of my own. Laveda's right, I can go anywhere and do whatever I please; I could think of plenty of stuff I'd rather do than spend the rest of my life knocking off people for The Group.

So I strip and pop a bean in my mouth, and do a little exploring. I explore my way right into Laveda's room, which turns out to be just down the hall. Coral's there, too. Just like I figured.

They're sitting around gabbing. Turns out, I'm the first guy they've done this number on. Laveda's tried it herself, a year ago, and Coral's saying how she'd like a crack at being invisible.

Laveda sort of puts her off. I think I know why, too. Reason she hasn't gone around making lots of her people invisible. It gives them too much power. She wants all the power for herself, wants to stay in control. She just made me invisible to get a job done for her. And I figure I'm probably expendable, she'll wipe me out once I get it done.

Well, they finally leave off their jabber and get down to rolling on the bed. You should've seen those two go at each other. Grunting and groaning, licking, eating each other out. I almost popped my load, just watching. Must've gone on for an hour. I wanted to jump right on 'em and stick it in the nearest hole, but I held off. Didn't want to mess with Laveda. The gal's bad news.

They finally get done. I see Coral making for the john, so

I get in quick ahead of her. She starts taking a shower. Okay, I know Laveda's out in the other room and if she gets me, I've had it. But I'm invisible, right? How's she gonna hurt me if she can't find me?

So I climb into the shower with Coral. She suspects something when the door slides open but, before she has a chance to yell, I bash her head on the tile and knock her out. More than out, dead. So then I lay her down in the tub and have my fun. You ever let it go after holding back for an hour? Nothing like it. Thought I'd bust, I came so hard.

Okay, I get out of the tub and dry off – don't want to be tracking water, you know. Then I get scared 'cause I see myself in the fuckin' mirror! It isn't me, really. The place is all steamy and there I am, like a hole in it. Bad news! I wanted to get outa there. So I hurried and finished drying, and snuck open the door a crack, just enough to see out. Laveda was on the bed. Looked like she was asleep.

I spent a lot of time watching her, wondering if I oughta turn off her switch. I mean, I knew I should. The bitch and her whole bunch would be after me for doing her playmate, and I'd be up shit creek if they ever got their hands on me. But I tell you what, I was scared. You'd be scared too. She's not what you'd call normal. I figured, what if I made a try for her and I couldn't kill her no matter what I did? She's got this magic, right? I finally figure I'm not gonna chance it. I'll just pull a vanishing act.

So I sneak out and get back to my room for the rest of the beans. Then it's *adios*.

No sweat at all, getting out of the compound. I walked right past the guards. Nothing there for them to see, except the beans in my hand, and those aren't big enough that anybody'd notice. The one in my mouth, that's invisible. Guess 'cause it's mixed up in my spit. I figured out, after a bit, I could pop 'em all in my mouth when I needed to hide 'em. Smart, huh? Better than leaving the things behind when I wanted to sneak in someplace: lost two, that way.

Okay, so I'm out of the compound and walking down this road. It's three miles, all of it through Group property, till I get to a highway. Remember now, I'm not only bare-ass, I'm bare*foot*. You try walking three miles barefoot, sometime.

I wanted a car bad. You get out in the sticks around midnight and see how many cars go by. Zip. And the ones that did come along, how was I gonna stop 'em? I finally made it to a farmhouse, dog tired. Speaking of dogs, that's where I ran into my first. I don't know if they can see me or what, but they sure as shit know where to find me. This one at the farm raised hell, even took a nip out of my leg before I killed it.

Farmer Joe came out to snoop around, and that gave me a chance to get inside. I waited till he was back in bed, then got a knife and went upstairs and slit his gullet. Got the wife, too. They had three kids. Just one was a girl. I had a good time with her.

After that, I wanted to sack out. But what am I gonna do with the bean in my mouth? Don't want it falling out while I'm asleep. So I just went ahead and swallowed it.

I woke up, after a couple of hours, when this car pulled up in front. There's Laveda, and half a dozen guys from the compound. The guys are wearing these weird masks. What they are, I figure out later, they're infra-red gadgets. Put on one of those suckers, and you can see me. See my heat image. Those bastards from The Group think of everything.

Okay, I figured they wouldn't know for sure I was there. They might think I just did my business and moved on, long as they didn't see me. So I hid. I ran over to the boys' room, and dumped the crap out of their toy box and hid in there. Sure enough, they didn't find me. Spent half an hour turning the house, then gave up.

But the fuckers set the place on fire. Insurance, I guess. Just in case they'd missed me. Tells you something, don't it? Sure told *me* something. Told me they wanted my ass dead.

I just about cooked, but I got out of that place. Their car

was gone. Great, I'm home free. Then I catch a slug in the shoulder and go down. This is it, Sammy. They'll move in now, and Lavenda'll get your dick just like she said. Except *they* don't move in. Just this one guy comes out from beside the garage, decked out with a rifle and those infra-red goggles. I play dead, and he's dumb enough to come close and it's bye-bye, dummy. I grab the rifle out of his hands and ram it through his teeth and blast off the back of his head.

Then I go over to the garage and hot-wire one of Farmer Joe's cars, and get the fuck out of there.

Lacey threw open the bathroom door. 'A car's coming!'

'Cops?' Dukane asked.

'I don't think so.'

She ran ahead of them, pressing her shirt to her damp breasts.

After cleaning the breakfast dishes, she had given in to her need to clean herself. She filled the sink with warm water, then checked the windows to be certain the snipers remained in their normal positions. Returning to the kitchen, she used liquid detergent to wash her hair. Bent over the sink to rinse, she worried about leaving the house unguarded, imagined the front door bursting open, men with guns rushing in. As soon as the soap was out of her hair, she grabbed a hand towel and again checked the windows.

Everything looked all right.

But she didn't like the kitchen, felt blind at its sink, and vulnerable. So she filled two pans with water and carried them into the living room. Facing the front window, she took off her clothes. She sponged herself with warm soapy water, and wiped the slickness away with cool water from the other pan. It felt very good. Maybe later, once the men were done in the bathroom, she would ask them to move Hoffman out and she could take a real bath. When was the last time? Yesterday? Just before going out to dinner with Scott. Only yesterday. It seemed like weeks ago.

She squeezed the sponge against the nape of her neck and felt the cool water stream down her back. It slid over her buttocks and between them, and trickled down the backs of her legs. If Scott were here, he could wash her back . . .

She imagined him coming into the room, and smiling with delight when he saw her. She would turn to face him. He would kiss her mouth, her neck, her breasts. His tongue would prod her nipples.

Rather lick me?

The memory of Hoffman's words smashed her fantasy. She tossed the sponge into the water and picked up a dish towel. She patted her legs dry. She rubbed between them. She looked around at the cut on her buttock. It was slightly red at the edges, but scabbed over. It hadn't been much more than a scratch, after all. But it itched more than the others that threaded her body. She resisted an urge to rake it with her fingernails, but rubbed it gently with the towel.

As she started to dry her arms, the sound of a car engine froze her. She glanced out the window. A black Rolls-Royce sped up the road toward the house.

Whipping the towel around her waist, she scooped up her shirt and raced for the bathroom.

Now Scott and Dukane were rushing past her, pistols ready. Scott checked the side window. Dukane kicked over a water pan as he dashed to the front. He crouched at the window.

Scott ran to the hall.

Lacey pulled her shirt on, grabbed her revolver off the rocking chair, and knelt beside Dukane. The car had stopped in front of the door – no more than ten yards away. Through its tinted windows, she saw moving, indistinct shapes.

A door flew open. A naked woman was thrust from the car. She fell facedown, and the door slammed shut.

Her back and rump were striped with raw, bleeding wounds. She pushed herself up. On her knees, she looked at the window. Lacey moaned, cold with sickness as she recognized the swollen, bloody face. Jan. The flesh of her chest and belly was tattered. Blood spilled from open wounds where her nipples should have been, flowed from her vagina, sheathing her thighs, forming a puddle on the ground between her knees.

The rear window slid down three inches. Lacey saw the crown of a bald head inside the car.

'We want Hoffman,' a man's voice called through the opening. 'Give us Hoffman, and we'll let the rest of you go. If you're . . .'

Dukane fired. With the first shot, the pale scalp erupted and dropped from sight. The second shot smashed into the window, halfway down, blasting out a cone of glass but not breaking through.

The car sprang forward.

Until that instant, Lacey didn't see the cord – the white electrical cord around Jan's left ankle and running up to the crack at the bottom of the car door. It snapped taut. Tugged Jan's leg from under her. Dragged her, spinning and bouncing, alongside the car.

Lacey's own scream drowned out the screams from Jan. Covering her ears, she lowered her head and shut her eyes tight.

Finally, she raised her head. The car had turned around and was now speeding back. Its body hid Jan from her view until it turned right and headed up the entry drive. Then she glimpsed the tumbling carcass.

Throwing herself away from the window, she grabbed the nearer pan and vomited into it. As convulsions wracked her, she realized vaguely that her towel had fallen away. It didn't matter. Her mind reeled at what she'd seen. Would they do the same to Nancy? To her? Lacey's stomach was empty, now, but she strained with dry heaves. Her mouth dripped hot stomach fluids. Her eyes dripped tears.

'You stay with Lacey,' Scott told Dukane. 'I'd better go in and get the rest of Hoffman's story.'

Dukane helped Lacey to the couch. Lying on it, she felt the soft fabric against her buttocks. She pulled a pillow down to cover her bare groin.

'What about Nancy?' she asked.

'There's nothing we can do.'

Dukane handed the panties and shorts to Lacey. 'We could give them Hoffman,' she said.

He turned away, and sat on an edge of the coffee table. As Lacey put on her clothes, he said. 'They won't let us go.'

'Why not?'

'Several reasons. First, we killed some of their people: the cops in Tucson, the sniper, the guy in the car just now. They can't let us get away with that. Second, we've been in contact with Hoffman and they've got to assume he talked, maybe gave out the formula for becoming invisible.'

'Did he?'

'He did. That, plus plenty of other information. The Group can't allow that. How many reasons is that?'

'Two.'

'Three, even if the other reasons didn't exist, they'd want us for the sport. The people in The Group are evil. I've had some prior experience with them. I know. They love the power, love to make people cringe at their feet, to torture and kill for their own pleasure.'

'Doesn't sound good,' Lacey said.

'It's not.'

Chapter Twenty-eight

Okay, I'm tooling along in Farmer Joe's car, keeping a sharp look-out for the bunch from the compound. But I never do see 'em. The farmhouse was north of the compound, so they must've figured I'd keep going that way. Well, I didn't. I went east. Got clean away.

But it gets to be daylight, and there's some traffic on the highway, and I start getting queer looks from the jerks in the other cars. Doesn't take me long to figure out why. I'm invisible, right? So who's driving my car?

I don't give much shit where I'm going – long as it's not back to the compound – so I pull into a Denny's and climb in back of the first car I find unlocked. Wherever they're going, I'll go. So I'm sitting there in the backseat and along comes not just momma and poppa, but three brats. Being invisible's no cinch. When the door opens, I knock this little bastard on his ass and get out of there. The kid's bawling, tells his dad somebody *pushed* him, and the old man gives him a whack for fibbing. Nice guy.

Next time, I play it safe. A guy comes in the parking lot alone. I make sure he doesn't lock up, then I go in Denny's, in the kitchen there, and heist myself a coke and a couple of burgers and polish 'em off while I wait for the guy.

He takes me into Iowa City, to this university there. I find my way into a girls' dorm. I tell you, thought I'd died and gone to heaven. Plenty of food for the taking, found me an empty room, and *man* the girls! You should've seen those hons in the showers.

There's one in particular, comes in for a shower every night around nine. A real honey, looks like a movie star, tits out to here. I'm sitting down so the steam won't give me away. Front row seat. Watching her rub herself all over with soap. I've got a hard-on feels like it's gonna bust.

Well, this one night I can see she's hot. Not just washing, you know, but feeling herself, rubbing her tits, playing around with her puss. Finally, she gets on her back with her legs up so the water's hitting her quiff. I move in with my mouth. I'm licking and sucking and sticking my tongue in, and she's so far gone she doesn't know, like she thinks the spray's doing it. Maybe she thought she was dreaming, I don't know. Well, she's squirming and moaning and rubbing her tits, and I just go ahead and put my dick right in. Should've seen her eyes bug out. Looks down at herself. Reaches down. I pull it out and give her a handful. She feels it up and down, like trying to figure out if it's what she thinks. She looks real confused and scared, at first. Then she gets this funny little smile on her face, and puts it back in.

I go ahead and hump the daylights out of her. She damn near screams when she comes.

After we're done, she starts drying herself off, frowning like she's trying to figure something out. Then she says, 'Are you here?'

I take the towel, and finish drying her.

'What are you?' she asks.

I don't answer.

'Am I . . . imagining you? I've never . . . here I am, talking to myself. Shit.' Then she reaches out and touches me, touches my dick. 'You sure don't *feel* like an hallucination.' She gets this funny smile again, and goes down on her knees and sucks me off. 'Don't taste like one, either,' she says when she's finished. 'Whatever you are, I hope you don't go away.'

'I'm the invisible man,' I whisper.

'No shit?'

'A government experiment went haywire. They're after me. 'Fraid I'll spill the beans.' A good one, right? Spill the beans? Anyway, I tell her I'm hiding out 'cause they'll kill me, which wasn't that far from the truth. If The Group ever got their hands on me . . .

Well, this gal's fascinated. Says I can hide out in her room, and she'll take care of me.

And she does. Man, does she take care of me! A real wild gal. Name was Robin, like the bird. The first couple days, she cut all her classes and stayed in the room with me. Only just left to get us food. Told all her friends she'd come down with something. It was like a fuckin' honeymoon. Didn't do nothing but play games.

That, and talk. A great talker, Robin. Name me a woman that isn't. She wanted to know the story of my life. I just made up a lot of shit, made me sound like a regular sweetheart. Most of all, she wanted to know how I got invisible, and what it was like. Said she wished she was that way, she'd do just what I did except she'd head over to the boys' shower room. I let her know it wasn't all fun and games, like how you freeze your ass off when it's cold out, and how tough it is to get places. Like how do you drive?

So she drags out her make-up and shows me how to put it on so I've got a face. Puts a wig on me. Presto, I've got a head. After a couple of days, I have her go out and buy me some clothes and sunglasses. Now I'm all set. I don't look like much. Look kind of weird, in fact, and even weirder when my mouth's open, but I figure at least I'll be able to get around at night like a human being.

Robin's got other ideas, too. She's full of ideas. It's June, see, and she's got final exams coming up. So she puts me to work hiding out in faculty offices and heisting exams. Stupid stuff, but it gave me something to do and kept her happy.

She also wants to even up a score. Her boyfriend dumped her for some bitch. They're living off campus, so she drives me out there to take care of them. She just wants me to do some tricks, move some furniture around, make stuff float, scare the shit out of 'em. But the gal turns out to be a fox so after I spook 'em for a while, I do the guy, tear him up, chase the gal around with his head, have my own kind of fun.

Well, Robin finds out all about it when she sees the

newspaper. Calls me a maniac, shit like that. Frankly, I think she's just pissed 'cause I fucked the gal. But she's also yelling about how the cops'll come looking for her, seeing as she was the jilted lover. I figure she's probably right. The cops'll pull her in and she'll finger me. So it's *adios* Robin. I break her neck and light out.

I take along her make-up, and the clothes she bought me, and my six beans. I hide in a utility closet till night, then get the hell out of the dorm and steal her car. She isn't gonna need it, right?

The car's hot, though. I'm no dummy. I know I've gotta dump it fast. So I drive downtown – what there is of it – and I see where a movie's just getting out. None of the gals coming out of the theater are alone, so I follow this guy. When he gets to his car, I bash him. I scoot him over to the passenger seat, and bring my stuff over to his car.

Smart, huh? Look at it this way: if I heist a car, somebody's gonna miss it and call the cops. Probably by morning. There I am, stuck with another hot car before I hardly get used to it. But if I take the guy with it, he's not gonna tell his car's gone, right? Dead men don't yap. And if a guy goes to the movies alone, you can lay odds he's single. Won't be a wife waiting up for him, worrying her tail off. So I figure I can use the car for a couple of days, at least, maybe longer. You ever need a car for a long haul, kill off the driver.

Anyway, once I've got the guy's car, I drive out in the boondocks, throw him in the trunk, and put on my make-up and clothes so I'll pass for a normal person.

I'm on the road a long time, after that. I drive at night. Rip off restaurants and houses for food. Sleep in the backseat when daylight hits, either that or take a house. I found one place where the folks were on vacation or something. Stayed there a week. But most of the time, the places weren't deserted and I had to do the people. Couldn't stay more than a day or two, then, 'cause sure enough somebody'd come around snooping.

Then it'd get in the papers. Goddamn papers. I know The Group, see, know they're watching out for stuff like that. Probably sticking pins in a map. Not gonna quit till they've got my ass nailed.

So then I get this bright idea. I grab a camper, an RV, off a couple of old farts I figure are retired and nobody's gonna miss 'em for a while. Then I head west. Keep my hands to myself, don't leave a trail for the fuckin' Group.

First thing you know, I'm in Phoenix. I figure, hey, how about paying a visit to my old friends in Oasis?

Chapter Twenty-nine

'Give us Hoffman!'

The voice startled Lacey awake. She raised her head off the couch and saw Dukane crouched by the front window.

'Give us Hoffman,' the tinny voice continued, 'and we'll let you live.'

Lacey rushed to Dukane's side. Looking out the window, she saw the black Rolls-Royce stopped in front of the house – perhaps thirty feet away. The doors on its far side stood open, but the body of the car hid whatever was being done.

'I warn you,' said the amplified voice. Lacey spotted its source: a man on a distant rise of land, speaking into a megaphone. 'Give us Hoffman, or you will all be annihilated. There is no escape for you unless you do as we ask. You have seen what we do to our enemies. Each of you will meet a similar end, if you continue to ignore our request.' The megaphone was lowered.

Lacey heard the bathroom door open. Scott rushed across the floor and knelt at the other window.

From behind the car came a heavy clank. A hammer striking metal? The pounding continued with a slow, even rhythm.

'What're they doing?'

Scott frowned at Lacey, and she saw anguish in his eyes. He backhanded speckles of sweat off his upper lip. 'Maybe you shouldn't watch.'

'You think it's Nancy?'

'Yeah.'

Dukane suddenly rushed from the room.

The pounding stopped for a few seconds, then started again. Lacey scurried over to Scott's window.

'Sounds like they're driving in stakes,' he said.

'Oh God.' Lacey sank down. Turning, she sat beneath the window with her back against the wall. She brought up her legs, hugged them to her breasts, pressed her mouth to one knee.

The slow pounding kept on.

Dukane returned to the room, crouching low, a wine bottle in hand.

'Nobody's moving in,' he said, and squatted near the other front window. 'Can you tell what they're doing?'

'Driving in stakes, I think.'

'Shit,' he muttered. He took a handkerchief from his pocket, tore it in half, and twisted one of the pieces into a strip. He stuffed it into the bottle's mouth, and drew it out. The pungent fumes of gasoline stung Lacey's nostrils.

He reversed the rag and stuffed it into the bottle again. Three inches hung out like a wick.

The pounding outside continued.

'Anybody got a match?'

Lacey hurled herself forward, scurried to the coffee table, and grabbed a lighter. She raced back to Dukane.

'When I open the door, light the rag.'

Lacey nodded, suddenly excited, eager to be striking back. Dukane jerked the door open.

Lacey lighted the wick. As fire bloomed from the dripping rag, Dukane pitched the bottle. He slammed the door shut and dived into Lacey, throwing her to the floor as bullets burst through the wood above them. Splinters rained down.

Dukane rolled off, and scrambled to his window. Lacey saw Scott take aim. She rushed to his side as the flaming car lunged forward, its far doors still open, leaving two men behind. One raced after it, yelling, his open Hawaiian shirt fluttering behind him like a cape. He turned a somersault as Scott's bullet smacked the back of his head. The other man, on his knees with a hammer when the car left him unprotected, sprang to his feet. He ran toward the house, waving the hammer overhead like the tomahawk of a demented Apache.

'Let him come!' Dukane yelled. 'We can use him.'

His naked body, as bony as a starved man, was streaked with blood. Not his own, Lacey assumed. What had he been doing? She was afraid to look away from him. He ran toward the window, shrieking, and looked about to dive through when a dozen bullets hit him from behind.

Scott threw Lacey back.

The man's head drove into the window as if trying to squeeze itself between two of the flat, open slats of glass. They burst, tearing his scalp, ripping the sides of his face and neck. His chin came to rest on the sill. Blood slid down the inside of the wall.

Lacey scooted backwards, unable to look away from the ghastly man's head. 'Get . . . get him *out* of here!' she stammered. 'Get him OUT!'

'Oh good Christ,' Dukane said. He was staring out his window. 'My God, those . . .!' Leaping away from the window, he took quick strides toward the dead man's protruding head.

'What did they . . .?'

'*Bastards!*' Dukane swung up his leg in a vicious kick, catching the man in the face. The head bounded upward. Lacey glimpsed its torn, mashed face. The eyes seemed to glare at her with hatred for an instant as the head smashed through three more louvers. Then it dropped backwards out of sight.

Scott ran to the window. He knelt beside it and looked out. 'Oh no,' he muttered. He turned to Dukane, his face ashen. 'What'll we do?'

'Nothing.'

'*Nothing?*'

'We can't get to her. They'd nail us before we got a yard.'

'We can't just leave her like that!'

'Want to put her out of misery?'

'No! My God, Matt! I don't think she's even hurt.'

'Hard to tell.'

'I think she's all right. But my God, we can't just . . . Stop!' he told Lacey, raising his hand like a traffic cop as she crawled forward. 'You don't want to see it.'

'What? What did they do to her? You said she's all right.'

'They've got her staked down. With Jan.'

'Jan?'

'What's left of her,' Dukane muttered. 'They're tied face to face.'

Chapter Thirty

I'm in the camper, right? I'm not gonna take it to Oasis, though. Suppose somebody digs up the old farts? I don't want their RV popping up where I'm at. So I ditch it at the Phoenix airport, along with my clothes and make-up, and don't take nothing with me but my four beans. I'd lost two, by then. But the one I'd eaten was still doing its job. Still is. That's close to two months, right?

Okay, I take a Greyhound to Oasis. Leave the driving to them. The thing was nearly empty, so I didn't have no trouble.

First thing I do when I get there, I look up my old pal Lacey in the phone book. Only her name ain't in it. I figure she's either unlisted, or she's got herself married, or she's moved on. I can't exactly stop someone on the street and ask, right? If she's in Oasis, though, I'm gonna find her.

So what I do, I head for the old lady's market. Too much going on in the Safeway, people gonna be tripping over me. The market's quiet, I know my way around. Hell, I damn near lived in that dump when I was a kid. After school, weekends. Beat the shit out of me if I gave 'em any lip about it.

Well, this is my chance to pay the old lady back. Spook her up, and do her. But first I'm gonna lay low. If Lacey's still in town, she's gonna pop up in the market sooner or later. Everybody does. Even the Safeway regulars, they show up for a frozen pizza or aspirin or some kind of odds and ends. So I'll just hang out and wait.

Only trouble is, the old bat's got ears like a hawk. I don't even make it through the first day, and she hears me moving around. It's night, about an hour before closing time, when suddenly she perks up and starts acting scared and looking all over for me.

Well, I like seeing her scared. Gives me a kick, throwing a fright into folks, but she's special. I'm thinking of all the times she used to slam me around, whip me with the ironing cord. Her and the old man both. Too bad *he* kicked off before I got a chance at him, the old turd. Anyway, she's plenty scared 'cause of the noises, so I throw another one into her by opening up the cash register. That does it. She closes and high-tails it.

I'm pissed, right? There goes my big plan for laying low and waiting for Lacey to show up. So I'm eating a steak and soaking up a bottle of red to make myself feel better when some asshole starts pounding on the door. I toss a fuckin' meat cleaver at him. Too bad I missed.

So what happens next? A whole troop comes piling into the store. The old lady, the jerk that was at the door, some other gal, and guess who? My old pal, Lacey. Things are looking up, right? Only they take one look at the cleaver stuck in the door, and run off like the joint's haunted.

I go after 'em. By the time I get to the door, though, they're packed in this car and taking off.

Well, at least I know Lacey's still in town.

A cop shows up, a little later. I just stand around and watch him search. When he takes off, I sack out in the storeroom.

That was Friday night. I figured the old cow'd be back in the morning, but she didn't open up all weekend. Spooked her good, I guess. Anyway, she comes in Monday morning and sees the mess I'd made. She always did hate messes. She wasn't so scared, this time. Just pissed off. People came in, she'd tell 'em it was vandals, probably kids. If they come back, she says, she's gonna fix their wagon.

So that night, some pal of hers shows up with a fuckin' watchdog. I get out of there till they leave, 'cause the dog's gonna go for me, you know. Well, once they're gone I sneak in again to take care of the mutt. It damn near got me, but I opened up its head with the meat cleaver and ripped the thing apart. Then I skinned it. Even tried some. I figure, shit, it tried to take a bite out of me. Turn-about's fair play. Didn't taste bad.

I figure all hell's gonna break loose when they find what's left of the dog, so I get out of there before morning.

Head over to the high school. Forgot school's out for the summer, till I got there. But it turns out they've got summer school going, and most of it's athletic stuff. So I'm okay, after all.

Guess where I go? Where else, the girls' shower room. I've got a thing about shower rooms, huh? When I was a kid, I used to always dream about getting into this one, grabbing a peek at all those hons, maybe copping a feel here and there. Used to wish I could turn invisible, and just spend all day with 'em. Well, I knew that was impossible. Impossible, right? So I thought I'd dress up like a girl and sneak in that way. Figured I'd get caught, though. Well, now I'm invisible and I make my dream come true.

These hons are a lot younger than the ones at the university. Some are still flat, some got these tiny little pointed tits that look like they're half nipple, and some got boobs out to here. Some haven't even got a bush, yet.

I have a great time watching, sometimes grabbing a little feel. Tell you how you do it. I worked out a system at the university. You go for where their hands are. They're rubbing soap on their pussy, you can get in a feel without them noticing. See what I mean?

Anyway, around noon, things slow down in the shower department. Only a few in there, rinsing off after their volleyball and stuff. One's this blond with nifty little pointed tits. I follow her home. The house is empty, which works out nicely. I don't want her knowing my secret, so I bop her on the head. Then I blindfold and gag her. Wait till she comes around before I start the fun and games.

You'll be happy to know I didn't kill her. No point. Just draw attention to myself, right? The way I did it, she maybe kept it to herself. You live in a little town like Oasis, you don't want it getting around you've been raped. People figure you brought it on yourself, you'll never live it down. So I just left her, and headed on back to the market.

Guess who's there. Not just my old lady, but the asshole that owned the dog. He's got himself a shotgun. And he doesn't go away. He's gonna blow the head off the bastard that put the dark on his pooch. So he says.

The store's full of people. They're all buying one or two things, just for an excuse to visit the scene of the crime. Must be eight o'clock before the joint clears out.

That's when I go to it. Start spooking 'em. The asshole almost gets me with his shotgun, though. Blows apart a coke display. Then I take his shotgun away and knock him on the head. I don't have time to finish the job, 'cause the old lady's screaming her face off and running for the door.

I catch up to her, throw her down, and tell her who I am. It's Sammy, her darling son, come back to give her a taste of what she'd given him.

She's crying and pleading with me, saying she's sorry. Man, is she sorry. Especially when I start snapping her fingers. I have to gag her to stop the screams. Then I drag her back to the meat counter.

She and the old turd taught me how to be a butcher, how to use the bone saw and cleaver. Made me sick. All that blood. But then I got to like it, and they'd catch me eating the raw meat and they'd say I was stealing and knock me around. Well, they got their way. Made me into a butcher.

So here goes the old bag, up on the chopping block. I go at her real slow, wanting to keep her alive for a while so she can see what a good butcher she turned out. I even use tourniquets on her stumps to keep the bleeding down so she'll last a while longer.

Hope she enjoyed it.

Packaged her up real nice in Cellophane, and laid her out with the rest of the beef. Then I went over to the guy. He's still out cold. I start with his arm. Hack it right off. And then I hear the front door open.

If it ain't my old pal, Lacey! This, I know, is gonna be a banner day. I let her snoop around some, then I go for her. Knock her out, strip her down, and do what I'd been wanting to do since I was a high school kid. Ah, she was fine, just fine. You oughta know, right? You haven't had a piece yet, you're missing a bet.

I don't kill her. No way. I've got big plans for her. So I leave. Only one car in the lot, that and a pickup truck. I knew the pickup belonged to the dog man, so the car has to be Lacey's. I get in, and lay down on the back floor.

It's a long wait. The cops come. I don't know, it's maybe an hour before she finally comes out. She checks the car real careful, almost like she knows I'm there. Doesn't see me, though. Course not. So she starts up the car and heads for home.

She lights up this cigarette, and I cough. God knows what she must've thought. Scared her plenty, though. Thinks I'm in the trunk, I guess. When she stops, she jumps on the trunk like maybe it isn't locked. Has her face pressed up against the back window and here I am, looking right at her with her cheek mashed in.

Then she runs off, goes in her house, and I get out of the car. I'm standing there, and out she comes with a revolver. Shit, this gal's got balls. She goes right to the trunk and opens it, planning to blast me to hell. Course, I'm not there. I'm over by her front door, now, waiting for her to come back and open it.

She gets it unlocked, and we're about to go in when this jock shows up. He's gonna play big hero and search around. So they go off together, and she doesn't bother to lock the door up, so I help myself and go inside.

Pretty soon, they come in. The guy looks all over the place. He wants to stay, but Lacey won't bite, so he runs off and she's finally alone.

Almost alone, right?

Gets herself some wine, and makes this call. That's how I find out she works for the paper. Cute call. Doesn't tell what I did to her. That's gonna be her secret. Just between her and me. Like I say, you can't let a thing like that get around, not in a town like Oasis.

So after the call, lo and behold, she locks herself in the john and starts to run the bath. Never even suspects I'm right in there with her. I have myself a great time watching her strip, check herself out in the mirror, lay down in the tub, soap herself up, sip her wine. I just stand there enjoying it for a while. I figure, she's mine now. I own her. I can do what I want with her, as much as I want.

Well, I finally decide it's time to spook her, start showing her who's running the show. So I turn off the light. I hear her splashing. Then she's out of the tub and pointing this pistol at her door as if I'm gonna come bashing through it. I just stand behind her and enjoy it. She's scared shitless. I can hear her gasping, making little whiny sounds. I leave her alone till she starts to get dressed, then I nail her. This time's better than before. It's better when they're conscious, squirming and crying. Adds a little flavor to the proceedings, you know?

By the time I'm done, I'm beat. Busy day, right? So it's time to hit the sack. I tie her to the bed and blindfold her. Don't want her walking off – or limping, as the case may be. And I don't want her learning my little secret till I'm ready to spring it on her. I want to see her reaction.

Next morning, after some asshole comes to the door, I have another go at her. She's better than ever, squirming and fighting. That should've given me a clue: the bitch has a lot more guts than I counted on. But I figure, once she sees I'm invisible, she's gonna know she can't win. She'll fall in line.

I let her know my plan. She's gonna be like Robin in Iowa, gonna take care of me and keep her mouth shut, and go on about her business just like nothing'd happened. I warn her what'll happen if she screws up. Then I go ahead and untie her and take off the blindfold.

First thing she does, when she sees she can't see me, is give me a kick in the nuts. Then she runs. But she's smart, gotta give her that. She doesn't try to run away, knows she can't get away from someone she can't see, so instead she goes in the kitchen thinking she'll finish me off. Throws flour on me so she can see where I am, and sticks a knife in my back.

That would've taken care of most guys, just like all the fuckin' bullets you pumped into me. But I'm not most guys, right? I've drunk at the river, all that shit. Got magic powers. So she hurts me and gets away, probably thinks she's killed me.

But she hasn't. I'm out of there and hiding by the time the cops show up. Well, I figure she'll come back sooner or later. I'll just wait her out.

That's what, Thursday? I hang around all day, and she doesn't come back. Then I hang around Friday. When she doesn't show up by Saturday, I figure it's gonna be a long wait if I don't get into action.

I know she works for the paper, right? So I figure somebody there's gonna know where to find her. Turns out, the cops are there. Somebody got offed with a letter opener, and there's a note makes it sound like I done it. Weird, huh? Anyway, I stick around till the cops go. There's only me and the editor. He's acting funny.

I get ready in case I have to follow him. Snatch a shirt and cowboy hat out of the cleaner's next door. Hide the stuff out back, then I nail some bitch that's getting in her car. I park it near the *Trib*'s lot, check her purse to see she's got some blush-on for my face – better than nothing – and put my clothes in her car.

I'm all set, right? I just wait a while, and the editor shows up. He checks his car real careful. Good thing I didn't hide in it, huh?

So I follow him to Tucson, and the rest is history. You know the rest. Except maybe how I got in the room, that second time. Lowered myself on a sheet. Man, that was hairy!

When you got away that time, I figured I'd flush you out with a fire. Used cleaning fluid. Started four fires, in all. Burned real good.

I would've had you and Lacey, only I got overconfident about the gun. Well, shit, can't win 'em all.

Chapter Thirty-one

'Might be good for you to listen, Lacey.'

'Why?'

'Know your enemy,' Scott said.

She nodded. She wished she could leave and avoid the presence of Hoffman – even his voice disgusted and frightened her. But she was curious. 'I don't know,' she said.

'You'll have to hear him a lot,' he said, 'if you're going to collaborate on the book with me. Might as well get used to the idea.'

'Yeah. All right.'

Scott started the tape. 'Okay,' Hoffman said. 'You want me to talk, I'll talk.'

Dukane stepped over to a front window. He knelt at its side, and peered out.

Looking at Nancy? Wondering if he could save her?

'The one I really wanted, it was Lacey.'

She tried not to listen. She thought about Nancy.

The girl had been out there for nearly an hour now. Dukane had spent most of that time looking at her. 'She's gagged,' he'd told Lacey. That explained why there were no screams.

He'd discussed shooting at the ropes or stakes that pinioned her spread-eagled to the ground. But even if he could free her that way, he supposed a fusillade would tear her apart before she could make the door – particularly since she was bound fast to Jan's larger body. Maybe after dark . . .

The tape played on. Lacey found herself listening, appalled by the list of Hoffman's victims, by the bragging and insolent tone of his voice. She listened with dread to the ghastly method of transformation, sickened by the image of the severed head, the beans being pushed through its eyes, the drinking of blood. When he described his attack on Coral, she shivered at the memory of herself in the dark bathroom of her home.

His tale of perversion and slaughter went on and on. Lacey thought about going into the kitchen, standing by the sink, running the water full blast to drown out the hideous sound of his voice. But she couldn't force herself to leave. She felt compelled to listen, much as she might be drawn to a grisly accident, horrified and worried about the victims but curious to see their broken remains.

Scott flipped the cassette over.

Then Hoffman was in Oasis, looking for her name in the telephone directory. She remembered the series of obscene midnight calls that had made her life miserable two years ago until she took an unlisted number. Thank God for those calls. The new number had at least postponed Hoffman's attack. If she'd only stayed away from the market . . .

She gagged as Hoffman described eating the dog.

Then he was in the shower room at the high school, secretly touching the girls, following one home to rape her. Lacey knew most of the people in Oasis. She wondered who the girl was. Pitied her. But it could've been so much worse.

When he told of breaking his mother's fingers, Lacey knew what was coming. She didn't want to hear about the butcher job. With a finger in each ear, she blocked the sound. But her mind saw him hacking Elsie apart, wrapping the pieces in

Cellophane. Scott, sitting only a few feet away, looked at her with sadness in his eyes. Then he blushed and turned away.

Lacey took the fingers from her ears. 'Ah, she was fine,' Hoffman said. 'Just fine.' Who did he mean? 'You oughta know, right. You haven't had a piece yet, you're missing a bet.'

Scott glanced at her, made a shy smile, and lowered his gaze to the floor.

Lacey, suddenly understanding, felt heat rush to her skin. Bad enough that Hoffman should violate her, but to *brag* about it, to suggest that Scott ... What could she expect from a bastard like Hoffman?

She listened to the way he hid in her car, how he sneaked into the house, how he stood close to her as she phoned James. With growing dread, she waited for his description of the attack. She watched Scott as Hoffman spoke. He sat with his legs crossed, his hands gripping his knees. 'This time's better than before. This time she's conscious, at least till the very end.' He stared at the floor, his face dark red. 'It's better when they're conscious, squirming and crying.' Scott raised his face. He looked at her, and she saw tears shining in his eyes.

My God, she thought, he's crying for me.

She hesitated only a moment, then crawled across the floor to him and sat at his side. He took her hand.

'First thing she does when she sees she can't see me, is give me a kick in the nuts.'

Scott squeezed her hand. He looked at her and grinned as Hoffman told how she stabbed him. Then they listened as he described following Carl to the hotel.

At last, it was over.

Scott turned off the machine.

Dukane turned away from the window, a strange pleased look on his face. He sat with his back to the wall. Grinning. 'Listening to him ... I got an idea. I know how we might save Nancy. It's a risk for all of us. It may not even work but it stands a decent chance. I think we owe it to her.'

'What's your idea?' Scott asked.

'Send Hoffman out for her.'

Lacey groaned as the words clutched her bowels. She felt numb all over.

'We'd have to let him loose,' Scott muttered.

'As I said, it's a risk. He might try to get away, or he might turn on us. In either case, he'd be hard to stop. But he's awfully worried about Laveda. I don't think he'd want to make a break, not with the place surrounded. By now, somebody out there might have a pair of those infra-red goggles.'

'The goggles could kill his chance of getting to Nancy.'

'We'd have surprise on our side. They probably aren't watching constantly with those things – if they have them at all. They certainly won't expect us to send Hoffman out for the girl.'

'I don't know.'

'Lacey?'

'I . . . He's a monster. He'll try something. He'll try to kill us or . . . if he does get away, all the innocent people he'll kill . . .'

'His chances of escape are remote,' said Dukane. 'I think he knows that. As long as he sticks with us, he has some firepower on his side. If I were him, I'd stick with us until I'm sure we've had it. *Then* I'd chance a break.'

'He's put Lacey through hell,' Scott said. 'If he does take you and me out . . . God only knows what he'd do to her.' He placed a hand on Lacey's knee, held it tightly. 'I don't want to risk that.'

'All right,' Dukane said.

'Wait.' Lacey covered Scott's hand and squeezed it. 'We can't leave her out there. She . . . as Matt said, we owe her. Let's give it a try.'

Lacey sat on the floor, her back to the couch, her legs drawn up protectively as Dukane led Hoffman in. One cuff was attached to Dukane's left wrist: the other stood out sideways.

Scott followed, several paces behind, with Jan's shotgun aimed toward the area above the floating cuff.

Lacey raised her revolver and aimed at the same empty space.

'If it ain't Annie Oakley,' Hoffman said. 'Don't look so worried, huh? I'm doing you guys a favor.'

As they approached the broken front window, Dukane removed the handcuffs. He slid a small carving knife from his rear pocket. 'Take this,' he said. 'But leave it outside once you've cut her free.'

The knife left his hand. He backed away.

'I'm supposed to go out the window, right?'

'Right. We'll open the door on your way back.'

'*If* I come back, huh?'

'If you don't, you'll end up in Laveda's hands. Sooner or later.'

'Yeah yeah.'

'Get going.'

The knife, hovering several feet off the floor, turned toward the broken window. The end of its handle lowered against the sill.

'Holy fuckin' shit,' Hoffman said. He sounded impressed. 'Look at them, will you?'

'We've seen.'

'You just want the one underneath, right?'

'Right.'

'Other's dead as a carp.' The knife raised and shot through the opening. 'Ha! Right on target. She can't feel it anyway, huh?' After a pause, he said, 'Look out, belowwww.'

Dukane crouched by the window.

As Scott hurried to the other one, curiosity overcame Lacey's distaste. She joined him, pistol ready, and peered out. Immediately, she regretted it. She gagged, but managed to swallow the bitter fluid that gushed up her throat.

She forced herself not to look away. The arms and legs of both women were spread wide and bound to metal stakes, but the mangled carcass on top hid most of Nancy from her view. Flies swarmed over the tattered skin of Jan's back and rump. The rear of her head had been scraped bald. A splinter of bone protruded from her left arm. Her left leg was dislocated and stretched far longer than the other; Lacey saw a knife embedded in its buttock.

As she watched, the knife slid out. It moved slowly over the ground to the staked foot, and sawed through the rope. Though Nancy's foot remained bound to Jan's, it was now free of the stake. It didn't move.

The knife crossed the area between the spread legs, and cut the next rope.

It dropped out of sight beside the legs, and reappeared sliding along the ground near Nancy's outstretched left arm. It cut through the rope, then returned over the ground to her side. It appeared again near the feet, crossed the space between them, and moved up the other side. It snaked the length of Nancy's right arm, sawed through the rope.

Dukane stepped to the door.

The women's feet wobbled slightly. Then they rose from the ground and the bodies jerked into motion. Gunfire broke the silence. Bullets kicked up dust around the dragging bodies. Dark matter burst from Jan's back. Her head jumped, pieces exploding away.

Dukane threw open the door.

The bodies bounced up the low stoop. More bullets smacked into Jan, splashing her like pebbles striking water.

Then they were inside. Dukane kicked the door shut. As slugs pounded through it, he lunged toward the raised feet of the women. The feet began to drop. He swung his pistol, but it swept through empty air. Scott raced to help. Dukane's head snapped sideways. He staggered and dropped to his knees. Scott clutched his own belly. As he doubled, his shirt collar and belt jerked taut. He was lifted high off the floor.

Lacey fired twice at the space beneath him.

Then he was slammed down. The tile floor pounded aside his hands and knees. His forehead hit with a thud.

Dukane shot over him. Four bullets hit the far wall, blasting holes in the plaster, knocking down a framed oil of a desert sunset. He came forward slowly, in a crouch, his head turning as if he thought he might see a target. The gun suddenly flew from his twisted hand. He grunted as the front of his pants dented in. His nose jerked sideways, spouting blood. Throwing himself forward, he reached out and fell.

Lacey fired above his back. Her bullet smacked the wall. She aimed over his head and fired again. His head jumped. For a sinking instant, she thought she'd hit Dukane. Then the head snapped down, thudding the floor. He went limp.

Lacey pushed herself to her feet. She stood with her back to the wall, pistol forward. Dukane and Scott both lay motionless on the red tile floor. She breathed hard. Her heart felt ready to explode.

'My turn,' Hoffman said.

From the left.

She shot at his voice. Splinters burst from the hall door-frame.

'Time for fun and games.'

She aimed again, then hesitated, realizing the six-shot pistol held only one more live cartridge. If she missed with this one . . .

She knew a target she couldn't miss.

With a quaking hand, she raised the pistol and pressed its muzzle to her head.

Chapter Thirty-two

'Go on,' said the voice in front of Lacey. 'I'll fuck you anyway. Only thing is, you won't get a chance to enjoy it.'

She tried to force her finger to move, to squeeze the stiff, curved metal of the trigger just a bit, just a quarter inch, just enough. But part of her mind resisted. She wanted to live. She gazed at Scott's unmoving body, and didn't want to leave him. She wanted to see him smile again, to hear his laughter, to feel his gentle arms around her. Even if only one more time. As she stared at Scott, he moved one hand slightly.

She thumbed back the pistol's hammer.

'*Adios*,' said Hoffman.

She stabbed the pistol forward, felt its muzzle stop against Hoffman, and jerked the trigger.

'Bitch!' he shrieked through the gun's roar.

Something clubbed her face, knocking her head back against the wall. Her hand stung. The pistol fell. Another blow struck her face. As she sagged, a hand clutched her throat. It held her to the wall. The neck of her tank top jerked out. The fabric stretched taut, popped, and tore down the front. Pain erupted in her breasts as he grabbed them and tugged her to the floor.

Her knees pounded the tile. He forced her backwards. Down beside Nancy. Beside Jan. She tried to raise her head, but had no strength. Warm fluid spilled onto her legs as the gym shorts were yanked down. Hoffman's blood! Her panties were ripped away.

Where's Scott? her mind screamed. He's alive. She'd seen him move. *Why doesn't he stop this!*

She gasped in agony as Hoffman shoved into her. He rammed hard, one hand gripping her breast as if to keep her from being shoved over the floor by the force of his thrusts.

A wetness splattered her shoulder as he plunged.

She should've . . . why hadn't she pulled the damn trigger on herself and ended it? Better that than . . .

He pushed her head sideways. As he chewed and sucked the side of her neck, she saw Jan's face inches away from her own. The blank, staring eyes. The flap of dark flesh hanging off her cheek. The torn lips baring her broken teeth.

Dead.

Better this. Hoffman grunting and slobbering, twisting her skin, battering her insides with his vile organ. Better this than like Jan.

She lowered her gaze to the wide, blinking eyes of Nancy. They were filled with terror, but alive.

Where's Scott?

Hoffman's weight was on her now, crushing her chest, his mouth mashing her lips, suffocating her as he pounded down with his pelvis. Then he was rigid. Lacey felt his jerking throb inside her, the spurt of fluid.

He lay on top of her, breathing heavily. At last, his weight lifted. She felt his organ slide out.

She raised her head enough to see Scott and Dukane still unconscious on the floor.

'Guess what's next,' Hoffman hissed.

Lacey shut her eyes and said nothing.

He grabbed her hair and pulled her to her feet. 'One guess, cunt.' He paused. 'No? Well, just watch and see.'

The door flew open behind Lacey. A hand squeezed the back of her neck. Another clutched between her legs. She was lifted off her feet and hurled outside.

She hit the ground hard, tumbling, gasping as gravel and cactus tore her skin. Then she lay still and awaited the hail of bullets.

Chapter Thirty-three

Dukane's head throbbed with fire. He lay motionless, feeling the floor under him, wondering what had happened. Slowly, he remembered. Guilt hit him like a club.

What have I done?

He forced himself to open one eye. The living room was bright with sunlight. Nearby was the sprawled body of Scott, hands cuffed behind him.

Dukane was tied with electrical cord. As he struggled to free himself, he heard a quiet sob.

'Scott?' he whispered.

The body rolled over. 'Matt?' His face was wet with tears. 'I thought you were dead.'

'Where's Hoffman?'

'I . . . I don't know. He took Nancy into the bedroom a few minutes ago. Probably in there. Matt, Lacey's . . . He choked back a sob. 'Lacey's gone.'

'Where?'

Scott shook his head. 'I came to . . . asked Hoffman. He just laughed.'

'Shit.'

'Oh God, Matt . . .'

'Take it easy.' He jerked his hands free. Grimacing as pain cut into his head like a lance, he rolled onto his side and untied the knotted cord at his feet. He scanned the room, and flinched. In the rocking chair facing the broken front window sat Jan. The shotgun rested over the sill, aiming outside.

'Beau Geste,' Scott muttered.

'Maybe the shotgun's loaded.' Dukane forced himself to stand. He took one step.

A tinny, amplified voice said, 'We want Hoffman. You've

got five minutes. Bring him out, and we'll let you go. If not, you'll all die. The girl first.'

'Lacey,' Scott whispered.

Dukane rushed to the window. As he reached for the shotgun, he looked out.

He saw Lacey. A hundred yards away. Sprawled across the hood of the Rolls-Royce. Her arms and legs were outstretched and tied.

A dozen men and women stood near the car, watching as a woman lashed her once with a thin, golden chain.

The woman was naked. Glossy, blond hair draped her back. Her gold arm bands glinted sunlight.

Laveda!

In spite of the heat, gooseflesh prickled Dukane's skin.

Lacey's quiet gasp of pain came through the silence as the chain struck again.

Dukane grabbed the double-barreled shotgun. He broke it open. The chambers were empty. Turning from the window, he looked for other weapons. The pistols were nowhere in sight. He quietly closed the breach.

'Four minutes,' the distant voice announced.

Dukane hurried to Scott. He fished a key from his pocket and knelt to unlock the cuffs.

'Is it Lacey?'

'Yes.'

'Oh God.'

'Come on.' Dukane tiptoed into the hallway, Scott close behind him. The bathroom door stood open. The bedroom door was shut. Almost.

He stepped quietly toward it. Stopped.

From inside came muffled grunting sounds, the creak of bedsprings.

Nancy lay on the bed, her sweat-slick body pounding against the mattress, arms stretched overhead, breasts oddly mashed, legs wide open and twitching, the lips of her vagina spread far apart like an open, sucking mouth. Dukane heard the slap of flesh, and wet, smacking sounds.

'Three minutes,' announced the amplified voice.

Dukane shouldered open the door. He ran for the bed, reversing the shotgun, raising it high by its barrels.

Nancy's wet eyes looked up at him. She turned her head away as he swung the shotgun down.

It stopped before hitting her, stopped six inches above her face, stopped with a crashing thud like a coconut hurled against concrete. The stock of the shotgun split on impact. Teethmarks appeared in Nancy's cheek – empty, ragged holes that quickly filled with blood.

Scott dived onto her. He groped above her left arm, grabbed, snapped a handcuff in place, closed the other bracelet around his own wrist.

'Got him!' Scott cried.

Chapter Thirty-four

'You have two minutes,' said the man with the megaphone.

Even as he spoke, the thin chain twirled over the head of the woman beside Lacey, its gold links flashing sunlight, and whistled down. She cried out as it cut fire across her breasts. A smile trembled on the woman's lips. Her nipples stood erect on her sweaty breasts.

She's getting off, Lacey thought.

It must've been at her command that the rifles hadn't opened up on Lacey, that instead the Rolls had come for her.

She'd watched it approach, too frightened to move, thinking *it's dead*, Dukane got it with a Molotov cocktail, how can it be coming? It bore down on her, its grill blinding in the sunlight. She thought it might crush her into the gravel, but it slipped sideways and its black front tire missed by inches. A door flew open. She was dragged inside the chilly, air-conditioned car.

Two men held her across their laps, pawing her as the car sped away.

The chain whipped down, lashing her belly.

The woman was breathing hard. But not from the exertion. She licked her lips, and struck again. Lacey jerked rigid as the chain cut her thighs.

It was the woman who ordered her tied to the car's hood. The sun-baked metal had scorched her, but the pain of the burnt flesh faded when the whipping started.

The chain whipped down, biting into her shoulder and breast.

A man suddenly threw himself onto her, licking the blood from her breast.

The woman lashed him. 'Not yet!' she snapped.

Others jerked him away.

'One minute,' said the man with the megaphone.

'They won't come,' said a stocky, red-faced man.

The chain slashed her belly.

'I did not expect them to come,' the woman said in a trembling voice. 'They threw her out. She's ours.'

'Will we drink?' asked a voice.

'When I am done with her.' Again, the chain whipped down.

Lacey bucked as it tore her.

'The dagger.'

A teenaged girl in a bikini and Dodger cap handed a knife to her. Lacey stared at its thin, tapering blade.

'The river flows,' said the woman.

'The river is red,' chanted the others.

'The river flows!'

'Flows from the heart.'

'The river . . .'

'They're coming out!' a man cried.

Lifting her head, Lacey stared over her torn body. Dukane and Scott were out of the house, walking slowly forward, tugging at the open space between them.

She glanced at the woman, saw a fierce smile on her face.

'Tell the snipers not to shoot. I want all three alive.'

A man spoke over his megaphone, ordering everyone to hold fire.

On both sides of the car, men and women lowered their weapons.

Lacey gazed at Scott, watched him struggle to hold his invisible, silent captive. The pain of her wounds was forgotten as gratitude and despair brought tears to her eyes.

They're doing this for me, she realized.

Sacrificing themselves.

If only she'd had the courage to end her life back at the house when she had the chance . . .

They were thirty yards away.

'Go back!' she yelled, but she knew it was too late.

The men kept coming, jerking and swaying as if the beast between them fought to free himself.

Twenty yards.

She could see the grim, determined look on Scott's face.

Ten yards.

A low laugh came from the woman. 'Bring him to me,' she called. 'I have waited a long time for Samuel Hoffman. And for you, Matthew Dukane. This will be a great day for me.'

'Every dog has its day,' Dukane said. One side of his mouth curled into a smile.

He and Scott sprang apart, diving sideways and rolling through the dust. Four pistols appeared from behind them. They stopped rolling, and their gunfire stuttered through the stillness in a deafening roar.

Bodies whirled and flopped. Dirt exploded around Scott and Dukane as their fire was returned. Screams tore through the din. A man clutched his belly and sat down hard. The ball cap and bloody matter flew from the head of the teenaged girl as she fired at Dukane. He tossed a pistol aside and kept firing his automatic. A man spun, crashed into the side of the car, and fell.

Dukane yelled as he was hit.

Scott rose to one knee, not even glancing at him, shoving a fresh magazine into the handle of his .45. Gravel kicked up beside his foot, but he didn't flinch. He worked the slide and resumed firing.

Dukane was on his knees, his left arm hanging limp, firing with his right.

A man raced forward, shooting. A bullet slammed him down.

Abruptly, there was silence.

Jerking her head from side to side, Lacey saw no one still standing. On both sides of the car lay crumpled bodies.

Scott ran forward in a crouch. Far off, a rifle cracked. Dirt spouted in front of him.

As Dukane dropped and crawled forward, Scott dived to the ground near a fat man. He grabbed the man's rifle. It had a telescopic sight. Settling himself in a prone position, he aimed toward the far left of the house.

A distant shot. The top of a cactus near Dukane exploded. Scott fired, then made a thumbs-up sign at Dukane. He swung the barrel to his right.

Dukane scurried forward. He reached the front of the car, and began to cut the rope at Lacey's foot.

A shot thunked the grill.

Scott fired. 'Watch it,' he called. 'Still one out there.'

Dukane freed Lacey's left hand, then rushed around the rear of the car and came up at her other side. As he sliced through the rope, a shot rang out. The bullet smacked the windshield inches above her head.

He scurried to the front.

Scott fired. 'Got him!' he yelled. 'That oughta be it.'

Lacey sat up. As soon as her right foot was loose, she scooted off the hood. Scott, hurrying toward her, passed the rifle to Dukane and pulled off his shirt. He draped the shirt over Lacey's back. Holding her by the shoulders, he looked down at her torn body. 'Oh God, Lacey,' he murmured. 'I'm sorry. I'm so sorry.'

With blurry, tear-filled eyes, she stared at his tormented face. She kissed him. Then she managed a smile. 'Who do you think you are, James Bond?'

'Max Carter and Charlie Dane.'

Dukane came up behind him. 'I think I deserve a kiss, too.'

He got one. Lacey hugged him, ignoring the pain of her own wounds, and kissed his dry lips.

'You guys are nuts, coming out like that.'

'The best defense . . .' Dukane said.

Lacey gasped, her joy suddenly turning to cold fear. 'Hoffman! You let him . . .' She staggered back, clutching the shirt tight to hide her nakedness, looking behind her as if she might somehow see him sneaking up.

'Hoffman isn't with us,' Dukane said.

'I know. You let him . . .'

'He's still in the house,' Scott interrupted. 'Securely handcuffed in the bathroom.'

'You mean . . .?'

'Pretty good act, huh?'

'Now,' said Dukane, 'how about attending to my arm before I bleed to death?'

'Oh,' Scott muttered. 'Forgot about that.'

'I didn't.'

Chapter Thirty-five

The bullet had smashed a bone in Dukane's forearm. Scott broke the stock off a rifle, and made ungainly splints from it. He used strips of Dukane's shirt to bandage the wound and lash the splints into place.

'We'd better get you to a hospital,' he said. 'Both of you, and Nancy.'

'All in good time. See if the car works.'

Scott helped Lacey inside.

'Right with you,' Dukane said.

As Scott climbed into the driver's seat, Dukane wandered from body to body, crouching over several of the women for a closer inspection.

Scott turned the ignition key. The car came to life, blowing cool, welcome air onto Lacey.

'What's he looking for?' she asked.

Scott shook his head.

Finally, Dukane climbed into the back seat. In each hand, he held a large gold band, the bands Lacey had seen on the arms of the woman who'd whipped her. 'I know I hit the bitch,' he said. 'Saw her go down.'

'Who?'

'Laveda. But she's not here now. Just her damn jewelry. Did you see anyone run off?'

'No,' Scott said. 'I thought we got them all.'

'Okay. Let's pick up Hoffman and Nancy, and get the hell out of here.'

The car sped forward, bumping over the rough earth, down a gradual slope, and up a rise to the flat area in front of the house. Scott turned off the engine. 'You can wait here if you want,' he told Lacey.

She didn't want to be left alone. 'I'll go in,' she said.

Scott pulled the key from the ignition and stepped out. Lacey opened her door. Stifling heat wrapped her like a blanket as she climbed out. She glimpsed the body of the man under the broken window, hammer still clutched in his outflung hand.

She entered the house behind Scott. Dukane followed and shut the door. The house was silent.

'Nancy?' Dukane called.

No answer.

He suddenly broke into a run, vanishing down the hall. Scott and Lacey rushed after him.

The bedroom was empty.

'Nancy?'

From the closet came a muffled sob.

Dukane jerked its door open.

Nancy sat crouched in a corner, half hidden behind hanging dresses. Her black hair clung to her face with sweat. Though the room was hot and she wore jeans and a wool shirt, Lacey could see her shivering.

'It's all right,' Dukane told her. 'It's over. Everything's fine.'

'No,' she gasped, batting away his hands as he reached for her. Her wide eyes blinked. 'Not over. Wanta hide.'

From behind them came a scream that washed over Lacey like a vile, chilling flood. It was the scream of a man.

'Get Nancy out of here,' Scott snapped, and ran after Dukane.

Lacey dropped to her knees. She tried to grab the girl's flailing hands. 'Stop!' she cried. Then she clutched a foot and dragged Nancy from the closet. She pulled the girl to her feet, tugged her into the hall.

From there, she saw Dukane slam the bathroom door, shutting himself and Scott inside.

Screams filled her ears as she led Nancy through the living room. 'Wait in the car,' she said.

Then she raced to the hall.

The bathroom door flew open. Dukane staggered backwards through it, and fell. The wooden hilt of a butcher knife stood upright in his belly.

As she ran toward him, she heard a *whup* like the sound of a wind-flapped canvas. Fire exploded through the doorway.

'Scott!' she shrieked.

The fire lapped her body, forcing her away from the door. She shielded her eyes and gazed into the inferno. Near the floor, she saw a hole in the fire as if a tunnel had been dug in the flames – a writhing tunnel shaped like a man.

A passage opened in the blaze. It rushed toward her. Smashed her aside. She tripped over Dukane. As she slammed the far wall, she saw a flaming figure race down the hallway, arms waving, hair ablaze.

Scott? She ran after it. As it lurched across the living room, she realized she could see through it: the fire blazed around a hollow shell. It fell against a window. The curtains caught fire. As it lurched out the front door, it turned and Lacey glimpsed its fire-wrapped face, its breasts.

She rushed back to the bathroom.

'Scott!' she cried out. '*Scott!*'

The wall of fire roared.

Chapter Thirty-six

Lacey circled the block twice, watching for strangers, then killed the headlights and steered the Firebird up the narrow driveway to her garage. She put it into the garage, and entered her house by the back door.

The lights were off. She left them that way.

Searching the dark house, she remembered how she and Cliff had gone through it that night so long ago – only a few days ago. They'd found no one then. Lacey found no one now. But she couldn't be certain she was alone: she could never be sure of that again.

Though filthy, she was afraid to use her tub.

Though dazed and weary, she was afraid to use her bed.

She arranged blankets inside her walk-in closet, and lay down there. It reminded her of the nest in the hallway that she'd shared with Scott.

Thoughts of Scott swirled through her mind as she tried to sleep. Other thoughts, too. Bad ones that made her shake.

Three times during the night, she heard sounds in the house that made her sweat and hold her breath. Afraid to investigate, she lay there rigid until exhaustion forced her to fall limp and gasp for air.

Once, as she drifted off, the closet door swung silently open. The dark figure of a man knelt over her. She quaked with terror until he spoke.

'It's just me,' he said.

'Scott?'

'I had a hard time finding you. What're you hiding from?'

'Everything.'

'Don't be afraid.'

'Oh Scott, I thought you were dead.'

Then he came down and kissed her, and his charred lips crumbled and filled her mouth with ashes.

She bolted upright, gasping, and found herself alone in the closet. Its door was still shut.

After a moment's hesitation, she pushed open the door. She studied the familiar night shadows of her bedroom, then crawled over the carpet to the alarm clock. Four-thirty.

Time to begin.

Lacey tiptoed through the dark silence of the house. She searched cupboards in the kitchen, found what she wanted, and stepped outside.

She entered her garage through a side door connecting it to the laundry room. A dim light went on inside the Firebird when she opened its door. Kneeling on the passenger seat, she reached out and drew its keys from the ignition.

The Firebird was one of the four cars she'd found after she ran from the burning house and discovered the keys of the Rolls-Royce were gone. She and Nancy had dashed up the long entry road, and come upon the cars of the dead people. She'd insisted Nancy take one of them, and leave her.

Now, keys in hand, Lacey crawled out of the Firebird. She left its door open for light, and walked over the warm concrete to the trunk. Taking a deep breath, she unlocked it. The lid swung up.

As dawn lightened the sky, Lacey twisted off the plastic cap. She raised the bottle to her lips. Its strong fumes made her throat clutch, but she filled her mouth anyway to wash out the other taste – the sour taste of the vomit that had flooded out after the blood.

She spat the brandy onto the loose earth at her feet, then upended the bottle. The amber fluid gurgled out, splashing onto the dirt.

When it was empty, she tossed it aside. It fell to the grass beside the Cellophane package of beans and the knife.

She put her clothes back on, covering her blood-spattered nakedness.

Then she picked up her shovel. She set it inside the laundry room. Shutting the door, she started for her house.

A man stepped around the corner.

Numb with fear, she staggered back.

The man didn't move.

She gazed at him, at his blackened face and torso, his hairless scalp, his scorched and tattered pants – and recognized the phantom from her nightmares. She pressed trembling hands to her eyes. At the sound of footsteps, she lowered them.

He was walking toward her, his sooty hands reaching out.

'Thought you'd be glad to see me,' he said. 'I know I look like a wreck, but . . .'

'Scott,' she muttered.

He clutched her shoulders and drew her against his body. His cracked, dry lips pressed her mouth. She felt the wetness of his tongue. His hands stroked her hair, the sides of her face.

'It *is* you?' she whispered. Scott's grimy, grinning face blurred as tears filled Lacey's eyes.

Chapter Thirty-seven

He guzzled half a bottle of Bud, leaned back on the kitchen chair, and sighed.

'That was Hoffman we heard screaming. When Matt and I ran in the bathroom, all we saw was this butcher knife jerking around right above the floor. And the handcuffs shaking. Laveda must've made herself invisible when the shooting started. Must've had a bean left over from the time she'd gone through the process a year ago.

'She went for Matt. That gave me a chance to douse her with gas and touch her off. The whole gas can went up, though. I thought I was cooked, but I dived out the bathroom window. The fall . . . it knocked me out cold. Don't think I was out for long, but by the time I reached the front of the house, I saw you and Nancy running off.'

'Why didn't you yell?'

He shook his head and took another gulp of beer. 'I figured

I could catch up later. The main thing was to get Matt out of the house.'

'You went back in?'

'Had to. Couldn't leave him in there. I got to him just before the fire did, dragged him out, patched up his stomach wound the best I could, and threw him into the car. When I drove up the road, you and Nancy were nowhere in sight. I figured you'd be all right, though, so I drove like hell back to Tucson and got him into an emergency room. I didn't think he'd make it, but he's a tough son of a bitch. They had him in stable condition by the time I left.'

'He's *alive*?' Lacey grinned. 'Well. What do you know?'

'When I got back to the house and couldn't find you, I suspected you might come back here.'

'I didn't know where else to go.'

'Not the greatest hide-out in the world.'

'I had a plan,' she admitted, and lowered her eyes. Until now, the plan had seemed like her only chance for survival. With Scott sitting across the breakfast table, it seemed ridiculous and perverse. She didn't want to tell him about it.

'In your place,' Scott said, 'I might've tried the same thing.'

'You know?'

'I saw the empty brandy bottle out back. And the sack of beans. And where you dug the hole.'

'The . . . the rest of the body's still in the garage. I found her . . . near where they'd left their cars. After I sent Nancy away, I . . . a bean was in the dirt by her mouth. That's what gave me the idea. If I were invisible, nobody could get me. I tried the bean, but it didn't make me invisible. So then I put her body in the trunk of a car and . . . God, it was all burnt and crumbly and . . .'

'It was Laveda!'

Lacey nodded. 'I guess so.'

Reaching out, Scott squeezed her hand. 'Then it's over.'

That night, he dug up the head. They drove far out in the desert, and poured gasoline over the remains of Laveda. The fire burned for a long time. When it finally dwindled, they dug two holes in the sand and buried the smoldering head a great distance from the body.

Dark Mountain

Part One

Chapter One

Cheryl heard it again – the soft, dry crunching sound that a foot might make in leaves. This time, it was very close.

She lay rigid in her sleeping bag, barely daring to breathe, gazing straight up at the dark slanting wall of the tent and telling herself to stay calm.

It's probably just an animal. Maybe a deer. A few days ago, camped in a meadow below the pass, they'd been awakened in the night by a deer wandering near their tent. Its hooves had crashed through the foliage, snapping branches and shaking the ground. Bambi the Elephant, Danny had called it.

This was different.

This was stealthy.

She heard it again, flinched, and dug her fingertips into her bare thighs.

Maybe something falling from a tree? Pinecones? They could make sounds like that, she supposed. Plenty of wind out there to shake them loose.

That's it. That has to be it. Otherwise, somebody is standing just outside the tent, and that can't be.

They'd seen nobody for two days. They'd reached Lower Mesquite Lake early in the afternoon. Except for this small patch of woods, the glacial lake was surrounded by barren rock. They'd hiked completely around it. They'd explored the woods. They'd seen nobody.

Not even when they hiked over a small ridge to Upper Mesquite.

Nobody.

Cheryl took a deep breath, trying to calm herself.

Go to sleep, chicken-shit.

Cheryl consciously relaxed her legs and rump and back, settling down into the warmth, and turned her head to stretch her taut neck muscles. She felt like rolling over. She wanted to turn facedown and burrow deep, but she was afraid to move that much.

A monster under the bed. Just like when she was a kid and *knew* there was a terrible monster under the bed. If she lay absolutely still, it would leave her alone.

I'm eighteen. I'm too old for this.

Slowly, she started to turn over. Her bare skin made whispery, sliding sounds against the nylon bag, almost loud enough to mask the other sound. She went stiff. She was on her side, facing Danny. The other sound came from behind her – a quiet hissing sigh, a sound such as fingernails might make scraping along the tent's wall.

She flung herself against Danny, shook him by the shoulders. Moaning, he raised his head. 'Huh? Wha—'

'Somebody's outside,' she gasped.

He pushed himself up on his elbows. 'Huh?'

'Outside. I heard him.'

'Who?'

'Shh.'

Neither of them moved.

'I don't hear anything,' he said in a groggy voice.

'I did. God, he's right outside the tent. He *scratched* on it.'

'Probably just a branch.'

'*Danny.*'

'Okay, okay, I'll go out 'n' have a look.'

'I'll go with you.'

'No point both of us freezing our asses. I'll go.' He rose to his hands and knees, still in the double sleeping bag, letting in the cold night air as he searched through the clothes and gear at the head of the tent. He pulled his flashlight out of his boot. 'Just be a minute,' he said.

Cheryl scooted away. Danny climbed from the bag and crawled to the foot of the tent. Kneeling there, naked, he pulled at the zipper of the mosquito netting.

Cheryl sat up. The cold wrapped around her. Shuddering, she hugged her breasts. 'Maybe you'd better not,' she whispered. 'Come on back.'

'Nah, it's all right.'

'Please?'

'I've gotta take a leak anyway,' he said, and started to crawl through the flaps. He was halfway out when he stopped. He uttered a low groan. One of his feet reached backward.

Cheryl heard a wet thud. Spray rained against the tent flaps.

Danny's legs shot from under him. He bounced up and down, knees pounding the tent floor, flopping in mad spasms that seemed to last forever. At last, he lay motionless.

Cheryl stared in horror as Danny began to slide through the flaps. His buttocks vanished. His legs dragged along as if he were being sucked slowly into a dark mouth.

Cheryl was alone in the tent.

But not for long.

Chapter Two

Meg staggered into the living room, a strap of her negligee sagging down her arm. 'Good grief, hon, what time is it?'

'Nighttime,' Karen said.

'Tell me. Christ, tell me. Call this a vacation?'

'I sure do.'

'Yeah, guess you would.' She flopped into a chair, hooked one leg over its stuffed arm, and stretched to reach for a pack of cigarettes. 'What time's he picking you up?'

'Five-thirty.'

'Gug. Want me to put on some coffee?'

'I don't want to be peeing.'

'Shit. Car full of kids, you'll be stopping every five minutes anyway.' She lit a cigarette.

'They're not exactly kids,' Karen said. 'Julie's sixteen. Benny's thirteen or fourteen.'

'Even worse. Christ, kiddo, you're in for it.'

'They're okay.' Karen propped the backpack against the sofa and shoved in the mummy bag.

'Who's this other family?'

'The Gordons. Never met them before.'

'They have kids, too?'

'Three.'

'Oh, you're gonna have a *swell* time. Hope you're not planning to screw the guy.'

'We'll see.' Karen buckled the leather straps of the cover, picked up the backpack, and carried it towards the front door. She leaned it against the wall.

'Sure sounds like a lot of fun. Wish I was coming.'

'You were invited.'

'Give me a break. I need a campout like I need a third boob.'

Karen dropped to the sofa and started to put on her hiking boots. They were Pivettas, scratched and scuffed. They had stood in the back of her closet, unworn since the summer she finished her MA four years before, but they felt comfortable and familiar, like good friends from the past – friends with stories of dusty switchbacks, the cool wind of mountain passes, desolate lakes, icy streams, and campfire smoke. She finished lacing them, and slapped her bare knees. 'This is gonna be great.'

'You're a masochist,' Meg said, and stabbed out her cigarette.

'You don't know what you're missing.'

'Sure I do. Sack time.' She pushed herself off the chair, yawned and stretched. 'Well, have fun if you can.'

'Right. See you next Sunday.'

'Give my regards to the chipmunks.' With a wiggle of her fingers, she turned away and left the room.

Karen glanced at her wristwatch. Five-twenty-eight. Leaning back, she stretched out her legs. Her plaid shirt was gaping open at the belly. She fastened the button, then checked the fly of her cutoff corduroys. All set. She yawned. Maybe she should've taken Meg up on that coffee. She inhaled, a deep breath that seemed to fill her whole body with a light, pleasant weariness. As she let it slowly out, she shut her eyes.

A whole week in the mountains with Scott. Kids or no kids, it would be wonderful. They would find time to be alone, if only at night. It'd be cold, and they'd snuggle together with the wind whapping the tent walls . . .

The blare of the doorbell shocked her awake. She shoved herself off the sofa and hurried to the door. She pulled it open.

Scott, standing under the porch light, smiled at her through the screen.

'Take your *Watchtower* and shove it,' she said, and shut the door. When she opened it again, his face was pressed to the screen.

'I want your body,' he whispered.

For an instant, face mashed out of shape, he looked like a stranger. Karen felt a tingle of fright. Then he stepped back and was Scott again, handsome and smiling. 'Ready for action?' he asked.

'Yep.' As she pushed open the screen door, she leaned out and glimpsed his car in the driveway. The headlights were on. The car's interior was dark. 'The kid's there?' she asked.

'Just barely. It was murder getting Julie out of bed. Benny was raring to go. I'm not sure he even slept last night. Then he decided he couldn't live without his binoculars and we couldn't find the damn things.'

'Did you?'

'We did. But it screwed up our departure time.'

'You're forgiven.'

'Thanks,' he said. He took Karen in his arms. He smelled of coffee and after-shave. With his mouth pushing gently against hers, she felt so comfortable that she thought she might doze off. Until his hands were under her shirt. She was wide awake as they moved up her back under her armpits and closed gently over her breasts. They circled. They caressed. Her nipples stiffened under their touch.

'Think I'll send the kids home,' he muttered.

'Mmm. I've missed you.'

He kissed her again, hugging her tightly. 'We'd better get it in motion. You all packed and ready?'

'All set.'

She bent to pick up her backpack. 'Allow me,' Scott said. As he lifted it, Karen hurried to the coffee table. She grabbed her handbag and floppy felt hat, and followed him out the door.

The morning air wrapped around her bare arms and legs, seeped like chilly water through her shirt. Shivering, she waved at the dim face peering out through the backseat window. In the blue-grey light, she couldn't tell whether it belonged to Julie or Benny.

'You can get in,' Scott said.

She shrugged, preferring to wait rather than enter the car without him. They went to the boot. She stood with her shoulders hunched, arms folded across her chest, legs pressed together, jaw tight to keep her teeth from chattering.

Scott smiled back at her as he unlocked the boot. 'The heater's on.'

'The fresh air feels good.'

He laughed, and placed her backpack on top of the others. Then he swung the lid shut. 'Forget anything?'

'Probably.'

He leaned back against the boot, looking relaxed and warm. Of course, he was wearing long pants and a flannel shirt. 'Sunglasses?' he asked.

'Got em.'

'Jacket?'

'In my pack. Wish I had it on.'

'Let's go.'

Karen headed for the passenger door, taking her time, waiting until Scott was in the driver's seat before she opened the door. She ducked inside and smiled over the back of her seat. 'Morning,' she said.

'Hiya, hiya,' Benny said, winking one eye in time with the words. He raised a closed hand to his mouth as if holding a microphone. 'And a good morning to you and thanks for tuning in. Have we got a shower for you!'

'Can it, Bonzo,' Julie said. She gave Karen a quick, tight-lipped smile and turned her face towards the window.

Karen sat down. She pulled her door shut. The heater blew against her legs. She sighed and settled back, enjoying the warmth as Scott backed out of the driveway.

'All right if I drive?' Nick asked.

His father shoved the station wagon's tailgate into place. 'Can you keep it under sixty?'

'If you don't care when we get there.'

'Well, our ETA's two-thirty. I think we can make it without breaking any speed records. You start getting tired, though, let me know.'

'Right.'

They climbed into the car. Nick started the engine.

His father twisted around. 'Any last-minute pit stops?'

'Gross,' Heather said from the backseat.

'Vile,' said Rose.

'I think we're all set,' Mom told him.

'Sunglasses? Hats? Tampax?'

'*Dad!*' the twins blurted in unison.

'Arnold!'

'High altitudes,' he said, keeping a straight face. 'Bleeding occurs.'

'*Nose*bleeds,' Rose said.

Heather giggled.

'Whatever,' Dad said. 'Can't be too careful. "Be Prepared," right, Nick?'

'I've got mine.'

His father burst out laughing, and slapped his knee.

'I hop you fellows get it out of your system before we meet the O'Tooles.'

'Scott's no prude.' He glanced at Nick. 'San Diego Freeway. Runs right into 99 just the other side of the Grapevine.'

Nick pulled away from the kerb.

'Everybody buckled up?'

Near the corner, Nick flipped on the turn signal though no other cars were in sight. With his father beside him, he planned to drive by the book. He slowed almost to a stop before making the turn.

'What's his girlfriend's name?' Mom asked.

'Sharon? *Karen*. Karen something. He ran into her at a Sav-On.'

'A checkout girl?'

'No, no, she was in line with him. I think he said she's a teacher.'

'Oh, yuck,' Rose said.

'What does she look like?'

'A real bow-bow. Floppy ears, hair on her face, a wet nose. Nice tail, though.'

'What *do* you know about her?' Mom asked.

'Not much. You know Scott. Keeps his cards close to the vest.'

'I hope she plays bridge. June was so fantastic.'

'Don't start on her.'

'Well, she was.'

'I don't think we want to discuss that person in front of the girls.'

'I don't know why you're so angry. She didn't run out on *you*.'

'My best friend. Same difference. Now I think it would be wise to drop the subject. You have a green arrow,' he told Nick.

Nick made the left-hand turn and headed down the freeway on-ramp, embarrassed that he'd let his mind drift away from the driving. In the past, he'd heard a few references to the O'Tooles' break-up, but never anything so close to an argument. He was intrigued. It was none of his business though. Driving was his business, and he'd better pay attention or his father would take over.

Nick liked to drive. He wished they were taking the Mustang instead of this clunker, but it would've been a tight squeeze with all of them plus five backpacks. Besides, Dad wouldn't want to leave it sitting out in the middle of nowhere for a week. Last year, up at Yosemite, someone had broken a window of the station wagon and had a party inside. They'd come back to find beer cans and a pair of torn, pink panties on the floor.

The break-in had frightened Nick, and he felt uneasy thinking about it now. It was bad enough that some creeps had fooled around in the car, but what if you ran into them on an isolated trail? What if they stumbled onto your camp?

Nothing like that had ever happened to them, but it could. Nick was glad that the O'Tooles were coming along this year. Like Dad, Scott O'Toole was a big man. If any trouble came up, they'd be able to handle it.

With a feeling of relief, he checked the side mirror, signalled, and slipped into the right-hand lane. He sped up the overpass. Before it curved over the Santa Monica Freeway, he eased off the accelerator. He picked up speed again on the way down, signalled a left, and drifted across three deserted lanes of the San Diego Freeway.

His father leaned across the seat to check the speedometer. The needle hovered between 55 and 60 miles per hour. With a nod of approval, he settled back. 'You get tired, let me know.'

Benny leaned forward. 'Hey, Karen?' he said to the back of her head. She turned in her seat and looked around at him. Her face, so near to his, made him feel funny – excited and warm and a little embarrassed. He stared at her, forgetting what he'd planned to say.

He'd never seen her from so close. Her eyes were clear blue like the water of the swimming pool. He noticed, for the first time, the light golden hair barely visible above her upper lip. His cousin, Tanya, with dark hair, had more of a moustache there. Hers looked a little gross, but this on Karen looked so soft and fuzzy that he wished he could touch it. Maybe there wasn't even enough to feel, not over her mouth anyway, but it looked a little heavier on her smooth, tanned cheeks.

'Do you know how to get down off an elephant?' he asked.

'No, how?'

'You don't. You get down off a duck.'

Karen smiled and shook her head slightly.

Then she turned away. He could no longer see her face. Sitting back, he stared at her. The rim of an ear showed through her hair. He wished she would look around again, but first he would have to think of another joke.

He'd only seen Karen once before today. Usually, his father drove off to meet her. But last Saturday, she came over for barbecued ribs. She'd worn white shorts and a loose shirt of shiny red with green and white flowers, and she'd looked beautiful. When Dad introduced him, she shook his hand and said, 'Very nice to meet you, Benny.'

She had a pale scar curved like a horseshoe on her forearm. He'd wanted to ask her about it, but didn't have the guts.

That day was overcast, so nobody went into the pool and

he didn't get to see her in a swimsuit. She sat across the table from him at dinner. It wasn't dark yet, but his father had lit candles. The light from the flames made her hair shine like gold. He thought she was very nice. Julie acted creepy, though. After dinner, Tanya took him and Julie to a movie. By the time they got home, Karen had gone. Dad said she would be coming along on the camping trip, and Julie went crazy. 'What do we need her along for? I don't even like her! I don't want to go if she's going.' Dad, looking unhappy, asked why she didn't like Karen. 'Oh, never mind!' she snapped.

'I think she's very nice,' Benny said.

'So do I,' Dad told him.

Sometimes, Julie could be a real jerk.

'Anyone hungry?' Dad asked.

'Me!' Benny said.

Julie shrugged and kept on reading her book.

'Julie?'

'I don't care.'

'I could use a bite,' Karen said, looking towards Dad. Benny saw the side of her face for a moment before she turned forward again. He sighed. Gosh, she was beautiful.

'Well,' Dad said. 'We'll be at Gorman in a few minutes. We'll stop there and have some breakfast.'

'Look out there,' Flash said, keeping his voice calm but pressing a hand to the dashboard as a semi swung into their lane. It was moving up the steep grade towards Tejon Pass at half their speed. They were closing in fast.

Nick slipped over one lane to the left, and sped past the truck.

'Stupid fucking bastard,' Flash muttered. He lowered his hand from the dash. Nick was looking nervous. 'You all right?'

The boy nodded and licked his lips.

'That . . . He had no business coming over.' Flash took a few deep breaths, and slipped at White Owl from his shirt pocket. His fingers trembled as he tore open the cellophane wrapper. He plugged the cigar into his mouth and lit it, then cranked open his window to let the smoke stream out.

'I tell you, Nick, Vietnam was safer than these freeways. Goddamn truckers. Run you down as soon as look at you. Best thing to do is stay out of their way.'

Nick glanced at him. The boy still looked shaky. 'Too bad this isn't an F-8,' Nick said. 'We could blow them off the road.'

'Thataboy. I tell you, we did our share of that, Scott and me. Nailed whole convoys along the Ho Chi Minh Trail. Blasted the shit out of 'em.'

'*Arnold*,' Alice complained from the backseat. She'd heard that one. He glanced around. The twins were asleep, Rose slumped against the door with Heather leaning against her.

'I'll keep it down,' he said in a quiet voice.

'Keep it clean.'

He tapped off a length of ash, and took a long draw on his cigar. Smoke swirled around his face. *Smoke filled the cockpit. 'Blue Leader, this is Flash. Caught a hot one.'*

He shook his head sharply, trying to dislodge the memory as his heart began to thunder and his stomach twisted into an icy coil. Oh, Christ!

The station wagon nosed downward, picking up speed.

'Take it slow,' he warned.

Nick looked at him and frowned. 'Are you okay, Dad?'

'Sure. Fine.' He wiped the sweat from his face. He started remembering again. 'Well well well,' he said quickly to block off the thoughts. 'We're over the hump now. The old buggy made it over the Grapevine once again. Gonna be hot as blue blazes in the valley. Good thing we've got our air conditioning.'

Chapter Three

'I offered 'em down, Ettie.'

She gazed at the naked bodies of the young man and woman stretched out side by side in front of the tent. The man was facedown, a terrible wound across the back of his neck. The woman, on her back, was bruised and torn. Ettie saw bite marks on her mouth and chin, on her shoulders and breasts. The left nipple was missing entirely.

'I offered *him* with a hatchet,' Merle said, rubbing his hands on the legs of his jeans and trying to smile. 'The gal, I plain choked her.'

'Looks like you did more than that,' Ettie muttered.

'She was pretty.'

'Merle, you haven't got the sense of a toadstool.'

Her son tugged the bill of his faded Dodgers cap down to hide his eyes. 'I'm sorry,' he said.

'What're we gonna do with you?'

He shrugged. He toed a pinecone with his tennis shoe. '*You* do it,' he argued.

'Only when He speaks to me.'

'He spoke to me, Ettie. Honest He did. I never would've done it, but He asked me to.'

'You sure you weren't just feeling horny?'

'No, ma'am. He spoke to me.'

'I saw you yesterday spying on these two. I was afraid you might pull a stunt like this, but I trusted you, fool that I am. I should've known better.' She glared at Merle. The bill of his cap rose for a moment as he looked at her. Then dipped down again. 'What did you promise me?'

'I know,' he mumbled. 'I *said* I'm sorry.'

'What did you promise me?' she repeated.

'Not to do it again without asking.'

'But you went ahead and did it anyway.'

'Yes, ma'am.'

'This is gonna make it hot for us, Merle.'

In the shadow of the ball cap, she saw a thin smile. 'You just can't take me anywhere.'

'Wipe that smile off your face.'

'It isn't *that* bad, Ettie. I already looked through their stuff. They didn't have any fire permit.'

'So?'

He tipped back the bill, no longer afraid of meeting Ettie's gaze. 'If they'd checked in with a ranger, they would've got one and said where they were going. But they didn't. So the rangers don't even know they're here.'

'Well, that's something.'

'Even if someone knows they're gone, nobody's gonna have the first notion where to look. We'll just bury 'em and take their stuff to the cave, and we'll be okay.'

Ettie sighed, folded her arms across her bosom, and stared down at the bodies. 'I'll put out a spell to ward off searchers, just in case.'

Merle looked doubtful. 'Maybe I better.'

'I can still conjure circles around you, boy, and don't you forget it. I got us safe out of Fresno, no thanks to you. If you'd had the sense to fetch me what I needed—'

'I was seen.'

'Wouldn't have taken you half a minute,' she said. Merle stood silent, watching as she knelt beside the man's body. She untied a leather pouch from her belt and opened it. 'Never should've taught you the Ways.'

'Don't say that, Ettie.'

'Made us no end of trouble.' She wrapped her fingers around a lock of hair, and yanked it from the man's scalp. She pressed the hair into the raw gorge at the back of his neck. Thick blood coated the strands. She twisted them into a string, knotted them once in the centre, and poked them into her pouch. Then she lifted his hand. The fingernails were chewed to the quick. She unsheathed her knife, pressed the blade to the cuticle of his index finger, and removed the entire nail. She dropped it into her pouch and stepped over to the woman.

Squatting beside the body, she ripped out a ringlet of hair. She squeezed the breast to force more blood to the surface, and dabbed the hair in it. She tied the sticky cord into a knot. She flicked it into her pouch, then picked up a hand. The plum fingernail polish was chipped. One nail was broken, but the rest were long and neatly rounded. She pared off the tips of four, catching them in her palm, and brushed them into her bag.

'Now, that's all there is to it,' she said, looking up at Merle. 'Wouldn't have taken you half a minute, and I could've laid down a dandy spell and we'd still be in Fresno today. You didn't even have to take blood. If you'd just had the good sense to bring me hair and nails, I'd have had the essence to throw a cover on us.'

'I like it here fine,' he mumbled.

'Well, I don't.' Her knees crackled as she straightened up. 'I like my creature comforts, Merle. I like a good meal and a cold beer and nice clothes and a soft bed.'

'And men,' he added, showing a sliver of a smile.

'That's the truth.' She pushed her knife into its sheath at the side of her dress, and started tying the pouch to her belt. 'You deprived me of all that 'cause you were horny and careless.'

'I told you, Ettie. He spoke to me.'

She didn't believe him. 'Don't go laying off your blame, Merle. Now, you take care of the burying and bring up their things to the cave. I'll come along and check before sundown, and I want to see this place looking like nobody was ever here. Do you understand?'

'Yes, ma'am.'

'And if you ever offer down again without my say-so, you'll be the sorriest young man that ever walked on two legs.'

He looked down at his feet. 'Yes, ma'am.'

Leaving him there, Ettie made her way along the rockbound shore. At the narrow, southern tip of the lake where its feeder stream splashed down from Upper Mesquite, she crouched and cupped water to her mouth. Even after spending a month up here, she still couldn't get over the cold, fresh taste of it. Hard to believe that water could be so fine. She knew she would miss it in September, when they had to leave. Wouldn't miss anything else, though: not the heat steaming off the rocks, or the mosquitoes, or the wind that tore around at night so loud it often kept her awake, or the cold when the sun went down, or the hard ground she slept on. She'd be glad to leave all that behind. Not the water, though.

She unsnapped the canvas bag of her canteen, and pulled out the aluminium bottle. After twisting off its cap, she upended it. The old water burbled out. She held the empty canteen under a lip of mossy rock, gripping it tightly as fresh water washed over her hand. When the bottle overflowed, she capped it, then slipped it back into the case. It felt heavy and good against her hip as she stood up.

Staying close to the stream, she climbed up pale, broken slabs of granite to the ridge between the two lakes. She turned slowly, scanning the slopes that rose high above her. Then she peered towards the trail slanting down from Carver Pass beyond the northern end of Lower Mesquite. Once every few days, backpackers hiked by. Until yesterday, when the two stayed and camped, Merle had been just fine.

Blast Merle. Damn and shit!

The trail was deserted now. More than likely, if anyone should show up today, it wouldn't be till the afternoon. The pass was a hard, three-hour climb from the nearest lake to the east, so Merle should have plenty of time to take care of the mess. Besides, there was the spell . . .

Stepping onto a flat surface of rock, Ettie unbuckled her belt with all its gear. She set it at her feet and opened the buttons of her faded, shapeless dress. She pulled the dress up over her head. Except for her heavy socks and boots, she was naked. She felt the sun on her skin, the caress of soft breezes. The air smelled hot. It smelled of scorched pine needles, of baking rock.

Bending over, she spread her dress across the granite. Then she sat on it. Through the thin layers of fabric, the rock felt hard and rough. The heat seeped through, stinging her buttocks as she removed her boots and damp socks.

When they were off, she untied the leather pouch from her belt. She crossed her legs and sat upright, with her back arched, her head straight forward. With both hands, she clasped the pouch to her breastbone.

'Into darkness,' she whispered, 'I commit the essence of my foes. As their essence is obscured, so let all traces of their presence be banished from this canyon, that those who seek them might find no cause to trespass here.'

Lowering her head, she opened the drawstrings of the pouch. She pulled out a bloody lock of hair and placed it into her mouth. She chewed slowly, working it into a sodden clump, and swallowed it. She did the same with the second coil of hair. She washed them down with water from her canteen. Then she dumped the fingernails onto her palm, raised them to her lips, and ate them. She drank some more water.

The rock was rough and hot through her dress. The hair felt thick and heavy in her stomach.

But she was done.

She smiled. She raised the canteen and poured its cold water over her head. It streamed down her face, her shoulders. It rolled down her back. It spilled over her breasts, dripped from her nipples, ran down her belly and sides. Moving the canteen, she let the water fall onto her crossed legs, her groin. She sighed at its icy touch.

Too soon the canteen was empty.

She stared at the glinting blue of Upper Mesquite. Why

not? She deserved a treat. Leaving everything, she skipped over the searing rocks to the shore. She waded in, shivering and gasping, and hesitated only a moment before plunging headlong.

Chapter Four

They stopped at a gas station in Fresno. Rolling down his window, Julie's father asked the teenaged attendant to 'fill her up with super unleaded and check under the hood'.

With the window open, heat rushed into the car. Julie fanned her face with her book.

'Guess I'll make a pit stop,' Karen said.

'Me, too,' said Benny.

They both climbed out.

'Julie?' Dad asked.

'I'll wait till they're back.' She watched them walk through the glaring sunlight towards the side of the station. Benny was smiling up at the woman, grinning and talking.

'Benny seems to really like Karen,' Dad said.

'I noticed.' The two disappeared around a corner of the garage.

'I think you'd like her, too, if you gave her half a chance.'

'What have I done?' Julie blurted.

'It's your attitude.'

'I can't help it if I'm not crazy about her. What am I supposed to do, worship the ground she walks on?'

'There's no call for sarcasm.'

'*I* didn't ask her to come with us.'

'Well, *I* did, and I'd appreciate it if you'd get your act together. You've been miserable all morning.'

'I am miserable.' Her throat tightened. She suddenly felt as if she might start blubbering.

Dad looked around at her. 'What's the matter, honey?' he asked in a gentle voice.

'Nothing,' she mumbled.

'What is it?'

'I don't see why I even had to come.' Tears filled her eyes. She stared out the window at the gas pumps. 'I should've stayed home with Tanya. You don't want me here anyway.'

'Of course I do.'

'No you don't. You've got Karen. You don't need Benny and me.'

'Look, if I'd wanted to be alone with Karen, would I have insisted you come with us? I could've left you home easily enough, but I wanted you and Benny along. Hell, it wouldn't be half as much fun without you two. Now come on, buck up, old girl. Let's see a smile.'

Julie wiped her eyes, but didn't try to smile.

'Come on.'

The squeak of a squeegee drew her eyes to the young attendant. He was grinning down at her through the passenger window as he scraped away the dirty water.

'Here they come,' Dad told her. 'Why don't you go on ahead?'

With a nod, she opened her door. She slid out and stepped towards the rear of the car.

'It's around back,' Karen said as they passed.

'Thanks.' Walking away, she glanced over her shoulder. The boy at the windshield met her eyes. She smiled at him, and continued on her way.

The heat brought sweat to her forehead. She wondered if the boy was watching, admiring the way she looked in her T-shirt and tight white shorts.

The restroom was shadowy and stifling. She quickly relieved herself. At the sink, she splashed tepid water onto her face and looked at herself in the mirror. Her eyes were rimmed with red from crying. Her hair was slightly mussed. She wished she'd brought her brush along. She combed her fingers through her hair and patted the swept-back sides. her T-shirt looked loose and baggy. Opening her shorts again, she pulled it down firmly and tucked it in. She looked down at herself. The shirt was taut over her breasts, emphasising them. The white lace of her bra was clearly visible through the stretched fabric.

She smiled at her reflection. She winked at herself. Then she stepped out of the restroom into the glaring sunlight.

The car was still at the pumps, but the boy was gone. She spotted him through the windows of the office. At the car, she put her hands on the sill of Karen's open window and looked in. 'Dad, could we get some Cokes or something?'

'Yeah!' Benny said.

'Sure. Why not?' Dad shifted his weight to reach for the wallet in his back pocket.

'Let me,' Karen said. 'My treat.'

'No,' Dad said. 'That's—'

'I insist.' She took a billfold from her handbag. After moment of searching she said, 'I guess I don't have any change,' and gave Julie a five-dollar bill. 'Why don't you pick up some chips or something, if they've got 'em?'

'I'll come with you,' Benny said, and burst from the car.

'What'll you have, Dad?'

'Root beer or Coke.'

'Karen?'

The woman smiled at her. 'Mountain Dew, or Dr Pepper. If they haven't got one of those, a cola'd be fine.'

Benny raced ahead of her to the office, and planted himself in front of the soft-drink vending machine. Julie, feeling a flutter of anticipation, took a deep breath and entered. 'Hi,' she said to the boy behind the desk.

He got to his feet and swept a hank of brown hair away from his forehead. 'Hi. Can I help you?'

Julie held the bill out to him. 'Could we have some change for your machines?'

He smiled 'Sure thing.' He leaned over the desk. As he reached out, his eyes lowered from Julie's face to her breasts to her extended arm. He took the money. 'You'll be wanting quarters,' he said. He broke a fresh roll of them into the open drawer of the cash register. The patch above his shirt pocket read TIM. 'Are you from around here?' he asked.

'From Los Angeles. We're on our way to the mountains.'

'Yeah? Camping?'

'We'll be backpacking out of Black Butte.'

'No kidding? I've been there. That's real nice country.' He counted out quarters, and dropped them four at a time into Julie's palm, his fingers sometimes brushing her.

'Thank you, Tim.'

He beamed, and nodded.

Turning away, Julie gave the coins to Benny. 'Here, you get the stuff. You know what everybody wants?'

'Sure.' With the quarters clutched in his hand, he stepped up close to the soft-drink dispenser. Julie went back to Tim.

'Do you work here all the time?' she asked.

'Whenever I can. My dad's the owner.'

'Don't you get awfully hot?'

'Oh, you get used to it.'

'I don't think I would.'

'It's not so bad.' He stepped around the desk and sat on its edge. 'You've got a nice tan,' he said, looking at her legs.

'Thanks.'

'I bet you go to the beach a lot, being in Los Angeles and everything.'

'Yeah.' She considered explaining about their backyard

swimming pool. Tim might think she was bragging, though. 'I really like the ocean,' she said.

'We've got the river,' he said, 'and some lakes. I'll go over to Millerton or Pine Flat. They aren't far. We take the boat over when—' The double ring of a bell interrupted him. He peered out the window. A pickup was rolling to a stop beside the pumps. With a sigh of disappointment that pleased Julie, he pushed himself off the desk. 'Well, I've gotta go. Have a good trip, now. Stop in on your way back if you get a chance.'

'Okay. 'Bye, Tim.'

He left the office. On his way towards the pickup, he looked over his shoulder and waved. Julie waved back.

Benny had set the four soft-drink cans on the floor to free his hands. He punched a number on the snack machine. Inside the display window, a clamp opened, dropping a small pack of barbecued potato chips into a trough.

Julie picked up the chilly, wet cans. Benny gathered up four packs of chips and Fritos. Together, they left the office.

At her door, Julie watched Tim lift the hood of the pickup. 'So long,' she called.

'Stop by again,' he said.

Then she climbed into the car. She passed around the drinks, poured the remaining change into Karen's hand, and thanked her.

As they pulled away, she looked out the rear window. Tim was wiping a dipstick with a red rag.

'He seemed like a nice young fellow,' Dad said.

'His father owns the station,' Julie said.

'Oh? Checked him out, did you?'

'I didn't "check him out." We were just talking, that's all.'

'Baloney and liver sausage,' Benny said.

'He looked like he was about Nick's age,' Dad told her.

'Nick?'

'Flash's son. You remember him? The company picnic?'

'Unh-uh.'

'Well, that was about five or six years ago. I think you ran the three-legged race with him.'

'Oh, *him*.' She smiled. 'We won that. He's Mr Gordon's son?'

'Yep. He's seventeen now.'

'Oh, yeah?' Maybe this wouldn't turn out to be such a rotten vacation after all.

'Ow!' Heather cried, clutching the back of her hand.

'Rose, play nice.'

'I didn't hit her hard.'

Alice Gordon gave her daughter a warning scowl. She considered calling a stop to the game, but Heather had already hidden her hand behind her back, ready to continue.

'One, two, three,' Rose said. Her open hand darted out.

Heather, at the same instant, swung her hand into view with two fingers extended. 'Aha! Scissors cut paper!'

Rose presented her hand. Heather slapped it hard, getting even.

'Didn't hurt,' Rose taunted.

They got ready for another match. 'One, two, three,' Rose said.

Heather came out with scissors again. As Rose's flat hand swung forward, it closed into a fist. 'Rock breaks scissors,' she declared.

'No fair!' Heather cried out. 'You cheated. Didn't she, Mom? You saw her! She was paper!'

Nick looked around from the passenger seat. 'Is Rose cheating again?'

'Yes!' Heather blurted.

'I think we've had enough of this game,' Alice said. 'Why don't you find something nice to play? Twenty Questions or Hangman.'

'I get to slap her!' Heather protested. 'She was paper!'

'No more slapping.'

'But I won!'

'Kids!' Arnold snapped. He was driving and didn't look back. 'Do as your mother says.'

'But, *Daaaad*!'

'You heard me.'

Heather sighed as if the world were unfair. She narrowed her eyes at Rose. 'Cheater.'

With a long-suffering smile, Rose offered her hand. 'Go ahead and give it to me.'

'Mom, can I?'

'Oh, I don't care. Just once, then I want you both to find something better to do.'

Heather slapped downward. Rose's hand shot out from under the path of the blow, and smacked the back of Heather's descending hand. 'Hey!'

Rose laughed. So did Nick. Heather punched her sister's knee.

'That's enough!' Alice snapped. 'Stop it!'

'I think I'll pull over and tan some hides,' Arnold said.

'No!' Heather yelped.

'We'll be good,' Rose said. 'Promise.'

'All right then. Now, do as your mother says and play something nice.'

'Better yet,' Nick said, 'take a nap.'

Rose rolled her eyes upward. 'Are we almost there yet?'

'A couple more hours,' Arnold told her.

The idea of a nap certainly appealed to Alice. She took the pillow from the space between her and Heather, fluffed it up, and placed it behind her head. Snuggling back against it, she closed her eyes. In quiet voices, the twins were discussing whether to play Hangman. She heard a rustle of paper. Good. That should keep them out of mischief for ten or fifteen minutes.

She wondered if Arnold had remembered to set the lamp timer before they left. No point bothering to ask, though. If he'd forgotten, it was too late now.

Her mind drifted to the last time she'd seen Scott O'Toole.

They'd gone over for dinner and bridge. Scott had compli-
mented her on her perm. That must've been over a year ago,
closer to two. How could June walk out on a man like him?
Must be more to it than meets the eye. Maybe he was fooling
around on the side. Sure had plenty of opportunity, being
away half the time. And those flight attendants. Everyone
knows how they are. June was no slouch, not by any stretch of
the imagination, but a guy like Scott'd be a real prize for lonely
girls. A lot of temptation there. Take a strong man to resist.

Thank God Arnold stopped flying. He might have to work
nights when the shift bid didn't go his way, but at least he
came home to his own bed and wasn't alone in hotels all
across the country. Would've been nice for him to have pilot's
pay and prestige, but she'd rather have him as he is. They got
by just fine, thank you, and she didn't have to spend all her
time worrying.

Poor June must've been worried sick, wondering if he'd go
down or get himself shacked up with some girl. Who was
that – Jack? – no, Jake. Jake Peterson. Had a whole second
family in Pittsburgh. Must've come as quite shock to his wife
– *both* wives. Wasn't even a Mormon, not that that would've
made it right, but . . . Alice's thoughts slipped away as sleep
overtook her.

The road up the mountainside had once been paved, but
winter snow, spring runoff, and summer sun had broken up
the asphalt, leaving a dusty shambles. The car bounced over
ruts and potholes as Scott steered slowly up the grade.

Ahead, a Volkswagen appeared around a bend.

'What now?' Karen asked.

'He's small.' Scott eased the car to the right until branches
squeaked against its side. He stopped.

'Hope he's careful,' Karen said. She was gripping the
armrest.

'If he's not,' Scott told her, 'he'll have a very thrilling ride
for a few seconds.'

A girl in the passenger seat of the VW had her head out the window. She was looking down, apparently contemplating just such a ride. From her perspective. Scott imagined that the sheer drop-off must look bottomless. After a moment, she pulled her head in and said something to the driver.

The VW crawled closer. The young bearded man behind the wheel grinned at Scott as he inched alongside. 'Lovely day,' he said.

'Yep,' Scott agreed. 'How far to Black Butte?'

'Take you an hour.'

'The road get any better up ahead?'

'No. Tell you what, though, there's an RV about a mile behind me.'

'Thanks for the warning.'

'Have a good one, friend.'

'You, too.'

The Volkswagen finished passing, took to the centre of the narrow road, and sped off with a cloud of dust.

'A camper?' Karen asked. She looked sick.

'What'll we do?' Julie asked from the back.

'I guess we'd do well to find a wider place in the road before he shows up.'

'No sweat. Right, Dad?' Benny asked.

'No sweat,' he said, and pulled away. He drove slowly, looking for a place to turn out. Ahead, the road bent back in an uphill hairpin. He took the curve. Now *they* were on the outside, the slope dropping away sharply to the right. 'Maybe a little sweat,' Scott admitted. He picked up speed. The car lurched and jarred as it rushed up the grade.

Should've played it safe, he thought. Should've stopped back at the bend. But now he was committed. What he could see of the road ahead didn't look good. The mountainside rose up steeply to the left, leaving no room for turning out. To the right, there was no more than a yard's width before the ground fell away. Even if he parked at the very edge, he doubted there would be room for a recreational vehicle to squeeze through.

'What'll we do?' Karen asked.

'If worse comes to worst, we can always back up.'

'Oh, wonderful.'

Scott's foot jumped off the accelerator as the camper came down the centre of the road straight at them. In a reflexive move, he pulled at the wheel as if to raise the nose and shoot above the oncoming vehicle. His car remained earth bound. He stepped on the brake, and eased to a halt.

The camper moved over close to the mountain's wall and stopped, blocking two thirds of the road. An arm poked through the driver's window. It waved Scott forward.

'Can you make it?' Karen asked.

'Sure,' he said. 'Just to be on the safe side, though, I want you out.' He looked over his shoulder. 'Everybody out.'

'I'm not scared,' Benny said.

'No arguments.'

With a sigh, Benny opened his door. When he, Julie, and Karen were outside the car, Scott unbuckled his seat belt. The trio walked ahead of him, Karen nodding and speaking to the man behind the wheel. At the rear of the camper, they stopped and turned around to watch. Karen straddled the road's edge, her eyes fixed on his right front tyre. Her lip were drawn back in a grimace. She wiped her hands on the sides of her corduroy shorts.

This must be really bad for her, Scott thought as he inched forward. Karen knows no one's immune to an accident. She'd barely escaped death in a car crash three years before, and her fiancé had been killed.

With the fingers of his left hand curled around the door lever, he steered alongside the camper. He watched its gleaming side as he slid past it, no more than an inch away. If the car should start to tip, he realised, he wouldn't be able to get his door open.

Not at first anyway. He might find an instant, though, just before the car slipped over the edge.

He glanced at Karen. Her hand was covering her mouth. Benny looked relaxed. Julie was squatting down, hands on knees, staring at the tyre.

Ice fishing when he was a kid, Scott drove out on the frozen Saint Lawrence River with his father. Sometimes, the ice creaked and groaned under the weight of the pickup truck. They always kept their doors open for quick escapes. Everyone did, driving on the river. Everyone but fools.

He wished he had his door open now. A little precaution like that could save a man's life.

The front of his car was even with the rear of the camper. He fought an urge to speed up, and kept to a steady crawl until he cleared the vehicle. Then he swung to the left and stopped in the road's centre.

Benny climbed in first. 'Boy, Dad, that was really close.'

'A piece of cake,' he said, and backhanded the sweat off his upper lip.

'Hope we don't have to go through *that* again,' Julie said.

Karen slumped in the passenger seat with her knees against the dash. She stared straight ahead. Her lips were a tight line.

Reaching out, Scott rubbed the side of her neck. 'You okay?'

'I guess,' she muttered.

After another traverse, the road curved around the mountainside to a high, wooded valley. A weathered sign, caught in a patch of sunlight, read: BLACK BUTTE RANGER STATION, 6 MI.

Chapter Five

The forest, pressing in close on both sides of the unpaved road, opened up. Karen saw two cars ahead parked under trees. One, a dusty Mazda resting at a rakish angle, had a rock at the base of each rear tyre to keep it from rolling.

'Guess we beat them to it,' Scott said.

'What do they drive?' Karen asked.

'Probably the Plymouth station wagon.'

Karen imagined a station wagon trying to squeeze past the RV on the thin strand of road along the mountain slope, and her stomach tightened.

Scott swung off to the left. He pulled forward slowly, the tyres crunching over fallen limbs and pinecones. He parked with the bumper close to an aspen, and shut off the engine. 'Let's leave everything here for now, and check out the ranger station. We can pick up our fire permit while we're waiting.'

They climbed out of the car. After the air conditioning, the heat outside felt stifling to Karen. But the air smelled sweet, and a soft breeze stirred the trees. She took a deep breath. She stretched, arching her stiff back, sighing with pleasure as her muscles strained. Then she followed Benny around the rear of the car, the thick mat of leaves and pine needles springy under her boots. 'This is really wonderful,' she said, joining Scott and Julie.

'Warm,' Scott said. He took off his flannel shirt, rolled it up, and tossed it into the boot. His T-shirt was tight across his chest, with a slight rip at the shoulder seam. 'Well, let's see if we can scout up a ranger.'

They walked alongside the tyre tracks towards a small log cabin in the clearing ahead. A Jeep was parked close to the cabin's side. The snort of a horse drew Karen's eyes to a corral at the left, where a man in a uniform was currying a brown stallion. 'That's probably the ranger,' she said.

They walked towards the corral. The man saw them and waved. He slapped the horse's haunch, tossed aside the curry brush, and climbed over the fence. 'Hello there,' he called in an eager voice. 'Hope I didn't keep you waiting. I was out on the trails, just got back.'

'No,' Scott said, 'we just arrived ourselves.'

'Well, that's good.' He smiled at Karen and Julie, winked at Benny. He looked to be barely twenty, with short blond hair and cheerful eyes. Though he wore a badge on his uniform shirt, he was unarmed and had a casual manner that put Karen at ease. 'Come on over to the office,' he said. 'We'll take care of your wilderness permit and get you on your way.'

They followed him towards the cabin.

'Where you folks from?' he asked.

'Los Angeles,' Scott told him.

'Dad's a pilot,' Benny said, looking proud.

'Oh? What do you fly?'

'L1011s, mostly.'

'No fooling? The big birds. My old man's a crop duster. He flies a replica of an old Fokker DR-1. The triplane?'

'Sure. Richthofen. The Flying Circus.'

'Yeah. My old man calls himself the Green Baron. He works out of Bakersfield.'

'Sometimes I wish I had three wings,' Scott said, stepping onto the porch after him.

'All that airfoil, he can glide for miles. Sometimes has to.'

They entered the dim, shadowy cabin. The young man stepped behind a counter near the door. On the wall was a huge topographical map of the area. A poster of Smokey the Bear hung over a two-way radio. Benny nudged Karen's arm, and pointed to a rifle rack on the wall across from them.

'Whereabouts are you heading?' the ranger asked.

'We're hoping to make it over to the Triangle Lakes area.'

'Some good fishing up there. Here's an *Angler's Guide* for you,' he said, and spread open a leaflet on the counter top. 'This map's a bit sketchy.'

'We'll be meeting some friends. They're got topogs of the area.'

'Fine. This one'll give you a nice overview, but it's weak on detail. You've got a nasty ridge here, for instance.' He tapped his ballpoint against a bare spot on the map. 'Looks like an easy jaunt from Wilson to Round, but don't you believe it. It'd take an hour of hard climbing. The topogs'll take care of that for you.'

He tapped the counter three inches from the bottom edge of the map. 'Okay. You're about here. You'll want to take the Juniper Lake trail. It's two miles to Juniper.' As he scribbled directions on an edge of the map, he said, 'That'd be a fine place to spend the night. Some nice campsites all around it. When you head out of there, you just follow the trail you came in on. It branches out at the head of the lake, and there's a marker there for Triangle Lakes. You just stay on it, all the way. Here's where it comes onto the map.' He drew a line along the trail. He circled a lake. 'This is Tully. It's beautiful, has a real nice waterfall at the western end. Just a couple of miles farther, you've got Lake Parker. They're a good day's hike from Juniper. I'd stick to one or the other if I were you. Once you leave Parker behind, you've got Carver Pass to look forward to. You'll want to be fresh when you tackle that. It's a good three- or four-hour climb, takes you up to eleven thousand feet.'

'Yuck,' said Julie.

The ranger grinned at her. 'About halfway up, if you're like most folks, you'll start wishing you were back home watching a ball game.' He marked zigzags on the map. 'You've got switchbacks you think'll never quit.'

'I'm ready exhausted,' Karen said, 'just hearing about it.'

'A great view from the top,' he told her. 'And a good, cool wind.' He lowered his eyes to the map. 'Right here, on the down side, you'll run into the Mesquite Lakes. I don't recommend you bother with those. You'll know what I mean when you see them.'

'The pits?' Julie asked.

'That's exactly what they are.' He drew his line along the trail. 'Wilson's just an easy three miles beyond the Mesquites, and it's fabulous. Wooded, good campsites.' He circled Lake Wilson. 'From there, you've got an easy shot to the Triangles. Get an early start from Wilson, and you should be there by noon.'

'Sounds terrific,' Scott said.

'Shall I put you down for Juniper, Parker, Wilson, and the Triangles?'

'Fine by me.'

He took out a form and began to fill in the information. 'So, we've got you into the Triangles on night four. How long will you stay there?'

'We'll want to be within an easy hike of here by next Sunday. Maybe spend Saturday night back at Juniper.'

The ranger marked it down. 'If you want to see some new scenery, you can make a circle by following the Postpile trail south out of the Triangles.' He marked the trail, describing the lakes along the way, explaining that the return route was shorter and mostly downhill.

'So, we'll figure on two nights at the Triangles, then a night at Rabbit Ears, a night at Lake Tobash, and then back to Juniper. Should be a fine trip.' The ranger reversed the permit form and pushed it towards Scott. 'Would you please read this and fill out the rest?'

Scott studied the sheet. He wrote his name and address, and the number of people in his party. He signed it, and paid the permit fee. The ranger tore off a section and gave it to him.

'Okay, you're all set.' He pointed at the screen door. 'About a hundred yards that way, you can pick up the trail.'

'Thanks for all your help,' Scott said.

'That's what I'm here for. Have a real good trip.'

They all thanked him and left the cabin.

'Well,' Karen said. 'That was painless.'

'The pain starts when we put our packs on.'

'He was neat,' Benny blurted. 'Did you see those neat rifles?'

'He had a nice Winchester in that rack,' Scott said.

'Do you suppose he lives up here all the time?' Julie asked.

'Should've asked him.'

She shrugged.

'I imagine he goes down before the snow closes the road.'

'It's probably beautiful here in winter,' Karen said.

'Yeah, at Christmas,' Benny added. Hurrying ahead of the others, he turned around and walked backward. He raised his hands like a choir leader. ' "Dash-in' through the snooow," ' he started to sing, waving his arms.

'Forget it, Mitch,' Julie muttered.

He ignored her and continued to sing until she hurled a pinecone at him. It bounced off his shirt. Laughing, he whirled away and ran the final distance to the car.

'He's so juvenile,' Julie said, as if to herself.

Scott smiled. 'Must run in the family.' He patted Karen's back. 'Do you think you can stand this for a week?'

'No sweat,' she said.

When they reached the car, Scott opened the boot and lifted out a pack. His T-shirt rode up as he crouched to set the pack down. Karen glanced at the revealed strip of bare skin and the band of his jockey shorts. She remembered Meg's remark, *Hope you're not planning to screw the guy*. We'll see, she thought, we'll see.

He took out the other packs and propped them upright against the rear bumper. He handed Karen her floppy felt hat. She put it on, and turned up the front brim.

'Gabby Hayes,' Scott said.

'Gee, thanks.'

As he opened the top of his Kelty bag to put his shirt away,

Karen heard a car engine. She looked up the shadowy road. A station wagon appeared, bouncing over the ruts.

'Is it them?' Benny asked.

'Yep,' Scott said. 'Looks like they made it.'

The driver, a broad-faced, florid man with a bald crown and a red fringe of hair over his ears, pulled in beside them and stopped. 'How'd you beat us up here?' he asked as he climbed out.

'Sheer skill,' Scott told him.

They shook hands.

'Karen, this is Arnold Gordon.'

'Call me Flash,' he said.

'Nice to meet you,' Karen said, and shook his big hand.

The others climbed from the car: a thin teenaged boy with his father's freckles and a full head of red hair; a short, rather chubby woman with a pixie haircut; two slim girls, maybe ten years old. Though twins, the girls were dressed differently; one wore her blonde hair in pigtails, while the other had a ponytail. That should help me keep them straight, Karen thought.

Scott and Flash introduced everybody around. Karen repeated the names to herself, and called up associations to help her memory. Flash Gordon was easy. Nick was Nick Adams of 'The Big Two-Hearted River,' a Hemingway story she'd taught last year. Alice was a toughty. Alice, malice, phallus – no, no. Well, she'd have to work on that one. Rose and Heather, flowers. Careful you don't call them Tulip and Dandelion. 'My Wild Irish Rose,' Scottish heather. Remember, Rose has the ponytail. Rosy pony. *The Red Pony*. That should do it.

'. . . three-legged race at the picnic,' Julie was saying to Nick.

'Oh, I remember that,' he said, blushing. 'And the egg toss.'

'Sure. It broke all over you.'

With a nod, he excused himself and turned away to help

his father unload the car. The entire family had matching red Kelty packs: two huge ones like Scott's, a slightly smaller one for Alice, and a pair of child-size packs for the girls.

'Arnold tells me you're a schoolteacher,' Alice said.

'Yes, that's right. High school.'

'Our Nick's quite the student. He makes straight A's in math and science.'

'That's very good.'

'I was at the top of the class in math myself when I was in high school. Of course, that was a long time ago. I planned to be a teacher, too, but then Arnold came along and I never got around to finishing college.' The challenging look in her eyes made Karen uncomfortable. Did she expect a reprimand for giving up school?

'From the looks of your children,' Karen said, 'you made the right choice.'

The hardness left Alice's eyes, and she smiled. 'Well, thank you.'

'We've already secured the fire permit,' Scott told Flash.

'They got a head around here?'

Scott pointed to an outhouse nestled in the shadows of trees a short distance away. 'All right, gang, let's hit the facility. Enjoy it, ladies. It'll be your last look at a toilet seat for the next week.'

Alice made a face at him.

'Gross,' said Rose of the ponytail.

Benny met Karen's eyes. He looked amused.

The entire group started towards the stone building.

'Is it all right to leave the gear over there?' Nick asked his father.

'Who's around to meddle with it?'

'How was your trip up?' Scott asked.

'That one-lane death trap was a bitch. Poor Alice, she nearly laid an egg. Did you happen to run into a camper the size of a bus?'

'Did we.'

'I had to back halfway down the mountain to let it by. A real bitch.

'Wasn't much fun,' Scott agreed.

Nick watched Julie waiting by the outhouse. Soon the twins came out, and she pushed in. When the door banged shut behind her, Nick turned away. He looked towards the two cars to make sure nobody was tampering with the packs.

There was no one in sight. For all he knew, the valley was deserted except for the nine of them and the ranger. But somebody had to belong to those other two cars, so it couldn't hurt to keep an eye on the equipment.

The last time he'd seen Julie she was just a skinny kid, a tomboy. Now she had breasts and everything. She was as cute as any cheerleader at Samo, and she would be camping with him for a whole week.

The thought of that made Nick very nervous. If only she were plain, or fat, or even ugly, he might be at ease with her and they'd have a good time. How could he manage to be himself, though, with someone like Julie around?

She would probably spend the whole week ignoring him. Probably goes steady with a football player. Messes around a lot, too. Girls like her always do. Just not with guys like me.

Who needs her?

Behind Nick, the door banged. He looked around. Julie was striding towards her father, her long legs slender and tanned, her hands flat inside the front pockets of her shorts, the white of her bra visible through her T-shirt. She glanced at Nick, but looked away quickly. Her hair bounced and swayed as she walked.

'Don't wear your eyes out,' his father said, coming up behind him.

Nick's face grew hot. 'I won't,' he muttered.

They headed for the car, walking well behind the others. 'She sure is something to look at.'

'She's all right.'

'All right, my ass. She's a knockout, and you know it. Now if I was in your shoes, I'd be right in there striking up an acquaintance.'

'Yeah, well . . .'

'You don't want her thinking you're stuck up.'

'I'm not stuck up.'

Approaching the car, Nick watched Julie pick up her backpack. She lifted it by the straps and swung it onto the trunk of her father's Olds Cutlass. Balancing it there, she turned around. Her eyes met Nick's for a moment, as if to make sure he was watching. Then she leaned back, hooking one arm through a strap, twisting, slipping her other arm into place. She leaned forward. The pack tipped against her. She stood up straight the pull of the straps drew her shoulders back. Nick found himself staring at her breasts, which seemed more prominent than before.

He turned away to put on his own backpack. When he looked again at Julie, she was wearing aviator sunglasses and a red beret that made her seem like some kind of commando.

That's a sharp hat, he could tell her. Sharp? She'll think I'm a turkey. An awesome hat. That's better. But he didn't say it. Instead, he picked up his walking stick.

'Hey,' Julie said, 'is that a real blackthorn stick?' She walked towards him.

Blushing, he nodded.

'Can I see it?'

He handed it to her.

'Hey, this is nice.' She ran her hands along its polished knobby shaft.

'I got it in Ireland.'

'Really? We've been there. Where did you buy it?'

'Some gift shop near Blarney Castle.'

'No kidding? We were there. Benny got a shillelagh at that place. Blarney Handicrafts?'

'Yeah, that's the place.'

She returned his stick.

'Did you kiss the Blarney Stone?' she asked.

'Sure.'

'How about the stairs going up there?'

'Pretty hairy.'

She laughed. 'Kissing the stone was a cinch after those stairs. Did you get the gift of gab?'

'I'm not sure it worked on me.'

'Let's get this show on the road,' Dad called.

Julie stayed beside Nick as they walked over to join the rest of the group. With Mr O'Toole and Dad in the lead, they hiked across a meadow. Ahead, Nick saw a wood trail sign.

'Have you ever been up in this area?' Julie asked.

'Not around here. We've been into Mineral King, Yosemite, lots of places. Parts of the John Muir Trail. How about you?'

She shook her head, making her blonde hair sway. 'I think it's really neat to go where you haven't been before.'

'Yeah, like exploring.'

'And you never know what you'll find.'

They reached the trail, a wide dusty track leading into the forest. The sign beside it read, JUNIPER LAKE, 2 MI.

'If it's all right with everybody,' Mr O'Toole said, 'we'll stop there for the night.'

'Fine by me,' Dad said.

The arrow pointed to the left. They started to walk. The straps felt snug on Nick's shoulders. The pack, though heavy, rode easily on his back. He took a deep breath. The hot air smelled of dust, and flowers, and pine, and he caught a hint of perfume from Julie. She stayed beside him as they walked.

She's not so bad after all, he thought. This could turn out good.

Chapter Six

Ettie's leg muscles trembled from the strain of squatting. Finally, she straightened up. She looked at what she'd done. With both hands, she scooped up loose soil. She sprinkled it onto the pile of her faeces. 'Into the dirt,' she said, 'I commit the essence of my foes. As their essence is obscured, so let all traces of their presence be banished from this canyon, that those who seek them might find no cause to trespass here.'

She brushed her hands on her dress.

'That'll do it,' she muttered.

She backed out of the crevice and sat on a block of granite. This high on the slope, she was still in sunlight. The shadow was not far below, creeping slowly upward as the sun sank closer to the opposite ridge.

There was already a nice breeze. It made her sweaty dress feel cool. Raising her arms, she let the breeze chill her sodden armpits.

Merle appeared, off to the right, mounting the crest of the small ridge that separated the lakes. He wore one blue back-pack, and carried another. As Ettie watched, he started climbing the shadowy slope. He didn't get far before abandoning the pack in his arms. With the other still on his back, he made his way higher, leaving the shade behind. He clambered over boulders, scurried up steep granite slabs, and finally vanished. From where Ettie sat, it looked as if he'd stepped through solid rock. She couldn't see the fissure that led into their cave.

A few moments later, Merle reappeared. He sprang down the slope, going to retrieve the second pack.

Though still angry with him, Ettie had to admit she looked forward to checking out the booty. If the couple's tent was any indication, they'd come well equipped. Probably had a camp stove and a couple of nice sleeping bags at least. A stove would come in real handy. Wouldn't put up smoke like the cook fires they sometimes built in the cave. And their ratty old sleeping bags weren't much good against the night's cold. There'd be food, too. Probably enough to keep them going for a few more days anyway. They'd been talking about another raid on campers over by Lake Wilson, just to snatch some food, but there was always the danger of giving themselves away, pulling stunts like that, so it was good not to try it too often.

In spite of the advantages, she wished Merle would learn to control himself. He was just like his father that way. Poor man got a taste of the power, and just couldn't stop. Took a policeman's bullet to stop him. She should've learned her lesson from that, and kept Merle ignorant. Seems a man just hasn't got the same control a woman does. It's that pecker, of course. Once that pecker gets heated up, nothing else matters.

I offered 'em down.

The gall of that boy, laying blame on the Master. The only call he got came from right between his legs.

She should've stopped him. When they saw those two swimming, she'd known Merle might go after the gal. She'd warned him against it. He'd promised to leave her alone. Ettie knew how weak he was. She had to admit she'd half expected him to break his promise. But when he fell asleep after dark, she'd figured it'd be all right. He must've been playing possum, just to put her at ease so she'd sleep and leave him free to sneak down.

Well, he wouldn't trick her that way again. Next time – if there was a next time – she'd keep herself awake all night.

As Merle disappeared again into the cave, Ettie stood up. Her rump was numb from sitting on the rock. She rubbed it, and the feeling returned with an aching tingle. Then she started down the slope.

She was eager to get to the cave and see what Merle had

brought in. First things first, though. She'd have to give the campsite a close look to make sure all the traces were gone.

Halfway down the slope, she left the sunlight behind. In the shade, the breeze felt chilly. Ettie hoped those folks had some nice parkas with them. Her sweatshirt up at the cave wasn't nearly warm enough once the sun went down.

She didn't descend all the way to the lake; that would mean more climbing. Instead, when she was about level with the low ridge at the northern end, she traversed the slope. She reached the ridge, leaped across the gap where the stream, far below, tumbled towards Lower Mesquite, and made her way down.

At the clearing among the trees where the campers had been, she found nothing. Even the circle of rocks piled up by previous visitors as a fireplace had been scattered, the ashes covered over. Where the tent had stood, the ground was now littered with pine needles and pinecones, sticks, and a few charred rocks from the fireplace. Merle had done a good job. But what had he done with the bodies?

Ettie wandered among the trees, saw nothing that looked suspicious, and returned to the campsite. Her eyes settled on the flat place where the tent had been. She stepped over to it. With the edge of her boot, she scraped a swath through the debris. She squatted down and pushed her fingers into the loose, grainy soil. Dropping to her knees, she started to dig. The hole deepened quickly as she scooped out handfuls of dirt.

At least if they're here, she thought, Merle planted them down far enough.

Her fingernails raked something soft. She cleared a small area at the bottom of the hole, uncovering an island of skin. Her nails had gouged furrows in it. Widening the hole, she discovered a navel. The skin around it was nearly hairless, so she figured this must be the girl.

She crawled forward, dug some more, and found the man's hip. Satisfied that Merle had buried them both, she filled in the holes. She stomped down the soil. She scattered pine needles over the area until it looked undisturbed.

She didn't much like the fact that Merle had buried them smack in the middle of the lake's only camping area. They were better than a foot under the surface, though. She supposed it'd be all right.

Chapter Seven

Back at the trail sign, Benny had thought two miles would be easy. After all, two miles was the distance from school to home, and he'd walked it a few times. He didn't remember it being hard. That was without a pack, though. And that was without an uphill climb that seemed to go on forever.

At first, he'd been able to keep up with Dad and Mr Gordon. When the trail started upward, though, his pack got heavier and heavier. The straps felt like hands on his shoulders, trying to shove him into the ground. Sweat made his glasses slip down his nose. Finally, he stepped off the trail. He dug into his pocket for the elastic band he used in gym class to keep his glasses from falling off. While he was busy attaching it, Karen and Mrs Gordon came long.

'Is it going okay?' Karen asked. She didn't look tired at all.

'Oh, my glasses,' he said. 'I'll catch up.'

'No hurry.' With a wave, she continued up the trail, walking slowly with long strides, leaning into the slope. Benny put on his glasses. He watched the backs of her slender legs.

While he was staring, the twins came up the trail. He nodded a greeting to them, and the one with the ponytail gave him a look like she thought he was a clod. What had he done, he wondered, to deserve that? After they passed, she whispered something to her sister, and both girls giggled a little.

Blushing, he made sure his zipper was up. It was.

They must've been making fun of him because he was resting. Or maybe because of his glasses. Four-eyes is pooped out.

He'd show them who's pooped.

Quickly, he pushed the loop of the elastic band onto his other earpiece. He glanced down the trail. Julie and Nick were coming towards him. He wouldn't give *her* a chance to knock him. Hanging onto his shoulder straps, he leaned into the weight and hurried up the trail.

He took long, steady strides like Karen. He closed in on the twins. 'Beep-beep,' he said. They glanced back, looking startled, and Pigtails fell in behind her sister to make room. He lunged past them.

One muttered, 'Turkey,' as he left them behind. He didn't look back.

Karen came into view as he rounded a bend. He kept up his speed until he was only a couple of yards behind her, then slowed his pace to match hers.

Turning sideways, she smiled back at him. Even in that funny hat, she was beautiful. 'Do you want through?' she asked.

'No, thanks. This is fine.'

It was real fine. He stayed behind her, watching her walk, listening to her voice as she talked with Mrs Gordon. He couldn't make out many of the words, but that didn't matter.

His shoulders hurt. His back was sore just above his rump where the pack rested. His leg muscles trembled. Sweat dripped down his face. His shirt and underwear felt glued to his skin. He was huffing for breath. But he didn't slow down. He stayed close behind Karen, well ahead of the snotty twins, and Julie and Nick.

No matter how awful he felt, he wouldn't fall behind. He wouldn't let himself.

Finally, the trail levelled out.

Then it sloped gently downward. He scanned the valley to the left, but saw only thick woods.

The lake's gotta be here someplace, he thought.

Two miles, the marker had said. They must've already hiked five. So where is it? Maybe the sign lied. Maybe there was a number one in front of the two and it was covered with dirt or something, and Juniper Lake is twelve miles. No, the ranger had said . . .

'Here we are,' came Mr Gordon's voice. He and Dad had stopped just ahead.

'How's it going?' Dad asked Karen.

'Whew,' she said. She took off her hat. It had matted down her hair. The strands across her forehead were wet and dark.

'It was a doozy,' Benny said.

She smiled at him, and wiped her forehead with the back of her hand.

'You did real good,' Dad told him. 'That was pretty tough going.'

He shrugged, and managed not to wince as pain streaked through his shoulders. 'It wasn't so tough,' he said.

While they waited for the others to catch up, Mr Gordon showed them the trail sign. It read, JUNIPER LAKE, but gave no distance. The arrow pointed to the left, where a narrow trail joined the main one and dropped away from the slope. Benny peered into the trees. He saw no trace of a lake.

'Where's the lake?' the ponytailed girl asked, frowning at her mother.

'Down there,' Mrs Gordon said.

'I don't see it.'

'Me either,' said the sister.

'Right *there*,' Benny told them. He pointed down the trail at the shadowy forest. 'Can't you see it?' he asked.

'No. Where?'

'See? Through there?'

Both girls scrunched up their faces and squinted into the trees.

'Maybe you need glasses,' Benny suggested.

'Do not.'

Quite a while later, well after reaching the bottom of the hill, Benny spotted a pale area through the trees ahead. The lake surface. About time.

'There it is!' cried one of the twins.

He grinned to himself, and kept on walking.

'Well now.' With a sigh, Flash slung his pack to the ground.

Scott took off his pack, too. The clearing, at the foot of the trail, was close to the shoreline. It had obviously been used often as a campsite. There were logs laid out as benches around a fireplace. There was a small pile of firewood. Plenty of flat area for sleeping.

Listening carefully, Scott heard the breeze stirring the leaves, the quiet lap of waves. But he heard no running water that would indicate a nearby stream.

'Why don't you all take a load off,' he suggested. 'I'll scout ahead. There might be a better place farther on.'

'This looks all right to me,' Flash said.

'Well, I'd rather be near a stream. Running water.'

'Good point,' Flash said.

'I'll come with you.' Karen swung her pack off, set it down, and joined him.

Benny, sitting on the ground against his pack, started to get up.

'You wait here,' Scott told him. 'We'll just be gone a few minutes.'

Looking disappointed, the boy settled back.

Karen followed Scott along a path near the shoreline. Without his pack, he felt nearly weightless. He walked with a springy step. The breeze was cool against his damp T-shirt.

And he was alone with Karen, at least for the moment. He turned to her. 'Howdy, stranger.'

She ducked under his outstretched arm, and leaned against him. He cupped her shoulder. They walked along the path, holding each other. 'Now, this is nice,' she said.

'You surviving the kids all right?'

'Sure. They're fine. Benny's quite a guy.'

'I think he's fallen for you. Can't blame him.'

'I've fallen for him, too.' She patted Scott's side. 'Good thing for you he's just a kid.'

'I wish Julie'd shape up. Maybe she will, now that Nick's around.'

'They seem to be getting along okay.'

'Yeah.' He sighed.

'What's wrong?'

'Well, I've been thinking about the sleeping arrangements. I really don't see how we can manage . . .'

'I know. I've thought about that, too. I guess I tent with Julie, huh?'

'I can't figure any way around it, what with the kids and the Gordons.'

'That's all right. Maybe we'll be able to sneak off, some time.'

'You can bet on it.'

Karen's hand moved down, and pushed into a rear pocket of his trousers. It stayed there, curved against his rump, caressing, as they walked along the path.

'If Julie gives you any trouble,' Scott said, 'let me know.'

'I'm sure we'll be fine. It'll give us a chance to get to know each other.'

'She's really not a bad kid. I've been trying to figure her out. It hit her pretty hard when her mother split. But it was never "How could she do that to me?" She only seemed upset that *I'd* been dumped on. She really holds it against June, won't even talk to her on the phone. Both kids are pretty bitter about what she did, but with Julie it seems to have spilled over onto you. It's not you personally. She'd have the same feeling towards any woman I got serious about. I'm sure of that. She seems to feel it's her duty to protect me.'

'Maybe she'll get over it once we know each other better.'

'I sure hope so. I feel bad, though, that you have to be put through this kind of thing.'

Karen smiled up at him. 'Hell, you're worth it.'

'Is that so?'

'That's so.'

They rounded a bend in the shoreline, and Scott heard the sound of rushing water.

'Success!' Karen said. She squeezed his rump, withdrew her hand from his pocket, and stepped ahead through a narrow passage between two trees. Scott watched her hurry forward. She bounded up a small, rocky rise, glanced down, then whirled around. *'Voila!'* she cried.

Scott climbed up to join her. A few feet below, a stream tumbled and swirled over rocks on its way to the lake.

They stepped down to it. Kneeling, Karen dipped a hand into the water. She cupped some to her mouth, and drank. 'It's luscious,' she said. As Scott tried the chill water, she splashed her face. Then, to his amazement, she unbuttoned her blouse. She spread it open, scooped up water with both hands, and flung it against herself. He watched it splatter her bare skin. It slid over her breasts, dripped from the jutting tips of her nipples, rolled down her belly. Bending over, she cupped more water to her mouth.

Scott reached across her back. He lifted the hanging side of her blouse out of the way, and curled his fingers around her breast. The skin was wet and cool, the nipple springy against his palm. She turned her face to him, and they kissed. 'We'd . . . better not.'

He kissed her again, then let go. As Karen buttoned her blouse, he caressed her back beneath it. Then they stood up. Scott filled his lungs with the fresh air. 'Well, let's see if there's a decent place around here to pitch camp.'

They leaped across the stream, walked up a low slope of broken granite, and looked down at a clearing. 'All *right*,' Karen said.

They made their way down to it. In the middle stood a nicely built-up stone fireplace with a grate across the top. Large, flat-topped rocks and smoothly sawed logs for stools were placed around it. Someone had even gone to the trouble of lashing branches together in the semblance of a table. Best of all, Scott saw plenty of level ground for the tents.

'It looks ideal to me,' Karen said.

'Me too.'

They headed back to tell the others.

'Let's get organized here,' Flash said, rubbing his hands together. 'Nick, you help me with the tents. Alice, why don't you and the girls scout around for firewood? We'll get this show on the road.'

'Benny,' Scott said. 'You want to go with them?'

The boy shook his head. 'I wanta do the tents.'

As Alice led the twins into the trees, Flash turned to Scott. 'Where do you want to set up? You should get first choice, since you found this place.'

'Makes no difference to me,' Scott told him. 'Right here's fine for one. Maybe pitch the other over there.' He nodded towards a level area closer to the lake.

'You want one that far off?'

'Sure. Why not? Give everybody a little breathing room.'

'Breathing room, eh?' He winked.

Scott looked amused as he pulled a tubular plastic bag from his pack.

'Which place do we get?' Benny asked.

'We should let the ladies pick.'

'How about it?' Karen asked Julie.

The girl shrugged.

'Over by the lake?'

'I don't care.'

'I wanta be close to the fire.' Benny said.

Karen grinned. 'You've got it. Julie and I'll take the scenic tent.' For a moment, her eyes met Flash's. There was mischief in them. Fooled you, they seemed to say.

Flash was fooled, all right. If he'd been in Scott's shoes, nothing in the world could've kept him from tenting with a woman like Karen. He hadn't put it quite that way to Alice, when they'd discussed it last night. He'd simply bet her a dinner at Victoria Station against a dinner at Casa Escobar that the couple would share a tent. 'I don't know about the girl,' she said, 'but Scott isn't that way.' Flash had smiled at that. He managed to refrain from telling about the time in Saigon when he and Scott, bare-ass and side by side, humped the daylights out of a couple of whores – then traded. No point in tarnishing Scott's image. Hell, Scott was about the only friend of his that Alice approved of. 'Aside from just good manners,' Alice had continued, 'he wouldn't put Julie and Benny together. They're too old to be sleeping together.' That point nearly succeeded in changing Flash's mind. Still, he hadn't called off the bet. Maybe they'd show up with three tents, one for one kid and . . .

'Over here?' Nick asked.

Flash turned around. His son was standing in a six-foot space between two spruces, a rolled-up tent in his arms. 'That'll be fine. Hold up a minute, though, till we clear the ground.'

Together, they brushed away the twigs and pinecones littering the area. Then they rolled out the red tent, and spread it flat. They joined the fibreglass wands, slid them in at the four corners, inserted the tips into eyelets at the top and bottom, and lifted the roof. In less than five minutes, the tent was up. All that remained was to tie out the guy lines and stake it down.

'I'll get the hatchet,' Flash said.

He headed for his pack. Scott, Karen, and Benny had nearly finished setting up a blue, two-man tent similar to his own. Julie was crouched by the fireplace, pouring fuel from an aluminium bottle into the base of a Primus stove.

Flash rummaged through his pack. As he looked for the hatchet, his stomach growled. He tried to remember the menu he'd worked out with Scott, but couldn't recall what was planned for tonight's meal. One of the Dri-Lite stews, probably. With pudding for dessert – either vanilla or chocolate. He hoped for vanilla. Nothing could beat that vanilla pudding, especially when it didn't get mixed up real good and still had some of those lumps in it.

He found the hatchet. As he walked back towards the tent, he saw Nick staring into space. No, not into space. At Julie. The girl was holding the small stove high, waving a lighted match under its base to warm the fuel for priming.

Wouldn't that be something, Flash thought, if Nick and Julie got together? He wondered if Scott would approve. No reason why he shouldn't. Nick's a fine lad, an Eagle Scout, a good student, and my son. The girl could sure do worse.

So could Nick. A lot worse. As far as Flash knew, the boy had never dated a gal half as attractive as Julie.

She shook out the match, turned a metal key to start the gas jetting, and frowned.

'I'll take care of the stakes, Nick. Go on over and see if Julie needs a hand with the stove.'

The boy shrugged.

'Go on. Maybe the nozzle's clogged.'

'Well . . . okay. Be right back.' He walked towards her. Julie smiled when she saw him approach. 'Having some trouble?' he asked.

'This thing doesn't want to cooperate.'

'Here, let me take a look.'

Go to it, boy, Flash thought, and picked up a stake.

Chapter Eight

Crouched by the stream, Karen shivered and gritted her teeth. Only a couple of hours ago, she'd been splashing herself to cool off. Then the water had felt like ice on her hot skin. Now, with the sun down and a chilly breeze blowing, the water seemed almost warm.

Except for Benny, everyone else had already finished washing their cook kits and returned to camp. He stood on the opposite bank, shaking and waving his aluminium dish to dry it while Karen scrubbed out the big pot. He was smart. He'd put on a jacket before coming over. Karen was still in her shorts and thin blouse. The blouse did no good at all. The cold breeze passed through the cloth as if it weren't there.

Benny sat down on a rock across from her. He wiped the dish across a leg of his jeans. 'Aren't you awfully cold?' he asked.

'I'm one giant goosebump.'

'You want me to get a jacket for you?'

'That's all right, I'm about done. Thanks, though.'

'It's funny how it gets so cold.'

'The altitude, I guess. You bake during the day and freeze at night.'

'Yeah. It's weird. It sure isn't like home.'

'That's one of the great things about camping,' she said. 'Home looks so good after you've been out here a while. You start dreaming about a hot bath, a soft bed . . .'

'Yeah!' Benny leaned forward, elbows on knees. 'Last year, we were out for a week and I got so I *had* to have a chocolate milkshake. I wanted one so bad I couldn't stand it. Then Dad stopped at Burger King on the way home and . . . gee, I think that was the best milkshake I ever had. I can taste it, just thinking about it.'

'Just thinking about it makes me cold.' Karen rinsed out the pot, stood up, and shook the water from it. 'Right now, I could go for some coffee.'

'We've got cocoa, too,' Benny said. Standing up, he brushed off the seat of his jeans. 'And marshmallows.'

'Maybe I'll have a marshmallow in my coffee.'

He laughed, and hopped across the stream.

'Thanks for keeping me company,' Karen told him as they walked up the granite slab.

'Ah, that's all right.'

The clearing ahead shimmered with firelight. Most of the others were seated close to the fire.

'Thought we'd lost you,' Scott called.

'Save me some coffee,' Karen called back. She handed the pot to Benny, and carried her cook kit down a gradual slope to the tent. 'Right with you,' she said over her shoulder.

Her backpack was propped against a rock near the tent entrance. She lifted the flap, dropped her kit into the darkness, and dug through the equipment trying to find her jeans and parka. They were near the bottom, of course. What you wanted was always at the bottom.

Clamping the jeans between her legs, she quickly shook open the parka and put it on. She sighed with relief at its warmth.

Then she crawled into the tent. It was very dark inside, but she didn't need her light for this. She sat on her soft, down-filled sleeping bag, took off her boots, and changed from her shorts to the long-legged jeans. Pushing into her boots, she left the tent. She hurried towards the fire, hoping she wouldn't trip on the laces.

Her cup was still on the stump where she'd left it after dinner. 'All set,' she said.

'Coffee?' Scott asked.

'You bet.' She held out the cup. Scott spooned in granules of instant from a plastic bag, then poured hot water into her cup and gave it a stir. Steam rose against Karen's face as she took a sip. 'Ah, that's good.' She sat on the stump, and drank more.

Benny, she saw, already had cocoa with a couple of marsh-mallows floating on the surface.

'How about some songs?' Alice suggested.

They started with 'Michael, Row the Boat Ashore.' Then it was 'Shenandoah'. Flash led them in 'Danny Boy', to which he knew all the words, and seemed almost tearful as he sang of the boy returning to his father's grave.

'Let's get into something more upbeat,' Scott said when that one ended. In a loud baritone, he started 'The Marine Corps Hymn' and everyone joined in, their voices booming.

'"The Caisson Song"!' Nick called out.

Then 'The Battle Hymn of the Republic', then, 'Dixie'. When that was done, the Gordons sang a song about a logger who stirred his coffee with his thumb.

'That puts me in mind of Robert Service,' Scott said. '"There are strange things done in the midnight sun . . ."'

'"By the men who moil for gold",' Karen said along with him, smiling that they both knew the same poem. They continued with it, line after line, one remembering what the other forgot until they finally got Sam McGee cremated on the marge of Lake LaBarge.

Their performance drew applause, and a two-fingered whistle from Julie.

Alice urged the twins to recite 'Stopping by the Woods on a Snowy Evening'.

'Sissy stuff,' Flash said when they finished. 'How's about this one? "You may talk o' gin and beer/When you're quart-ered safe out here,/And you're sent to pennyfights and Aldershot it . . ."'

Karen knew 'Gunga Din' by heart, but she kept silent as he proceeded. He messed up the middle badly. Nobody seemed to notice, though.

'Bravo!' Scott called, clapping as he finished. 'Benny, why don't you do one?'

The boy shrugged. He glanced shyly at Karen.

'Come on,' she urged him.

'Well. Is "The Raven" okay?'

'Great! I love Poe.'

Benny leaned forward on his rock, and set his empty cup on the ground between his feet. 'Well, here goes.' He began to recite the poem in a low, ominous voice. When the raven spoke, he screeched its 'Nevermore' like a demented parrot.

Rose giggled. Heather elbowed her for silence.

Benny ignored them. He spoke slowly, a haunted look on his firelit face as if he'd become the lonely, tormented man of the poem. He grew frenzied, then furious. '"Quit the bust above my door!"' he cried out. '"Take thy beak from out my heart and take thy form from off my door!"'

When he finished, there was silence. Everyone looked a bit stunned. Until he stood up, grinning, and bowed. Everyone clapped. Even Rose. Even Julie.

'Terrific,' Karen told him. 'That was great!'

'Do you know some others?' Rose asked.

'Maybe,' he said. 'Maybe tomorrow night.'

'Let's tell stories,' Julie suggested. 'Anybody know a really scary one?'

'How about "The Hook"?' Nick asked.

Rose wrinkled her nose. 'That's an old one.'

'I could tell you something,' Karen said, 'that happened to a friend of mine. It happened just a few years ago when she was camping with some friends – not very far from here.'

Heather's eyes widened. She looked frightened already. Flash leaned forward, took a burning stick from the fire, and lit a cigar. Benny turned to face Karen.

'We don't want to give the kids nightmares,' Scott told her, smiling.

'I'd better not tell it.'

'Come on,' Nick said.

'Yeah,' Julie said. 'You can't quit now.'

'Well ... they were camping in the mountains not far

from here. It was a cold night, with the wind howling and moaning through the trees. Sandy – that was her name – sat close to the campfire with her two friends, Audrey and Doreen. I would've been along, but I'd sprained my ankle a few days earlier and had to stay home. Lucky for me, as it turned out.'

'Is this really a true story?' Benny asked.

'Let her talk,' Julie said.

Karen leaned closer to the fire. She felt its heat on her face, the cold on her back. 'The three of them huddled close around the fire to keep the cold away. They sang and told ghost stories, none of them wanting to leave the fire's cheery warmth. Slowly the flames dwindled. Sandy put on the last piece of firewood. Soon, that, too, was nearly gone. "Well," Sandy said, "why don't we hit the sack?" The others were against it, though. They'd frightened themselves so much with the ghost stories that the tent, off in the darkness, looked like a creepy shadow.'

'"What if someone's hiding inside?" Doreen asked.'

'"Oh, that's ridiculous," Sandy said.'

Karen glanced at Benny. He was staring, wide-eyed, at his tent across the clearing.

'Well, they decided to stay up for a while longer. But the fire was nearly dead, only a few flickers still lapping around the charred remains of wood. If they were going to stay up till their jitters passed, they would have to replenish the supply of firewood. Since nobody wanted to go alone into the dark woods around the campsite, they decided to all go together.'

'But they had no flashlight. The flashlight was in the tent. "I'm not going in there," Doreen said.'

'"Me either," Audrey said.'

'Sandy was frightened, too, by this time, but she told herself it was silly. So she volunteered to get the flashlight. She left Audrey and Doreen sitting by the fire, and crossed the dark clearing towards the tent. She crouched in front of it. Her heart was pounding like crazy, but she wasn't about to let herself be scared off. Then she got an idea that made her grin. She almost laughed, but kept quiet and lifted the tent flap. Inside, it was as black as a cave. She almost lost her nerve, but took a deep breath and crawled in.'

'Suddenly, she screamed. She screamed again, a piercing shriek of terror so loud it made her ears hurt. "No!" she cried out. "No! Please! *No!*" And then she let out a howl of horror and agony that made her own flesh crawl.'

'What was it?' Benny whispered. 'What got her?'

'Not a thing,' Karen answered. 'This was Sandy's idea of a practical joke. Like lots of practical jokes, though, this one backfired. Once she was done screaming, she found the flashlight. She crawled out of the tent, all set to yuck it up about the great gag she'd pulled on her friends. But they were gone.'

'She scared 'em off,' Nick said.

'That's what Sandy thought. She walked around the clearing, calling out to them. "Hey you guys!" she yelled. "I was kidding! Come on back!" But they didn't come back.'

'Sandy sat by the campfire. Only a glow remained, by now, and she was cold. "Come on," she finally called. "Enough is enough." But Audrey and Doreen still didn't return.'

'At last, she left the campsite and walked into the dark woods, calling out for her friends. With each step, she half expected the girls to leap out at her screaming, to pay her back for the scare. But they didn't. She kept searching, wandering farther and farther from the camp.'

'Finally, she spotted them in a moonlit clearing. They stood motionless as she hurried towards them. "What're you doing way out here?" she asked. They didn't answer. They didn't speak a word. When she reached them, she stared. She began to whimper.'

'The two figures wore the clothes of Doreen and Audrey, but the arms and legs were made of sticks. They were scarecrows with heads of bloody fur.'

'Yuck,' Rose muttered.

'Somehow, Sandy found her way back to the camp. She sat by the dead fire. The wind moaned around her. She stared into the darkness. She waited and waited. Audrey and Doreen never returned.'

'Never?' Benny asked.

'Never. Some hikers wandered into camp a couple of days later and found Sandy still sitting there, her wide eyes gazing into the woods as if looking for her lost friends.'

'What *did* happen?' Nick asked. 'To Audrey and Doreen.'

'Search parties looked everywhere for them. They were never found. Nobody will ever know what became of them after they ran out into the woods that night. Maybe it's best that way.'

There was silence. Heather peered over her shoulder. Rose leaned closer to the fire.

'On that cheerful note,' Flash said, 'I think it's about time to call it a night.'

Chapter Nine

'Hey,' Nick said. 'I'm gonna sleep under the stars tonight. You want to?'

'That'd be neat. I'll have to ask Dad first.' Turning around, Julie spotted him with Karen and Benny. The three were heading away from the campsite, apparently on their way to the stream. 'Wait up!' she called, and ran after them. She quickly caught up with her father. 'Can I sleep outside tonight?' she asked.

'Do you have a choice?'

'I mean by the fire. Instead of in the tent. Nick's gonna sleep out, too.'

'Just the two of you?'

'I don't know.' She sighed. 'Jeez, Dad, we're not gonna *do* anything. I hardly even know the guy.'

'I wasn't thinking about that. Now that you mention it, though . . .'

'*Dad.*'

He laughed softly, 'No, it's fine with me.'

'Great!' She whirled away and rushed to tell Nick. She found him crouching over his backpack, pulling out his sleeping bag. 'It's okay,' she told him.

'Fantastic.'

'Meet you by the fire.'

Well away from the campsite, in the woods beyond her tent, she brushed her teeth and washed her face using water from her plastic bottle. As she capped the bottle, she heard a quiet crunching sound. Not far away. A footstep? Holding her breath, she stared through the trees. She saw only black trunks, bushes, a few dim clusters of stone.

Nobody's there, she told herself.

Still, she felt exposed standing in a bright patch of moonlight. With a sidestep, she moved into the dark. She listened. She heard only the breeze in the treetops, the quiet lapping sound of the lake, a few indistinct voices from the camp.

'Damn story,' she muttered. Karen's story, and nothing more, was responsible for her jitters. 'Wasn't even scary,' she said.

But as she lowered her pants and squatted, she scanned the darkness. Ridiculous. Dumb story. She was a jerk to let it bother her.

Here I am, a jerk. Staring into the woods like a fool, half expecting Audrey and Doreen to dash by. Dumb.

She stared and shivered. This was taking forever. Why the hell had she drunk so much coffee?

Finally, she finished. She hurried back to camp. Nick, in

his sleeping bag near the fire, waved at her. 'Right with you,' she called.

In the darkness of her tent, she changed into the hooded warm-up suit she'd brought along for sleepwear. She put on clean wool socks, then slipped into her sneakers. She rolled her mummy bag into a loose bundle, grabbed her foam-rubber mat, and crawled outside.

Nick watched her approach. She felt self-conscious, naked under her snug jacket and pants. He can't tell, she thought. Besides, she was holding the bulky bag in front of herself.

'You ought to put down a ground cloth,' he suggested.

'Yeah. I'll get my poncho.' She spread out the rubber mat, piled her bag on it, and walked back across the clearing. Let him look, she thought. Nothing to see. For all he knows, she could be wearing long johns under her suit. Her uneasiness, however, was mixed with a tingle of excitement at the idea that he might be watching and wondering.

She crouched over her pack. The pants drew taut against her rump and slipped down a bit. She felt a strip of cold above the elastic band. Nick can't see. It's dark.

She took out her poncho, water bottle, and flashlight and fastened down the cover flap for the night. Standing, she hiked up her pants. Then she returned to the fire.

'Can you use a hand?' Nick asked.

'That's okay. I'll just be a minute.' She spread her poncho over a fairly smooth patch of ground several feet away from Nick's bag. He was wearing a T-shirt. 'Aren't you cold?' she asked.

'Just what you can see. I'm toasty warm from there down.'

'Toasty warm?'

'Snug as a bug in a rug.'

'Good grief,' she muttered.

Nick laughed.

Knees on the poncho, Julie straightened out her rubber pad. It was just wider than her shoulders, just long enough to cushion her from head to rump. She spread her sleeping bag over it. Sitting on the puffy surface, she pulled off her shoes. She placed them near the head of the bag, propped her water bottle between them, and slipped her flashlight inside one. Then she lowered the zipper of her bag halfway. She drew back the top as far as she could and struggled to get in, rolling onto her back and drawing up her knees nearly to her chin before she could work her feet under the edge. 'Graceful, huh?'

'Yeah.'

She used the inside tab to pull the zipper up. Then, nestled in warmth, she sighed.

'Okay.' It was her father's voice, a short distance away. 'See you in the morning.'

'Bright and early,' Karen answered.

''Night,' Benny said.

'Go on ahead, I'll be right with you.'

Raising her head, Julie saw Benny turn away from the adults. They walked towards Karen's tent, the one she would've been sharing with Julie. In the darkness near its front, they embraced. They kissed. Julie turned her face away.

''Night,' Benny said as he walked by.

'Yeah,' she muttered.

'Good-night,' Nick said.

Dad came along a while later. At least he didn't go in the tent with her. 'Sleep tight, you two,' he said as he passed.

''Night, Dad.'

'Good-night, Mr O'Toole.'

'From here on, it's Scott. Okay?'

'Sure. Good-night.'

Soon Dad reached his tent. Julie heard his voice and Benny's, but she couldn't make out the words. Quiet voices also came from the tent where the twins were. They had a flashlight on, its beam making a pale disk that showed through the red wall. Julie smiled.

'Something funny?' Nick asked.

'I think that story really threw a scare into the twins.'

'Yeah. They scare real easy.' He scooted down until only his head was visible. 'You know what'd be neat? We oughta get up and run behind their tent.'

'Are you kidding?'

'It'd scare the hell out of them.'

'Cold out there,' Julie said. She felt cosy in her sleeping bag, but the idea of rushing through the woods with Nick sent a shiver of excitement through her.

'It'd just take a minute,' he told her. In the shimmering glow of the firelight, his face looked eager.

She grinned back at him. 'We'll get in trouble.'

'I don't mind.'

'Me either. It'd be worth it. But we've gotta do Benny, too.'

'What about Karen's tent?'

'Why bother?'

'Just the two tents, then.'

'Right. Let's do it.'

Slowly, as if someone might be watching, they unzipped their mummy bags, Julie's throat felt tight. She clamped her teeth together to stop her chin from trembling, and sat up. As she reached for her shoes, she saw Nick swing his bare legs free of his bag. He was wearing blue shorts. Boxer underwear? No, she decided, must be gym pants. He wouldn't dare run around in nothing but his undies. 'You're gonna freeze your tail off,' she said in a shaky whisper.

'You're telling me.' He turned towards her and started putting on his shoes. She noticed, with a mixture of relief and disappointment that the shorts had no fly. She caught herself trying to see up the leg holes, and quickly lowered her gaze. She stared at her shoes as she put them on.

'All set?' he asked.

Julie nodded. She stood up, feeling the cold seep into her clothes. As she tugged at the bottom of her jacket, she saw the thrust of her nipples through the tan fabric. Nick saw too. He was staring. 'Take a picture,' she muttered. 'It lasts longer.'

He met her eyes for a moment, looking stunned and hurt, then turned away. He shook his head.

'Hey,' Julie whispered.

'Never mind, let's just forget it.' He knelt on his sleeping bag.

'Come on, don't chicken out on me.'

'It was a dumb idea.' He reached back to pull off a shoe.

Julie squeezed his shoulder. 'Come on. I'm sorry. It wasn't your fault. I was a jerk.'

'No you weren't.'

'Hey, you can look at me all you want. I was looking at you.'

'You were?'

'Sure. Come on, let's scare the crap out of everyone.'

The flashlight no longer beamed through the side of the twins' tent. Julie heard no talking. 'Hope they're not asleep,' she whispered.

Nick took the lead, striding quietly across the clearing. They stopped beside the tent. He began to pound his feet on the earth. Julie joined in. Shoulder to shoulder, they ran in place, their shoes crunching the dry pine needles and twigs and pinecones. Through the noise, Julie heard frantic whispers from inside.

In a high, trilling voice, she called, 'Hellllp meee. Pleeeease hellllp meeeee.'

Screams erupted from the tent.

Nick slapped a hand across his mouth, apparently to hold in a giggle, and dashed into the trees just behind the tent. He cut to the left, Julie close on his heels. Running through the dark, with the girls still screaming, she felt a strange quivering tightness in her chest as if she needed to scream herself. They passed the tent of Nick's parents, then raced towards the rear of her father's tent.

'Helllp meee!' she called in a shrill voice. 'Hellllp meeeee!'

Their feet crashed through the undergrowth.

'Pleeeease hell—'

'It's all right,' came her father's voice. 'Julie!' he yelled. 'It's not funny!'

'It's Doreeeeen!' she cried, and rushed by.

As they raced for their sleeping bags, Mr Gordon scurried out of his tent. 'What the fuck's going on!' he bellowed.

Julie dived for her bag. Nick hit his, laughing, and burrowed inside.

'For Chrissake,' Mr Gordon said. 'No more of that, Nick, or you're in for it.' He muttered, 'Infantile.'

Peering out of her sleeping bag, Julie saw him crouch at the entrance of the twins' tent. 'It's all right, girls,' he said in a loud voice. 'Just a couple of morons.'

'He called me a moron!' Julie whispered.

She heard Nick laugh.

Scott listened to Benny's slow, deep breathing. Finally asleep. About time. Julie's stunt had thrown quite a shock into him, keeping him awake for a long while afterwards.

Good old Karen. She really opened a can of worms with that story of hers.

Good old Karen.

He opened the side of his bag so slowly that the zipper popped open with quiet, individual clicks. Then he silently climbed out.

If Benny wakes up, he thought, I'll just tell him that nature is calling. Won't even be a lie; nature *is* calling.

Naked except for his jockey shorts, he shivered as he crawled to the foot of his sleeping bag. He relaxed his muscles, and the shaking stopped. That's it. Calm. Stay calm. He opened the mosquito screen and crept through the opening. On hands and knees, he scanned the camp. The fire was out. Except for a few pale tatters of moonlight, the area was dark. The two sleeping bags were black bulges near the low stone circle of the fireplace.

He stood up and brushed off his knees. Then he walked quickly to Karen's tent. He unzipped the front and crawled in. Her sleeping bag was stretched lengthwise along the righthand side. Her face was a vague blur at the far end. Her breathing was slow and steady.

He lay down on the cold floor of the tent, and kissed one of her closed eyes. She moaned. 'It's me,' he whispered.

'Mmmm.' She rolled onto her back.

Scott found the zipper at the side of her bag, eased it down, and slid his arm into the warmth. He touched her. She was wearing something loose and thick and soft. A sweatshirt? His hand moved over it, feeling her heat through the fabric, feeling the smooth curves of her belly and ribs and breasts.

Without warning, a hand grabbed his wrist. 'Password?' came a whisper.

'"Open sesame"?'

'"Pumpernickel." Close enough.' She raised her head. 'What are you wearing?'

'Not much.'

'So I gather. Jeez, get in here.' She lifted the cover of her sleeping bag, and Scott crawled in. She snuggled against him. Her lips brushed his as she said, 'How nice of you to join me.'

'Very thoughtful of Julie to sleep outside.'

'Yes.' They kissed. Karen flinched as he slid a cold hand under her sweatshirt. She pushed her tongue into his mouth. She touched the band of his shorts, slipped her hand in, and caressed his buttocks.

She sighed when he touched her breast. He stroked its smoothness, filled his hand with it, gently squeezed. She sucked a trembling breath as his thumb pressed her nipple. Then she pulled off her sweatshirt. She was bare and warm and sleek to the waist. She squirmed, rubbing herself against him.

His erect penis felt trapped in his tight shorts. She freed it. Her fingers curled around it, slid down the length of it and up again. Scott moaned as the sensation threatened to break his control. He moved lower, easing out of her hand. His mouth went to her breast. He kissed the rigid nipple, tasting the slight tang of salt on her skin.

Karen rolled onto her back, and he tongued her other breast while his hand roamed down the velvety skin of her belly. He plucked at the drawstring of her sweatpants, opening the bow. He slid his hand down. He felt the soft coils of hair. Her thighs parted to make room. She was warm and slick. Her breath became ragged. She clenched his hair, forcing his mouth hard against her breast as she raised her knees and writhed under his sliding fingers.

'Oh God,' she gasped. 'Oh my God.'

He took his hand away. She let go of his hair, and he rolled aside. While she struggled out of her pants, he shoved his shorts down and tugged them off. Then he was on top of Karen, thrusting his tongue into her mouth, squeezing a breast, pushing into her. She sheathed him, tight and slippery. She whimpered as he slid in deep. 'Hurt?' he whispered.

'Oh, Jesus!'

'Is that a yes?'

'No,' she gasped. 'It's a no,' she dug her fingers into his buttocks, pulled, and shuddered as he pushed the rest of the way in.

A few endless moments of mad lunging, burying himself in her dark hugging warmth, in her and enclosed by her and part of her, she strained against him for a deeper joining as if she ached for him to penetrate a secret place just out of reach. Scott sought that place. He plunged for it. He rammed for it. Just beyond him and now he couldn't hold back. He pumped, spurting into her, and knew that his fluid was finding that secret place, making that connection joining them. Karen quaked under him. Then she held him motionless and tight.

Chapter Ten

'Keep on going,' Ettie muttered. 'Don't you stop here.'

Dropping to her rump, she scooted down the steep side of the boulder she'd been standing on. The granite felt like hot sandpaper through her dress. She pushed off, fell a short distance into a nook among the rocks, and stretched out flat on an uptilted slab. From there, she watched the hikers stride up the distant trail.

They were heading up towards Carver Pass. Three of them. This far off, they were no more than tiny shapes. Something about the way they walked made Ettie suspect they were girls, but she could only be sure about one; the figure of that one made it obvious.

The person in the lead, who wore a cowboy hat, stopped and turned around, waiting for the others to catch up.

'No,' Ettie whispered when the leader pointed down at the lake.

The three stood close together on the trail, gesturing and nodding, apparently discussing the matter. Then the one in the cowboy hat started down the steep path towards the lake. The other two followed.

'Damnation,' Ettie muttered.

Squirming forward on the sun-baked granite, she spotted Merle. He was far below, seated on his favourite rock, fishing. With a high outcropping to his right, he was hidden from the intruders, at least for now. They would need to come halfway up the opposite shore to notice Merle in his recess. By then, he was sure to hear their voices and take cover.

'You better behave, boy,' she said. 'You better just leave 'em be, or I'll skin you.'

Before yesterday, there hadn't been much cause to worry on Merle's account. Folks had come down every now and again to rest by the lake, explore it, take a swim, or do some fishing, but Merle always stayed out of sight and left them alone. He'd even behaved the few times campers stayed the night. None of the overnight people had been pretty young women, though, until that last. Easy enough to behave when there's no temptation. But the first pretty girl comes along, he rapes her and kills her and lays it on the Master.

I offered 'em down.

Bullsquat.

Ettie turned her gaze to the hikers. They were already at the bottom of the slope, walking single file along the lake-shore. They were heading towards the area where Merle had buried the bodies. With its trees and shade, it stood out like an oasis in the desolate basin. No one came down without settling there.

A fine place to plant those folks, Ettie thought. We oughta dig them up and stick them someplace out of the way.

Sure enough, the three hikers stopped in the shadows and swung off their packs. One red pack was lowered within a yard of the graves.

As they opened their packs, Ettie heard them talking and laughing. From the sounds of their voices, she was sure that all three were girls.

Merle must hear them, too. She looked towards the boulder where he'd been sitting. He was on his feet, leaning out, trying to see around the jut of rock. He stood motionless for a few moments, then leaped across the narrow band of water, set down his fishing pole, and scrambled up the slope. Near the top, he crouched low, then raised his head enough to see over.

Only the width of the lake separated him from the girls. That couldn't be more than a hundred feet, Ettie figured. Merle could swim the distance in half a minute, if he had a mind to.

'You just let 'em be,' Ettie whispered.

She looked at the girls. They were sitting close together

269

on rocks, passing a couple of small bags back and forth, eating the contents.

Stopped for lunch, Ettie thought. She hoped that was all, that they would finish up quickly and be on their way.

The one in the cowboy hat, who sat with her back to Ettie, took off her checkered blouse. The straps of her bra were white against her tanned skin. She stood up and stretched, as if she liked how the breeze felt. Bending over, she set her hat on a rock. She rubbed her short brown hair, then turned away from the other two girls and walked to the shore. There, she knelt and flipped a hand through the water.

Ettie looked for Merle. He was gone.

The girl returned to her friends. Moving her hat off the rock, she sat down again and began to untie a boot.

'Oh, you fool,' Ettie muttered. She studied the opposite shore, but still couldn't see Merle.

One of the other girls, a skinny thing in jeans and a faded blue shirt, got up and stuffed a bag into her pack. Then she took off her shirt. Her breasts were small mounds, white except for their dark tips.

'Oh, Merle, Merle.' The temptation would be too much for him.

She considered rushing down to the girls, yelling and trying to scare them away. That might ruin everything, though. They'd be sure to tell someone – maybe a ranger – about the wild woman who chased them off. A spell might take care of that, but why take chances? A good spell's hard to call down, and you can't always count on one to take care of business.

Be better off to find Merle and stop him before he did something foolish.

She looked at the girls. The one who'd tested the water was on her feet, pulling down her shorts. The buxom one had her T-shirt off, and was reaching behind her back to unhook her bra. The skinny one sat right where Merle had planted the bodies, and tugged off her boots.

Ettie still couldn't spot Merle. She guessed he was across

the lake from the girls, spying on them, probably hard as a club by now and going crazy.

She scurried across the slope, staying low. She squeezed through crevices, slid down steep slabs on her rump, ducked behind every rock cluster offering any concealment, making her way slowly across the end of the lake. When she paused to catch her breath, she found all three girls stark naked. The one in the lead was knee-deep in the lake, walking backward, urging her friends to come in. The skinny one eased in a foot and jerked it out quickly. The other squatted down, breasts bulging against her knees, and tried the water with her hand.

Ettie left the sheltering rocks. The area ahead was a barren slab of granite that angled slightly downward. It offered no protection. If the girls happened to look towards the end of the lake, they would see her crossing. She squirmed along on her belly, watching them.

The girl in the lake had started to swim. The one crouched on the bank was scooping up water and rubbing it on her shoulders and breasts as if to get used to its cold. The skinny one, cringing and hugging herself, was wading in slowly. None of them so much as glanced in Ettie's direction.

She reached the end of the open space without being seen, and crawled behind a rock. She peered over its top. The small inlet where Merle had been fishing was no more than thirty feet away. Plenty of shelter between here and there. As quickly as she could, she rushed down to it. From the recessed shore, the girls were out of sight. She heard splashing and voices, then a sudden outcry that knotted her stomach before she recognised it as a shriek of laughter.

They're having a great time, stupid bitches. If they knew . . .

She hoped across the water on stepping stones, and crouched at the base of the outcropping. Merle's abandoned fishing pole lay against the rocks in front of her, a shrivelled bit of beef jerky on its hook.

Ettie worked her way up the slope, then peered over the top, first at the swimmers, then at the rocks along the bank. From this height, she expected to see Merle crouched behind a boulder.

She didn't see Merle. But she saw his scattered clothes.

A movement caught her eye. To the left. In the water. Just below a jutting clump of rocks. All she saw, at first, were rings, rippling outward as if a stone had been tossed in. Then there was the pale blur of a body sliding along beneath the surface.

Rage seized Ettie. She wanted to scream and yank Merle from the water. The fool! The *fool!*

She scrambled to the top of the outcropping and stood up straight. The first girl was floating on her back, arms out to the sides, her wet breasts shiny in the sunlight, her matted pubic hair glistening as she kicked closer and closer to the long, gliding form of Merle. The boy couldn't be more than a few inches below the surface, but he hadn't come up for air, yet, and none of the girls knew he was there.

'You!' Ettie shouted. 'Girls!'

Three wet, astonished faces snapped towards her.

'Get out! There's snakes! Poison snakes. Water moccasins!'

Two of the girls screamed and started splashing for shore even while Ettie yelled. The third, the one who'd started it all by leading her friends down to the lake, trod water and looked around. 'I don't see any,' she called.

'There!' Ettie snatched up a stone and hurled it. The girl turned to her right as it smacked the water. Not far to the left, Merle's head broke the surface. 'Right there! See it?' His head turned towards Ettie, then quickly submerged.

He knows he's found out, she thought. Sure enough, the pale blur of his body turned beneath the water and started back.

'Tracy!' called one of the girls.

'Come on, Tracy,' yelled the other. 'Let's get out of here!'

Both girls stood on the far shore, cowering and clutching

themselves, trying to hide their nakedness from the intruder as they yelled to their friend.

Tracy frowned up at Ettie. 'You're some kind of a nut,' she said. Then she swam casually across the lake.

Merle, still underwater, reached the cluster of rocks where he'd started. His head popped up. 'Stay down,' Ettie snapped.

The girl waded ashore on the far side. Before rushing to join her friends, she thrust her middle finger at Ettie.

'Mom?' Merle sounded pathetic.

'Stay down. I'll tell you when to come out.'

He waited, only his head out of the water, while Ettie watched the girls get into their clothes, swing their packs on, and start towards the far end of the lake. 'Okay now?' he asked.

'No. Stay where you are.'

The trio, often glancing back, reached the footpath and started striding towards the main trail. Ettie turned away. She climbed down the rocks, snapped the baited hook off the line, and picked up the springy stick Merle used as a fishing rod.

She carried it up the slope. When the girls were out of sight, she stepped down and walked along the shore to where Merle was waiting. 'Okay,' she said. 'You can come out now.'

'You gotta look away.'

'Get out!'

He sighed. 'Yes, ma'am.' He stood in the waist-deep water and waded ashore, both hands cupped over his groin.

'You haven't got no sense at all, boy.'

'The Master, He—'

'Don't you go laying it on the Master! Weren't nothing but your pecker wanted those girls. Bend over.'

'Ettie, please.'

'Do what I say.' He bent over, and she swung the fishing pole hard against his rump. Crying out, he clutched his buttocks. 'Move your hands.' He was sobbing. As his hands dropped away, Ettie saw a red stripe across his skin. Her throat constricted, and Merle went blurry as tears filled her eyes. She drew back the switch to strike again, but instead of swinging, she threw it down. 'Go on and get dressed,' she said in a shaky voice. 'And don't you ever nothing like that again, or you'll be the sorriest man that ever walked on two legs.'

'Yes, ma'am.'

Ettie walked away.

Chapter Eleven

'Hey, look!' Julie's arm swung up, and she pointed.

Nick gazed up the shadowy trail. Off to the side, he saw a small cleared area between two trees. It was a patch of raised ground, roughly rectangular, enclosed by a border of small stones. A weathered plank of wood tilted from the earth at its far end.

'A grave,' Julie whispered.

'Naw.'

'Sure looks like one.'

Leaning into the straps of his heavy pack, Nick hurried towards the mound. Julie stayed close to his side. He was nervous and excited, as if they were the first ever to discover this forbidden site. He stopped at its foot. The hump of ground was roughly the size of a small man. Words had been carved into the wooden marker. His eyes followed them as Julie read aloud in a hushed voice: '"Beneath this earth lies Digby Bolles. Poor man ran out of Dr Scholl's."'

Nick felt a mixture of relief and disappointment. 'It's a joke,' he said.

'I guess so.'

'Somebody went to a lot of trouble for a practical joke.'

'Some people do,' Julie said, and gave him an amused look. '*Doreeeen*,' she called softly. '*Audreeee*.'

Nick nodded. He thought of their brief, wild run behind the tents, the screams of the twins, how daring he'd felt through the whole experience. Running in only his T-shirt and shorts, Julie close to him in the dark. The way he'd wanted to grab her and pull her tight against him, and kiss her.

'We'll have to do that again sometime,' she said.

'We'd catch hell,' he told her. 'I wouldn't mind, though.'

'Whatcha got there?' Dad called from behind. He was trudging up the trail with Mom at his side. The girls were a short distance back.

'A grave,' Julie said.

'No kidding? Not a *real* grave?'

'Have a look,' Nick said. He and Julie stepped aside to make room for them.

'Holy Toledo,' Dad said.

'Who is it?' asked Rose, pushing forward.

'A poor guy named Digby Bolles.'

Mom read the epitaph aloud.

Heather wrinkled her nose. 'Who's Dr School?'

'It's not a who. It's a brand of foot powder.'

'And the guy died when he ran out?'

'No, honey. It's just a joke. Nobody's buried here.'

'We oughta get a snapshot of this,' Dad said. He swung down his pack. While he opened a side pocket, Rose and Heather stared at the plot of ground.

'Someone's there, all right,' Rose said.

'How do you know?'

'I just know.'

'A grave,' Benny gasped, arriving out of breath.

'Mom says it's not really,' Heather told him.

He frowned as he read the inscription. Then he grinned. 'Hey, that's neat.'

'I better use the flash,' Dad said. 'All these shadows. Want to make sure the saying comes out.' Everyone moved out of his way. He crouched at the foot of the mound. The flash cube made a quick burst of silvery light.

'What's all the excitement?' Scott asked. He was striding up the trail, Karen close beside him.

'It's Digby's grave,' Benny explained.

They walked over to it. Karen read the verse aloud, and laughed softly. 'That's a shame.'

'He should've been more careful,' Scott said.

Benny looked up at him. 'What do you think's down there?'

'Digby Bolles.'

'I mean really.'

Julie glanced at Nick. Her eyebrows went up and down. She turned to her father. 'What-say we dig it up and find out?'

'What-say we don't?'

'Come on, aren't you curious?'

Halfgrinning, he said, 'Noooo.'

'What about you, Karen?'

'I think we should let him rest in peace.'

'Now, let's stop all this talk,' Mom said. 'It's scaring the girls. We all know there's nobody buried here.'

'Yes, there is,' Rose told her.

'See what I mean? It's just somebody's rotten idea of joke.'

'We've got a lot of ground to cover,' Dad said. 'I say we haul ass.'

'Arnold!'

'Why don't you guys go on ahead?' Julie suggested. 'I'll catch up later.'

'Julie . . .'

'Why not? What'll it hurt? I'll put everything back just the way it is.'

'What are you hoping to find?' Scott asked.

She smiled mysteriously. 'Answers.'

'Oh, for heaven's sake,' Mom muttered. 'Nothing's there.'

Dad was smiling, obviously pulling for Julie. 'Wouldn't hurt to know for sure, though.'

'Arnold!'

'I'll stay and help,' Nick said.

'This is absurd,' his mother muttered.

'Hell, let 'em satisfy their curiosity, Alice. You said yourself they won't find anything.'

'That's right,' she said. 'They won't. But if they want to waste their time and energy, far be it from me to stand in their way.'

'Atta girl.'

She gave him a quick, humourless smile.

'Don't stay too long, kids,' Dad said.

'We'll catch up as soon as we can.'

Heather gazed at Nick with wide, frightened eyes. 'You gonna dig it up?'

'Probably nothing there but an old shoe,' he told her.

Rose narrowed her eyes. 'You'll be sor-ry,' she said in a singsong.

Both girls turned away and hurried to catch up with their mother and father.

'You want to stay?' Scott asked Benny.

The boy made a face as if he'd been invited to taste a worm. 'I don't want to see any stiffs,' he proclaimed.

'I don't blame you,' Karen said.

Scott turned to her. 'Shall we be off and leave Burke and Hare to their grisly chore?'

'I'm with you.'

The three of them started up the trail, leaving Nick and Julie by the grave. 'Mission accomplished,' Julie said. Nick grabbed her pack while she slipped her arms out of the straps. 'Thank you, sir,' she said, then took it from him and set it down. He swung his own pack to the ground. 'I've got a little shovel in here someplace,' she told him, propping her pack against his. Crouching, she slid a plastic clamp down its tie cord and peeled back the cover.

Nick stepped behind Julie as she rummaged inside. Her T-shirt clung to her back with sweat. The tint of her skin was visible through the fabric. So was the narrow white crossband of her bra, and the thin straps running up to her shoulders. He could see the bumps of her spine pushing out the material and remembered the way her nipples had shown last night. *Hey, you can look at me all you want. I was looking at you.*

'Here we go.' She stood up, a green plastic trowel in her hand.

'Perfect,' Nick said.

They stepped over to the mound. 'Where'll we dig?'

'In the middle?'

'Good a place as any.' She smiled, looking a bit nervous and knelt beside the border of stones. Nick stepped around her, and dropped to his knees. Her shoulder brushed against him as she reached out with the trowel. Using its edge, she scraped away a layer of pine needles to expose a patch of earth. With its point, she scratched out a pair of crossing lines. 'X marks the spot,' she whispered. She pushed the plastic blade into the soil, and hesitated. 'You don't . . . you don't really think anyone's down there, do you?'

'Naw.'

'Me either.' She pried out a heap of dirt, and dumped it next to the small hole. 'I mean, who'd bury someone out here?'

'I don't know.' Nick's mouth was dry. His heart beat fast. He didn't know whether he felt so tense because of the grave or because Julie was so close to him.

'What if we *do* find a body?' she asked, frowning at the tiny hole.

'It's unlikely.'

'It's possible, though.' She turned her face towards him. Her eyes were so blue that even the white seemed to have a faint bluish colour. There was a smudge of dirt on her cheek. Her tongue curled out from a corner of her mouth and caught a trickle of sweat. 'It is possible,' she said.

Nick felt breathless. 'Yeah,' he managed.

'Oh, what the hell.' Her face turned away, and she reached out with the trowel. Its tip hovered above the hole, quivering slightly. She sighed. 'You know, I'm not sure this is such a hot idea after all.'

'We don't have to do it,' Nick told her.

'We said we would.'

'That doesn't matter.'

'They'll say we chickened out. Not that I give a rat's ass what anybody says, but . . . I don't know, if there's a real live actual corpse –'

'A *live* corpse?'

'Okay, a dead one. It's be sacrilegious to mess around with it.'

'Not to mention gross.'

She laughed softly. 'Yeah, that too.' She looked at him again. Her eyebrows lifted. 'What do you think?'

'Let's forget it.'

She shook her head a bit. 'This is really weird. I mean, we both know there's nobody under here. So what're we afraid of?'

'I don't know.'

With the edge of her trowel, she brushed the small pile of soil back into the hole. She patted it down. 'There you go, Digby. Rest in peace.'

They stood up. Julie brushed dirt and pine needles off her knees. 'I guess that's that,' she said.

'Guess so.'

They returned to their packs. Nick watched her crouch down to put away the trowel and close her pack. Like before, he stared at the way her T-shirt clung to her back.

'I'm a chicken, all right,' he thought. 'If I weren't a damn chicken, I would've kissed her.

Do it now.
No. I can't. I just can't.

'That's quite a scar you've got there,' Flash said, taking a trail
cookie from the bag in Karen's hand. The scar was a pale
horseshoe on her forearm. 'How'd you pick it up?'
'A car accident,' she said. She looked away quickly, and
offered a cookie to Benny, who was sitting at the other end of
the fallen trunk. 'What to pass them around?'
Benny took the bag. 'Was it a *bad* accident?' he asked.
'Very bad,' she said.
Benny got up from the log, and gave cookies to the others
sitting on the ground against their packs. There was an uneasy
silence. Flash bit into his cookie and chewed. Obviously, he
shouldn't have mentioned Karen's scar. 'I've got a couple of
doozies myself,' he said. He started to tug his shirt out of his
pants.
'*Arnold*,' Alice said in her warning voice.
Ignoring her, he pulled up his shirt. He stood up an turned
so Karen and Benny could see the small puffy crater in the
flesh just above his hip. Karen wrinkled up her nose. Benny
looked impressed. 'That's from an AK-47 bullet I caught in
'Nam.' He turned around. 'See there? That's the exit wound.'
'How'd it happen?' Benny asked.
'Well, your dad and I were on a strafing run when I
caught a SAM. A surface-to-air missile. Knocked me right
out of the sky. I hit the silk – ejected, you know – and found
myself behind enemy lines.' His head suddenly felt light.
He let his shirt fall, and took deep breaths, fighting the
dizziness. 'Anyway, I spent nine days alone in the jungle . . .
working my way south, dodging pa—' He blinked. Benny's
silhouette was surrounded by a brilliant blue-silver halo.
Shit, he thought, I'm gonna . . . He staggered backward, sat
down heavily on the log, and lowered his head between his
knees.
'Are you all right, honey?' he heard through the loud

ringing in his ears. Alice. 'I knew he shouldn't get started on that. He tries to put on that it was a big adventure, but—'

'Stop,' he mumbled.

'Well, you shouldn't have brought it up.'

He felt a hand on his back. 'Here.' Scott. 'Drink some water.'

Flash nodded. The ringing faded. He raised his head, and blinked. His vision seemed okay again. The girls, beside Alice, were staring at him with wide eyes. Alice was frowning. 'Just a little dizzy spell,' he said. 'Probably the altitude.' He took the canteen from Scott, nodded his thanks, and drank a few swallows of cold water.

'Maybe you'd better lie down,' Alice suggested.

'I'm fine. Think I'll just . . .' He gave the canteen back to Scott and stood up. He still felt shaky, but the dizziness was gone. Walking carefully, he made his way to the shore of the lake. He stepped out on some low, flat rocks. Crouching, he dipped his hands into the chilly water and splashed his face.

Damn, but he'd made a fool out of himself back there. Should've known better.

He heard the crunch of footsteps behind him. Scott stood on a rock to his left. 'You okay?'

'Shit.'

'What was it the sweats?'

'Yeah. Happens now and again. Shit, you'd think fifteen goddamn years'd be enough to get over it. The damn thing's fucked up my whole life.'

Scott tossed a pebble into the water. It made a soft *plip*. 'I guess none of us got out of it unscathed. I have plenty of bad times myself, and I wasn't even shot down.'

'God, I used to love to fly.'

'You were one of the best.'

'I'd probably be a captain, now, like you, if . . . You know what really gets me? It's all in my head. All in my fucked-up head, and there's not a thing I can do about it. Like there's some damn stranger inside here.' He tapped his fingertips against his temple. 'Just hiding in here, scared shitless, and every once in a while he has to pop up and let me know he's still at the controls.' Flash forced a smile. 'Could've been worse. I'd been a grunt, I might be scared to walk.'

Scott smiled. 'Always a bright side.'

They stood up, and turned away from the shining lake. As they walked back towards the others, Flash saw Nick and Julie coming up the trail. 'Dig him up?' he called out.

'Sure did,' Nick said.

'Boy, was he a mess!' Julie added.

Flash sat down on the log and watched the two approaching. Nick's hand was out, closed as if he were holding something.

'He was all dismembered,' Nick said.

'What?' Karen asked, looking stunned.

'All cut up in little pieces.'

'That's not amusing,' Alice said.

Nick and Julie smiled as if it were. Nick stepped in front of the twins, who were resting against their packs with their legs outstretched. 'I brought you girls a souvenir,' he said. 'One of Digby's fingers.'

'Nick!' Alice snapped.

'Catch, Rose,' he made an underhand toss. His sister shrieked as a finger-sized object fell on her lap. Julie cracked up.

'*Nick!*'

'You creep!' Rose yelled, and hurled the stub of wood back at him.

Heather started to laugh. Everyone laughed except Rose and Alice. 'Really juvenile,' Alice said, scowling.

'So,' Flash said, 'what did you really find?'

'Nothing,' Nick told him. 'We decided to leave the thing alone.'

'Poor Digby's been through enough,' Julie explained.

'You didn't find out what's buried there?'

'I guess we'll never know,' Nick said.

Julie nodded. 'One of life's unsolved mysteries.'

Flash looked at Scott and shook his head. 'Our kids, I'm afraid, are a couple of chickens.'

Scott grinned at him. 'As my pappy used to say, "Better a chicken than a ghoul." '

Chapter Twelve

'Must we?' Alice complained. 'Why don't we play cards instead? Do you play bridge, Karen?'

'Not very well, I'm afraid.'

'I want a story,' Rose protested.

'Me, too,' said Heather.

'You girls were frightened out of your wits last night.'

'It was *neat*.'

'Too windy for cards,' Arnold said. He broke a dead branch over his knee, and placed both pieces on the fire. 'I'm for a story.'

Alice sighed. She didn't want to be a stick in the mud. On the other hand, she certainly didn't want a repeat of last night's shenanigans. The story itself hadn't bothered her. Not much anyway. But her idea of fun did not include being startled from a half sleep by the hysterical screams of her daughters. 'It's all right with me,' she said. She stared across the blazing fire at Nick. 'No funny stuff tonight. Promise?'

'Cross my heart,' he said.

'Who's got a story?' Scott asked.

'A real scary one,' Benny added.

'Karen?' Arnold asked.

'Someone else's turn. I did my damage.'

At least she had the good sense to realise she'd caused all the trouble.

Scott leaned towards the fire, grinning. 'There is, of course, the true story of Digby Bolles.'

'Oh, Dad.' Julie smirked at him.

'Go on,' Alice urged. This story should be harmless enough.

'Is it scary?' Benny asked.

'Listen and find out. Digby came to the mountains, insane with grief, to look for his missing daughter, Doreen.'

'*The* Doreen?' Karen asked.

'The very Doreen who vanished with Audrey so mysteriously earlier that summer. Well, Digby wandered the trails and woods and the high, barren passes, looking everywhere. Soon, his food ran out. But he didn't turn back. He kept searching. He lived on chipmunks and squirrels, which he ate raw.'

'Yuck,' Rose said.

'Squirrel tartare,' said Julie.

'October came, and a terrible blizzard hit. But Digby continued his search. He couldn't find any more squirrels. He was starving to death. Then one night he saw the light of a campfire in the distance. He trudged through the knee-deep snow, and came upon a lone camper. He staggered up to the man, who was kind enough to offer him a bowl of stew. But Digby had lost his taste for stew. The man, who happened to be a surgeon on a fishing trip, looked very appetizing to Digby. And he tasted as good as he looked.' Scott leaned back, folded his arms across his chest, and grinned.

'Is that all?' Benny asked.

'Great story, Pop,' Julie muttered, shaking her head.

'What happened next?' Rose demanded.

'Well, poor Digby eventually starved to death. He ran out of Dr Scholl's.'

'Boo,' Julie said.

'That's awful,' Karen gasped as she laughed.

'Wasn't even scary,' Benny complained.

'The best I could do on short notice.'

Heather looked up at Alice, frowning. 'I don't get it.'

'That's all right, honey. It's just as well.'

'He *ate* the guy, stupid,' Rose explained.

'I know that. What I mean is, if he ate up Dr Scholl's and then died, who buried him?'

'We'll never know,' Scott said. 'One of those great unsolved mysteries of life.'

'It's just a story,' Alice told the girls. 'None of it really happened.'

'But we saw his grave,' Heather said.

'Don't be a dork.'

Alice glared at Rose. 'Watch your language, young lady.

'I want a real story,' Benny said. 'That wasn't even scary. It was okay, but it was just a joke. I want a scary one.'

Nick suddenly sat up straight and slapped his knees. 'I've got it! Let's all get our flashlights and go on a Doreen and Audrey hunt!'

'Neat!' Benny blurted.

Julie looked eager. 'They've gotta be around here some place.'

'Can we, Mom?' Rose asked.

'Not me. I'm perfectly comfortable where I am.'

Arnold turned to Scott. 'What do you think?'

'I'm all for letting the kids go, if that's what they want.'

'Somebody might get hurt,' Alice said. She wanted to protest more strongly, but since Scott seemed to think it was all right . . .

'We'll be real careful,' Nick told her.

'And no funny stuff. I don't want you trying to scare the girls.'

He raised three fingers. 'Scout's honour.'

'Don't go wandering off too far,' Arnold said. 'We don't want to lose you.'

'We'll just circle the lake.'

'Maybe one of us should go with them,' Alice suggested. 'Just in case.'

'Jeez, Mom, nothing's gonna happen.'

'Nick's old enough to take care of things,' Arnold said.

She sighed. 'Well, be very careful. Somebody could fall and break a leg.'

'We'll be careful,' Nick assured her.

A flashlight shone in Benny's eyes as he hurried through the darkness. 'What took you so long?' Julie asked.

'I couldn't find my flashlight.' He shielded his eyes from the beam.

'Have you got it?'

'Yeah.'

Julie lowered her light. It made a pale disk on the ground at her feet.

'Okay,' Nick said. 'Let's stay close together.' Benny heard a slight tremor in the older boy's voice.

He was shivering himself. It was partly the cold, but he felt shrivelled and shaky inside. I'm not scared, he thought. Just excited.

'Now watch where you're walking,' Nick said. 'We'll catch hell if someone gets hurt, and they won't let us do it again.'

'Maybe we can do it *every* night,' Benny said, thrilled by the idea.

They started walking single file along a footpath near the shore. Nick was in the lead, with Julie close behind him. The twins followed Julie. With hoods up, their hair was out of sight, so Benny couldn't tell which was which.

Looking over his shoulder towards the clearing, he saw the glow of the campfire. He wished Karen had come along. It would be a lot more fun with Karen, even if she was grown-up.

He took his flashlight from a pocket of his parka, and

turned it on. The beam lit up the red jeans and sneakers of the girl in front of him. He shone it into the trees to his left. The weird, lurching shadows made him nervous. He swung his light down across the path, over pale rocks along the shore, and onto the water. The surface of the lake was rough from the wind. He swept the beam back and forth over the waves. He made curlicues. It was fun at first. The he thought, what if a hand reaches up out of the water and nobody sees it but me? That's stupid, he told himself. But the image of a dead pale hand rising out of the murky lake wouldn't go away and he began to feel certain he would see it if he kept watching. His skin was prickly with goose bumps. He turned off the flashlight.

'Doreeeen,' Julie called in an eerie voice. 'Audreeey! Come on, everybody.'

Nick took up the call. Then the high voices of the twins joined in. With a shrug, Benny started calling out, too. Their voices rose, mingling with the noise of the wind.

Somebody'll hear, Benny thought. But he kept on shouting, unwilling to be the only silent one of the group. Besides, he told himself, there's nobody around to hear us. Nobody we know about. He glanced over his shoulder, but saw only darkness behind him.

He began to wish he weren't last in line. It'd get him first. Nobody would even know. He'd yell his head off, but with all the others calling for Doreen and Audrey, they wouldn't even hear him. It'd drag him away and . . .

Benny jerked his foot back, but it was too late. The girl yelped and stumbled forward, leaving her sneaker behind. She crashed into the other twin, and they both fell sprawling. 'Jeez, I'm sorry!' he blurted.

'Get off me!' snapped the one on the bottom, pushing her sister.

Benny picked up the shoe.

'What happened?' Nick asked. 'You okay?' He and Julie helped the girls to their feet.

'I tripped,' said the girl Benny had stepped on. She had to be Heather.

'I stepped on her,' Benny admitted.

'Four-eyes!' Rose snapped.

'You klutz!' Julie said. 'Goddamn it!'

'I'm sorry.'

'Jesus, why don't you watch where you're going?'

His throat felt tight. He fought to keep himself from crying as he handed the shoe to Heather. 'I'm awfully sorry.'

'It's okay,' she told him. 'It doesn't hurt much.'

'Stupid jerk.'

'That's enough, Rose,' Nick said. 'It was just an accident. You both all right?'

The girls nodded. Heather put on her shoe.

'Okay, let's get going.'

'Don't walk so close,' Julie warned Benny.

'Maybe I'll just go back to camp.'

'Good idea. Why don't you?'

Turning away, he looked down the dark trail. They were near the end of the lake. There was no sign of the campsite.

Someone tugged the sleeve of his parka. 'Come on,' said a girl's voice. 'It's all right.' He looked around, and saw one of the twins behind him.

'I'm sorry I stepped on you,' he mumbled.

She smiled up at him. 'That's okay. Don't go back, okay?'

'I guess not,' he said. 'Thank you.'

They started walking again. Benny grimaced as he noticed that Heather was limping. He was careful to stay well behind her until the narrow path curved upward and vanished in the rocks at the lake's end. There, he stepped up beside her. She looked at him and smiled. Side by side, they walked over the low slabs of granite near the shore.

With no trees to cast heavy shadows, the night seemed very bright. The lake still looked almost black, but the bare rock was pale, as if painted with milk. Benny was amazed that he could see so well. He saw Julie's hair blowing in the wind, the pattern of Nick's plaid jacket, even the three stripes on the side of Rose's left sneaker. No colours, though. He couldn't make out any colours. Even Heather's jeans, which he knew were bright red, appeared to be a dark shade of grey. He wondered about that. You can see colours with a flashlight, but not by moonlight. It seemed strange.

Nick stopped and took hold of Julie's arm. 'Look,' he said, pointing high.

'What?' Julie asked.

'Way up there. Near the top.'

Benny scanned the pale slope. He saw patches of darkness, a few scrawny trees scattered about like solitary watching men.

'Oh, yeah,' Julie said.

'I don't see anything,' Heather muttered.

'I do,' Rose said. 'Are they dogs?'

'Coyotes,' Nick explained.

Then Benny spotted a pair of lean, grey shapes strutting stiff-legged across a ledge high on the slope. They had long snouts, and tails as bushy as a squirrel's.

'I still don't . . .' Heather began.

Benny crouched to her level and pointed.

'Oh, gosh,' she said.

'Don't worry,' Benny told her. 'They don't hurt anyone.'

'Is that so?' Julie asked. 'A coyote killed a four-year-old girl, last year, in her own backyard.'

'Where?' Nick asked.

'Back home, in L.A. One of those canyon areas. It just came down from the hills behind their yard and mauled her to death.'

'Let's get out of here,' Heather whispered.

'It's all right,' Nick said. 'They're way up there. Besides, they wouldn't try anything with five of us.'

'Unless they're hungry,' Julie added.

Nick laughed nervously, and started walking again. Soon, Benny saw the glow of the campfire on the other side of the lake. When they were directly across from it, he could see the tents and the adults sitting around the fire.

'Hel-lo!' Julie called.

Nobody answered. The wind must to be too loud, Benny thought.

They kept moving. Benny stayed close to Heather. She continued to limp slightly. Sometimes, when they had to climb over clusters of rock, Benny went first and gave her a hand. He liked helping her. She wasn't a snot like her sister. And she still seemed nervous about the coyotes. Every few steps, she looked back. 'I don't like it here,' she said after a while.

'There's nothing to be afraid of,' he told her.

She glanced behind her. 'What's *that*?'

Benny spun around, his heart thudding. 'That? Just a bush.'

'Are you sure?'

'Sure I'm sure,' he said, but he kept staring at the dark, hunched shape. It was barely visible in the shadows of an outcropping no more than two yards away. It *was* a bush, wasn't it? An icy feeling of dread crept up Benny's back. 'Come on,' he said. He took Heather's hand and pulled her away. She sidestepped behind him, still looking back. They hurried to catch up with the others.

Benny was glad to see that they had almost reached the end of the lake. Just below an outcropping ahead, the forest would start again. They would merely have to pick up the trail there, follow it around a bend in the shoreline, and hike straight back to the camp.

Nick, in the lead, disappeared over the top of the outcropping. Julie followed. Rose waited for Benny and Heather, then started down.

Benny looked back. Nothing was approaching from the rear. He let Heather go ahead of him. As she climbed down, Nick, at the bottom, suddenly lurched backward and swung an arm against Julie. With a yelp, Rose whirled around and began to scurry up the rocks. 'It's *them*!' she cried out. 'Doreen and Audrey!'

Heather twisted around. Benny saw terror on her moon-washed face. She lunged up and he grabbed her outstretched arm and yanked her to the top.

Julie pressed a hand to her thumping heart. 'Christ, you scared the crap out of us.'

'We were . . . uh . . . getting a trifle nervous ourselves,' said the buxom girl in the sweatshirt.

'We heard you coming,' said the one in the cowboy hat. She had a husky, confident voice. Her face glowed as she sucked on a cigarette. 'You from the campfire?'

'Yeah,' Nick said. Turning away, he called to the twins and Benny. 'It's all right! Come on down.'

'We didn't know anyone was around,' Julie said. 'Are you camped here?'

'Just off in the trees,' said the one in the hat.

'Don't you have a fire?' Nick asked.

'I wanted one,' said the other.

'A fire just makes you colder. And it kills your night vision. And it lets everyone for ten miles know you're there. Not real healthy when you're three girls camping alone.'

'Three of you?' Nick asked.

'Barb's back at camp.'

'You're not Doreen and Audrey, I take it,' Julie said.

'Who?'

'I didn't think so.' At the sound of footsteps behind her Julie turned around. Benny and the twins were coming slowly forward. 'They're not Doreen and Audrey,' she said.

The girl in the cowboy hat tapped ash off her cigarette. 'This Doreen and Audrey, you looking for them or something?'

Julie explained, telling briefly of Karen's story and how they'd used it as an excuse, tonight, to explore the lake's shoreline.

'Something like a snipe hunt,' said the girl in the hat.

'More like a ghost hunt,' said the other.

'If we'd known, we could've screamed it up for you.'
'I almost did anyway. Still jumpy from that nut case.'
'What's that?' Nick asked.
The girl folded her arms across her sweatshirt and looked at her friend. 'We'd better warn 'em.'
'Which way are you guys heading?'
'Over to the Triangle Lakes area,' Nick said.
'Then you'll be heading over Carver Pass, tomorrow. You know the area?'
'Just from maps.'
'Well, there's a couple of lakes just the other side of the pass. The Mesquites. We stopped at one of them for lunch today, and ran into some crazy old bag.'
'A real weirdo.'
'We went in swimming, and she popped up out of nowhere and started raving about water snakes.'
'Scared the hell out of us.'
'Speak for yourself. Anyway, I didn't see any snakes. I think she was just some kind of lunatic trying to get rid of us. I wouldn't worry much about her, if I were you guys. She might even be gone, by now.'
'Might not,' her friend countered.
'If you stop there, just don't be too surprised if you run into her, that's all.'
'Sounds like a good place to avoid,' Julie said. The ranger, she remembered, had already advised them to pass up the Mesquites. Did he know about the crazy woman? That didn't seem likely.
'I mean, we don't want to scare you,' said the girl in the sweatshirt. 'She didn't *do* anything. Just yelled at us. But she was definitely creepy. She had this look in her eyes. And she wasn't even dressed like a camper. I mean – do you believe it? – she was actually wearing a dress!'
'Sort of a housedress,' added the other girl, mashing her cigarette stub on the sole of her boot. 'A faded old thing.'
'And hiking boots.'

292

'Did you see her knife?'

'Knife?'

'On her belt. Looked like a bowie knife. A *huge* sucker.'

'Lovely,' Julie muttered. 'A crazy woman with a bowie knife. I think we'll stay away from that lake for sure.'

Chapter Thirteen

Karen hung upside down in the overturned car, clawing for the seat-belt buckle, unable to find it. 'Buckle up for safety, buckle up,' the old jingle taunted her. 'I'll warm you up,' said a voice from the window.

She knew what she would see if she turned her head, and the thought of it terrified her. She didn't want to see. But she couldn't stop herself. Her head turned slowly towards the open window. Go away! she thought. I'll shut my eyes and he'll go away. She shut them, but her eyelids were transparent and she gazed at the charred face. Wisps of smoke curled out of its empty sockets, the hole where its nose should have been, its mouth.

'Turnabout's fair play,' it said, blowing smoke into her eyes. The mouth twitched in a blistered grin, cracking the black flesh of its cheeks.

'No!' she cried. 'It wasn't my fault!'

He thrust a gasoline spout at her face. The foul liquid gushed out, stinging her eyes, filling her nostrils. She opened her mouth for a breath and gasoline filled it, choking her.

He grabbed her shoulder. She tried to pry the fingers

loose. They were dry and brittle, and she knew they would break off if she pulled hard enough.

'Karen!'

She woke up, gasping. Scott was kneeling beside her, hand on her shoulder. 'Are you okay?' he whispered.

'Thank God you woke me.'

'Must've been a hell of a nightmare.'

'It was.' With trembling fingers, she found the zipper tag inside her sleeping bag and slid it down. She rolled onto her side to make room for Scott. He climbed in, pulled the zipper shut, and took her into his arms. Like last night, he wore only jockey shorts. His back was smooth and cold under her hands.

'You're shaking,' he said.

'So are you.'

'I'm frozen.'

'I'm just scared out of my wits.' She hugged him tightly.

'Chased by boogeymen?'

'Something like that.' She let out a deep sigh. 'I haven't had one like that in a long time.'

'Sleeping on the hard ground'll do that to you. I've been having some pretty wild dreams myself. Mostly about you.'

'Not nightmares, I hope.'

'No indeedy.' He pulled her sweatshirt up so she was bare against his belly and chest. Gently, he stroked her back. 'I'll tell you mine if you tell me yours.'

'You don't want to hear mine.'

'Might help to talk about it. Maybe we can figure out what it means.'

'I know what it means. And what brought it on, too – that business about the scars this afternoon.'

His hands stopped moving. They pressed Karen closer against him. 'Your accident?' he whispered.

'Yeah. Only it's not Frank trapped in the car, it's me. He was crouched by the window . . . all burnt up. He sprayed me with gas . . .'

'Good Christ.'

'You woke me up before he got a chance to light it.'

'Must've been awful.'

'I've had it worse, sometimes. I usually wake up about the time he strikes the match, but a couple of times . . . I'm on fire and he crawls in through the window and . . .' She suddenly gagged.

Scott stroked the back of her head. 'It's all right,' he said. 'Shh.'

'Sorry.'

'It's all right. I'll tell you about my dreams.'

'Yours are nice, right?'

'Very nice. This morning – yesterday morning? – I dreamed it was raining and you came out of your tent in a clear plastic poncho, and nothing else.'

'You're making this up.'

'No. Honest. The rain was coming down real hard. Your hair was all matted down. Your face was slick and dripping. Water was streaming down the outside of your poncho, and I could see gooseflesh underneath. And your nipples were erect.'

'Like now?'

A hand went to her breast. 'Like now.'

She sighed as he fingered the nipple.

'One thing was weird, though.'

'What?'

'You know how dreams are.'

'Weird.'

'Right. Well, you didn't have any pubic hair. You'd shaved it off.'

'This dream of yours is getting me hot.'

'Me, too.' His hand slid down, caressing her belly. It pushed inside her sweatpants. Slowly, it moved lower. 'Just a dream,' he said.

'I could shave it.'

'It's nice this way.'

'Hey, if you dream it's shaven, that's an expression of a

frustrated desire, right? I'll do it. One of these days. It'll be a' – his sliding finger took her breath away – 'a surprise.'

'Want to hear the rest of the dream?'

'There's more?'

'Sure.' His hand moved away, drawing a slick trail up her skin. He started pulling at the bow in her drawstring. 'I said, "You must be cold. What happened to your clothes?" And you told me Julie had stolen them.'

'Significant, that.'

'She told you she'd hidden them so you'd have to stay in the tent.'

'Away from you?'

'Could be.' The drawstring loose, he pulled at Karen's sweatpants. She helped by kicking them down her legs. The inside of the sleeping bag felt cool and slippery on her bare skin. Scott caressed the back of her leg. His hand slid up her buttock, held it gently. 'Anyway, I said I didn't want you to freeze. We went into my tent so I could get you some warm clothes, but the only clothes you wanted were the ones I was wearing.'

'You have very peculiar dreams.'

'Don't I? So you made me lie down on top of my sleeping bag. You took off your poncho and knelt over me and started to undress me.'

'I stripped you naked?'

'Very slowly.'

She hooked her fingers under the waistband of his shorts, eased the elastic away from his body, and pulled downward. She felt him spring free. With the back of her hand, she caressed the underside of his rigid penis. She tugged the shorts lower. Then she curled her fingers around him, feeling his hardness and his heat. 'Did I do this?' she whispered.

He answered with a moan.

'And did I use my mouth?'

'Yes.'

Her encircling fingers glided up the smooth length of him.
'And did you use your mouth?'

'Yes.'

'Where?'

His hands showed her where, rubbing, fingers sliding in.
She trembled as heat surged through her body. 'Unzip the
bag,' she gasped.

'We'll freeze.'

'Did you freeze in the dream?'

'No, but—'

'Wouldn't you like your dream to come true? Better yours
than mine, right?'

'You don't know everything we did.'

'Show me.'

He did.

'This is when I woke up,' he finally gasped.

'Oh. Oh, Christ. Well, don't stop now!'

'But . . . this is when I—'

'Ad-lib.'

When they were through, Scott pulled the cover of
the sleeping bag over them. They held each other, panting
and sweaty. 'Quite a dream,' Karen whispered, and kissed
him.

Later, he fell asleep. Karen lay cuddled against his long
smooth warmth, feeling his breath on her face, feeling the
slow rise and fall of his chest. She was lazy and content.
She wanted to let herself slip into sleep and wake up in the
morning with him, but she couldn't.

It had always been that way. During their months together,
she constantly longed for him to stay, to spend the whole
night. In the morning, she would make him breakfast. It
would be so wonderful, so complete. Instead, he always had
to leave her bed and hurry home. For the kids. She certainly
didn't blame him, but she wished it were different. Someday,
maybe.

She kissed his eyelids, his mouth. He stirred against her.

His hand moved up her side. It closed gently over her breast. 'You'd better be going,' she whispered.

Scott groaned. 'I'd rather not,' he muttered.

'I know.'

He held her for a long time. He kissed her. Then he eased away and left the sleeping bag. 'Woe, it's cooold,' he gasped, pulling on his underwear.

'Do you want my sweatshirt?'

'No, that's—'

'Please. I don't want you freezing out there.' She tugged it from under her shoulder, and held it out to him. 'You can bring it back tomorrow night.'

'It's a deal.'

As he pulled it over his head, Karen sat up. The cold wrapped her bare skin to the waist.

'Tight fit,' he said. Then he leaned closer and hugged her. She felt his warmth through the softness of the sweatshirt. 'Sleep well,' he said. He kissed her again, then released her and crawled out through the tent flap.

Karen snuggled down in her sleeping bag. She heard his quick footfalls in the leaves, and imagined him rushing towards his tent. She was glad he'd taken her sweatshirt. It was as if part of her had gone with him. She wondered if he would keep it on once he was in his own sleeping bag. Would he wear it and think of her?

Curling up, she reached under her legs and found her sweatpants. She pulled them free. Instead of putting them on, she pressed the limp legs between her thighs. She smoothed the fabric over her belly and breasts. It was soft and warm. With the pants hugged against her, she fell asleep.

Chapter Fourteen

Scott woke up with a bad need to urinate. Lying motionless, he forced one eye open. The tent was murky with morning light. Benny was still asleep, breathing deeply, the red of his stocking cap all that showed of him at the top of his mummy bag.

After returning from Karen's tent, Scott hadn't bothered to put his own cap on. He should've. His head was cold, and the rolled-up jeans he used as a pillow felt hard.

He scooted lower until his head was covered, and brought up an arm to cushion it. A thick, soft sleeve pressed against the side of his face. Karen's sweatshirt. He sniffed it. There was a mild, fresh scent that brought a memory of crawling into her sleeping bag, huddling against her warmth, lifting the sweatshirt up over her breasts. She was without it now. He imagined how she would look wearing only the grey sweatpants. That gave him an erection. Swell, he thought.

He concentrated on how to conceal the sweatshirt. If the kids should see it . . . but Benny was still asleep and he heard no one stirring about the campsite. If he got up now, he could hide it in his pack, which was just outside the tent. He might wrap the sweatshirt in something, just to be safe. No telling whether Julie would actually be asleep.

Hell, if Julie *was* still sleeping, he could take the sweatshirt right over to Karen's tent and . . . no, too risky.

He didn't want to leave the snug warmth. He could just stay here. Take off the sweatshirt and leave it hidden in the bottom of the bag until later. Wait right here until the nice hot sun broke over the ridge . . . But that might be an hour. My teeth are floating!

Quickly, he pulled off the sweatshirt. He shoved it down low in the bag, unzipped the side, and climbed out. He gritted his teeth so hard his jaw ached. Funny, he thought, how the cold didn't bother him so much when he was sneaking out at night. It's all in the mind, he told himself. Sure. Feels more like it's in the bones. Sitting on the slick cover of his sleeping bag, he unrolled his jeans. He pushed his legs in, and leaned back slightly. He stifled a yelp as his shoulders met the cold, wet wall of the tent. Ducking away, he grabbed his cotton shirt and pulled it on.

He snatched up his hiking boots. Fresh socks were tucked inside them. He willed his hands to stop quaking, but they didn't obey. Finally, he managed to tug the socks over his feet. He shoved his feet into the boots. The cold of the boots, still damp from yesterday's sweat, seeped through his socks.

Why the hell does anyone go camping? he asked himself. We're a bunch of damn masochists.

He tucked the laces under the boot tongues. Even if he wanted to tie them, his hands were shaking too badly.

He crawled towards the tent flap, then remembered Karen's sweatshirt. He glanced at Benny. Still asleep. Reaching into the warmth of his sleeping bag, Scott pulled out the sweatshirt. He tucked it inside his shirt, and crawled outside.

He glanced at the two sleeping bags, some twenty feet away, stretched out side by side near the circled rocks of the fireplace. They didn't seem quite as far apart as the first night. Interesting. The tan hood of Julie's warm-up suit was all he could see of her. He quickly opened his pack, stuffed the sweatshirt deep inside, and rushed off into the trees behind the tents.

When he returned, he felt a lot better. If he could just get a fire started, he knew he would feel terrific. Fooling with it, though, he'd be sure to wake up Julie and Nick.

Their sleeping bags were no more than a yard apart. Very interesting, that. He was glad Julie seemed to like the boy. The way the trip had started, he'd been afraid of a disaster. Since meeting Nick, however, she'd been acting civil. Her resentment of Karen's presence seemed to have faded to the point where it was hardly noticeable. He supposed he could thank Nick for that.

And for picking up Julie's spirits in general. After getting dumped by that turkey, Clemens, she needed a friend.

O'Toole the matchmaker.

He took a small satchel and towel from his pack, and walked silently past the tent, heading for the stream. He smiled as he walked.

Julie would croak if she knew he'd planned it this way. When Flash first mentioned taking his family on a week-long backpacking trip, Scott had imagined spending time in the high mountains alone with Karen. It'd be a shame, though, to leave the kids home. Maybe a trip would help to pull Julie out of her depression . . . Then he thought of Flash's son, a handsome, reliable kid, a bit on the quiet side, but only a year older than Julie. If the two should hit it off at all, Julie might forget about that rat Clemens and start enjoying life again. So he'd suggested to Flash that their families join forces for the trip, and Flash had jumped at the idea.

Seems the little scheme had paid off.

The two kids were getting along pretty well – even better than Scott had expected. They didn't act smitten, but it was obvious that they enjoyed each other's company, and who knew what might be going on in their minds? Better, maybe, not to know. Just be glad Julie's back to normal.

At the stream, he spotted a place where sunlight slanted down through a gap in the trees. The bright swath, hazy with dust motes, fell upon a cluster of rocks not far away. He tramped through the bushes and stepped out onto the rocks. For a long time, he stood motionless, letting the warmth seep into him.

When he felt sufficiently thawed, he took off his shirt. He crouched low and cupped the cold water into his mouth. Then he brushed his teeth. He managed to raise a thin lather on his face, using a biodegradable soap, and began to shave with a straight razor.

'You're a terrible disappointment.'

He looked downstream. Karen, in her sweatpants and parka, was standing on a log bridge, arms folded across her chest, staring at him. 'Come on over here where it's warm,' he called. He continued to shave while she hurried towards him. She leaped onto a flat rock beside him.

'Oh, this is better.'

'And why am I such a disappointment? Or don't I want to know?'

'Using a razor,' she said in a mocking tone. 'I would've expected a macho guy like you to shave with a dull knife.'

'Tried it once. Half my face came off with the whiskers. This is far superior. Gives a nice, close shave without the inconvenience of a bloodbath.' Smiling up at her, he said, 'Did you come by for a shave?'

A blush darkened her face. 'My legs, you mean?'

'Also your legs, if you like.'

'Nasty man.'

'Is that a no?'

'Other people are up and around.'

'Damn.' He swirled the blade through the water, wiped it dry across a leg of his jeans, and folded it shut. He splashed water on his face. When the soap was rinsed off, he picked up his towel. 'Sleep well?' he asked as he dried his face.

'Like a rock.'

'No more dreams?'

'Not bad ones. How about you?'

'I'll tell you about mine tonight.'

'Oh ho-*ho*!'

'When I bring back your sweatshirt.' He stood up and lowered the zipper of her parka. She wore nothing under it. He slid his arms inside and around her back, and pulled her against him. She was smooth and warm.

'Good morning,' she said.

He kissed her.

Then there were voices in the distance. Reluctantly, Scott eased away from her.

'Nobody's here yet,' she said, and lifted his hands to her breasts. She held them there. Her nipples were firm under his palms. She sighed and her head tilted back, eyes shut against the sun.

'Wanton woman,' Scott whispered.

'Wantin' you,' she said. She pressed his hands firmly against her, then let go.

Scott moved his hands down the undersides of her breasts, down her ribs, inward as her velvety skin sloped to her belly. Then he pulled together the lower corners of her parka and fitted the zipper into its slot. He raised the tab about three inches. 'There.'

'Oh, charming.'

Someone came tramping through the bushes. With an exaggerated look of alarm, Karen jerked the zipper to her throat. The footfalls grew louder.

Scott had time to turn away, crouch, and slip his razor into his satchel before Flash appeared downstream near the log bridge. The man was already dressed in his knit shirt, plaid shorts, and boots. His mussy fringe of red hair was the only clue that he'd just crawled out of his sleeping bag. He squatted by the stream and dipped an aluminium pot into the water.

'Morning!' Karen called.

He looked over and waved. 'Tally-ho, mates!'

Scott grinned up at Karen. 'Mates?' he asked.

'Nautical jargon,' she said quietly.

'Ah. Afraid he was being a wise guy.' Standing up, Scott yelled, 'Ahoy and avast, are ye of a mind to weigh anchor?'

'Ain't had me coffee yet,' Flash called back.

'Then we'll sail for Java.' To Karen he said, 'Shall we be off?'

'Aye, matey.'

'Meet you in the galley,' Scott called.

They made their way back to camp. Julie still in her

warmup suit, was feeding sticks to the fire. Nick's sleeping bag was empty, but he was nowhere to be seen. One of the twins was walking into the woods with a roll of toilet paper. Alice, bundled in her coat, was tearing open a plastic bag of powdered eggs with her teeth.

'Back in a jiff,' Karen said, and headed for her tent.

In his own tent, Scott saw that Benny was still asleep. 'Up and at 'em,' he said, finding a foot through the down-filled bag and giving it a small shake. The boy raised his head and looked around, one eye covered by his red stocking cap. 'Sleep well?'

'Yeah.' Benny reached into the boot by his head, and pulled out his glasses. The lenses were fogged up. He tugged off his cap and put the glasses on anyway, then scrunched up his face as if that might help him to see better. 'Where'd you go?'

'What?'

'I woke up and you weren't here.'

'I've been up for a while,' Scott told him.

'No, I mean last night.'

Oh, Christ, he thought. He couldn't lie to his son, but how could he tell the truth? 'I took a little walk,' he said.

'See any coyotes?'

'Not one. You better haul yourself out of there and get dressed. Breakfast'll be ready before you know it.' Before Benny might be tempted to question him further, he backed out of the tent.

'Ahoy!' Flash said, walking by with a full pot of water.

'Avast,' Scott said. 'I'll get my stove going.' He took his Primus stove from his pack and carried it over to the fire.

Julie was there, stretched out on her sleeping bag to squeeze the air out before attempting to mash it into its stuff bag.

'Have a good night?' he asked her.

'My feet froze, but aside from that . . .'

'Maybe wear an extra pair of socks.' Hanging onto its key chain, he dangled the stove over the flame to heat the fuel. Thank God that Julie, at least, wasn't aware of his nighttime forays. The truth probably wouldn't upset Benny, but Julie

... If Benny should mention his disappearance last night she'd guess at once what he'd been up to. She might no throw a fit, but her resentment would surface and she would do her best to make everyone miserable. Probably even start sleeping in the tent just so it wouldn't happen again.

Should've just tented with Karen in the first place. Well, with the Gordons along they couldn't have done that anyway.

He swung the stove away from the campfire flames, and set it inside its aluminium holder.

'You got that sucker going yet?' Flash asked, coming up behind him.

'Stand back and get ready to duck.'

Flash scraped the last of his scrambled eggs and bacon bits from the bottom of his dish. 'Ah, that was good stuff. Want me to polish off yours for you?' he asked Rose.

'No.'

'Aw, come on. It'll only weigh you down.'

'Daddy!'

'Let her finish it,' Alice said. 'Have some Grape Nuts if you're still hungry.'

'Bleah.'

'It's good roughage.'

'So is bark. Doesn't mean I want to eat a tree.' He looked at the twins. 'Everything out of your tent?' They nodded as they shoved forkfuls of egg into their mouths. 'Let's get to it, Nick.'

Nick, on the other side of the fire, took a sip of coffee, nodded, and stood up. They went over to the tent and started taking it down. They worked in silence, pulling the guy lines, Flash holding the front upright while Nick folded the rear forward, then easing the front backward. When the tent was flat, they removed the collapsible rods, pulled out the stakes along its sides, and folded it into thirds. Flash rolled it up with the rods inside. Nick held the plastic stuff bag open, and Flash shoved the tent into it.

They stepped over to the other tent, and began to repeat the process.

'So long, over there,' a voice called.

Looking up, Flash saw three teenaged girls through the trees. They were on the main trail, hiking single file.

''Bye,' Nick yelled. 'Have a good trip back.'

'Watch out for the crazy woman,' warned the girl in the lead. Then the three vanished among the trees.

Nick eased the rear of the tent forward.

'Those the gals you ran into last night?' Flash asked.

'Yeah.'

'What's this about a crazy woman?'

'Nothing much,' Nick said. He shrugged as if it were unimportant, but his eyes looked worried. 'They told us they ran into some weird old lady yesterday at a lake the other side of the pass. I guess she yelled at them, or something.'

'What for?'

'I don't know. They just thought she was crazy.'

'Takes all kinds, I guess.'

'Hope we don't run into her.'

'Don't worry about it. Any crazy old bag gives us any lip, we'll stomp her. Right?'

Nick gave a nervous laugh. 'Sure thing.'

Heather grimaced, lips drawn back and teeth clenched, she pushed her left foot into her boot. 'What's wrong Alice asked.

'Nothing.'

'Let me see.' She squatted down beside the girl. 'Take your boot off.'

'Really, Mom, it's all right.'

'I'll be the judge of that.'

With a reluctant sigh, Heather pulled off her boot. She peeled the wool sock down her ankle. The skin above her heel was grey, as if smudged with dirt. She winced when Alice pressed it. 'Arnold, would you come over here?'

He was crouched over his pack, securing its flap. He looked over his shoulder. 'What's wrong?'

'We have an injury here.'

'Oh, shit,' he muttered. He hurried over.

'A bruised Achilles tendon,' Alice said.

Arnold gently rotated the foot. Heather's face showed pain. 'It's all right,' she insisted.

'How did this happen?' Alice asked.

Heather shrugged.

Rose, who'd been sitting on a rock nearby and watching, said, 'I'll tell you. It was that klutz, Benny. He kicked her last night.'

'He didn't *kick* me, he *stepped* on me.'

'Shit.'

'Arnold!'

'Does it hurt much?' he asked.

'No. Really.'

'I thought I saw you limping,' Alice said. 'Good heavens, Heather, why didn't you tell us about it?'

The girl shrugged, and pulled up her sock.

'I bet,' Rose said, 'she just didn't want to get Benny in trouble. She's got a crush on him.'

'I do not!'

'Do, too.'

'Knock it off,' Arnold muttered. He frowned at Heather. 'You can walk on it okay, though, right?'

'Yeah. It's fine.'

'Well, we'll try to take it easy today. If it gives you too much trouble, we'll figure something out.'

'Let's leave her behind,' Rose said. 'So the coyotes can eat her.'

'That's enough out of you, young lady.'

'All right,' Arnold said. 'Let's haul it. I've got a feeling this'll be a long day.'

Chapter Fifteen

Nick stopped at the trail sign. It read, CARVER PASS, 2 MI. Leaning against a rock to ease the weight of his pack, he looked down into the valley. Lake Parker was there in the distance, as blue as the sky, its north shore hidden among the trees. The south shore was mostly barren rock. He spotted the outcropping he'd climbed down last night, and felt a small tremor of the fear that had numbed him when he came unexpectedly upon the two girls. Then he smiled, remembering Rose's shriek and the way she'd scurried up the rocks. It had been quite a little adventure. Damn it, though. Poor Heather. They should've just stayed in camp after all.

'Hand me my water bottle?' Julie asked.

'Sure.'

She turned away. Nick unzipped a side pocket of her pack, and pulled out the green plastic container. He watched Julie tilt the bottle to her lips and drink. Her face was burnished with sunburn, her nose peeling a bit. The leather band of her beret was dark with sweat. When she finished drinking, she offered a drink to Nick. He took a few swallows, and slid the bottle back into her pack.

'This is gonna be a bear,' she said.

'Yeah. Especially for Heather.'

'That idiot brother of mine.'

'Looks like it'll be switchbacks from here to the top.'

'Don't you just love switchbacks?'

'On the bright side, it'll all be downhill to Lake Wilson.'

'If we can just make it to the top.'

Down the trail, Scott and Karen appeared, hiking side by side through the shadows. 'Let's hold it up,' Scott called. 'Wait for the others.'

'How's Heather doing?' Julie asked.

'Holding her own.'

They waited. Soon, Nick saw Rose coming up the trail. His father and mother were a short distance behind the girl. Dad was carrying Heather's red backpack like an unwieldy grocery bag. Nick hurried down. Taking the pack from his father, he saw Benny and Heather. They were far back. Heather, limping along with the aid of Nick's blackthorn stick, laughed at something Benny said. A good sign. At least she wasn't whimpering with pain.

Nick turned away. He trudged up the trail ahead of his parents.

'Is that pretty heavy?' Julie asked.

'Not as bad as ours.'

Karen stepped towards him. 'Let me feel.' She took Heather's pack from his arms. 'Why don't we split up what's in it? We'll each carry some, and nobody'll be stuck with lugging around a full pack all day.'

'Not only pretty, but brilliant,' Dad said. 'Any objections?'

Rose wrinkled her face, but nodded with defeat. Everyone else acted as if it were a great idea. Heather watched, looking embarrassed, while packs were opened and rearranged to make room for her belongings. When her father started to lash her empty pack to his own, she finally objected. 'I can carry that.'

'No trouble,' he told her.

'I'll carry it,' Benny said. His voice was a little whiny. 'It's all my fault.'

'Hey, those things happen,' Dad consoled him. 'Don't blame yourself.'

Benny looked around as if searching for a hole to crawl into. Finding none, he let out a deep sigh. 'I'm sorry, everybody.'

'No sweat,' Scott told him.

'Sure,' Julie said. 'It'll be fun carrying a little extra weight.'

Scott scowled at her.

'I knew we shouldn't have let them go off last night,' Mom said. 'Nobody listens to me. Next time—'

'Let's get this show on the road,' Dad interrupted. 'We've got a mountain to climb.'

Shouldering their packs, they started up the trail again. The trees thinned out, leaving fewer patches of shade, then no shade at all.

Nick and Julie, in the lead, paused often to wait for the others to catch up. Finally, near noon, they stopped at one of the flat areas where the trail turned back on itself in its zigzag up the mountainside. They shed their packs and sat on a boulder. Scott and Karen were a distance down the trail, slowly trudging closer.

'Who ever said backpacking's fun?' Julie asked.

'Not me.'

'Shit.' She lifted the front of her T-shirt and rubbed her sweaty face. Nick glanced at her bare midriff. She pulled the shirt down again. It clung to her. 'Feel like I'm gonna die.'

'At least there's a little breeze.'

'How'd you like to dive in a swimming pool about now?'

'I'd dive into anything that's cold,' Nick said.

'You and me both. Man, this is the pits. How'd we get into this? We could be home right now, having iced tea by the swimming pool.'

'A hamburger and chocolate shake at Burger King.'

'On the other hand . . .'

'What?'

'Well.' Julie looked at him, and shrugged. 'If we weren't up here in this godforsaken armpit of a wilderness, we wouldn't . . . I wouldn't have got to know you. I mean, I'm glad about that anyway.'

The words made Nick's heart pound fast. 'Maybe when we get back, we could – I don't know – go to the movies or something.'

She met his eyes. She smiled slightly. 'By then, you'll be sick of me.'

'Maybe,' he said.

Julie laughed.

'I doubt it, though.'

Karen called, 'Where's the top?'

'Up there someplace,' Julie answered.

'That's the rumour,' Nick added.

'You guys are really burning up the trail,' Scott said. Julie nodded. 'Regular roadrunners.'

Scott and Karen took off their packs. Scott looked as if the strenuous hike had barely fazed him. He wasn't even breathing hard. Karen looked just as good. She fluttered the front of her plaid shirt, then opened the three lower buttons. She gathered up the shirttails and made a knot just below her breasts. 'Nice breeze,' she said. She lay down against her pack, and fanned her face with her floppy hat.

'We thought,' Julie said, 'that this'd be as good a place as any to have lunch.'

'Sounds good,' Scott said.

After a lunch of gorp, dehydrated fruit slices, shortbread cookies, and Tropical Chocolate bars, they resumed the hike. At first, the weight of his pack felt unbearable to Nick. His shoulders and back throbbed with pain, and his legs seemed barely capable of supporting him. He felt like collapsing, but forced himself to take one step after another. Slowly, the torment faded, as if his body were giving up its rebellion, accepting its role as a beast of burden.

He walked behind Julie and matched his stride to hers. Her boots were powdered with trail dust. One sock was slightly lower than the other. The seat of her white shorts had two half-moons of yellow-brown dirt from sitting down, and he could see the outline of her panties through the thin fabric. The panties were very brief. Like a bikini bottom. 'Did you bring a bathing suit?' he asked.

'Sure. You?'

'Yeah.'

'Water's so cold, though. We'd freeze our butts.'
'Those girls swam.'
'Must be polar bears.'
'Probably not bad, once you're in it.'
'Depends. Some lakes aren't so bad.'
'Warmer if they're shallow,' Nick said.
'Depends on the runoff, too.'
'Way I feel, I'd swim in ice cubes.'
'We get to Wilson in time, I'd give it a try.'

They trudged along in silence. Looking up the slope, Nick could see where the mountainside ended. It didn't seem far above them, but he realised that the view might be deceiving. The area that appeared to be the top from here might turn out to be a shelf, the rest of the mountain farther back and out of sight. He tried not to let his hopes get too high.

He and Julie were still a distance below the apparent top, however, when the trail, instead of switching back, continued forward and curved around the slope. A strong, cool wind blew against Nick. Julie stopped. He moved up beside her. She smiled at him. 'What do you know,' she said.

'Didn't think we'd ever make it.'

Ahead of them, the trail wound over a flat, barren area between two bluffs. Then it dropped out of sight. In the distance, Nick saw peaks shrouded by clouds. A few minutes of hiking took them across the level area. They shed their packs and sat on a block of granite. From there, the trail started gradually downward along a narrow ridge. To the right of the ridge was a deep ravine. To the left was a shallow valley with two lakes. The lower lake, no more than a hundred feet below their perch, was larger than the other, bounded by rocky slopes except for a small stand of pine at its western shore. The upper lake, just above its southwest end, looked treeless and even more desolate.

'Must be the Mesquites,' Nick said.
'The ranger was right. They're the pits.'
'I don't see anyone down there.'

'The Madwoman of the Mesquites?' Julie asked.

'She's probably moved on. I mean, who'd want to camp there? Looks like the backside of the moon.'

'I hope Lake Wilson's better than these.'

'The ranger said it was nice. Besides, it's about a thousand feet lower.'

'What is it, three or four miles?'

'Something like that.'

Nick followed the trail with his eyes. It passed above Lower Mesquite, and vanished behind a steep wall of granite. 'At least it'll be downhill,' he said.

'Sometimes that's worse.'

'Yeah. Gets you in the toes.'

'And everywhere else.'

Scott and Karen arrived. They took off their packs, and settled down on a nearby boulder. Karen lifted her blouse again and tied it in front as she'd done when they stopped for lunch. 'Ah,' she said, 'that wind's terrific.'

'I don't like the looks of those clouds,' Scott said.

The clouds hugging the distant peaks were thick and grey. Nick figured that they must be at least ten miles away.

'I don't think I'd mind a little rain,' Karen said.

'It'd put a damper on dinner.'

'Maybe it'll miss us,' Julie said.

Scott shook his head. 'Looks like they're coming our way. These mountain storms are unpredictable, though. Could pass over us without leaving a drop. Or we might be in for it. Only time will tell.'

'Time wounds all heals,' Karen said.

Time's like hiking, then,' Scott added.

'Like Benny,' Julie said. 'He's the greatest heel wounder of all time.'

Scott looked pained. 'Why don't you ease up on that? Benny feels bad enough without your help.'

'He's not here.'

Scott ignored the remark and stared out over the valley.

Karen leaned back against her pack. She folded her hands on top of her head, mashing the soft crown of her hat. 'I wonder,' she said, 'if Heather can make it as far as Wilson.'

Chapter Sixteen

Ettie watched with despair through a crevice in the rocks. Luck had sure turned against them. Maybe the Master was dishing out punishment, paying them back for what Merle did to those other two campers – claiming he offered them down when he did no such thing, but just went at them for his own need and then laid it on the Master.

Then again, maybe Ettie wasn't judging the matter right. Could be a test. Maybe even an offering. She'd have to find out for sure, so she'd know what to do.

One thing was sure: the campers were fixing to stay. They were down in the clearing by the trees, setting up four tents, a kid in glasses rounding up rocks to build a fireplace.

Ettie eased away from the crevice and made her way across the slope to the cave entrance. Turning sideways, she squeezed through the opening. The murky light inside seemed very dark after the brightness, but she saw the dim shape of Merle sprawled out on one of the sleeping bags. She sat down on the other bag. Sunlight from the fissure overhead made a hot band along her crossed legs. She leaned back slightly against the cool granite wall.

'You awake, Merle?'

'Just laying here. I sure like this sleeping bag. It's the softest thing.'

'We've got some folks down by the lake.'

He sat up so fast that it startled Ettie.

'Just stay put,' she warned.

He was almost to his feet, but he dropped down again as if his legs had gone soft. 'Can't I see 'em, Ettie?'

'Just sit still.'

'Who are they?' he asked.

'How'd I know that?'

'They snooping?'

'They're putting up a camp. One's soaking her foot in the lake. She came limping in pretty bad. I guess she hurt herself in the pass. I figure that's maybe why they stopped.'

'A girl?'

'Don't get your heat up. They got three men along.'

'Can't I just look?'

'I'll tell you when you can look. We're gonna stay put till I've got it figured out.'

'Well, how many are there?'

'Nine.'

'Nine, and just three of 'em men?'

'There's some kids, don't look older than twelve. And three women.'

'How old are they?'

'Never you mind.'

'Are they pretty?'

'Fetch me the coyote skin.'

Obediently, Merle crawled past the head of her sleeping bag. He rummaged through a dark pile at the far end of the chamber and came back with the pelt of a coyote he had snared two weeks before. 'What're you fixing to do?' he asked.

'Read the signs. Maybe these folks come here by chance, or maybe the Master sent them.'

'Think He wants 'em offered down?'

'I don't know what to make of it. Could be we're out of favour and He sent them to punish us.'

'Why'd He do that, Ettie?'

'Not saying He *did*. I'm saying He might've. Now you just shush, and let me find out.'

She got to her knees and spread the coyote pelt on the sleeping bag. Then she unsheathed her knife. 'O great Master,' she intoned, 'Shadow of the Dark, give us a sign that we, Your servants, may know Your will.' With the knife, she carved a crescent on her left forearm. Blood spilled out, pattering on the coyote skin. 'Give us wisdom, Master, that we may abide by Your way.' She slowly waved her cut arm back and forth over the skin, then held it steady while she sheathed her knife. 'Count backward from thirteen,' she told Merle. Together, they counted down. When they reached one, she swung in her arm and tied a kerchief around the wound.

She stared down at the hide. The band of sunlight made a bright path across it, showing streaks and pools of blood on the pale skin. Except for the sunlit area, the rest was in deep shadow.

'What'd He say?' Merle asked.

'Get me matches.'

He dug a book of matches out of his jeans and gave it to Ettie. She plucked a match free, struck it, and bent low over the hide. By the light of the wavering flame, she studied the pattern of her spilled blood: its trails of shiny droplets, its loops, the way its shiny threads connected larger blotches, the shapes of the small puddles. A cold, sick feeling spread through her as the meaning became clear. She moaned.

'What's wrong?'

'Shh.' She shook out the match, lit another, and once again studied the map of blood. No, she hadn't been mistaken. She dropped the match. A spatter of blood killed its flame in a hiss.

'Is it bad, Ettie?'

She stared at her son. He was on his knees, looking down at the pelt. His face was a dim blur in the shadows. Reaching out, she patted his cheek. 'Nothing's gonna come of it, honey.

It's nothing to fret over. We're just gonna stay hidden here till they go away.'

As Merle reached for the pelt, Ettie swept a hand across it, smearing the blood.

'Shit!' he cried.

'It's not for your eyes.'

'Wouldn't of hurt nothing,' he said in a pouty voice.

Ettie folded the pelt over. She pressed down on the fur with both hands, and rubbed it hard.

''Least you can do is tell me what it said,' Merle complained. 'Must've said more than just stay in the cave.'

'*It* didn't say to stay in the cave, *I* did.'

'Well, what'd the blood say?'

'Said we better not mess with the folks down there. They brought death.'

Merle was silent. He stared down at the pelt for a while, then picked it up and peeled it open and moved it through the path of sunlight, squinting at the red smears. 'Is that what it really said?' he asked, sounding doubtful.

'You calling me a liar, son?'

'Well, no. But maybe you didn't read it right.'

'I read it right. Now, you got any notions about the women down there, put them out of your head, or you'll get us both killed. Do you understand?'

'I guess.'

'That's not much of an answer, Merle.' She crawled along her sleeping bag to the dimly lit gap of the cave's entrance. There, she sat down and crossed her legs, blocking the only way out.

'You don't gotta do that,' Merle whined.

'I'll do it, just the same.'

Chapter Seventeen

With a sooty rock in each hand, Julie stepped over to the fireplace. 'Here's a couple more for you,' she told Benny, and dropped them to the ground beside him.

'Thanks,' he muttered. He didn't look up. He lifted one of the rocks and added it to the low, circular wall he was building.

'Don't look so pitiful,' Julie said.

'It's all my fault.'

'That's right, Bonzo. Look on the bright side. At least you didn't break her foot.'

'Thanks. You're real nice.'

'Ain't I, though?' Trying to brush the black from her hands, she walked towards the lakeshore. Nick was there, sitting on a rock beside his sister while she soaked her left foot. 'How's it going?' Julie asked.

'Fine,' Heather said.

'Haven't seen any water snakes,' Nick said.

'Well, that's a relief. Any crazy old women?'

'Not a one.'

'Terrific.' She stepped out onto a low flat rock, squatted down, and washed her hands. The water felt cold, but not numbing. 'Still interested in a swim?' she asked.

'Sure.'

'Can I swim, too?' Heather asked.

'Better check with Mom.'

Julie shook the water from her hands and leaped ashore. 'See you in a couple of minutes,' she called over her shoulder.

Benny, still crouched by the fireplace, raised his head as Julie approached. His nose was wrinkled, upper teeth bared, like a snarling dog. Just his way to keep his glasses from slipping off. He shoved them up with a forefinger and stopped snarling.

'We're going for a swim,' Julie said. 'Wanta come?'

His head tilted sideways. He looked confounded. 'Are *you* going in?'

'That's the picture.'

'What about the water moccasins?'

'If you're scared, stay here.' In front of the tent, she dug into her backpack and dragged out her towel. It was still slightly damp from that morning's washing up. She hung it over a shoulder, and continued to search until she found he bikini at the very bottom.

Dropping to her knees, she crawled inside the tent. The tent had only been up for a few minutes, but already the trapped air felt stifling. Karen's sleeping bag was laid out. It looked thick and soft. Had it belonged to anyone but Karen, Julie would've sat on it while she changed. Instead, she sat on the tent floor, the ground hard under her as she stripped off her clothes.

She was on her back, naked, legs in the air, pulling the small white bottom of her bathing suit over her feet when the tent flap opened. Sunlight spilled onto her.

'Sorry,' Karen blurted. The flap dropped, shutting out the light.

Julie muttered, 'Shit.' Raising her rump, she pulled the pants into place. She sat up. Her heart was thudding. With shaky fingers, she knotted the strings of the top behind he neck, stretched the flimsy fabric of the triangles down over her breasts, and reached behind her to tie the back. 'Okay,' she called. 'You can come in.'

Karen ducked inside. She had a one-piece black swimsuit in her hand. 'Sorry about that,' she said. 'I didn't realise you were in here.'

'You could've asked,' Julie muttered, still fumbling with the strings at her back.

Karen sat down on the bag, and started to unlace her boots. 'Hot in here,' she said.

'You going in the lake?'

'Yeah. Benny and your dad are getting into their trunks.'
She tugged her boots off, and sighed with pleasure. 'That
water's gonna feel awfully good.'

Julie got the strings tied, but didn't move. She watched the
woman peel off a sock and inspect her foot in the murky blue
light. 'Well, no blisters on this one. How're your feet holding
out?'

'That's *my* business,' she said.

Karen stared at her. In the gloomy light, Julie couldn't tell
whether she looked angry or just hurt. 'Sorry,' Karen finally
said. 'I was just trying to be friendly.'

'Don't bother.'

In a quiet voice, she asked, 'What are you afraid of?'

'I'm not afraid of you, that's for sure.'

'You're afraid of liking me, I think.'

'What, you're so irresistibly charming I've gotta be a nut
case if I'm not kissing the goddamn ground you walk on?
Forget it. I just don't like you, that's all. I wish Dad had never
met you.'

'Your father and I . . . we love each other.'

'Ain't that just dandy,' Julie said through a tightness in her
throat.

'You knew that, didn't you?'

'I'm not blind.'

'We love each other, Julie, but don't think for one instant
that he loves you or Benny any less because of that. You're his
daughter. He's been with you all your life, and he'll love you
as long as he lives, no matter what. You'll always be part of
him in a way I can never be. I'm not taking him away from
you. I couldn't even if I wanted to.'

Julie stared down at her folded hands.

'Would you be happier if I stopped seeing your father?'

'I don't know,' she mumbled. 'I guess not.'

'What would make you happy?'

'I don't know.' She gnawed her lower lip as tears filled her
eyes. 'I don't want him hurt, that's all.'

'You think I'd hurt him?'

Shrugging, she wiped her eyes. 'Everything was fine till you came along.'

'Your dad wasn't fine. He was lonely.'

'He had us.'

'And he had a wife who'd run out on him. That left a big hole inside. Maybe he didn't let you see the hurt because he didn't want to make things worse for you and Benny, but it was there. And it isn't so bad any more.'

'Thanks to you, huh?'

'Thanks to the way we feel about each other.'

Julie took a deep, trembling breath. She picked up her towel, and rubbed the tears from her face. 'Nick's waiting for me,' she muttered.

'You'll make his day when he sees you in that bikini.'

'Trying to butter me up?'

'Yep. It's the truth, though. Look, Julie, I'm going to be your friend whether you like it or not. Because I love your father and I like you.'

'You like me, huh? Sure.'

'I do. And you'll get to like me, too, sooner or later. Before you know it, you and I are going to be buddies. Do you know why?'

'Why?'

'Because I'm irresistibly charming.'

Julie cracked a smile. 'My ass,' she said, and crawled out of the tent. The bright sunlight made her eyes ache. Standing, she brushed some dirt and pine needles off her knees. She felt strange – her mind vague, her muscles weak, her legs trembling. As she walked towards the lake, she tried to make sense out of her encounter with Karen. Her mind couldn't hold steady on it. Maybe everything had changed. Or maybe the talk had just confused her.

Nick, standing at the shore, was watching the twins wade in. He had a towel draped around his neck, and wore blue shorts that looked like the ones he slept in. When Julie walked closer, he turned around as if sensing her approach. He gazed at her. She blushed, uncomfortably aware of her near naked-ness and the way her breasts jiggled with the motion of her walk. 'All set?' she asked.

Nick smiled thinly, nodded, and quickly turned away.

Julie realised that she liked how she'd felt while he was staring. Beneath her uneasiness, there'd been a kind of thrill. She found herself dashing past Nick, the chill water splashing up her legs. Knee-deep, she spun around, scooped up water with both hands, and flung it at him.

'No!' he cried. He raised his arms to block the cold shower, and cringed as it splashed against him.

Julie stood up straight. She frowned with pretended concern. 'Oh, I'm sorry. Did that get you?'

He looked astonished for a moment. Then, laughing, he lunged forward, drove his hands into the water, and launched an icy barrage that pelted Julie from face to knees. Staggering away, she lost her footing. She yelped and fell, flapping her arms and hitting the lake flat on her back. She shuddered as the chill water closed over her. After the first shock, though, it didn't feel so bad. She pushed against the rocky bottom and sat up.

'Are you okay?' Nick asked. He sounded worried.

She wiped her eyes clear, and blinked up at him. 'Was it a graceful entry?'

Rose and Heather were giggling.

'Beautiful,' Nick told her.

'I'm so glad.' Her bikini top felt slightly awry. She made sure her breasts were still in it, gave the front a small adjustment, and stood up. Nick stared as the water streamed off her.

'How's the water?' Dad called from behind him.

'Cold,' she answered.

Karen was walking along close beside Dad, holding his hand. Her one-piece black suit clung to her like shiny skin. It was open in front with a wide, deep V that extended down to her belly. The lower part of the suit seemed even more revealing, cut so high at the sides that it left her hipbones bare and formed a long, lean triangle down to her groin.

Benny, off to one side and slightly behind Karen, was agape as he stared at her.

Someone whistled. Julie spotted Flash near one of the tents, his arms loaded with firewood. The whistle caught Nick's attention. He looked over his shoulder at the same time that Karen turned around to say something to Flash. Julie sighed. The suit was backless and almost bottomless, so narrow down the buttocks that it left the sides of her cheeks bare. They were lean, and smooth.

'Come on, Nick.'

He kept staring.

'Forget it. She's already taken.'

He faced Julie, innocently raising his eyebrows as if he'd been caught daydreaming by a teacher.

'Besides,' Julie said, 'isn't she a little old for you?'

His eyebrows dropped to their normal level, and the corners of his mouth turned up. 'Yeah,' he said. 'She's sure something to look at, though.'

'Tell me about it,' Julie muttered, feeling a little sick.

'She's gorgeous, in fact.'

'Not to mention irresistibly charming.'

Nick opened his mouth to speak, but Julie whirled away and dived, hitting the water flat out and swimming hard. Bastard, she thought. Damn it all to hell. The bitch *is* irresistible. Has Dad head over heels, and Benny damn near swooning. Even Nick's got the hots for her. Parading around damn near naked. Flash whistling at her. He didn't whistle at me. What am I, dog food? Damn her! Wants to be my friend. Sure, sure.

Julie realised she was crying, sobbing into the water. She choked and came up for air.

Wonderful. Drown yourself.

She kept her head above the surface, but continued to

swim as hard as she could. She didn't look back. She was near the centre of the lake, so she turned to the right and swam parallel to the shore.

She saw a small inlet where a slab of granite slanted out of the water. She sidestroked towards it. When she reached the rock, she crawled up it and lay down flat. She crossed her arms under her face. The surface was hot and gritty against her skin. The sun on her back felt good. She panted for air, and tried to stop sobbing.

Then she heard splashes. Someone swimming not far away. Coming closer.

Go away, she thought. Whoever you are, go away and leave me alone.

Down near her feet, the splashing stopped. She didn't bother looking around.

'You're pretty fast.' Nick.

'A regular speed demon,' she muttered.

'Mind if I come up and join you?'

'I don't care.'

She heard a swoosh of water, then dribbling sounds as he crawled up the rock. He sat down close beside her and leaned back, bracing himself up with stiff arms. His slim belly, streaming with water, heaved as he gasped for breath. 'You mad at me?' he asked.

'Why should I be mad?' Julie muttered, and turned her head aside so she wouldn't have to look at him.

'I don't know. Because I made you fall?'

'It wasn't that.'

'Then you *are* mad at me. What'd I do?'

'Nothing,' she mumbled.

'I don't get it.'

'That's okay. You don't have to get it.'

'Is it because I was staring at you? Like the other night when you yelled at me?'

'I didn't yell,' she protested.

'You said, "Take a picture. It lasts longer." If that's it, I'm

sorry. Really. It's hard not to stare, though. You're so . . .' He
hesitated.

'What?'

'Well, you know – beautiful. I keep trying not to stare, but
then you come along in something like . . . like what you're
wearing, and . . .'

She raised her head and looked at Nick. He was frowning
out at the lake. 'You think I was angry because you were
staring at me?'

'Well, yeah.'

'I didn't mind that.'

'Are you sure?'

'I'm sure.' Julie rolled over. She folded her hands under
her head to cushion it. Her heart was racing, and her mouth
was very dry. She licked her lips. Nick continued to gaze
forward. 'I got upset, if you really want to know, because you
were staring at Karen instead of me.'

He shook his head as if rejecting the idea, then turned and
met her eyes. He seemed to be frowning and grinning at the
same time. He looked very confused. 'Are you *serious*?'

'I know I shouldn't blame you. I mean, you're a guy and . . .
like you said, she's gorgeous. And that bathing suit of hers . . .'

'You won't . . .' Nick paused, shaking his head some more.

'I won't what?'

'Never mind,' he muttered, and looked away.

'Come on, tell me.'

'It's too embarrassing.'

Julie smiled. 'Embarrassing for who?'

'Me, I guess. Maybe you, too.'

She braced herself up on her elbows. 'Go on.'

'Well . . . about Karen's suit. When I was looking at her?
You won't believe this but I was imagining how it would look
on you.'

'You're kidding,' Julie said. Her voice came out in a
whisper. Her heart was thundering, and she was short of
breath. She sat up straight to breathe better.

'I'm not kidding,' Nick said. 'I mean, it's nothing against your bikini. I just, uh, tried to picture how you'd look in . . . I *told* you it'd be embarrassing.'

'A little bit,' she admitted.

He leaned forward, put his hands on his knees, and hung his head. 'I guess I'm kind of a lech.'

'I guess you are,' Julie said. For the first time, she noticed the sounds of distant laughter and splashing. An outcropping of rock, however, blocked her view of those in the lake. She put a hand on Nick's back. He flinched slightly startled by her touch, and looked into her eyes. For a long time, while her hand moved slowly up and down, they gazed at each other. His eyes lingered on hers, studied every part of her face, followed the curve of her neck, glanced at her breasts, and returned quickly to her eyes as if asking permission. A slight smile trembled on Julie's lips. Twisting herself sideways, she reached out and took hold of his far shoulder. She leaned towards Nick as she turned him. She held him motionless, and he stared down, his gaze roaming from one breast to the other. He looked again into her eyes. He reached under her outstretched arm, lay his hand against her back, and eased her closer. His other arm went around her. He turned her some more. Julie felt herself start to tip. Nick's eyes widened with alarm. Then he was flat on his back, still holding her. She lay across his chest. 'Whoops,' she said.

For a moment, he looked as if he might laugh. Then his face went serious. 'Julie,' he whispered.

She kissed him gently, briefly on the mouth. 'We'd better get back in the lake,' she whispered.

'Yeah,' he said. But when Julie tried to push herself up, he held onto her. 'One more?'

'One more.'

This time, his hand went behind her head. His fingers thrust into her hair and he pressed her close, kissing her again and again, his lips firm and warm and urgent, as if he had needed to kiss her for a long time and feared he would never get another chance.

Julie mashed her lips against his. She wanted it never to end, but there were those in the lake who might see them. So she turned her face. Nick kissed her cheek, her ear. 'We've gotta stop,' she gasped.

'Okay.' His hand slid out of her hair.

She raised her head. Nick's face was beaded with sweat, his eyes somewhat vague, as if he were in a daze.

'Well,' she said.

'Yeah.' His arms fell away from her.

She pushed herself up. Nick lay spread-eagled at her knees, his skin glossy with water and sweat, his chest heaving. His damp, clinging shorts bulged as if he'd slid a length of pipe down the front. A thick pipe. A long one. If it were any bigger, Julie thought, it would push right up under the elastic waistband and . . .

'Take a picture,' he said. 'It lasts longer.'

Julie grinned down at him. Nick grinned up at her.

'Come on,' she said. 'Let's go swimming.'

Chapter Eighteen

'I gotta pee, Ettie. Let me go out. I won't do nothing.'

She shook her head. 'Any business you got, you just do it right here. You can't go out till they're gone.'

'How you know they're still here?'

'Folks don't put their tents up and move on in an hour. They're staying the night. And you're staying right where you are.'

'I gotta *pee*,' he whined.

'Use a pot.'

'You're here.'

'Hon, you got nothing I ain't seen before. I'm the gal used to change your diapers.'

'Let me go out. Please.'

Ettie pushed herself away from the gap in the wall, crawled forward to the candle between their sleeping bags and blew it out. The cave went black. 'There. Now you don't gotta be shy.' She backed up quickly to block the opening. 'Go on ahead, Merle.'

Though her eyes were open, she could see nothing. She heard him sigh, then the soft hiss of fabric as he made his way along the sleeping bag. A match snicked and flared. Merle, kneeling at the far end of the chamber, was tossing around clothes and plastic packs of food to get at the cooking utensils. With a scrape and clatter, he pulled out a small saucepan. He waved it. 'This okay?'

'Just fine,' Ettie said.

He shook out his match.

'I'll dump it when you're done.'

'You said we have to stay here.'

'*I* can go out. You're the one goes around offering folks down for no good reason.'

'He told me to.'

'Horseshit.' She heard Merle's zipper slide down. 'Careful you don't miss,' she said. 'Hold it up good and close.'

'Don't know why I can't go out,' he muttered as his stream started hitting the aluminium. 'I wouldn't do nothing. You just don't trust me, that's all. I'd leave 'em alone.' He was talking fast, as if trying to cover the other sound. 'I just wanta see 'em, that's all. What'm I gonna try with three men down there? Think I'm a fool? Don't see why we can't both go out, and you keep an eye on me if you think I'm so crazy. I just wanta see 'em, that's all.' The splashing stopped.

Ettie waited until she heard his zipper, then crawled

forward and lit the candle. Merle scowled at her as she picked up the pan. 'I'll be right outside,' she said. 'You just stay put, you hear?'

'Yes, ma'am,' he mumbled.

She backed away on her knees, then got to her feet and squeezed through the crevice, the back of her thick parka whispering against the rock. Outside, she crouched low to empty the pan. She set it down and stood up straight, stretching her stiff muscles.

In spite of the cold wind blowing through her dress, Ettie was glad to be out of the cave. She pushed her hands into the pockets of her parka, and leaned back to block the narrow entrance.

The night was very dark, as if a heavy blanket had been spread across the sky to hide the moon and stars. The only light came from the campfire down by the lake. It fluttered, yellow-orange, and cast a glowing aura that shimmered on the campers seated at its far side. Those on the near side of the fire were black silhouettes.

Staring at them, Ettie felt herself knot up inside. She groaned, and pushed her fists against her belly. If the blood signs had been right ... Maybe she'd read them wrong. She could've missed something, reading them by match light.

They showed Merle dead. They showed her dead. Killed by some of the folks sitting down there so peacefully around the campfire.

These things are never certain, though. Even if you read the signs right, there's always a little room for doubt, so you take precautions and don't give up hope. If it weren't for that, there'd be no point in hiding away.

Always a chance, at least, that things won't turn out the way the blood signs say. A small chance.

She might go ahead and try throwing a spell to shield her and Merle. She'd given a lot of thought to that, while waiting in the cave, but it hadn't seemed too practical. She was sure the Master sent these folks as punishment, so He wouldn't let her magic work anyway. But what if He didn't send them? He *did* give a warning in the blood signs. Why warn her if he meant the folks to kill them? Just to torment her?

Maybe they weren't out of favour after all, and a spell would do the trick. Sure worth a try.

Ettie picked up the saucepan. She turned it over and gave it a few hard shakes. Then, with a last look at the figures huddled around the distant fire, she entered the crevice. She sidestepped, squeezing through the tight gap. 'Merle,' she said, 'we're gonna cast a Spell of Obscurity over us.' He didn't answer.

She was near the chamber now and expected to see a fluttering glow of candlelight. The area ahead was black. 'Merle, what happened to the candle?' He still didn't answer. Ettie's heart started thudding.

'You answer me, Merle. None of your foolishness.'

The walls no longer pressed against her. She tossed the pan forward. It landed with a soft *whup* on one of the sleeping bags. Her hands free, she dug into a pocket and pulled out a book of matches. Her left ankle was grabbed and jerked sideways. She pitched forward, falling through the darkness. Her parka and a sleeping bag cushioned her impact. As she started to rise, a body dropped onto her back and drove her down. 'Merle!' Cold fingers dug into the sides of her neck, squeezed. 'No!' she cried out.

She reached up, clutched the wrists, struggled to tear the hands away. Merle was too strong. Her ears were ringing. The blackness in front of her eyes glowed red.

Later, she woke up.

Her head was throbbing with pain. She was lying on her side. When she tried to move, Ettie realised that she was bound with rope – wrists tied behind her back, legs bent at the knees, ankles lashed tight. She attempted to straighten her legs, but her wrists were tugged down as her feet moved.

'Merle?' she asked.

She heard only hew own breathing and heartbeat, and the moan of the wind outside.

'Merle, are you here?'

A stupid question, she thought. Of course he's not here. He's gone after the women.

Chapter Nineteen

Flash blew steam away, and took a sip of his coffee. Across the fire, Benny leaned forward with a demented look on his face as he continued his poem:

'And I cried, "It was surely October/on *this* very night of last year/That I journeyed – I journeyed down here/That I brought a dread burden down here/On this night of all nights in the year,/Ah, what demon has tempted me here?"' His glasses reflected the firelight, hiding his eyes behind leaping flames. '"Well I know, now, this dim lake of Auber – /This misty mid region of Weir – /Well I know, now, this dank tarn of Auber/This ghoul-haunted woodland of Weir."' He leaned back, took a deep breath, and smiled.

Heather, who'd been gazing spellbound, started to clap. The others joined in. 'Terrific,' Karen said. Flash clamped his hot mug between his knees, and applauded.

'Did you learn that for school?' Karen asked.

'No, just for myself.'

She shook her head as if amazed, and Benny's welled up with pride.

'Sure was a *creepy* poem,' Nick said.

Julie turned to Nick, hunched her shoulders, and contorted

her face. In a low, moany voice, she said, '"The ghoul-haunted woodland of Weir."'

Nick made himself look frightened. 'Yeeeeahh!' he cried, and covered his face.

'Why is it,' Alice said, 'that we insist on trying to frighten ourselves? Why doesn't somebody say a *nice* poem?'

Flash grinned. 'Nymphomaniacal Jill used dynamite to get her thrill—'

'Don't you dare!'

'Gross,' Rose said.

Flash peered at his daughter, surprised.

'Why don't I start a story,' Alice suggested, 'and we'll go around the campfire and everybody add onto it?'

'Bleah,' Rose said.

Nick nodded. 'That's a drag, Mom.'

'Why don't we give it a try?' Karen said. 'Might be fun.'

Scott nodded. 'Sure. Go ahead, Alice.'

Alice looked grateful for their approval. 'All right,' she said. 'Once upon a time, there was a fair maiden who lived in the woods, all alone except for . . .' Pausing, she turned her head towards Rose.

'Mick Jagger,' Rose said.

She got plenty of laughs except from Alice. 'Be serious.'

Rose sighed. 'Okay. Except for her mean mother.'

Alice rolled her eyes up, and Flash took a drink of coffee to hide his grin.

'One day, the maiden got so tired of her mother always spoiling her fun that she ran off into the woods and met . . .' She turned to Heather.

Heather looked across the fire at Benny as if asking for help. With a shrug, she said, 'And met a . . . gee, I don't know.'

'The gee-I-don't-know,' Nick continued, 'was an ugly hairy thing with one eye where its nose should've been.'

'And two noses,' Julie added, 'where its eyes should've been. The noses were upside down, so it wore a big cowboy hat to keep itself from drowning during rainstorms. Whenever it sneezed, it blew its hat off.' She turned to Benny, who stared at her as if she were crazy.

'When the maiden found the gee-whatever-it-is,' he said, 'it was crawling around looking for its contact lens. She helped it, and finally they found the lens.' Shrugging, he looked at Karen.

'With the contact lens back in its eye, the gee-I-don't-know stared at the maiden. She was the most beautiful creature it had ever seen. "Gee, you're purty," it said.' She grinned at Scott.

'The maiden blushed,' he went on. '"You're not too shabby yourself," she said. "And with those two noses. I bet you smell a lot better than me."' He raised his eyebrows at Flash.

'So the gee-I-don't-know picked up the fair maiden and carried her deep into the wood. They came to his hut, and went at it hot and heavy.'

'*Dad,*' Rose muttered.

'Before you know it,' he continued, 'the little hut was crowded with little gee-I-don't-knows, so they packed up and moved to a condo in Palm Springs and lived happily ever after.'

'What a dumb story,' Rose muttered.

'I thought it was kind of cute,' Karen said.

'Why don't you tell a story?' Benny asked her. 'Do you know another scary one like "Doreen and Audrey"?'

'Afraid not. That was my entire repertoire.'

'How about you, Dad?' Julie asked.

'My last one didn't go over too well.'

Julie wrinkled her nose. 'Yeah, that's right. Forget I asked.'

'I've got one,' Flash said.

Alice raised an eyebrow. 'Is it clean?'

'Sure.'

'Go on,' Nick said. 'Let's hear it.'

Flash finished his coffee, and set the aluminium cup on the ground between his boots. 'Maybe I'd better not,' he said. 'Your mother has this thing about creepy stories.'

'Don't make *me* the villain,' she protested. 'If you think the story's appropriate, go ahead and tell it.'

He grinned. 'Well, if you insist.' Reaching inside his jacket, he took a cigar from his shirt pocket. He tore off the cellophane wrapper, crinkled it into a ball, and tossed it into the fire. 'This happened to me a long time ago, back when I was in high school.'

'The Dark Ages,' Nick said.

'Right.' Clamping the cigar in his teeth, he lifted a twig from the fire. With one hand shielding the small flame from the wind, he lit up. 'My dad, my brother, Cliff, and I were on a fishing trip up around Land O'Lakes, Wisconsin. We'd heard about a string of axe murders in the area. Seems some lunatic was running around giving the whack to folks he found in the wood. They called him the Chopper. Maybe a frustrated tree surgeon.' Flash grinned at his joke, and stared at the glowing tip of his cigar. 'There were four or five bodies they found in the woods. All of 'em were dismembered. Some had arms cut off. Some were missing a leg. Two of 'em were beheaded.'

'Arnold,' Alice said in a warning voice.

'You said I could tell it.'

'I imagined you'd use some discretion.'

'Want me to stop?'

'Keep going,' Nick said. 'It's neat.'

Alice sighed. 'Just tone it down, all right? There are children present.'

'Tone it down, okay. Now, where was I?' He sucked in some smoke, let it drift out of his nostrils. The wind whipped it away. 'Oh, yeah. So the Chopper was on the loose, and they'd found some of his handiwork in the woods, but there were a few other folks who'd just disappeared, so they figured the body count would get even higher. We were a little jumpy, camping out in the neighbourhood. Dad was packing a .22 revolver, though, so we figured we'd waste the sucker if he showed himself.'

'I tell you, though, we didn't get much sleep that first night. We were the only campers on the lake. It was mighty dark and silent. Every now and then, we'd hear a rustle in the bushes. Me and Cliff were sure it was the Chopper sneaking in close. I tell you, that was one of the longest nights I ever spent. Before the war anyway,' he added, and felt his chest tighten as he saw himself cowering in the jungle.

'Did he get you?' Scott asked.

'Huh? No. No, we made it through the night okay.' Flash took a deep breath. 'We spent the next day on the lake. Rowing around and fishing.' It was sunny and hot. Real nice. Dragonflies, loons cackling. Real pleasant. And we had a lot of luck, fishing. Brought in a whole string of bluegill and sunfish, a couple of bullheads. We fried them up for dinner, and had a real feast. Then we went out in the rowboat again for some night fishing.

'I guess we were all glad to be on the lake after dark. Out here, we didn't have to worry about the Chopper. My God, it was nice out there. Warm, just a little breeze. The moonlight looked like silver on the water. There were lightning bugs. We were all greased up and stinky with 6–12, to keep the mosquitoes off.' He sighed. 'Anyway, we were drifting near the north end of the lake, maybe fifty yards from shore, when I felt a sudden tug on my line. Man, I was excited! I started reeling in, thinking I'd hooked a real whopper. Felt heavy, you know? My rod was bent almost double. But I started to wonder, because I wasn't getting any play. You know how you can usually feel the fish flipping around down there? Well, this one didn't seem to be moving at all. Just a dead weight.'

'Cliff shined his flashlight on the lake where my line was in. The beam only went in a little way. I remember how dirty the water looked. Like it was full of dust, or something. Then, as I cranked the reel, this pale hand came up like there was somebody reaching for the light. I tell you, I damn near croaked. But I kept reeling in, and Cliff held the flashlight steady, and a second later I had a severed arm swinging from the end of my rod. It was cut off at the elbow. My hook was in its wrist. We all just stared at the thing. It hung there, dripping and swaying.'

'My God,' Julie muttered.

Alice said, 'I thought you promised to tone it down.'

'I'm just telling what happened,' Flash said.

'This didn't happen,' she said.

'Didn't it? Ask Cliff next time he's over.'

'How come you never mentioned it?'

'You know how you are about these things.'

'Why'd you have to bring it up, then?'

'The kids wanted a story.'

'Mother of God.'

'May I continue?'

'You mean there's more?'

'I haven't got to the good part yet.'

'Oh, for crying out loud.'

'Go on,' Nick said. He was leaning forward, elbows on knees. 'What'd you do with the things?'

'I wanted to cut my line and get rid of it, but Dad said we had to keep it for the authorities. He told me to swing it over to him. He was sitting in the stern. I swung it over, and grabbed the line and lowered the arm into the boat and cut the line. Then Cliff rowed us back to camp.'

'By the time we got there, most of the shock had worn off. We were all pretty excited, acting as if we'd landed a record-breaking muskie or something. We figured, you know, that it must be the arm of a Chopper victim. Dad put it in a grocery bag. He wanted to take it to the police right away. The nearest town was about an hour's drive, though and we had lots of good camping gear we didn't want to leave behind while we went in. Cliff volunteered to stay a guard the stuff, but Dad wouldn't let him. We finally decided to break camp and take everything with us. We figured, you know, we wouldn't be too eager to stick around another day anyhow.'

'We didn't bother making a campfire. I lit the Coleman

lantern, and we kept it by the tent while we gathered up our things. We worked real fast, but it seemed to take forever. The car was parked about a hundred yards away. Dad left me and Cliff a couple of times while he carried stuff over. We didn't much like it when he was gone. We kept looking over our shoulders at the bag with the arm.'

'Anyway, he was carrying the cooler and tackle box to the car and Cliff and I were busy folding the tent, our backs to the lake, when we heard this splashing sound behind us. Like somebody wading slowly out of the water. We leaped to our feet and spun around. And Jesus, there was a man coming at us!'

Heather covered her eyes.

'He was kind of stumbling along like he was drunk. He was just a dim shape in the darkness at first. When he got closer to the lantern, though, we could see him real well – too well. He was a skinny guy, about forty. He was wearing jeans and a plaid shirt. His sneakers squished with each step. He was dripping from head to foot. The top of his head was split open like a broken watermelon, and his left arm was gone.'

'Right beside the lantern, he stopped and stared at us with these blank eyes. Then his mouth opened. He tried to say something, and about a gallon of water gushed out of his mouth like he was throwing up. When the water stopped pouring out, he said in this kind of choked, gurgling voice, "My arm. I want my arm." '

'Cliff and I ran like hell, too scared even to scream. When we got back to the camp with Dad, the guy was gone.' Flash sighed. He tapped a length of ash off his cigar. 'We followed his footprints to the edge of the lake. For a long time, we stared out over the water. We couldn't see the guy, but we knew he was out there. Somewhere down below. In the dark, murky water. With his arm.'

Chapter Twenty

The struggle had left Ettie's wrists and ankles raw, but the ropes binding her were as tight as they'd been when she started. Her blood made them slippery, but still she couldn't pull free.

Her only chance was to cut herself loose. Either that, or wait for Merle to release her. But he might not come back. If the signs had been right . . . Maybe it was already too late to save him. Or herself. Maybe this is how it would end, with Merle meeting his fate at the hands of the campers and Ettie starving to death, helpless in the cave.

'No,' she said into the darkness.

She would get loose. She had to!

She knew, from rolling onto her side, that her sheath knife was gone. Merle must've taken it. But what about the Swiss Army knife they'd found among the gear of the dead campers? If he'd forgotten about it, the knife would be somewhere in the heap of equipment at the far end of the cave.

Slowly, moaning as she strained with stiff muscles, she began to squirm forward. The journey seemed to take forever, but finally she was lying in the jumble of boots, plastic bags, backpacks, cook kits. She felt cloth against her cheek, nudged it aside, felt cool metal. The butane cylinder? She wondered if she might try to burn the ropes off, then quickly abandoned that idea; with her limited mobility, it would be far too risky. Maybe as a last resort.

The packs, she knew, were empty. Merle had dumped out their contents the day he'd brought them in. So the knife had to be lying loose here, someplace.

She continued to search, using her face to push away invisible objects, exploring some with her tongue. She bit and dragged aside soft fabric, a button between her teeth.

She lowered her face where it had been, and felt a metallic tube against her lips. She ran her tongue up the ribbed surface. The tube bulged at one end. A flashlight? She rolled it, and felt the switch against her cheek. A flashlight.

They'd used it only once, testing it when it came tumbling from the pack two days before. Its beam had been dusky yellow, the batteries weak, and she'd told Merle they should save it for an emergency. After that, she'd forgotten about it.

Ettie pushed the switch with her chin. The dim beam spilled out, revealing a rumpled pair of jeans. Gripping the flashlight in her teeth, she struggled to her knees. She turned her head slowly, shining the beam over the packs, a sweatshirt, tennis shoes, a collapsible plastic water bucket, foil and cellophane packets of food, a Primus stove, a wallet, a first-aid kit. Her mouth, stretched wide to hold the flashlight, ached badly. She could breathe only through her nose. She felt as if she were suffocating. She gagged, and her eyes teared, but she kept her bite on the metal.

The red plastic handle of the knife was nowhere to be seen.

Inching forward, she crept into the heap. Her left knee nudged a hard object hidden under a flannel shirt. She pushed the shirt aside, and tucked her chin down to shine the light at her knees. The murky yellow beam fell on a hatchet.

Relief swept through Ettie. She forced her mouth open wide, and let the flashlight drop. It hit the granite floor with a dull thud. The cave went dark.

Ettie writhed and twisted until her fingers found the hatchet. Gripping the blunt end of its head, she pressed the cutting edge between her wrists and began to saw the rope.

Chapter Twenty-one

Nick shoved aside a sawed-off stump and a rock that had been used as seats at the campfire. Then he spread out his ground cloth. He opened the straps, keeping his rubber mat in a tight roll.

'Are we sleeping out?' Julie asked.

He looked over his shoulder. She was approaching from between two of the tents, a toothbrush and tube of toothpaste in her hand, her water bottle clamped under one arm. 'Don't you want to?' he asked.

'What about the rain?'

He held out his open hands. 'What rain?'

Julie smiled. Her sun-burnished face glowed copper in the firelight. 'I'm game if you are,' she said. Grinning, she turned away. Nick watched her stride towards the far tent and crouch over her pack. When she vanished inside the tent, he finished arranging his sleeping bag.

His parents were down by the shore with the twins, washing and brushing teeth. He went to his pack, took out his shorts and T-shirt, and crawled into their tent. His shorts felt cool when he put them on, as if they were still damp from swimming. He knew the sun had dried them, though, and his T-shirt had the same moist feel against his skin. Shivering, he hurried outside, stuffed his clothing into his pack, and rushed to his sleeping bag. His teeth chattered as he tugged off his untied boots and his socks. He put them at the head of his bag, and scurried into it. The slippery fabric was cold at first. Slowly, it filled with warmth. By the time Julie came out of her tent, he'd stopped shaking.

'You look cosy,' she said.

'I am. Sort of.'

She spread her poncho on the ground beside him, rolled

out her foam rubber mat, and tugged open the drawstrings of her stuff bag. The sleeping bag bloomed as if inflating when she pulled it free. On her knees, facing Nick, she bent over to spread it out. He watched the way her hair, hanging from under the edges of her hood, brushed against her cheeks like wisps of gold in the firelight.

'You sleeping out?' Scott called. He appeared from behind one of the tents, Karen and Benny at his sides.

'Sure,' Julie said. 'It's not gonna rain.'

'I hope you're right.'

When they were gone, Julie unzipped her sleeping bag, crawled in, and pulled the zipper up to her shoulder. She rolled onto her side. She pillowed her head on her bent arm, and smiled at Nick.

'We'll wait till they're all in their tents,' he whispered. 'Then we'll run around yelling, "My arm! Where's my arm?" '

She laughed softly. 'Forget it. I'm not moving a muscle till the sun comes up.'

'Unless it rains?' Nick asked.

'If it rains, I think I'll murder you.'

'Hope you two've got your Mae Wests on,' Dad said, coming back from the shore.

'You're gonna drown,' Rose informed them.

'You people have no confidence,' Nick said.

'I'll move in with the girls.' Mom said. 'If the rain starts, young man, you hightail it into your father's tent.'

'Fine,' he said.

At last, everyone vanished into tents. Nick lay on his side, staring at Julie's face a yard away. She was looking at him, too. He wished there was more light.

'You ought to wear a hat when you sleep,' Julie said.

'I burrow down.'

'You're not burrowed now.'

'If I burrow, I can't look at you.' He could hardly believe he'd said that. But he was glad. As the silence stretched out, he felt his heart beating fast. His stomach was fluttery.

Julie moved her sleeping bag closer. 'How's that?' she whispered.

His throat felt tight. He nodded. 'Great,' he managed. Julie's face was dim in the faint, shimmering glow of firelight, her eyes glistening. He felt the warmth of her breath through the cold air. 'Do you know what?' he whispered. His thundering heart felt as if it might explode.

'What?' she asked.

'I . . .' He backed down. He couldn't say it.

'What?'

'I've never known a girl like you.'

'How do you mean?'

'I don't know. I'm not very . . . I like you an awful lot, Julie.'

'I like you an awful lot, too.'

'You do?' He felt a trembling warmth spread through him.

'Yeah, I do. I . . . hell . . .'

'What?' he asked.

Her lower lip curled in. She clamped it between her teeth. Then she let the lip go, and sighed. 'I think,' she whispered, 'that maybe I love you.'

The words stunned Nick. He went breathless and dizzy. He felt like shouting with joy, like weeping. He said, 'Jesus.'

'The name's Julie.'

'God, Julie. You really . . .'

'Really.'

'Oh, Julie,' he whispered. 'Julie, I love you.' He pressed his mouth gently to her parted lips.

Scott stared at the slanting dark walls of the tent above him and listened to the sounds of Benny's breathing. He didn't think the boy was asleep yet. As he waited, he stroked the sweatshirt spread over his chest and belly. He imagined Karen wearing only her sweatpants.

'Dad?' Benny asked.

'Huh?'

'Do you think it was true?' The boy sounded nervous. 'About the guy and his arm?'

'No, of course not.'

'He said it was true.'

'It's not. Dead people do not get up and wander around.'

'Have you ever heard of zombies?'

'I think so,' Scott said, smiling in the darkness.

'They're dead people who get brought back to life with voodoo. They're supposed to really exist. You know, like in Haiti? I've read about 'em.'

'You oughta be reading *The Hardy Boys* instead of all that weird junk.'

'You don't think there are zombies?'

'I sincerely doubt it.'

'What about witches and vampires and werewolves and ghosts?'

He wrapped his arms around the soft sweatshirt. 'It's awfully late, Benny. Can't we pick up this conversation in the morning?'

'If you want,' he said. He sounded disappointed.

Scott sighed. 'I just think it's all people's imaginations. Stuff they made up to frighten each other, like Karen's story about Doreen and Audrey, or Flash's about the guy and the arm. Just stories.'

'I don't know,' Benny said.

'Well, it's just my opinion. I haven't read a hundred books on the subject the way you have. But I've been around thirty-eight years and my life's been relatively free of things that go bump in the night. If there are ghoulies and ghosts out there, they've been minding their own business. I haven't lost any sleep over them – until now.'

'I guess you want me to be quiet.'

'We have a lot of hiking to do tomorrow.'

'I'm not very sleepy.'

Terrific. 'Try to think about something pleasant,' Scott said.

'Okay. I'll try. Good-night.'

' 'Night, Benny.' He heard the boy sigh and roll over.

Turning onto his side, he eased the sweatshirt up against his face. He wondered if Karen was cold without it. No, the sleeping bag would keep her warm. And soon he would be with her. If Benny ever fell asleep.

Karen wondered if he would come tonight. Maybe not. He might be worried about the weather. If he came and it started raining, Julie would catch them. That'd be an embarrassment for everyone.

But he'd whispered, 'See you later,' when he kissed her good-night. He obviously planned to take the chance. He could've changed his mind, though.

It was still early. He couldn't leave his tent until Benny was asleep. He had to worry about Julie and Nick, too. Give all of them time to conk out.

Might be a long wait.

One of her shoulders was cold. She slid down deeper into the bag, the slick fabric making whispery-sounds against her skin. She crossed her ankles, folded her hands on her belly, stared up into the darkness, and smiled. Scott would be in for a pleasant surprise when he found her already naked.

If he comes.

He'll come, she told herself. Oh, yes.

She wished she could sleep. Though every muscle ached from lugging her pack up that awful trail, she wasn't the least bit tired. She was wide awake and eager, trembling slightly.

At last, she heard a soft crushing sound behind the tent. It was barely audible over the noise of the wind. It might have been nothing more than a pinecone falling to the ground, but it might have been a footstep. She let out a shaky breath, and listened. For a few moments, she heard only the wind rushing through the trees and mountain gaps. Then came another quiet crunch. She was sure this time that it was a footfall.

He's being very cautious, she thought. Maybe he's not certain Julie's asleep.

With a shaky hand, Karen unzipped the side of her sleeping bag.

The footsteps stopped at the front of the tent. She heard the rustle of the flap being eased aside. Shutting her eyes, she waited. Her heart was pounding hard. She lay motionless, breathing deeply, trying to feign sleep.

He was inside now. She could hear him crawling along the tent floor, coming slowly closer. He stopped beside her.

He smelled bad. Like sweat and urine.

Her eyes flew open. The face above her was a dim, grinning blur in the darkness and it didn't belong to Scott. She opened her mouth to scream. A hand slapped across it. The other hand swept down. Something crashed against the side of her head.

Scott propped himself up on one elbow, and stared at the dark bulk of Benny's sleeping bag. He listened carefully. The boy was breathing in a slow, steady rhythm.

Finally.

He opened his sleeping bag, and felt the cold slide over his skin. He sat up. He folded Karen's sweatshirt and tucked it under one arm. As he started to rise, he heard a soft tapping sound on the taut wall of the tent. Then another. Suddenly, the tent was being pattered by a thousand raindrops.

He muttered, 'Shit,' lay down again, and zipped himself into his bag.

'Ohhhh crap!' Julie wailed.

Nick's eyes fluttered open. He wrinkled up his face as raindrops smacked it.

Julie kissed him quickly on the mouth. 'Better inflate your Mae West,' she said.

Then they were both scurrying out of their sleeping bags. Julie shoved her feet into her boots. The rain soaked through the back of her warm-up jacket as she gathered up her bag. 'Oh, damn damn damn damn!' she cried.

Nick grinned at her.

She snatched her rubber pad off the poncho, and raced for her tent. The flaps weren't zipped. She lunged inside, flopped forward, and landed on the soft heap of her sleeping bag.

There was a startled grunt.

'Sorry,' she gasped, and raised her face. Beside her, near enough to touch, was a bare rump. The legs were wedged between another pair of legs.

He's screwing Karen! The thought hit her like a punch in the stomach, knocking her breath out. She shoved herself off the bag and crawled backward. He reached out and grabbed her wrist. 'Let . . .' Then she saw his face. She screamed and wrenched her hand free. She flung herself away, falling through the tent flaps. Rain splashed her face. She started to squirm away. The flaps flew open and a naked man dived out, a huge knife in one hand. He landed on Julie, slamming her flat on the ground. He clutched her throat, holding her down while he pushed himself up and straddled her hips. He plunged the knife into the earth by her face. He yanked the neck of her jacket, found the zipper, and tugged it down. She bucked with pain and screamed again as a rough hand squeezed her breast. The hand went away. It jerked at her pants. She felt the wet ground under her buttocks. Then he had both her arms pinned down and he was heavy on her and shoving his knees between her legs to force them apart and his mouth was on her, mashing her lips. She heard a yell, and his head snapped back as a bare foot shot past her eyes.

Her father was there, grabbing the man's hair, ripping at it so the head bent back, chopping with his other hand at the bridge of the man's nose. Blood spouted, mixed with the rain hitting Julie's face. The man rolled off her. He scrambled away on hands and knees.

She rolled onto her side. As she pulled up her pants, she watched her father dash towards the man. The man was on his feet now, trying to run, but Dad was gaining on him fast.

Then there was a pale figure sprinting in from the side. *Nick!* In his upraised hand was a hatchet.

Dad slipped on the wet ground. He windmilled, trying to get his balance, and went sprawling headlong. As he skidded, he grabbed for the man's foot. He missed. The man glanced back at him. He crouched and picked up a rock and took a step towards her father, then saw Nick an staggered back. Nick swung. The hatchet caught the stranger high in the chest. Nick tore it free and prepared to strike again. The man took a few wobbly steps backward, and fell.

Nick dropped to the ground and vomited.

Flash, running towards him, yelled, 'Stay with the girls!' over his shoulder to Alice. He stopped over the body. 'Oh, God,' he gasped.

Julie got to her knees. She tried to fasten her zipper, but her hands shook too badly, so she hugged the jacket shut.

Benny was walking slowly forward, unsteady, hands out as if to help his balance.

Dad pushed himself up. He stared for a moment at the body, then ran towards Julie. 'You okay?'

She nodded. 'He – he hurt Karen.'

Chapter Twenty-two

Scott fell to his knees. Karen was lying motionless on her open sleeping bag, arms and legs spread wide. He pressed a hand below her rib cage. He felt the rise and fall of her breathing, and he started to cry.

'Karen?' he whispered. She didn't stir.

In a boot near her head, he found a flashlight. He turned it on, and shone the light on her face. Her eyelids trembled, but didn't open. Her left cheekbone was swollen. Her face was slick in places. Teeth marks on her cheek, her mouth. It was all blurry through Scott's tears. Sobbing quietly, he backhanded the tears from his eyes.

'Dad?' Julie's voice. 'How is she?'

'Alive.'

'Can I come in?'

'Yeah.'

Julie crawled through the flap, and knelt beside him. 'Is she unconscious?'

'Yeah.' He moved the beam down her body.

Julie groaned as it lit wet shiny places and crooked teeth marks on Karen's left shoulder and breast. 'God,' she murmured.

Fingers had put scratches and red imprints on her skin, but Scott saw no blood, no stab wounds.

'Is everybody okay?' Benny called from outside.

'Yes,' Scott answered. 'Stay out there.'

The marks ended at Karen's rib cage. He nudged Julie. She leaned out of his way and he bent over her body and shone the light on her vagina. There was no blood, no semen. Her legs looked okay.

'Dad?' Julie whispered. 'He raped her.'

He nodded.

'Do you think she'll be all right?'

'I don't . . .' His voice cracked. 'I don't know. Here.' He gave Julie the flashlight. 'Go over to my tent. Get her sweatshirt. It's in my sleeping bag.'

Without a word, she hurried from the tent.

Scott found Karen's sweatpants in the space behind her boots. They were folded neatly.

God, she must've been lying here naked, waiting for him. If only Benny had fallen asleep a few minutes earlier . . . if the rain hadn't come . . . if he hadn't been so damned worried about everyone else, and simply tented with her all along . . .

He stroked the length of her outflung leg, slipped his hand under her calf, and lifted it. He slipped the sweatpants over her foot and drew in her other leg. By the time Julie returned, he had the pants in place. Together, they lifted her to a sitting position and pulled the sweatshirt over her head. Scott worked her limp arms into the sleeves. He lowered her gently, and smoothed the cover of the sleeping bag over her.

Julie was kneeling beside him, staring down at the dark bundle. He put an arm around her. 'How are you doing tiger?'

'Okay.'

'Jesus.'

'Are *you* okay?'

'Yeah.'

'You're gonna freeze.'

He realised, vaguely, that he was naked except for jockey shorts. He was wet and shivering. 'I'm okay,' he said.

'I guess the guy's dead.'

'Yeah. I'm sorry it was Nick. He didn't have to. I – it's too bad.'

'I'll go see how he's doing. If you don't need me any more.'

Scott nodded.

Julie eased away. She brought her own sleeping bag over, and wrapped it around him. 'Benny and I – we'll stay in the other tent.' She kissed him lightly on the cheek, and left.

Benny grabbed Julie's arm as she stood up outside the tent. He stared at her, the rain splashing on his glasses. 'Is she okay?' he asked.

'She's unconscious.'

'What'd he do to her?'

'He knocked her out.'

'I know, but . . .'

'Why don't you go back to the tent? You're drenched.' His chin started to shake. 'I gotta know how she is!'

'She'll be fine.'

'Goddamn stinking rotten dirty bastard!'

Julie put her hand on Benny's cold, dripping cheek. 'She'll be all right. You'll see.'

'*He* won't! *He's* dead! I wish *I'd* killed him!' Benny suddenly threw himself against Julie and hugged her tightly. She wrapped her arms around him. He was sobbing out of control. His stocking cap was sodden and cold against her cheek.

Beyond his head, Julie saw Nick sitting on a rock by the dead fire. He was wearing a hooded poncho. He was slumped forward, staring at his feet.

Her own poncho, which she'd left on the ground when the storm hit, was spread over the dead body. It was barely visible through the darkness and sheeting rain. She thought of what was under it, and turned her eyes away.

Flash, in a clear plastic rain slicker, was crouched in front of the far tent, apparently talking to Alice and the girls.

He shouldn't have left Nick alone.

'Come on,' Julie said. 'Dad's gonna stay with Karen. If you're staying outside, why don't you go get your poncho? And try to find Dad's for me. Okay?'

With a nod, Benny backed away and walked towards the other tent. Julie went over to Nick. He looked up as she stopped in front of him. 'How are you doing?' she asked.

'I still feel a little sick. How about you? Did he hurt you?'

'Bruised me a little. He got Karen pretty bad, though. He raped her.'

'God. How is she?'

'Unconscious. He hit her with something. Maybe the knife handle.'

'Will she be okay?'

Julie shrugged. 'You were great, going after the guy that way.'

'I heard you scream,' he said. His voice sounded flat, as if his mind were far away. 'I saw you on the ground. And your dad hit him. I didn't know what was going on. I just knew I had to get him. I didn't plan to . . . kill him.' He stared up at

Julie with wide, unblinking eyes. 'I don't know. I guess I did want to kill him. I just knew he'd hurt you and I grabbed the hatchet. I feel kind of strange.'

She stepped between his knees and pressed his face against her body. 'Don't feel bad. If you hadn't done it. I think Dad would've.'

'That's what my dad said. He said the guy was "dead meat." '

'Here it is,' Benny said.

Julie stepped back. She shook open the wrinkled plastic sheet, and pushed her head through its hooded hole. As she snapped the sides under her arms, Flash approached. He squeezed her shoulder. 'How're you doing, young lady?'

'Fine, I guess.'

'What about Karen?'

'She's beat up some. She's unconscious.' With Benny standing there, Julie didn't want to mention the sexual assault. 'He messed her up pretty good.'

'Well, Nick messed *him* up pretty good. She'll be all right, won't she?'

'I guess so.'

'That's good to hear. How you holding up, Nicky?'

'Okay,' he muttered.

'I know it's not easy. I've put the nix on a couple of guys in my day. It's never easy. Nothing to worry about, though. A clear case of self-defence. What I think we'll do is get some snapshots of the body. We can't exactly pack it out with us. We'll wrap it up good and tight, and bury it here. Let the authorities come back for it.'

Julie watched him reach into his clear slicker and pull an Instamatic from the pocket of his jacket. 'You kids can wait here. No need for you to watch.'

He walked to the front of the tent where the man had struggled with Julie. The knife was still embedded in the muddy ground. He tugged it free, and went to the dark bundle. With the point of the knife, he swept the poncho aside.

Julie was ready to look away, but the ground where the corpse should have been sprawled was bare.

Benny groaned.

Julie felt a shiver crawl up her spine, squirm on the back of her neck.

Nick muttered, 'Holy shit,' and leaped to his feet. He ran towards his father, Julie and Benny following close behind.

Flash was walking slowly towards the shoreline. He stopped at the edge of the water. When they caught up to him, he was standing motionless, arms hanging at his sides, eyes staring out at the black ruffled surface of the lake.

'Dad?'

Flash shook his head. His voice came out in a whisper barely loud enough to hear over the sounds of the wind and rain. 'He was dead. I know he was dead.'

Chapter Twenty-three

With a sudden intake of air, Karen sat up straight. Scott put a hand on her shoulder. She flinched and looked at him with wide, pale eyes. 'It's all right,' he said. She raised a hand to her face, and moaned. Then she lunged forward, scurried out of her sleeping bag, thrust her head through the tent flap, and vomited.

Scott found her water bottle propped up between her boots. He took it to her. She was on her hands and knees, half outside the tent. She'd finished throwing up, and had raised her head. She was staring through the rain. Scott saw four dark figures with flashlights wandering among the rocks and trees to the right.

'What are they?' Karen muttered.

'I don't know.' He gave the water bottle to her. As she washed out her mouth and took a long drink, Scott gazed at the place where the body had fallen. He saw a rumpled shape on the ground. Good, they'd covered it. He patted the wet back of Karen's sweatshirt. 'Let's get in where it's dry.'

She crawled backward and sat down on her sleeping bag. She pulled off her sweatshirt and used it as a towel to dry her hair. Then she lay down. Scott covered her. 'Come in with me?' she asked. Her voice was quiet, but pitched high, like that of a child about to cry.

Scott crawled in beside her. He closed the zipper. Rolling against her, he embraced her gently.

'What happened?' she asked in the same high voice.

Scott caressed her back. Her skin was damp and cool near the shoulders, smooth and dry and warm lower down where the rain hadn't found her. 'You don't remember?' he asked.

'I remember waiting for you. I didn't know if you would come. Who did this to me. Scott?'

'I don't know. A stranger.'

She hugged him tightly. She burrowed her face against the side of his neck.

'You don't remember any of it?'

'No,' she murmured. 'I know what he did, though. I . . .' She started weeping. Her tears moistened Scott's neck. She shook with small sobs. 'I can . . . feel what he did.'

'I'm sorry,' Scott whispered through the tightness in his throat. Tears burned in his own eyes. 'I'm so sorry, Karen.'

'Are they . . . looking for him? Outside?'

'No. I don't know what they're doing. He didn't get away.'

Karen stiffened. 'Where is he?'

'He's dead.'

She pressed herself against Scott.

'He attacked Julie, too.'

'Oh, no. Oh, no.'

'She's okay. She came in when the rain started, and found him with you. She screamed. I came running, and so did Nick. Nick got him with a hatchet.'

'Dear God,' she murmured.

'Yeah. I feel bad about that. Nick's just a kid. I feel bad that he killed the guy. It should've been me. I should've done it. Nick beat me to it, that's all.'

'Will he be in trouble?'

'Some, I guess. There'll be an inquest, I suppose. Nobody's gonna be arrested, though, not with something like this.'

'I guess it's self-defence.'

'Something like that. I just hate it that Nick's gonna have to live with killing a man.'

For a long time, they lay motionless, holding each other tightly and saying nothing. Scott listened to the patter of raindrops on the tent, to the quiet sounds of her breathing. He felt her warm breath on his skin. Sometimes, when she blinked, her eyelashes tickled his neck. He wished she would sleep and forget, at least for a time, what had happened to her. But her heart was pounding fast. He could feel it against his chest.

Then she whispered, 'He didn't come in me. I mean, that would've been worse.'

'Yeah.'

'I feel so filthy. It's like I can still feel where he . . .' Her voice died. Later, she said, 'Will you still want me?'

'Of course. I love you.'

'But . . . will it make a difference?'

'I guess it already has. Knowing I could've lost you tonight. He had a knife. I thought I might find you . . . I don't know what I would've done.'

'Will you make love to me?'

He fondled her hair. He didn't answer.

'Please. Please, I need you. I can still *feel* him. I want it to be *you* I feel.'

'I might hurt you.'

'I don't care. You want me, don't you?'

'Of course I do.'

Pushing a hand inside her sweatpants, he stroked the warm smooth skin of her rump. He slid his hand up to the curve of her hip, down to her sleek thigh. She stiffened when he touched her pubic hair. 'Don't stop,' she said. He eased his hand lower, gently cupping her mound, fingers curling in, caressing. She raised a leg slightly opening herself to him.

She pulled the waistband of Scott's shorts away from his body and down, freeing his erect penis. He moaned as her fingers gripped him.

Then they were both naked. Scott braced above her on elbows and knees, touching her only with his lips while her hands roamed down his back, stroked his buttocks.

'Is something wrong?' she asked.

'I don't want to hurt you.'

A hand went away from his rump. Fingers took his penis and guided him lower until he pushed into soft folds. He slid slowly into Karen, deep into her hugging sheath. She sighed. She wrapped her arms around his back, and pulled him tightly against her.

After searching the area around the campsite, they followed Flash to the fireplace. He sat on a stump, rested the bowie knife across his lap, and put his flashlight into a pocket of his slicker. 'You kids might as well turn in,' he said. 'I'll stand watch.'

'Do you think he'll be back?' Nick asked.

'Who the hell knows? I thought he was dead. Maybe he wasn't, but I know for damn sure he was too far gone to get up and run off. Might've dragged himself a few yards maybe even as far as the lake. Or maybe he *was* dead, and somebody carted him off when we weren't looking.'

Benny mumbled something.

'What?'

'I said, maybe he's a zombie.'

'Give us a break,' Julie told him.

'Like the guy in your story who came out of the lake to get his arm.'

'That was just a story,' Flash said. 'It didn't happen.'

'What about the woman?' Julie asked.

'What woman?'

'Yeah!' Nick said. 'That's right.' He looked at Flash. 'Remember I told you this morning about a crazy woman who yelled at those girls? They ran into her right here, yesterday.'

'The girls said she had a knife like that.' Julie pointed at the weapon on Flash's lap.

Nick frowned. 'They didn't say anything about a guy.'

'He could've been hiding when they were here.'

'I've got it,' Benny blurted. 'The guy and the woman are the same person! Like that guy in *Psycho*. He dresses up—'

'Then who took the body?' Julie asked.

'The woman took it,' Nick said. He sounded very sure of himself. 'She was a friend of his, maybe his wife. She saw what happened to him. Then she waited for her chance, and snuck over and got him.'

'She would have to be an awfully strong woman,' Flash said, 'to walk off with that guy's body.'

'She didn't. She dragged it over to the lake, and towed it away in the water.'

'I guess that's possible,' Flash admitted.

Julie's face suddenly contorted.

'What's wrong?' Nick asked.

'I just thought of something.' Her wide eyes looked from Nick to Flash. 'Those girls – they just saw a woman. And we just saw a man.'

'So?' Flash said.

'What I mean,' Julie continued, 'is how do we know there aren't *more* people here? Maybe another man. Maybe a whole bunch.'

Flash stared at her. 'Damn, I wish you hadn't said that.'

'It's possible,' Nick said.

Benny started looking around, searching the darkness through his dripping glasses.

'That's all the more reason we'd better keep watch. Even if it's just a woman, we don't know but that she'll try to get back at us. The rest of you go on and hit the sack.'

'I'll stay up with you,' Nick said.

Flash considered insisting that the boy turn in, but he liked the idea of having company.

'I wouldn't be able to sleep anyway, and if something does happen' – Nick shrugged – 'it'd be better if there's two of us.'

'I guess you're right. Okay.'

The hatchet swinging at his side, Nick walked Julie and Benny to their tent. Benny crawled inside. Julie faced Nick, put her arms around him, and kissed him. The kiss was not brief. Flash felt he shouldn't be staring, so he went over to the poncho he'd used to cover the body. Pools of water had formed on its rumpled plastic. He picked it up and flapped it, shaking off as much water as he could. When he turned around, Julie was gone, and Nick was walking towards him. 'This'll help keep us dry. We'll sit back to back so we've got a three-hundred-sixty-degree view.'

They moved two stumps together, sat down, and draped the poncho over their heads. The rain made loud, hollow sounds as it struck the plastic. Flash stared through the downpour, moving his gaze slowly over the black lake, the dim pale rocks along the shoreline, the place where the body had fallen, the rocks and trees beyond the border of the clearing, Karen's tent, the pines close behind it, the gap between it and the next tent. Awfully dark behind the tents. A lot of trees. A small rocky rise farther back. Plenty of cover for someone sneaking in. Someone with a knife . . .

'I'll check around,' Flash said. He left the sheltering poncho. With the knife in one hand and his flashlight in the other, he walked to the far side of Karen's tent. He stepped behind it, being careful not to trip over the guy line. He shone his light on the blue fabric long enough to see that it hadn't been rent. Then he swept the beam across the pines the bushes, the head-high clump of broken granite. The light threw squirming shadows that sent a chill up his back, but he saw no one. He moved on. Behind the next tent, a sudden voice made him jump.

'Who's there?' Julie asked.

'It's me.'

'Something wrong?'

'No. Just checking around.'

The tent after that was his. He knew it was deserted but he flashed his light across its rear, just in case. It looked all right. He stepped to the last tent. 'Just me,' he said quietly in case Alice or the girls should be worried. There was no response. They must be asleep, he thought, but he felt a stab of fear. He put his light on the tent. The red fabric, shiny with running water, was intact.

He made a last check of the trees and rocks behind the tent, then hurried around to the front. The flaps were zipped shut. He opened them. Ducking low, he swept his light over the three crowded, motionless shapes. The looked okay. He shut the zipper, and walked towards Nick.

'Is everything all right?'

'So far. We'd better check once in a while, though. We're awfully vulnerable back there.' He sat on the stump with his back to Nick, and pulled the poncho forward to shield him.

For a long time, Flash stared into the darkness. His eyelids grew heavy. His mind drifted. He imagined he was riding through the rain, fighting hard to stay awake. Alice cried out, 'Don't hit him!' and there was a one-armed man staggering up the road, pale in the headlights, a hatchet embedded in his chest. Flash shot his foot at the brake pedal. The heel of his boot skidded on the wet ground and he snapped awake as he started to fall. He caught himself. He wondered how long he'd been out.

Twisting around, he saw that the stump behind him was deserted. He spotted Nick behind the tents, the flashlight beam sweeping over the rocks and trees.

'Everything shipshape?' Flash asked when the boy returned.

'No problem.' Nick sat down and covered his head. 'Maybe she won't try anything.'

'Sure hope not. We've gotta stay on our toes, though.' The warning was more to himself than to his son. He was ashamed of falling asleep. He wouldn't let it happen again.

When he felt himself becoming groggy, he went into his tent for cigars. He returned to the seat, unwrapped a cigar, and clamped it between his teeth. He pulled the poncho forward enough to shield the cigar from the rain. To save his night vision, he shut his eyes when he struck the match. Then there was only the soft red glow of his cigar. Flash smoked slowly. When only a hot, bitter stub remained, he tossed it down and crushed it under his boot. 'Still with us?' he asked Nick.

'I'm awake.'

'I'll make the rounds.'

He stood up, and stretched his stiff back. His light probed the darkness ahead of him. A shape lurched from behind one of the pines, and his heart seemed to jump. Nothing but a shadow. He satisfied himself that no one lurked among the trees or crouched in the tumble of rocks, then turned his beam to the back of the tent.

For an instant, he thought the two-foot vertical slash was another trick of light – nothing more than a shadow. Crouching, he set the knife by his foot and touched the slit. It parted, and his fingers slid in.

He muttered, 'Jesus.'

Shoving the flashlight through the gap, he tugged the fabric wide. It split more. He dropped to his knees and peered inside.

Scott squinted up at him. He looked alarmed. His forehead was smeared with blood.

'It's me,' Flash said.

'What the hell are you doing?'

Karen, beside Scott in the sleeping bag, raised her head. She squeezed her eyes shut when the light hit her. The left side of her face was swollen and discoloured. So was her mouth and chin. A speck of fresh blood glistened above one eyebrow.

'Flash?' Scott said.

'Someone was here. I've gotta . . .' he shoved himself away from the tent, staggered backward, and caught his balance, 'Nick!' he yelled. 'Check Julie!' He rushed past Julie's tent, glimpsing its gashed fabric. His own was the same. He fell to his knees at the rear of the last tent, rammed his flashlight through the split, and yanked a wide opening. Alice lurched upright.

'It's me.'

Her forehead was bloody.

'What's going—'

'See if the girls are okay.'

Rose was already lifting her head. She blinked into the light. There was blood on her right cheekbone.

Alice shook Heather awake. The girl was buried in her sleeping bag. As she scooted forward, Flash saw a small patch of blood at the top of her head.

Alice touched her daughter's bloody hair, then looked at her finger. 'What's going on?' she asked in a low, frightened voice.

'I don't know,' Flash said, 'Somebody—'

'They're okay!' Nick called. 'They're both cut, though.'

'Get dressed,' he said into the tent. 'We're getting out of here.'

'Tonight?' Alice asked.

'Right now. As soon as we can break camp.'

Chapter Twenty-four

Benny, sitting on top of his sleeping bag, shoved his foot into a boot as Julie slipped a poncho over her head. She started crawling towards the tent flap held open by Nick. Benny blurted. 'Don't leave me here!'

'All right. But hurry.' She stopped. 'Do you know what's going on?' she asked Nick.

'I don't know.'

Benny got his other boot on. 'Ready,' he said. Grabbing his poncho, he followed Julie outside. He stood up and donned the poncho, thrusting his head through the hooded hole.

Mr Gordon came around from behind the last tent.

'Is everybody okay?' Nick called.

'Just cut. Nothing serious. Christ!'

'They're *all* cut?' Nick asked.

'All of 'em.'

'I don't get it.'

'Neither do I.'

The front of Karen's tent bulged and Dad crawled out, wrapped in a sleeping bag. Karen came out next. She wore grey sweatpants and a quilted parka that reached only to her waist. Her floppy hat covered her head. Her feet were bare.

Looking at her, Benny got a hollow ache in his chest. 'Are you hurt much?' he asked.

'Not bad,' she said. She slipped a hand from her pocket and held it out to him. He clasped it gently.

'I think we should haul ass outa here,' Mr Gordon said. 'What do you think?'

'Is everyone okay?' Dad asked.

'So far. But who knows what we're up against? We're too damn vulnerable here. I say we move out. Once we're on the trail, we can see what's coming. The trip's shot anyway, right?'

'I'd say so,' Karen muttered.

'Leave the body here?' Dad asked.

'It's gone,' Julie said.

Benny felt Karen's fingers tighten around his hand.

'Either the guy wasn't dead,' Mr Gordon explained, 'or someone snuck in and made off with him.'

'It had to be that woman,' Nick said.

'What woman?' Dad asked.

Nick repeated the story about the three girls who'd been swimming here yesterday until a weird woman yelled at them and frightened them away. 'She must be the one who slashed the tents, too,' he added.

'Why would anyone do that?' Karen asked. 'It'd make sense if she wanted to cut our throats, but . . .'

'Just one woman,' Mr Gordon said, 'couldn't have killed everyone. Not with two or three to a tent, and me and Nick on watch. She might've got a couple of us, but we'd have nailed her.'

'Why just scratch us, though? What does that accomplish?'

'You don't suppose . . .' Julie's lips drew back, and she shook her head.

'What?' Nick asked.

'It's crazy.'

'What's crazy?' Dad asked.

'Well . . . maybe her blade was poisoned.'

Benny's stomach knotted. 'Curare,' he muttered.

'Nobody's got curare out here,' his father said. 'And if they did, we wouldn't be standing around talking about it.'

'Maybe something,' Karen said. 'Some kind of poison or germs.' With her free hand, she touched the cut on Benny's face. 'I don't feel any swelling. There'd be swelling with snake venom. Besides, it'd take quite an amount to do much damage.'

'Rabies?' Nick suggested.

Julie groaned.

'I don't want to get creepy,' he went on, 'but all it'd take is some saliva or blood from a rabid animal—'

'I'd say it's pretty unlikely,' Dad interrupted. 'This had to be a spur-of-the-moment thing. Who's gonna have a rabid animal on hand?'

'A crazy old woman,' Julie said.

'Pretty remote chance.'

'It's possible, though,' Mr Gordon said. 'You'll admit it's possible?'

'Anything's possible.' Dad sounded annoyed.

'It does seem a little farfetched,' Karen said, 'but something like that, at least, would explain why she cut us. Otherwise, what's the point?'

'I don't know,' Dad admitted. 'I just hate to think that . . . I guess we'd better play it safe.'

'We'll hike straight out,' Mr Gordon said. 'I bet we can reach the roadhead in a day, if we really push it.'

'It's mostly downhill,' Julie added.

'Right,' Dad said. 'We'll lighten our packs. We can leave most of the food behind.'

'What about the tents?' Nick asked.

'Forget 'em,' Mr Gordon said. 'They're ten pounds each, and they're fucked anyway. We can make better time without 'em.'

'I'm with you,' Dad told him. 'Leave the things. Let's pack up fast and—'

'*Murderers!*' The shrill outcry made Benny jump. Karen jerked her hand away and whirled around. Benny staggered backward a step. Through the sheets of water he saw a woman perched on a boulder near the shore. He felt warm urine spill down his leg, and fought to stop it.

Everyone stood motionless, staring at the woman. She stood with her feet spread apart, dress clinging to her legs, face a thin pale mask streaked with ropes of dark hair, arms raised overhead. The blade of a small knife jutted from one hand. From the other hung a pouch the size of a baby's head.

'*Murderers!*' she shrieked again. 'You're cursed!' She shook the pouch. 'I have your blood and hair! You killed my son and you'll die, every one of you! Cursed! My curse is on you!'

She leaped off the rock and took a few steps sideways, waving the pouch. Then she turned away and started to run.

Mr Gordon lunged forward, but Dad grabbed his arm. 'Let go! I'll nail her!'

Benny saw the woman dash behind an outcropping.

'Just wait,' Dad told Mr Gordon. 'What if she's not alone? What if someone's waiting to pick you off?'

Mrs Gordon rushed from her tent, Heather and Rose following close behind. They wore yellow slickers and rain hats, and Benny couldn't tell which was Heather until one of the girls waved at him. 'Who was that?' Mrs Gordon asked.

'Some crazy old bag,' said Mr Gordon.

'Apparently the mother,' Dad explained, 'of the guy who attacked Karen and Julie.'

'A witch,' Benny said.

The others acted as if they didn't hear him. 'What did she want?' Mrs Gordon asked.

Her husband shrugged. 'God only knows.'

'Is she the one who took the body?'

'She didn't say.'

'She put a curse on us,' Benny said loudly. 'A death curse. She's a witch.'

'Bullshit,' Mr Gordon said.

'Bullshit or not,' Karen told him, 'that woman did, in fact, put a curse on us. In a way, though, it's a relief. I don't think she cut us to infect us – just to get blood for her hex or whatever.'

'That *is* how it sounded,' Dad admitted. 'The gal's obviously a nut case. Unless it was all a show to lure us after her.'

Benny took a deep breath. His glasses had slipped down the bridge of his nose. He shoved them back into place, and wrinkled his nose to hold them there. 'Do you want to know what I think?' he asked.

'I think we'd better get out of here,' Mr Gordon said. 'Rabies or no rabies, the quicker we get back to the cars, the better. We don't want to spend another night out here if we can help it. A loony like that gal, there's no telling what she might do.'

'Especially,' Julie added, 'if she's not alone.'

'Can I say something?' Benny asked again.

'What's this about rabies?' Mrs Gordon asked.

'Probably a false alarm, but—'

'Benny has something to say,' Karen broke in.

'Shoot,' Dad told him.

'I know I'm just a kid and everything, but I think we better not leave here till we get our stuff back.'

'What stuff?' Dad asked.

'Our blood and hair. She's got it in that pouch, I think.'

'She's welcome to it,' Dad said.

'She'll *use* it. You know, like with a voodoo doll? You need the person's hair or clothes to make it work. If she's got our hair and blood, she can use it like that.'

'To make voodoo dolls?' Karen asked.

'Or something. I don't know. I just know she can't mess with us if we take our stuff away from her.'

'For cryin' out loud, Benny.'

'What if he's right?' Nick asked. 'I mean, I'm not saying I believe it, but—'

'You'd certainly *better* not believe it,' Mrs Gordon scolded. 'It's blasphemy.'

'It's bullshit.'

'Please, Arnold.'

'Can't we just get out of here,' Julie said, 'before anything else happens?'

'We can't get away from a curse,' Benny warned. 'I'm telling you, we'd better—'

'Spare us, okay?'

'Look, Benny,' Dad said, 'I understand you're worried about this thing, but a curse is in the same category as zombies and vampires and ghosts. It's make-believe. It doesn't really exist. All it can do is frighten us it can't really hurt us. Guns and knives and hatchets can hurt us, but a curse is just words. Okay? So let's just try to forget about it and move out of here before we have something *real* to contend with.'

Benny shrugged. He knew it was pointless to argue. 'All right,' he muttered. 'But we'll be sorry.'

Part Two

Chapter Twenty-five

'Good grief, hon, you're a wreck.'

'Tell me about it,' Karen said. She swung her pack to the floor, crossed to the couch, sat down, and started to unlace her boots.

'A disaster, huh?' Meg lowered her husky body into a chair, and hooked a leg over one of its padded armrests. She took a cigarette from the side pocket of her housecoat. 'How'd you get the shiner? Bump into a tree, or did Scott smack you around?'

'A guy attacked me.' Karen pulled off her boots and leaned back against the soft cushions.

Meg groaned as she lit her cigarette. She inhaled deeply and blew smoke out her nostrils. 'How do you mean attacked?'

'He raped me.'

'Good Christ! Are you kidding? Are you okay?'

'Mostly bruises.'

'My God,' she muttered. 'Jesus Almighty Christ, that's . . .' She shook her head. Her face was twisted with disgust. 'How could it happen? There was a whole army with you.'

'I was alone in the tent.'

'Must've been . . . Karen, Karen.'

'I don't remember any of it. He knocked me unconscious. Scott was with me when I came to.'

The cigarette trembled in Meg's fingers as she raised it to her lips. 'What happened to the bastard that did it?'

'He was killed.'

'Good. I hope he died slowly. I'd have cut of his dick.'

'Then I'm glad you weren't there,' Karen said. With a moan, she lifted her feet and propped them on the coffee table. She folded her hands on her belly. 'I'm sore all over,' she muttered. 'We hiked out of there in one day – a night and a day. Then spent half a day at the sheriff's office. Then a few hours at some damn hospital for rabies tests.'

'Rabies tests? Was the bastard rabid?'

Karen shook her head, wincing at the pull of her stiff neck muscles. 'We were worried about his mother's knife.'

'His *mother*?'

'Yeah.' She explained about the tents being slashed open, the head cuts on everyone except Flash and Nick, the mother showing herself and cursing them.

'Like a fuckin' horror film,' Meg said. 'What was she, some kind of witch?'

'That's what Benny says. He's pretty spooked about the whole thing.'

'And you're not?'

'I'm not gonna lose any sleep over a curse. Sleep, ha! Wonder what that is. Feel like I haven't slept for a week.'

'Maybe you'd better hit the sack.'

'Funny, I'm not sleepy. Just kind of shaky and spaced out, and like I might vomit. But, anyway, I've gotta take a bath first. Probably turn the water black.'

'Can I do something for you? Fix you something to eat?'

'No, thanks. We ate on the road.'

'How about a drink? You could probably use a stiff one.'

'Yeah. A good belt of Alka-Seltzer. I'll get it.' She pushed herself forward, stood up, and limped towards the kitchen. Meg, hurrying ahead of her, turned on the light and went to a cupboard. 'Any trouble with the cops?'

'They're sending out a team to search for the body. I guess there won't be an inquest or anything unless they find something.'

Meg ran cold water from the tap, and filled the glass.

'Nobody's really sure the guy's dead. We think so, but the way the body disappeared . . .'

'Good Christ.'

'We think the mother took it. Anyway, they're investigating the whole thing.' She accepted the glass from Meg. 'They said they'd be in touch.'

'What a mess.'

'Yeah.'

Meg returned to the living room. Karen carried her glass up the short hall to the bathroom. Leaning against the sink, she opened the medicine cabinet and found a packet of Alka-Seltzer. Her hands shook badly as she tried to tear the foil. Finally, she ripped it with her teeth. She dumped the two tablets into her glass.

While she waited for them to dissolve, she stared at herself in the mirror. She looked as bad as she felt. Her blonde hair was dark and stringy. Her face was puffy and smudged with bruises. There were shadows under each eye. The eyes themselves were like those of a dazed, haggard stranger. She touched the cut above her right eyebrow, and felt the tiny ridge of scab. Combing her hair down with her fingers, she found a swath that was too short.

I have your blood and hair.

The bitch wasn't kidding.

Karen lifted the glass. The cool fizz tickled her nostrils as she drank. When she was done, she stripped off her filthy clothes. Many of the bruises on her neck and shoulders and breasts were shaped like teeth marks.

Beautiful. That's what the female deputy had said while inspecting the marks. Karen had blushed then, and she blushed now at the memory of it. The surge of blood made the pounding in her head hurt worse.

'Beautiful?' she'd muttered.

'The fella would've been an orthodontist's dream. These are nearly as good as fingerprints.' Then the deputy had taken an endless series of photos – long shots and close ups of each injury. 'And you're positive there was no ejaculation?' she asked when she finished.

'Does it make any difference?'

'Yes and no. It's rape irregardless, so long as he penetrated without your consent. A semen specimen can be typed, though, if he's a secreter. By that, I mean his blood type can often be determined from a semen sample. That'd be good evidence in court.'

'He didn't ejaculate.' Scott had. A specimen, if any traces could still be found, would only serve to confuse the situation.

The deputy had shrugged. 'We can live without it.'

'We can live without it,' Karen muttered to the bruised face in the mirror. 'Jeez.' She turned away. Her head throbbed as she bent over the bathtub and turned the faucets on. When the water was hot, she twisted the shower handle. There was a pause, then water sprayed down. She stepped over the side of the tub, into the hot rush, and pulled the plastic curtain shut.

The water felt wonderful splashing against her, matting her hair and spraying her face, running hot down her body. She turned slowly, sighing as it struck the back of her head, her sore neck and shoulders. Its gentle force massaged her, eased the pain in her head, brought a languor that made washing seem like too much effort.

Finally, she forced herself to shampoo. Her arms ached as she rubbed the suds into her hair and scrubbed her scalp. When she finished rinsing, she stood motionless, arms hanging limp, letting the spray hit her, feeling the hot streams slide down her body. She didn't want to move, except to lie down in the enveloping heat. But she needed to be clean first, to soap away the grime of the trails, her own sweat, the filth of the man who'd soiled her by his touch.

Stepping away from the shower so the water fell just against her calves, she began to rub herself with a bar of soap. Except for a patch of skin out of reach in the centre of her back, she lathered herself from neck to ankle. She set the bar in its dish. She felt as if she wore a suit of slick, hugging suds. With a wet washcloth, she began to scrub herself. She did it hard, despite the flickers of pain as she scoured the bruised areas.

Squatting, with the spray on her back, she swabbed between her legs. Tomorrow, she thought, she would stop by the Thrifty and buy a douche. She wished she didn't have to wait that long, but the store would be closed by now, so there was no choice.

She stood up and rinsed, cleaned her face and ears, and was done.

Crouching, she stoppered the drain. The sound of the shower changed immediately: a loud sound, hollow and plopping, not unlike the drum of rain on a tent.

It hadn't been raining when the man entered her tent. It had been raining when she came to. When Scott made love to her, the noise of rain smashing the tent was all around them, part of it all, as close to them as the sound of their heartbeats and breathing.

It was a good memory.

Karen sat down in the pooled water and slid herself backward until the spray enveloped all but her outstretched legs. Drawing them up, she wrapped her arms around her knees. She sat there, huddled under the hot shower, the water level rising, the sound like the rain hitting the tent two nights before when Scott was with her, so gentle, so hesitant, afraid of hurting her, finally filling her and making so much of the real hurt go away.

She wished she could be with him now. He'd asked her to come home with him, but it hadn't seemed right. 'I'm such a mess,' she'd objected. 'You'd better take me to my place.' Even as the words came out, they'd left a hollow, lonely place inside her. She'd wanted, more than anything, to go home with Scott. She didn't want to leave him. She didn't want to leave Benny or Julie. But they deserved time to be together as a family, time away from her. Even if they wanted her in their home tonight, she knew she would feel like an intruder.

The water splashing on Karen seemed less hot than before. Sliding forward, she twisted the shower handle down. The spray ceased, and water gushed from the faucet. She stopped all the cold, and continued to fill the tub, a hand under the spout until the falling water started to cool. Then she shut it off.

She lay down, her head against the rear of the tub, all but her face submerged in the warmth. The enamel was slick against her back, but she felt the washcloth under her rump. She pulled it free, wrung it out, and spread it over her face.

Wrapped in heat, she felt tranquil and lazy. The soreness seeped from her muscles. Her limp arms were buoyed up. She forced them down, and slid her fingers beneath her buttocks to stop them from rising.

Her mind began to drift. She was crouching by a mountain stream, splashing herself with water so cold it stung. She saw Scott's eager eyes, felt his hand cup her breast. When he pulled off her shirt, she reminded herself that he hadn't done that; they'd kissed and moved on and found the compsite for their first night. But now he did. He pulled off her shirt and kissed the teeth marks on her breasts. There shouldn't be teeth marks, but there were, and he kissed them gently. He plucked open the drawstring of her sweatpants. She'd been wearing shorts that afternoon, but never mind. They were off and she was sprawled naked on a hot granite slab beside the stream, with the spray of the tumbling water icy on her skin, and the sun hot. Scott, standing between her spread legs, wore only a grey sweatshirt. Karen's sweatshirt. It was much too tight. He struggled to take it off, but couldn't, so he slit it up the front with a straight razor. He knelt down. 'I've got a surprise for you,' he said. Reaching into a bowl, he scooped out a handful of white lather. He spread it on her groin. 'Are you going to shave me?' she asked. Scott didn't answer. He rubbed her with the thick, slippery cream, then piled a huge heap of it on her belly. As he smeared it over her skin, he said, 'It's not what you think.' She asked, 'What is it?' He swirled it over her breasts, made tiny white peaks on each nipple, and licked them off. 'Whipped cream,' he said. 'I'm going to eat you up.' He raised his face and grinned, but he wasn't Scott any more but a gaunt, wrinkled old woman with watery eyes and crooked brown teeth. There were dabs of whipped cream on her lips and the tip of her nose. 'No! Get away!' Karen gasped. The awful face darted down. She tried to twist away, but the teeth clamped on her breast and sank in. The old woman shook her head like a savaging dog, jerked free, and loomed over Karen's face, chewing a clump of flesh; blood and whipped cream spilled onto Karen's lips. Karen started to scream. Her mouth filled with water.

The choking startled her awake. She spat out a mouthful of water as she lurched upright. The washcloth peeled away from her face. She curled forward, muscles afire as a fit of coughing racked her body.

Gasping and coughing, she thrust herself out of the water. She swept an arm towards the shower curtain, then grabbed a wet fold as her right foot skidded out from under her. The curtain yanked taut, ripped free. Her legs shot out and she was falling. She heard a heavy splash an instant before her head seemed to explode. She slid down. Water covered her eyes, and then she saw nothing at all.

Chapter Twenty-six

Kneeling on his bedroom floor, Nick unstrapped his sleeping bag from his pack frame and rolled it aside. Right now, he thought, he would be lying next to Julie high in the mountains, if only . . . 'Damn it,' he muttered.

He opened his pack and began to empty it, tossing his dirty clothes into a heap for the laundry hamper, setting aside his cook kit, utensils, and water bottle for a trip to the kitchen, making a third pile of equipment – compass, first-aid kit, rope, toilet articles – that would need no attention and could simply be returned to the pack for the next time.

The next time?

After what had happened at Mesquite, he doubted he would ever want to go backpacking again. But you never know. Always in the past, when he stayed away from the mountains too long, he'd been hit with a longing to return, a strong aching need like homesickness. Maybe he wouldn't get that feeling any more.

Maybe nothing would ever be the same again.

He'd killed a man. He knotted up at the thought of it. Everyone – even the sheriff deputy after hearing the story – had told him it was all right, that the guy had it coming, that Nick had performed a service by ridding the world of him. Nick had told himself the same thing, over and over, and part of him was glad he'd done it – avenged Karen and Julie, stopped the man from attacking Julie's father with the rock, made it so he would never hurt anyone again. But deep inside he felt a steady tight sickness at the knowledge that he had ended a life. The man was dead. Dead. He would never again feel the sun on his face, or . . .

Or rape another woman.

If he'd been dead a week ago, he couldn't have attacked Karen or Julie. He couldn't have messed up their lives, and my life.

And if he'd got away, there might've been campers tonight or next week or next year to terrorize, maybe kill.

I did the right thing, Nick told himself. I shouldn't have to feel like shit. It's not fair.

'Nick?'

He looked over his shoulder. His father, dressed in a bathrobe, was standing in the doorway.

'Phone call.'

He felt a cold edge of panic. From the look on Dad's face,

though, he realised he had nothing to fear. 'Who is it?'

'A certain Miss O'Toole.'

Nick got to his feet, wincing with the ache of sore muscles, and hobbled down the hallway behind his father.

'You can take it in the den, but stay off the couch in those jeans or your mother'll throw a fit.'

'Right,' he said.

Dad limped into the master bedroom, and Nick hurried ahead to the den. He snatched the phone off its cradle and said, 'I've got it.' The bedroom extension went dead. 'Hello?' he asked.

'Hi.' Her voice sounded slightly different over the phone, but familiar enough to send a warm rush through Nick.

'Hi, Julie. How are you?'

'Long time no see, huh?'

'Yeah.'

There was a long pause. Nick tried to find something to say, and wondered if Julie were having the same trouble. Even with the silence, he liked the feel of being close to her.

'I just thought I'd call,' she finally said, 'and make sure you got home okay.'

He smiled. 'Afraid the curse might've got us?'

He heard her quiet laughter. 'Pardon me while I barf,' she said.

'Benny still at it?'

'We had about two hours of peace after we left the hospital. That's because he fell asleep. Then Dad had to stop at Denny's so we could feed our faces, and Benny spent the rest of the time trying to convert us. The kid's warped.'

'We're not allowed to talk about it. I brought it up once, and Mom nearly went through the ceiling. You know the first commandment?'

'Whose?'

'God's. You know, to Moses? The stone tablets?'

'Oh, those commandments. I know the eleventh is, "Don't get caught." '

Chuckling, Nick started to sit on the couch. He stopped himself in time, and sat on the carpet instead. 'Anyway, the first commandment says, "Thou shalt have no other gods before me" – something like that. According to Mom, that means it's a sin to believe in occult stuff.'

'Like curses?'

'Like curses, ghosts, Ouija boards, palm reading, astrology, witches and goblins and gremlins.'

'What the hell's a gremlin?'

'I don't know, a fairy.'

'Something that lives in San Francisco and lisps?'

'And eats quiche.'

'We oughta go on Letterman,' Julie said.

'It hurts to laugh.'

'Me, too. Gets my stomach muscles.'

'Yeah. So stop laughing.'

'You, too.'

'Right. Anyway, where was I? Oh, yeah, Mom and the curse.'

That brought a snort and gales of laughter through the phone. 'Oh,' Julie finally gasped. 'I'm sorry. I' – she giggled – 'I think I'm . . . a bit giddy. No sleep.' He heard her take a deep breath. 'Okay. I'm all right. Continue.'

'I think I was done.'

'Oh. All right. So. What've you been up to?'

'Just unpacking.'

'I'm saving that for tomorrow morning. I don't even want to *look* at that junk. The first thing I did was get in the shower.' He pictured her naked under a hot spray, rubbing her breasts with soap. 'Man, it sure feels good to be clean again. Now I've got Ben-Gay from head to foot.'

'Bet you smell terrific.'

'The fumes make my eyes water. And my nightgown's sticking to me.' He pictured her in a flannel nightgown. Of course, it probably wasn't flannel. Not in the middle of summer. Something light and transparent, and clinging to her breasts. He wondered if she'd put any Ben-Gay on her breasts. '. . . like a real person again,' she said. 'The Long Hike almost did me in.'

'Almost did us all in.'

'How's Heather getting along?'

'Not bad. The doctor says she'll be sore for a couple of weeks, but it's nothing to worry about. Mom's got her in the kitchen, soaking it.'

'Maybe she oughta try some Ben-Gay.'

'Yeah. Couldn't hurt.'

'At first it's pretty hot, but you get used to it.'

'Maybe I'll try some. After my shower.'

'You're still yucky, huh?'

'Yeah. I got last shot at the bathtub. I'm still waiting for Rose to get done. She takes forever.'

'Just as well. What if I'd called while you were in the shower?'

'I would've called back.'

'I might've been in bed by then.'

'Wouldn't you have waited up?'

'Maybe, maybe not. A girl's gotta get her beauty sleep.'

'Good thing I wasn't in the shower, then.'

'A very good thing.'

There was a long silence. Nick suspected she was getting ready to hang up. He clutched the phone tightly.

'Well . . .' she said.

His heart was thudding and his mouth was parched.

'. . . I guess I'd better let you—'

'Julie?'

'Yes?' she asked in a hushed voice.

'Look, I want to see you.' There. It was out.

'That would be nice,' she said.

'Tomorrow? Tomorrow night? Maybe we could go to a movie or something.'

'I'd really like that.'

'Great.' He let out a nervous laugh. 'This is so weird.'

'What's weird?'

'Asking you for a date. I mean, like we were almost strangers or something.'

'We're the same people who were in the mountains, Nick.'

'I know. I guess so.'

'You guess so?' She laughed softly.

'It's just that, you know, now we're back. It's strange.'

'I haven't changed. I still feel the same about you.'

A smile trembled on Nick's lips. 'I feel the same, too. really miss you. How about seven o'clock?'

'Fine. Just let me check with Dad. Hold on a minute.'

Nick waited. He took a deep, shaky breath. He'd done it, he'd asked her and she'd seemed as eager as he was. *I still feel the same about you*. It was almost too good to believe. He was already nervous, anticipating the date.

'Okay,' she said. 'It's all set. Tomorrow night at seven.'

'Great. I'll see you then.'

'Do you know how to find the house?'

'No, but Dad . . .' He didn't want to lose the sound of Julie's voice. 'Maybe you'd better tell me.'

There was blue terry cloth under Karen's face. Her lungs felt on fire, pain blasting through her body as a spasm of coughing shook her. Someone's hand was rubbing her back. As she lifted her head, nausea swept through her. She managed to get to her knees and twist around, briefly meeting Meg's worried eyes before scurrying to the toilet and vomiting.

When she finished, she sat on the toilet seat, sobbing and coughing, gasping for breath. Through teary eyes, she watched Meg fold up the bloody bathmat. She unrolled some tissue, wiped her eyes, her mouth and chin.

'How's the noggin?' Meg asked in her low, husky voice.

Karen groaned. She drew fingers through her wet hair, and felt a lump above her ear.

'Thank God I heard you yell. I was about to turn on the TV.' Meg opened the medicine cabinet. She took down a box, slid a tampon out, and tore off its wrapper. She handed it to Karen.

While Karen inserted it, Meg pulled the bathtub stopper. 'I tell you, kiddo, you scared the shit out of me. How're you feeling? Should I run you over to emergency?'

'I'm okay,' she muttered.

'I was gonna give you about ten more seconds to wake up, and then I was gonna call the paramedics.'

'How long was I out?'

Meg shook her head. 'No idea. Maybe three or four minutes, I don't know. I just knew your ticker was still ticking and you were breathing. I figured you'd come around, sooner or later, but I started to have my doubts.'

'What a mess.'

'The bathmat's a goner. I'll clean up the rest after you're in bed.'

'No, I'll—'

'You're in no condition to do anything, kiddo.'

Karen looked down at herself, wrinkled her nose, and unrolled more toilet paper. As she rubbed away streaks of blood, she said, 'I've gotta take another shower.'

'I suppose you do. Sit tight for a second.' Meg hurried from the bathroom. Karen continued to clean herself. Soon, Meg returned with a spool of tape. Reaching up, she worked at securing the shower curtain to its rod. 'Think it was the curse?' she asked.

'I *know* it was the curse.'

Meg chuckled.

'A week early.'

'Stress'll do that. On the bright side, at least you know the bastard didn't knock you up.'

'I knew that before,' she said.

When the curtain was in place, Meg ran the water. Karen clung to her arm for support, and staggered on wobbly legs to the tub. At her friend's urging, she didn't try to stand while she washed. She sat under the hot spray. With Meg waiting on the other side of the curtain, she shampooed and soaped herself and rinsed.

Meg stood by, hands out to catch her, while she climbed from the tub and dried. 'Safe now?'

'Yeah. Thanks.'

'You finish drying. I'll get us a little something.'

'A little what?'

'I'll surprise you.'

Left alone, Karen wrapped herself in the towel. She washed down two aspirin tablets with a glassful of cold water. She brushed her teeth. Then she drew a comb through her hair, wincing as she snagged tangles.

'In your room,' Meg called from the hallway.

Karen went to her bedroom. Meg, just inside, greeted her with a wink. The covers of her bed had been pulled back, showing her flowered blue sheets. Her chair had been dragged close to the bedside. On its seat rested a tray adorned with crackers, a wedge of cheddar, a small wheel of Gouda, and a cheese knife. Two wine goblets stood on the lamp table, and beside them was an open bottle of white wine.

In spite of her aches, Karen managed a smile.

'Medicine,' Meg said. 'Cheese and crackers to settle your gut. A Masson Sauvignon Blanc to help you sleep.'

'You're really fantastic.'

'I know.'

Karen put on her nightgown. She climbed into bed, pulled up the top sheet, and eased herself against the headboard. Meg poured the wine. She set the tray across Karen's lap, they lifted their glasses. 'Here's how,' Meg said.

'Here's to you,' Karen said. 'You saved my life.'

Meg blushed. 'What are roommates for?'

They clinked their glasses, and drank.

Chapter Twenty-seven

'A decent meal,' Arnold proclaimed, pulling up his chair to the breakfast table. He sniffed his plateful of bacon and fried eggs, and sighed loudly. 'Ah, the comforts of home.'

Smiling, Alice set a plate down in front of Heather. 'I didn't see you turning up your nose at your other breakfasts.'

'You even wanted mine,' Rose reminded him.

'I'll eat anything in the mountains. But this, now – this is real food.'

'I wonder what's keeping Nick,' Alice said.

'He's probably getting ready for his big date.'

'At nine in the morning?'

Arnold laughed, and started to cut his bacon.

Alice carried the final two plates to the table, then went to the kitchen doorway and called for Nick.

'Right there!' he yelled.

'Your egg'll get cold,' Alice warned. She returned to the table, sat down, and sighed, glad to be off her feet. She didn't look forward to grocery shopping, walking the aisles with stiff legs and blistered feet. There wasn't much choice, though. Not if they wanted supper tonight.

She heard the shuffle of Nick's moccasins on the kitchen floor. He came up behind her, and sat at the table. He gave her a quick smile. His eyes had a jittery look. 'Are you all right?' Alice asked.

'Sure. I didn't sleep too well, that's all.'

'Nervous about the big date?' Arnold asked.

Shrugging, Nick picked up his fork. It quivered in his shaky hand. He started to cut his eggs with the edge of it. Alice felt uneasy watching him, as if his tension were contagious. She started to eat, but barely noticed the taste of her food. Obviously, the boy was bothered by more than anxiety over tonight's date with Julie. He'd been through a nightmare, and she couldn't begin to guess how deeply it might've affected him. Julie might help take his mind of the rest of it.

'Where'll you be taking her?' she asked.

Nick shrugged. 'I don't know. I'll have to check the paper. There's all kinds of movie theatres in the Valley.'

'Plenty of drive-ins,' Arnold said.

'I don't want you taking her to a drive-in.'

'Why not?' Rose asked. 'They're neat.'

'Nick knows why not.'

'*We* go,' Rose persisted.

'That's different.'

'Why?'

'Just you never mind, young lady.'

'We used to call them passion pits.'

'Arnold!'

Rose tilted back her head and smiled, showing a mouth full of chewed bacon. 'Oh, I get it.'

'What?' Heather asked.

'Mom doesn't want 'em making out.'

'Some of my fondest memories . . .' Arnold started.

'That's enough.' She turned to Nick. He was staring at his plate as if oblivious to the conversation, swabbing up the last of his egg yolk with a bit of toast. 'You will not take Julie to a drive-in. I'm sure her father wouldn't approve, either.'

'I'm not arguing,' Nick said.

'Especially on a first date—'

'He's not arguing,' Arnold interrupted.

'Okay. I'm not one to nag. I just want to be sure we understand each other.'

'I understand,' Nick said.

'So,' Arnold said, 'what's on the agenda for today?'

'I, for one, have to go grocery shopping.' Alice got up from the table. 'Who wants to come along?' She picked up the coffeepot.

'Me,' Rose blurted.

'Me, too,' said Heather.

'You'd better stay home,' Arnold told her, 'and keep off your feet.'

'Oh, Dad.'

'He's right,' Alice said, stepping around the table to refill his mug. 'The more you stay off that foot, the quicker it'll heal.'

'Time heals all heels,' Nick said, and smiled. His first real smile of the morning.

Alice poured him more coffee, then refilled her own mug and took the pot back to the counter. 'Anything special I need to pick up at the store?'

'Vodka and Dos Equis,' Arnold said.

'Of course.' She sat down and took a sip of hot coffee, pleased that she'd turned the conversation to a less objectionable direction. 'I think I'll pick up a new Ace bandage. The old one's a disgrace.'

'I used up the Ben-Gay last night,' Nick said.

Arnold sniffed. 'So that's what I smell. Thought it was Rose's breath.'

The girl made a face at him, and Heather laughed.

'I think I lost my comb,' Nick said.

'Better buy him two or three,' Flash said. 'A young man in love is lost without his combs.'

Rose made an O with her mouth. Heather giggled. Nick's face turned as red as a ripe tomato. 'Jeez, Dad,' he muttered.

Arnold was beaming. 'Oh, did I say something wrong?'

'How's your dandruff shampoo holding out?' Alice asked her husband.

'Fine,' he said. 'A little low on the pit-slick, though.'

'May I be excused now?' Nick asked. 'I want to air out the sleeping bags.'

'Just throw them over the line,' Arnold said.

Nick left the kitchen. Arnold met Alice's gaze, and shrugged. 'You embarrassed the boy half to death,' she said.

'Is he really in love?' Heather whispered.

'Your father was just being his usual obnoxious self.'

Arnold chuckled.

'I bet he is,' Rose said.

'Regardless,' Alice warned. 'It's nothing to poke fun at. Being in love is a very serious matter.'

'Especially when you're seventeen,' Arnold added.

'Come on, Rose, help me clear the table. I want to beat the crowds to the supermarket.'

Benny held a plate under the kitchen faucet, and watched the steaming water melt away the clumps of sugar left over from the cinnamon rolls. When the plate looked clean, he handed it to Tanya. She put it into the dishwasher, and he grabbed another plate. 'Do you think they'd let a kid use the library?' he asked.

'What library?' his cousin asked.

'At the college.'

'What is it you're looking for? Maybe I could find it for you.'

'Just some stuff.'

Tanya set two coffee mugs upside down in the machine, and stared at him. She raised a dark eyebrow. 'Occult stuff?' she asked.

'Yeah,' he admitted. 'Witches and things.'

'Did you try your bedroom?'

'Yeah, last night. I haven't got that much, though. Nothing with the details. And the public library stinks.'

'They probably don't want to corrupt the youth.'

'Anyway, what I was thinking was that maybe I could go along with you and take a look around while you're in class.'

'For two and a half hours? Aren't you afraid you'll get bored?'

'I never get bored. Dad says boredom's a sign of a weak mind.'

Tanya grinned, brushed a lock of hair away from her

forehead, and took the plate from Benny. 'Well, you're welcome to come along, if that's what you want. But you'd better check with your dad first. He might have some chores for you. Go on ahead. I'll finish with the dishes.'

'Thanks,' he said, and hurried outside. His father, in his faded blue swimming trunks, was down on one knee beside the pool, checking the thermometer. 'Hey, is it okay if I go over to the college with Tanya? It's all right with her if it's all right with you.'

'Fine with me. What's up?'

'Nothing. I just want to fool around in the library.'

Dad's mouth curved in a half smile. 'The only known copies of the *Necronomicon* are said to reside in the Miskatonic University library and—'

Benny laughed. 'You know about that?'

'You'd be surprised what your old dad knows. I ain't completely illiterate, boy. Anyway, go ahead if you want. Be warned, though. Karen'll be showing up in an hour or so.'

Benny's eagerness faded. He didn't want to miss Karen. On the other hand, this was too important to delay. Maybe he wouldn't find anything helpful in the college library, but he had to give it a try. 'Well,' he said, 'I'd better go anyway. We'll be back around one.'

'Karen should still be here. She's staying for supper, I imagine. Good hunting.'

Chapter Twenty-eight

They were on a quiet, tree-shadowed lane no more than six blocks from home, Rose fooling with the radio dial to bring in a rock station, when a German shepherd wandered out from behind a parked car. Alice gasped. She threw an arm across Rose's chest, knocking the girl backward as her foot shot down on the brake pedal. The tyres shrieked. The dog swung its head around, seemed to glare at Alice, made no move to get out of the way. The hood hit it from view an instant before it was struck. The impact jolted the station wagon. Alice whimpered as the left front tyre bumped over the dog.

'Oh, Mom!' Rose cried. She had a look of horror in her eyes.

Alice glanced at the rearview mirror. The shadowy lane was deserted behind them. She didn't know what to do. She wanted to drive on and get far away from it all, but she couldn't do that without a rear tyre passing over the dog. The thought of that sickened her. Her right leg, still stretched out and mashing the brake pedal to the floor, started to bounce in a frenzy as if its muscles had all gone berserk.

Rose fumbled with her seat belt.

'Just wait a—'

'We've gotta help it, Mom!' She flung open her door and leaped out.

'Rose! Damn it!'

The girl, paying no attention, was running around the front of the car. With a shaky hand, Alice turned off the ignition. She set the emergency brake, struggled to free herself from the seat belt, and shoved open her door. Her jumpy right leg started to collapse when she put weight on it. She hung onto the door to hold herself up. 'Rose!'

It was too late. The girl was standing rigid by the front tyre, staring down, her pretty features twisted hideously, palms pressed to her ears as if to block out a terrible noise.

Alice glanced down at the crushed remains of the dog. She raised her eyes quickly to Rose. 'There!' she snapped. 'Are you happy? I *told* you not to look!' She hadn't, not really, but she'd tried. 'I wish, damn it, just once, you'd *listen* to me when I tell you something!'

The girl kept staring at the dog. 'Oh, Mom,' she muttered, and dropped her hands to her sides.

'Did you hear anything I told you?'

'We've gotta help it,' Rose said again, and started to cry.

'Oh, Rose, Rose.' Alice hugged her daughter fiercely. She started to cry. 'I'm sorry, honey. I'm sorry I yelled. I just didn't want you to see. I'm sorry.'

'We've gotta help it.'

'It's beyond our help, honey. It's with God now.'

'No. Please. It can't be dead.'

'I'm sorry, honey.'

'We've gotta take it to a vet.'

'It's dead. There's nothing a vet can do for it.'

'Please. If we don't try . . . We've gotta *try*!'

'Trouble?' someone called.

Alice spotted a young, bearded man striding down the nearest driveway. Please, she thought, don't let it be his dog. 'It ran out,' she said. 'I couldn't stop in time. It just . . . ran right out in front of me.'

He stepped past the front of the car, and looked down. 'You sure creamed it, all right. What a mess.'

Alice wiped her eyes. 'Do you know who it belongs to?'

'Never seen it before.' He crouched down close to the remains. 'Doesn't seem to have a collar. A stray maybe.'

'We're gonna take it to a vet,' Rose said.

The man raised his eyebrows. 'You want to put *that* in your car?'

'No—'

'Yes! We have to, Mom. Please.'

'Honey, it's dead.'

'No, it's not!'

'Looks pretty dead to me,' the man said. He sounded a bit amused. 'I'm no authority, but the way its guts are spread around—'

'Stop that!' Alice snapped.

'Sorry. I didn't . . . Tell you what. If you really want to take it with you, I'll give you a hand. Let's not mess up your car, though. You want to hang on a minute, I've got some Hefty bags out in the garage. Go ahead and open your tailgate. I'll be back in two shakes.'

Alice stood mute while he hurried away. She didn't want the awful thing in her car. But she felt trapped. She couldn't drive away without running over it again – not unless she first dragged it out from under the car. Besides, Rose would never forgive her.

She supposed that she did have a certain responsibility for the poor creature. She couldn't blame herself for killing it – she'd been driving under the speed limit and it had stepped out right in front of her and nobody could've stopped in time. But she had been the one to kill it, even if it weren't her fault. As much as she hated the idea, she supposed that hauling its corpse to a veterinary hospital would be the right thing to do.

Let them dispose of it properly.

They could leave it here for the Department of Animal Regulation to pick up. But other cars might . . . Maybe the man would move it out of the road.

Hell, she might as well take it. Make Rose happy. Unless she was mistaken, there was a veterinary hospital on Wilshire, just a block from their dentist's office.

She saw the man striding down his driveway with a garbage bag and a shovel. A *shovel*. 'Get in the car, honey.'

As the girl obeyed, Alice took the keys from the ignition and stepped to the rear of the station wagon. She lower the tailgate. Hearing a car behind her, she rushed to the driver's door and shut it. The car swung into the other lane. Alice looked down so she wouldn't see those inside the car as it passed. She was relieved that it didn't stop. Once it was gone, the road was clear.

'You sure you want to take this thing?' the man asked. 'I could drag it over to the curb, have the pound come for it.'

'No, that's all right. My daughter—'

'Yeah. Kids. You're always better off going along with them. Hey, they're usually right anyway.'

He spread the plastic bag flat on the pavement, its edge an inch from the blood puddle. Standing on it, he put on a pair of garden gloves. He spread his feet wide, pinning down the bag, and dragged the dog forward by its front paws. Horrified, Alice saw that some of its insides stayed behind, as if glued to the street. She gagged and turned away. She heard crinkling plastic, then the raspy scrape of the shovel. 'There y'go,' the man said. To the dog? 'You hanging in there? Ma'am? You all right?'

Alice nodded.

'Do you think you can lend a hand? We don't want the bag to tear.'

'Of course,' she muttered. She faced the man, and tried not to look at the dog. 'What should I do?'

'Let's drag it to the back. If you can lift that end of the bag a bit, take some of the weight off . . .'

She stepped around the man. Crouching, she grabbed the edge of filmy plastic. The man lifted his end and waddled backward, dragging the awful load. The dog was very heavy. To keep from looking at it, Alice focused on the man's head. Though he appeared no older than thirty, his black hair was thin on top. That explains the beard, she thought: balding men often wore beards.

Finally, they reached the rear of the station wagon.

'Lift?' he asked.

'I'll try.'

'Got a good grip on it?'

She adjusted her hold. 'Okay,' she said.

'*Now.*'

They lifted. She felt the plastic stretch as if melting over her fingertips and knuckles. It spread and tore, but then the weight was gone, the dog supported by the tailgate.

The man crawled into the rear of the wagon. He tugged he bag, sliding the dog in after him. Turning away, he climbed into the backseat and left through a passenger door.

Alice shoved the tailgate shut.

'Okay,' the man said. He plucked off his gloves and picked up his shovel. 'All set. You can probably get someone at the vet's to take it out for you.'

'Well, thank you so much for helping.' She wondered if he should offer him money. That would be embarrassing, specially if he refused. 'We really appreciate it.'

'Anytime,' he said, and made a wry smile. 'Hey, if it pulls through, let me know.'

Sick, Alice thought. 'I will,' she muttered.

Then the man was walking away with a sprightly step, the shovel over one shoulder. She half expected him to start whistling like one of the Seven Dwarfs.

'Hurry, Mom,' Rose called.

She climbed in behind the steering wheel. The girl was on her knees, looking over the back of the seat towards the dog. She was sniffing, dabbing at her nose with a wad of blue Kleenex. 'Turn around and strap yourself in,' Alice said. While Rose sat down and fastened her safety harness, she buckled herself in and started the car.

She drove forward slowly to the end of the block. At the stop sign, she checked the intersection carefully before proceeding.

'Drive faster, Mom. Please!'

'There's no hurry,' she said.

'Yes there is!'

On the front lawn of a house just ahead, a boy in overalls

was cavorting with a cocker spaniel. Alice watched them as she approached. Thank God it had been a dog, she thought, and not a child. That was too awful even to contemplate. What was wrong with the mother of this boy, letting him romp unattended in the front yard? The spaniel suddenly made a lunge towards the road. Alice shot her foot to the brake pedal, but the dog stopped at the sidewalk, wheeled around, and scampered back into the yard. Sighing with relief, Alice drove past.

The steering wheel was slick under her sweaty hands. She let go, one hand at a time, and wiped them on her skirt.

The shopping trip, she decided, was out of the question. After this ordeal, she was in no condition to face the super-market. It could wait, or Arnold could go. Either way, she had no intention of leaving the house again today. When she got home, she would shut herself up in the bedroom with the new Sidney Sheldon book and not come out until . . .

From behind Alice came a low, rumbling growl. The back of her neck prickled.

'It *is* alive!' Rose blurted joyously, starting to turn around.

In the rearview mirror, Alice saw the German shepherd, forepaws on top of the backseat, fangs bared, bloody saliva hanging in strings from its snout. With a raging snarl, it sprang forward. Rose shrieked. Alice jammed on the brake pedal. The car lurched to a stop, throwing them both into their harnesses, slamming Alice's forehead against the steering wheel. The dog tumbled onto the cushion beside her, its entrails slopping down after it, teeth snapping shut on Rose's wrist as the screaming girl tried to unbuckle her safety belt. It released her wrist and lunged at her throat.

Alice fumbled with her own buckle. She flung the straps aside and threw herself onto the huge beast, hooking an arm around its neck as Rose cowered against the door and shrieked and tried to hold off its snapping jaws. Alice squeezed the thick, furry neck in the crook of her elbow. She shoved her other hand into its mouth, cried out as the teeth tore into her, but clutched the snout and pulled it towards her, away from Rose. Then she was falling backward, the squirming dog heavy on her chest, the teeth still grinding into her hand. 'Rose!' she yelled. 'Get out!'

The dog writhed and jerked, trying to roll but unable to free itself from Alice's grip. If she let go, she knew it would flip over and go for her throat. Her hand was afire with pain, her fingers weakening, but still she held on.

The door behind her head swung open.

Rose, standing above her, grabbed one of the dog's kicking forelegs. 'Let go!' she cried.

'Rose!'

'Let go!'

She opened her fingers, felt the teeth release her. The dog stretched its head up, trying to snap at Rose.

Rose was trying to pull it out of the car! Didn't she realise . . .

'No!' Alice yelled. The wet fur of the dog's back muffled her outcry.

It was half out of the car, and didn't Rose realise it would go for her? Alice wrapped her arms around its open belly, trying to keep the beast from getting out.

The body suddenly quaked as a thudding, crushing sound filled Alice's ears. The car rocked a bit. The sound came again. Again. Each time, the car swayed and the dog jerked and trembled.

Then it was motionless on top of her.

'Mom? Are you okay?'

As the body was dragged off Alice, she realised what the thudding sound had been – *her daughter slamming the car door three times on the German shepherd's head.*

Chapter Twenty-nine

'What've they got him for?' Benny asked as a young man standing beside a guard shack waved them ahead.

Tanya smiled at the man, and drove slowly past him. 'He's supposed to keep out undesirables,' she said. 'People who don't have any business being here. You get all kind of crazies hanging around if you aren't careful. Flashers, rapists, that kind of thing. It's because there are so many women around. Every college has trouble like that.'

'Really?' Benny asked.

'Sure. Berkeley had about a dozen rapes when I was there. That's one reason my folks were so eager to have me transfer down here and live with you guys.'

'I didn't know that,' Benny admitted. 'I thought you did it just to help Dad.'

'Oh, that was part of it, too.' She swung into an empty space next to a VW van. 'There were all kinds of reasons,' she said. She reached for the spiral notebook and the heavy volume of Shakespeare plays on the seat beside her, but Benny grabbed them first.

'I'll carry them for you,' he said.

Tanya smiled, and Benny felt a blush spread over his face. She really was so beautiful. Not as beautiful as Karen, though. He wished he could be home when Karen arrived.

He climbed from the car and joined Tanya on a walkway that led down the side of the parking lot. Not far ahead, he saw several buildings: some looked low and modern, all stucco and windows like his junior high; others were ancient, square structures of red brick. The buildings were far apart, separated by broad lawns with more trees than a park. In fact, Benny decided, the campus looked very much like a park. There were even benches. 'This is nice,' he said.

'I like it,' Tanya told him.

'Better than Berkeley?'

She shrugged.

'Not as much?' he persisted.

'I don't know,' she said. 'I think I like this better. Berkeley was so huge, I felt lost. There'd be a couple of hundred students in some of my lecture classes. You know this Shakespeare class? Fourteen students. It's great.' She glanced at her wristwatch, and groaned. 'Cutting it close,' she said. Instead of hurrying, she stopped. She nodded to the right. 'My class is over that way. You'd better go on to the library without me, or I'll be late. I'll meet you there when class is over, so we can check out any books you want. Okay?'

'Fine.'

She pointed straight ahead. 'See the third building down? That's the library.'

Benny flipped up his clip-on sunglasses and counted the structures. 'The one with the pillars?'

'That's it. Kind of a dreary place. If you get sick of it, the student union's directly across the quad. You can get yourself a Coke or something. I'd better get moving.' Benny gave her the notebook and the thick text. 'Good luck,' she said, and hurried away. She cut across the grass, walking quickly, her rump shifting inside her tight blue shorts. Then she waved and called out, 'Steve!' A guy climbing the stairs of a distant building turned around, waved back, and waited for her. Tanya jogged forward to meet him.

Benny watched until they disappeared through a glass door. Feeling abandoned, he lowered his sunglasses into place and started towards the library. The few students he passed on the walkway seemed to be in no hurry. Apparently, they were between classes. A young couple was sitting on a bench, holding hands and talking. On a rise off to his left, a girl in shorts and a halter was lying on a towel, sunbathing while she read a paperback. A Frisbee landed near her. She ignored both the Frisbee and the shirtless guy who raced up and scooped it from the ground. The guy sailed it over Benny's head, and ran across the walkway to rejoin his friends.

Benny was glad that nobody seemed to notice him. He felt out of place here among these college kids, an intruder in their special world. He half expected someone to challenge him and throw him out.

A skinny, middle-aged woman in a pantsuit approached, scowling through her tinted glasses. 'Excuse me, young man,' she said in a sharp voice.

His heart quickened. 'Me?'

'Yes, of course you. Which way is the administration building?'

'Gee I don't know.'

'You don't know,' she said with disgust. 'The *administration* building,' she repeated, more loudly this time as if to penetrate his deafness or stupidity. 'Weller Hall.'

'I don't know him, either,' Benny said. The whiny sound of his voice embarrassed him.

'It's not a *he*, young man. *Weller Hall*. It's the name of the administration building.'

'Oh.'

She huffed through her nose, and Benny eyed her nostrils, expecting snot to fly out.

'I don't know where anything is,' he admitted. 'Just the library and the parking lot.'

'If I'd wanted the library or parking lot, I would've asked. I'm looking for –'

'Weller Hall,' Benny interrupted.

'Are you being smart with me, young man?'

'No, ma'am.'

'See that you're not,' she snapped, and hurried off.

Shaken by the encounter, Benny quickened his pace. What was she, crazy? Couldn't she tell, just by looking, that he didn't belong here? Crazy old bag.

Crazy old bag. Somebody – Julie? – had used those words about the mountain woman. The witch.

Benny glanced back.

Gone! She was nowhere in sight. A creepy feeling scurried up his spine.

Probably she just went into the building back there.

But what if she is the witch? What if she followed us down from the mountains, followed us home?

As he climbed the steps towards the library door, he pictured the witch in the dark with her arms high, shouting her curse over the noise of the wind and rain. He tried to imagine how she might look in a grey pantsuit, wearing fashionable glasses, her hair fixed up. With a sick feeling, he realised she might look very much like the woman he'd just met. If only he'd had a better look at the witch's face.

'Don't be dumb,' he said to himself out loud.

Then he took off his clip-ons and pulled open the library door. Carpet silenced his footsteps as he walked towards the circulation desk, where a young woman was reading. She had a felt-tipped pen. She wore a white blouse with a frilly collar, and had golden hair like Karen. Benny saw nothing threatening about her. She looked up as he approached, and smiled. 'Hello,' she said.

'Hi,' Benny whispered. 'Is it all right if I look around for a while? I'm waiting for my cousin. She's in class.'

'Certainly. No problem. If you want to look at some magazines, the periodical room's over behind those stacks.' She pointed to the right.

'Thank you.'

'Help yourself. If you have any questions, I'll be right here.'

Benny thanked her again, and walked over to the card catalogue. Nobody else was using it. Except for a few students seated nearby at long tables, reading or scribbling notes, the big room was deserted.

He studied the drawer labels. Finding one marked WIKWIZ, he slid the drawer open. He flipped through the cards towards the back of it. Soon, he came to a card marked *Witchcraft in*

Salem Village. Behind it was *Witchcraft Through the Ages*, then *Witchery Ditchery Doc*, a novel. No good to him. He flicked that card forward. *Witches and Warlocks*. That sounded useful. But the next card set his heart racing: *Witch's Spells and Potions*.

He looked at the call number, and frowned. Instead of Dewey decimal numbers, which he understood, there was a series of letters.

Well, the librarian *had* offered to help.

Taking the ballpoint from his shirt pocket, he started to write the letters on the heel of his hand. The pen skipped badly. Then he noticed a small tray of scrap paper on top of the catalogue. He took down a piece, and wrote out the call letters, author, and title.

Then he returned to the circulation desk. The woman finished marking a passage with her yellow felt-tipped pen, and smiled up at him.

'I'm sorry to bother you again,' Benny said, 'but do you know where I can find this book?'

She glanced at the paper. 'Oh, that'll be downstairs. Are you familiar with the Library of Congress system?'

'No, I—'

'Well, you just go alphabetically along the shelves. They're all labelled. Then, when the books are all lettered the same, you go by the numbers underneath. It's pretty simple, really.'

'Fine. Thank you. Uh . . . it's downstairs?'

Nodding, she swivelled her chair around and pointed. 'Right through those double doors.'

'Thank you,' he said again. Taking the scrap paper, he walked alongside the counter and pulled open one of the doors. It swung shut behind him. The landing was dimly lit. Benny looked up at the fixture, a globe with the debris of dead bugs showing through its frosted glass. Wrinkling his nose, he started down the stairs. They seemed to be concrete, but rang under his footsteps as if there was metal inside. The echo made him uneasy. He tried to descend more quietly. As he neared the next landing, he imagined taking off his shoes to muffle the noise. That would be dumb. And what if somebody saw him? 'Hey, kid, put your shoes on. What're you trying to pull?' Besides, why should he worry about making a little noise?

When he reached the landing, he looked down the final flight of stairs and hesitated.

It was dark down there.

The globe overhead cast its light on the first few steps, faded, and left the lower ones in murky gloom. The fixture below was a dull, grey ball, its bulb either turned off or dead.

He'd seen a movie last summer, where a monster lurked under a staircase. He leaned over the railing and peered down. There did appear to be an open space beneath the stairs.

Don't be a jerk, he told himself. He took a deep breath and charged down into the darkness, more certain with each clamouring footfall that he was not alone in the stairwell. The bottom of the stairs took him by surprise. He thought there was one more step, but there wasn't. His right foot pounded down hard on the floor, sending pain up his leg. He stumbled forward, his shoulder driving open the door, and fell sprawling as the door slammed the wall with a stunning crash.

He picked up his glasses and glanced at the lenses. They hadn't broken. He put them on, and slid the clip-ons back into his shirt pocket. Then he got to his feet. Rubbing his sore knee, he looked down the long aisle ahead of him. He glanced to the sides, down narrow lanes between bookshelves. He saw no one. More important, no one had seen him; he felt like a clumsy idiot.

Klutz.

It was like the night he'd tripped Heather.

Good thing Julie wasn't here to ride him about it.

On the other hand, he almost wished she *was* here. Except for a buzzing sound from the fluorescent lights, the room was silent. It's supposed to be silent, he reminded himself. This is a library. But somehow it seemed too silent. He strongly suspected that nobody was down here but him.

With a glance at the lettering on the shelves to his left, he realised that the witchcraft book was probably somewhere down that aisle. He should find it, grab it, and hurry upstairs. But the thought of the stairwell sent a shudder through him.

Sooner or later, he would have to face it. Unless he waited down here long enough for Tanya to come. The librarian knew where he was. She'd tell Tanya, or maybe she'd come down herself in a while. Or some students might show up and . . . For all Benny knew, there might already be students down here, silently searching the shelves. If he found one, he could follow him out.

This is really dumb, he thought, as he started walking slowly up the centre aisle. He glanced each way into the narrow spaces between the shelves.

There's nothing in the stairwell. I'm just yellow.

So I'm yellow. If there just happens to be someone else down here and I just happen to see him leaving, I'll just happen to follow along. No harm in that. Nobody has to know what I'm doing. Nobody will ever know, if I don't tell.

He was halfway to the end of the aisle without spotting anyone when he noticed a sound like someone panting. He froze. The sound seemed to come from his right, somewhere not far ahead. Between those shelves. If he took just one big step, he could probably see.

It was a quick, harsh gasping sound that someone might make after running hard. Then a moan that made his skin prickle.

He knew he should take that single step forward. Or better yet, stride boldly by and just happen to glance over as he passed. But he couldn't. Instead, he backed silently away.

After several paces, he ducked into the stacks to the left. Hidden by the ceiling-high shelves, he made his way quickly to the far wall. There, he turned left and rushed back the way he'd come. He passed between the final set of shelves. Crouching at the end, he peered down the centre aisle. He saw no one. He glanced behind him at the door to the stairs, only a couple of yards away.

Maybe he should run for it. The stairwell frightened him, but now it seemed no worse than the room itself. He had to get out of here before . . . The book. He needed the book. If he left without it, all this would've been for nothing.

He eased backward. The scrap paper was a crumpled sodden ball in his hand. He picked it open, spread it out, and compared the series of call letters to those on a book near his shoulder.

He must be close. Standing, he sidestepped away from the aisle and scanned the labelled spines. The search led him deeper into the stacks, farther and farther from the door. As his eyes moved over the books, he listened intently, ready to bolt. He heard nothing but the buzz of the fluorescent lights.

On tiptoes, head tilted far back, he squinted at the top row of books. He couldn't quite make out the lettering. It's probably up there, he thought. If it is, I'll have to climb for it. The shelves were metal, about four feet long, deep enough to hold books on both sides, secured at each corner to upright rods. They looked very sturdy. Benny grabbed a forward edge, and tugged it. There was no wobble at all. He wouldn't try climbing, though, until he was sure he had to.

He stepped to the left, dropped to his knees, and stared at the bottom row of books. The first line of letters was right, but the numbers below . . . Turning his head, he read the titles: *Black Magic, A Practical Guide to Sorcery, Step into Darkness, Tarot Made Easy, Witches and Warlocks, Witch's Spells and Potions.*

Great!

He didn't see much use for the tarot book, and he had no idea what *Step into Darkness* might be about. A glance at the table of contents . . . No, he could do that once he was safe upstairs. He'd take it, and the other four.

As he reached for them, the books shot forward, knocking

into his hands and tumbling against his knees. A bony, blue-veined hand snatched him by the wrist.

The lights went out.

Shrieking, he thrust his other hand forward, ramming books from the higher shelf into the darkness, hearing volumes fall on the other side. He tried again, this time finding the shelf's edge, shoving at it, trying to brace himself as the fierce grip drew his lower hand forward.

She wants to drag me through!

With all strength in his left arm, he tried to hold himself back. 'Let go!' he yelled. '*Help!*' The tugging grew more powerful until he felt as if it might rip his arm from the socket. His other arm gave out. He flew forward, head bashing the edge of the upper shelf, then fell onto his back.

'No!' he cried as he was dragged between the shelves.

In a frenzy of panic, he reached out with his left hand, felt the dry stiff fingers clutching his other wrist, pried on away. There was no yell of pain. Just the sharp brittle *pop*, like the snap of a twig, as the finger broke off. The grip loosened. He jerked his wrist free, whipped his arms down, and grabbed the bookshelf edge above his chest. With a quick yank, he thrust himself out. The metal edge scraped the top of his head as he sat up.

He lunged to his feet, turning in the direction of the door – he hoped. To the left? Yes! It had to be! He reached through the darkness, slapping at the books to keep his bearings. Then the books stopped. He threw himself against the wall, felt along it, found the door. He flung it open and plunged into the stairwell.

Clawing blindly, he smashed his forearm on the banister. He grabbed the railing. Hand over hand, he followed upward. The entire stairwell was dark. At the first landing, he dared to glance back. Only blackness. He blinked to be sure his eyes were open. He heard nothing but his own rasping breath and thudding heart, but a chill spread over his skin like a spray of ice water. She's there, she's coming!

He charged up the next flight of stairs, trying not to scream, and saw a thin strip of light from under the door. He shouldered the door open.

The librarian flinched, swivelled in her chair, and opened her mouth. She said nothing, though, as Benny sprinted past the desk in his mad race for the exit.

He shoved open the glass door. He ran down the steps to the walkway and he didn't stop running until he reached the car.

Chapter Thirty

Benny was lying across the backseat, sweltering in the locked car, when Tanya finally arrived. She opened the driver's door, and looked down at him. 'Are you all right?' she asked.

Nodding, he sat up.

'I got worried when I didn't see you in here. Thought I'd lost you.'

'Sorry,' he muttered. He climbed out. After the oven of the car, the air outside felt fresh and cool. He mopped the sweat off his face, and put on his shirt. Tanya, leaning across the front seat, unlocked the passenger door for him. He opened it, and rolled down the window before getting in.

She handed him a small, black book. Benny stared at the cover. *Witch's Spells and Potions*. 'You got it?' he asked, amazed.

'Kristi did. What went on anyway?'

'Huh?'

'At the library.'

'I had some trouble,' he muttered.

'So I heard. When I showed up, Kristi said you'd run off

like a bat out of hell. What were you doing down there? She said the lights were off, and you'd thrown books all over the floor. She was a little ticked.'

'I didn't do it.'

Tanya glanced at him with disappointment, reached forward, and started the car. 'Nobody else was down there, according to Kristi.'

'Somebody was,' he said, trembling now with the memory of it. He held his right hand towards Tanya. His wrist was ringed with faint bruises, raw furrows where fingernails had raked his skin.

Tanya stared at the injuries. 'Who did that to you?'

He shrugged.

'My God, Benny! You should've told someone. Who did it? Did he try to—'

'She.'

'We'd better tell campus security.'

'They won't find her. She's a witch.'

'That's crazy, Benny, and you know it.'

'Yeah,' he muttered. 'I figured you'd say that.'

'We can't tell security that a witch—'

'I'm not gonna tell 'em anything. They'll just say I'm crazy, too.'

With a sigh, Tanya shifted to reverse and backed out the car. She started driving towards the parking lot exit. The air coming through the open windows felt good to Benny. 'I know you're not crazy,' Tanya told him. 'But you've got witches on the brain, and a very active imagination.'

'Did I imagine this?' he asked, holding up his hand.

'Of course not.'

'You think I did it to myself?'

'Did you?'

'No.'

'Okay, I believe you. Now why don't you tell me what happened down there?'

'All right.'

* * *

'And then her finger broke off,' Benny said. 'Right in my hand.'

'Broke *off*?' Scott asked. 'Are you sure?'

'Yeah.'

'Bullshit,' Julie muttered.

Scott frowned at her, and glanced at Karen. She was staring into her Bloody Mary, a look of disgust on her bruised face. 'Okay,' Scott said. 'Then what happened?'

'Well, she let go and I got away.'

'You never saw her at all?'

'It was pitch black.'

Scott leaned back in his lounge chair. He wiped the wet bottom of his cocktail glass on his trunks, but it dripped anyway as he took a sip. On the sun-heated skin of his chest, the splash of icy water felt like a knife prick. He rubbed it with his fingertips. 'Sounds like you had a rough time of it, pal.'

The words of sympathy seemed to hit Benny hard. His chin started to shake. He pressed his lips into a tight line.

'You sure all this really happened?' Julie asked. 'You weren't just dreaming or something?'

'It wasn't a dream,' he mumbled.

Tanya, sitting cross-legged with her back to the pool, said, 'The library worker went down to look around after Benny took off. She told me the lights were off and there were books on the floor. She thought Benny did it. According to her, nobody else was down there.'

'I wonder how well she looked,' Karen said.

'Did she happen to find a finger?' Julie asked.

'A finger doesn't normally just break off,' Scott said. 'Even if the bone . . . there are muscles, tendons, flesh.'

'And blood,' Julie added. 'There'd be blood all over the place.'

Shaking his head, Benny turned his hands over as if looking for stains. He said nothing.

Scott sipped his Bloody Mary. 'Well,' he said, 'whatever happened, it was pretty bizarre. I don't know what to think. But at least you're okay, Benny. That's what really counts.'

'What if it happens again?' he asked in a hushed voice.

'I don't imagine . . . well . . .'

'You should be all right,' Karen said, 'as long as you're with someone. Just don't go anywhere alone for a while, if you can help it. That way, if something funny happens again, you won't have to face it by yourself.'

'Maybe he needs a bodyguard,' Julie suggested.

Benny stared at her, blinking rapidly. 'You won't think it's so funny when it happens to you.'

'Spare me.'

'It was the curse,' he blurted, 'and you're part of the curse, too. All of us are, except Tanya. She's gonna try to get us all.'

'Who, Tanya?' Julie asked, smirking.

'The witch! She's got our stuff and I *said* we've gotta get it back and nobody listened. I'm just a crazy little kid and there's no such thing as witches and curses. Only there is, and she put a curse on us and it's gonna get us all if we don't *do something*!' He shoved himself off the chair and raced into the house.

Julie blew softly through her pursed lips. 'He oughta see a shrink.'

'That'll be enough out of you,' Scott snapped. 'The kid's been through God-knows-what and what he *doesn't* need is lip from you.'

Julie flinched, her smirk falling away. 'Excuse me,' she muttered, and walked towards the house.

Tanya, looking embarrassed, stood up and brushed off the seat of her shorts. 'I'll see how Benny's doing.'

'Thanks.' When she was gone, Scott turned to Karen. 'I shouldn't have lost my temper like that.'

'Happens to the best of us. God knows, it was mild compared to some of my tirades at school. I've been known to go totally berserk.'

Feeling better, Scott turned his chair to face her. She was leaning back, bare legs outstretched and crossed at the ankles, one hand curled around the glass resting on her belly. The front of the oversized, faded blue shirt she wore over her swimsuit had a patch of darkness from the glass's moisture.

'You deal with teenaged kids all the time,' he said. 'What do you make of my two?'

'I'd say, for starters, that Julie's scared, probably very upset about what happened to Benny.'

'Has a funny way of showing it.'

'The sarcasm's just a defense mechanism. She seems to use it all the time when she has trouble facing things. I don't think she's callous or insensitive. If anything, maybe she cares too much. The sarcasm's like a safety valve for her.'

'All right. I'll give you an A for that one. She's always been that way, hiding behind it. Just gets hard to take sometimes.'

'Look on the bright side – at least she doesn't go hysterical.'

'I guess that's a blessing, of sorts. Okay. What about Benny?'

'I'd say he's extremely imaginative and sensitive, and handling the situation remarkably well. I'd be a total basket case if I'd gone through what he did. So would most people. They'd freak out totally.'

'Do you think it really happened?'

'Yes.'

'All of it?'

'Yes.'

'How do you explain—'

She shook her head. 'I can't explain any of it. That's why I would've freaked out if it'd happened to me. I think Benny's fortunate, in a way, that he can blame the curse. It gives him a frame of reference that lets him deal with it. In terms of curses and magic, anything can happen, nothing is illogical.'

'*You* don't believe in that stuff?'

'The important thing is that Benny does. It's part of his reality. So this business in the library makes sense to him.

Otherwise, God knows how he might've reacted.'

'Look, we don't believe in that nonsense. *I* don't, anyway. How am I supposed to figure out what happened?'

Karen grinned mischievously. 'Just keep telling yourself there's got to be a logical explanation. Write it fifty times on the blackboard.'

'What do you think?'

'There's got to be a logical explanation.'

'Like what?'

'Damned if I know.'

Scott laughed. 'You're a lot of help.'

She drained the last of her Bloody Mary.

'Refill?' Scott asked.

'Sure. Why not? While you're gone, maybe I can dream up a theory.'

'Try,' he said. 'Try very hard. I would appreciate a good, solid, down-to-earth explanation.'

'Right. I'll work on it.'

He took Karen's glass. Bending over her, he kissed her gently on the lips. Then he went into the house. Instead of turning towards the kitchen, he walked down the hall to Julie's room. Her door was open. She was lying on her bed under a Bruce Springsteen poster, staring at the ceiling, wearing her earphones. When she saw him enter, she pulled off the headset. 'Hey,' Scott said, 'I'm sorry I yelled at you.'

She answered with a shrug.

'I guess we're all kind of edgy.'

'It's okay,' she muttered.

'Why don't you give Nick a call, see if he'd like to come over early and have dinner with us? Say around five? I'll be doing steaks on the barbecue.'

'Okay,' she said, smiling slightly. 'That'd be nice. I'll check with him.'

'Fine.'

In the kitchen, Scott took an extra steak from the freezer. Then he prepared the Bloody Marys. He carried them outside. After the air conditioning of the house, the hot sun felt good. Karen was standing, taking off her shirt as he walked up behind her. She wore the same skimpy black swimsuit she'd taken camping. Except for crisscrossing straps, her back was bare to the waist.

'Ready for a dip?' Scott asked.

She grinned over her shoulder at him. 'Ready for a sip,' she said. She draped her shirt over the back of the chair.

Scott handed a drink to her, and they both sat down. 'I dig your outfit,' he said.

'Does it flatter my contusions?'

The bruises were yellow-green blotches on the tanned skin of her shoulders and breasts and arms. The teeth marks were darker than the discoloured skin surrounding them. Looking at them brought back the horrible night – finding her motionless in the tent, the dread when he didn't know whether she was alive or . . .

'Do you have to stare?'

'Can't help myself,' he said, managing a smile. 'You're damn near naked.'

'You're staring at the bruises.'

'Nope, at your full, firm breasts.'

She laughed and took a sip of her drink, shutting her eyes as her face tilted towards the sun.

'I talked to Julie. She's inviting Nick over to have dinner with us.'

'Oh, that'll be nice.'

'Even nicer that they're going out tonight. Now, if I can just get Tanya to take Benny to a movie or something . . .'

'Do you think that'd be a good idea?'

'Sure. We'd have the house to ourselves for a few hours.'

'He might be better off staying home.'

'Ah, you don't *want* to be alone with me.'

'I'm serious, Scott. He went through a hellish experience this morning. If I were him, I wouldn't want to go out tonight. I'd want to stay here safe with my dad.'

'Yeah, I guess I shouldn't push it. With you here, he wouldn't want to leave anyway. In fact, when he found out you'd be coming over, he almost didn't go to the library.' Scott raised his hand, forefinger and thumb a quarter inch apart. 'He was that close to staying home. If I'd just—'

Karen shook her head, stopping him. 'There are always those ifs when something goes wrong. We can't blame ourselves. It's just a bunch of little choices that don't mean anything till the shit hits the fan, and then you look back and see how you got there. And you find a whole string of ifs going back forever.'

'I suppose. But if Benny'd stayed home this morning—'

'He wouldn't have needed to go looking for a witchcraft book at all if we'd never gone camping. And we wouldn't have gone if you and I hadn't met.'

'There's an if I'd hate to change,' Scott said.

She smiled at him. 'Me, too. But you've got to admit it's one of the links in the chain. If we hadn't met, Benny wouldn't have been attacked this morning.'

You wouldn't have been beaten and raped, he thought. From the sombre look on Karen's face, he wondered if she were thinking the same thing. If we'd never met . . .

Frowning, she took a drink. Scott watched a drop of water fall from her glass, splash the glossy skin of her chest, and roll down between her breasts. She wiped it away. 'Anyhow,' she said, 'it gets slightly ridiculous when you think about it too much. The ifs are endless.'

'I suppose so,' Scott admitted. 'So, have you come up with any marvellous theories about what happened to Benny?'

'I thought of something. He said the lights went out a second after the hand grabbed him. Unless we want to accept magic as the explanation, there must've been another person involved – someone to turn off the lights while the other attacked him.'

'I wonder if it might've been a practical joke,' Scott said.

'A couple of students figuring it'd be a kick to throw a scare into him. After he ran off, they hid themselves somewhere.'

'That still doesn't explain the finger.'

'Well, if it didn't actually break off . . . Benny must've been in a panic, disoriented. He could've just bent it back, maybe even broken it, but only *imagined* it came off.'

'He sounded pretty sure.'

Scott sighed. 'I just don't—' He heard a door slide open behind him. Looking over his shoulder, he saw Julie step out. She walked forward, frowning down at the concrete deck. She'd left the door open, but she seemed lost in thought, troubled, so Scott didn't tell her to shut it. She turned a deck chair towards him and Karen, and sat down without speaking.

'What is it?' Scott asked.

'I called up Nick,' she said in a distracted, barely audible voice. She was hunched over, elbows braced on the armrests of her chair, staring down with half-shut eyes.

'Can't he make it?' Scott asked.

'Maybe. He's not sure. He's . . . gotta stay home with Heather. His dad's at the hospital.'

'Flash? My God, what happened to him?'

Julie shook her head. 'Not him. They got a call, and he went over. It's Alice and Rose.' She looked up at Scott with confusion in her eyes. 'They were attacked by a dog. This morning. It was supposed to be dead, I guess. Alice hit it with the car, and she was driving it to a vet's to have it . . . taken care of. Then it attacked them. I guess it bit them up.'

'Jesus,' Karen muttered.

'How bad are they?' Scott asked.

'Nick said they're operating on his mom's hand. It got her worse than Rose. Neither of them . . . they're in pretty good shape, I guess, except for bites on their hands and arms. Nick said they'd probably be home this afternoon.'

'Alice is in surgery?'

'Just for her hand. Some tendons or muscles or something have to be fixed.'

'Well . . .' Sighing, Scott gazed at the shiny surface of his drink. 'Thank God it's nothing worse.'

Julie rubbed her face with both hands, and leaned back in her chair as if exhausted. 'Maybe Benny's right,' she mumbled.

'It's just coincidence, honey.'

'Is it?'

'Of course. Come on, you don't actually believe that a curse . . .'

'I don't want to believe it,' she said in a tired voice. 'But Benny, and now this.'

'I admit it's a bit weird, both things happening the same way, but it's just a freakish coincidence.'

'*Two* is a coincidence,' Karen said, frowning down at her Bloody Mary. 'Three is . . . I was nearly killed last night, myself.'

Scott gazed at her, stunned.

'I realise accidents happen all the time, people falling in the bathtub . . . but I've never done it before. Oh, I've probably slipped a couple of times, but last night I took a real header. If Meg hadn't pulled me out when she did . . .' Karen made a crooked smile. She stirred her drink with a forefinger, the cubes clinking on the sides of the glass. 'I was out cold under the water when she found me. A couple more minutes . . .' She shrugged a bare shoulder. 'I wonder if they really put a tag on your big toe. It seems so . . . *ludicrous*, doesn't it? I suppose they do. Who's gonna object right?'

'My, God, Karen.'

'Anyway . . .'

'Are you all right?' Julie asked.

'Well, I'm here to tell the tale. Yeah, I'm okay.' Looking at Scott, she raised her eyebrows. 'What do you think?'

He felt dazed. He could think of nothing to say. He shook his head.

'Coincidence or the curse?' she prodded.

'I . . . I just don't know.'

'She said she'd get us,' Julie muttered.

'On the bright side,' Karen said, 'at least nobody's been seriously hurt or killed.'

'Not yet.'

'Look,' Scott said, 'curse or no curse, sometimes you have bad luck and accidents. These things just happen. We'll only make matters worse if we start thinking that gal's causing it all.'

'But what if she *is*?' Julie asked. 'What if this is just the beginning?'

'I don't know,' Scott said. 'What's your answer? If you're so sure it is the curse, what do you suggest we do about it? Hide? Stop taking showers? Stay home the rest of our lives? Maybe you'd better forget about going to the movies with Nick tonight. The curse might get you.'

'You don't have to get nasty.'

'I mean it. Where does it take us? Do I quit my job? God knows I'd damn well better not take up an L 10-11 with three hundred passengers aboard if this gal's put a whammy on me.'

'When's your next flight?' Karen asked. She looked serious.

'Come on, I was just—'

'When is it, next week?'

'Tuesday. I'm taking the eight-forty to Kennedy.'

'This is Thursday. If things keep happening—'

'They won't.'

'One way or the other,' Karen continued, 'we should have a pretty good idea where we stand by then.'

'You sound like you're already convinced.'

'I'm getting there fast.'

'What about you, Julie?'

'I'm going on my date, no matter what.'

Chapter Thirty-one

Benny finished his grilled-cheese sandwich and Coke in the kitchen with Tanya, then excused himself. He carried his book into the den. Through the sliding glass door he saw the others outside. His father and Karen were just beyond the door, Dad reading while Karen was stretched out on a sunbed.

Her hands were folded under her head. Her eyes were shut. Her skin looked slick and shiny from her suntan oil. Benny stared at her breasts, only their middles covered by the taut fabric of her swimsuit, their glossy sloping sides clearly visible. They were beautiful except for the bruises. The bruises gave Benny a sick feeling. He wished they were gone.

The black suit clung like skin, showing the curves of her ribs, her flat belly, even the small depression of her navel. It left her hipbones bare, and slanted in sharply down to her groin. Benny stared at the smooth hollows where her legs joined her body. One of the hollows creased as she raised her knee.

He knew that if he watched much longer, he might lose control. So he turned away. He moved a chair so he could till see Karen, and sat down. The view wasn't very good from here. But he felt guilty about spying on her, especially about getting aroused. By crossing a leg, he eased the tight feeling. He opened the book.

Really lucky that the librarian had remembered the title. He'd thought she was nice, from the start, but it took a very special person to bring the book upstairs for him in spite of he way he'd run off leaving such a mess.

His mind returned to the attack. He felt his penis shrink as if trying to hide. As the fear tightened its grip, he forced himself to read the title page.

Witch's Spells and Potions: A Handbook for Witches and Warlocks by Jean Du Champes. He turned to the table of contents, and ran his eyes down the chapter headings:

Chapter 7, on countermagic, sounded as if it might be what he wanted. Maybe he should start at the beginning, though, and work his way up to it. He riffled through the pages, glimpsing weird diagrams and charts, a strange drawing that looked like a tree woman, lists like recipes, all kinds of poems and chants. He flipped back to the page with the tree woman. It was labelled MANDRAGORE. A leafy bush seemed to grow out of her head. Her body, with outstretched arms and legs, was formed by the root. Benny gazed at the crudely drawn breasts and vagina. Then he was staring out the glass door at Karen, trying to imagine how she would look without her swimsuit. A couple of times he'd accidentally seen Julie naked. But that was different she was his sister. To see Karen . . . He forced himself to look away from her, and turned to the end of the book. The last page was numbered 264.

He was not a fast reader. At about twenty-five pages an hour, it would take him at least ten hours to wade through the whole volume. He'd better start with the important chapter. Later, if he had time, he would go back and read it all. That part about love spells. Maybe he could . . . No! This is bad stuff. It's wrong to mess with it. Dangerous, too. It's okay to use magic to fight the curse, but to put a spell on Karen ... The idea excited him, but gave him a heavy, disgusted feeling.

I won't! No matter what!

He flipped back to the table of contents, checked the page number for the countermagic chapter, and quickly turned to it. He found the end of the section. Thirty pages long. With a sigh, he began to read:

> Beware! Sooner or later, as you tread through the dark passages of magic, you are bound to arouse the enmity of practitioners unfriendly to your art, who will use their powers to foil you. Taken unaware, you will be totally at the mercy of your adversary, open to potent attacks that might prove injurious, even fatal. To insure your safety, you must take precautions that will throw a curtain of safety around yourself, your loved ones, and your home.

The protective spell required that he walk around the outside of the house during a new moon carrying a chalice of purified water, chanting about an earth goddess named Habondia. On completing the circle, he was to sprinkle some of the water in each room of the house. He should see chapter 3 for instructions on how to purify water. But there would be some moon tonight, so he didn't bother checking on that. He kept on reading.

He could hang a holystone on the hearth. If he had one. Or he could protect himself with a lodestone or a cross-stone. But where was he supposed to find such things?

The more he read, the more frustrated he grew. Every spell, every amulet or talisman or potion, called for strange rocks, herbs he'd never heard of, or planetary positions that made no sense to him. He slammed the book shut.

Then he opened it again. He'd only read ten pages of the

countermagic chapter. He would read the rest of it. There had to be something in it that would help.

Had to be.

Chapter Thirty-two

When Julie woke up, the towel beneath her was sodden. She used a corner to wipe her face, and lifted her head. Down at the end of the pool, Karen was stretched out on a chaise longue, apparently asleep. Her father, sitting nearby, was reading a book.

Julie reached down at her sides, found the dangling cords of her bikini top, and tied them behind her back. Sweat streamed down her hot skin as she sat up. The concrete apron of the pool seared her feet. She slipped into thongs, and walked towards her dad. In a soft voice, so she wouldn't wake Karen, she asked the time.

Dad checked his wristwatch. 'A little after three. Nick phoned while you were asleep.'

'Oh, no! Jeez, why didn't somebody wake me up?'

'He just left a message with Tanya, said he'll be here at five.'

'How's his mom?'

'He didn't say. Things must be going all right, though, or I doubt if he'd be coming.'

'Yeah, I guess so.' She sighed, disappointed about missing the call. 'Anyway, are you gonna be sticking around for a while?'

'Yep. Why?'

'Nothing. Just thought I'd go in for a dip to cool off.' With a casual shrug, she added, 'Don't let me drown, huh?'

Dad raised his eyebrows. 'If you're so concerned, maybe you should stay out of the pool.'

The remark hurt. 'Jeez, I was just kidding, for God's sake.'

As she walked away, he said, 'I'll keep an eye on you.'

'Thanks,' she muttered. At the edge of the pool, she kicked off her thongs and stepped down the stairs into the shallow end. The water felt cool and refreshing as it wrapped around her legs. She waded forward, sucking in her breath when the water touched her groin, wondering how she'd managed to stand the icy lake in the mountains. When the level reached her belly, she eased forward and left her feet. The chill water closed over her. After the first mild shock, it felt good. She swam beneath the surface to the far end, came up for air in the shadow of the diving board, and glanced a her father as she made her turn. The book was closed on his lap. He was watching her.

She backstroked slowly, keeping an eye on the pool side, trying to judge her distance so she wouldn't bump her head when she reached the end. Stopping, she glanced over her shoulder and found the wall two yards away. She sighed, annoyed with herself for being overly cautious, and plunged forward. Her muscles, sore from hiking, ached as they flexed and stretched. It was a good feeling. When she reached the deep end, she thrust herself away from the wall with such force that the water tugged her bikini pants down a couple of inches. She pulled them up and kept on swimming. When she reached the shallow end, she pushed off more gently.

If nobody else were here, she could forget about the suit and speed through the water naked. It was such a fine, wild feeling. Especially at night. Hell, though, if she were alone, she'd probably be afraid to go in the pool at all. That damn curse. Probably just bull, but how do you explain what happened to Benny, to Alice and Rose, even to Karen? Okay,

Karen slipped in her tub. That happens to everyone. But what about . . .

She touched the wall at the deep end, and tucked. Her feet found the tile. Gripping her pants with one hand, she shoved. She skimmed through the water, let go, and began to stroke. With her first kick, a muscle spasm locked her right leg. Crying out silently into the water, she clutched her cramped thigh. She rubbed it hard, pounded it. Though the pain was bad and her lungs started to burn, she was rather pleased that she felt no panic. She'd had leg cramps before. She was only a few yards from a side of the pool. The main thing was to ignore the pain, use her arms and her good leg to surface, and get the hell to one of the walls. Forcing herself to release her thigh, she paddled upward and kicked. With a shock of agony, her left leg froze. Both legs were drawn up, paralysed. Her weight shifted backward as she clawed her way up. Her arms broke the surface, slapped it hard, but without enough force to bring her head out. Through inches of frothy water, she saw the diving board wavering above her. Though she flailed her arms, she kept sinking. The board became a hazy blur. Even her fingertips no longer could reach the surface.

This is insane!

Shit, I'm really . . .

Something stopped her right arm. Another cramp? No, his felt different, like a tight cuff around her wrist. Pulling. In an instant, her head popped through the surface. Gasping for air, she turned and saw her father in the pool, one hand clutching her, the other hanging onto the edge. Beyond him, Karen was kneeling, face twisted with fear.

Dad eased her forward. She hung onto the concrete lip of the pool while he climbed out. Together, he and Karen pulled her from the water. She lay on her side, rubbing her stricken thighs.

'Cramps?' her father asked.

'Yeah.'

'Both legs?'

She nodded.

'God,' Karen muttered.

'It's crazy,' she said.

'You were pushing it pretty hard, honey.' Crouching beside her, Dad started to knead her right thigh. Karen worked on the other. Soon, the pain began to ease. The muscles loosened, and Julie straightened out her legs.

'I guess I'm okay now.'

'You'd better lie down for a while,' Dad said. He and Karen helped her stand up. Holding her by the arms, they walked her towards the lounge chair. Her legs were trembling and weak.

When she was stretched out on the cushion, Dad bent over her. He stroked her forehead, smoothing aside wet strands of hair. 'Are you sure you're all right?'

She nodded. 'I guess I shouldn't have gone in after all.'

'You just pushed it too hard.'

'I guess so. Hey, thanks for pulling me out.'

He pressed his lips together tightly, and nodded. His eyes were red and wet. He patted her cheek. 'Take a little nap now. I'll wake you up in time for Nick.'

'Let me know at four, okay?'

'Sure.'

Karen gave her shoulder a gentle squeeze, and smiled down at her. Then she and Dad walked towards the recliners, talking quietly.

Julie shut her eyes against the sunlight. She flexed her leg muscles, and felt them tremble. Then she relaxed. She was drained of energy. The heat was a comforting blanket. She tried to think about what had happened to her, but her mind strayed. She was stretched out on a hot granite slab by the lake, Nick's body wet against her, his lips caressing her mouth.

A hand shook her awake. 'It's just past four,' Dad said.

'Thanks,' she murmured. She lay motionless for a little while after he left. She felt groggy, and weighted down by the heat of the sun. Then thoughts of Nick's arrival pushed away her weariness. She sat up, sweat trickling down her body, small puddles spilling from the hollows of her throat and her navel. She looked for her thongs. They were still at the shallow end of the pool where she'd left them. Clutching her towel, she raced over the burning concrete to the house.

Benny, seated in the den, looked up from his book as she slid open the door and entered. He wrinkled his nose to hold his glasses up. 'Are you okay?' he asked.

'Sure. Dad tell you about it?'

'Yeah. I was in the john when it happened. Wish I'd seen it.'

'Too bad. It was quite a spectacle – your sister nearly drowning. You'd better keep on your toes so you don't miss any more fun.'

'I just meant maybe I could've helped.'

'Sure.' Chilled by the air conditioning, she wrapped herself in the towel. 'Where's Tanya?'

'I think she's in her room studying.'

Julie left the den and went to Tanya's bedroom. She found the older girl at the desk, bent over her big volume of Shakespeare. 'How do you feel?'

'Not bad.'

Tanya shook her head. 'Can't believe it. *Both* legs seized up on you?'

'Dad says I was pushing it.'

'Benny thinks it's the curse.'

'What else is new?'

'He's in there, boning up on remedies.'

'Looking for a hex remover?'

'Something like that.'

'It's just a lot of bull.'

'You still think so?' Tanya asked.

'Hell, I've had leg cramps before. But since there does seem to be an epidemic of accident proneness going around, I was just wondering ...' She sighed, wondering how to proceed. Tanya waited, eyebrows raised. 'Nick's coming over pretty soon, and I've gotta get cleaned up. I need to take a quick shower. Did you hear about Karen falling in her tub last night?'

'You're kidding.'

'No, she almost drowned, but her roommate got to her just in time.'

'There *is* an epidemic.'

'I'll say. Anyway, I was wondering if you'd mind taking a little break from your Shakespeare and kind of keeping an eye on me while I shower.'

Tanya frowned up at her. 'You really *are* worried.'

'Well, I'm still a little shaky on my feet. I guess it's kind of ridiculous. I mean, I'm not spooked or anything. I just thought, to be on the safe side . . .' She stopped fumbling with words as Tanya set her pen down on the open book and pushed her chair back. 'I'll be quick, I promise.'

'No, that's all right. You can take your time. I'm pretty Shakespeared out.'

'I really appreciate it.' With a grin, she added, 'I'll do the same for you sometime.'

'Hey, forget it. There's no curse on *me*.' She made a playful, scowl. 'You don't suppose it's contagious?'

'You'd have to ask Benny about that.'

In her own bedroom, Julie tossed her damp pool towel onto her bed. She grabbed her robe, and hurried down the hallway to the bathroom. Tanya was already there, waiting on the toilet seat. 'Maybe you've had your run of bad luck for the day.'

'I sure hope so,' Julie said. She crouched and ran water into the tub. When it felt right, she turned the shower on and slid the glass door shut. She took off her bikini, blushing slightly as Tanya watched.

'Think you got enough sun today?'

'Too much, probably. Hope I don't peel.'

'Put some lotion on, afterwards.'

She nodded. She pulled the door partway open, tested the

water with her hand, then carefully stepped into the tub. A foot slipped. She clung to the door.

'Christ, be careful!'

'I'm all right.' Then she was standing in the tub with the door shut, the spray hot on her back. Through the frosted glass, Tanya was a vague, blurred shape. 'Hope you know CPR,' Julie called.

She couldn't quite hear Tanya's reply over the noise of the shower.

'You know, maybe I'd better take a fall, just to make this look good. I'm gonna feel like a jerk if nothing happens.'

She turned slowly, enjoying the feel of the water as it splashed her body and streamed down. There was no stinging sensation, so she knew she wasn't badly sunburned. Her tanned skin had a glossy look, a slight reddish hue. Even her breasts looked rosy, but that was from the shower, not the sun. If she could find more time to sunbathe naked . . . In a way, though, she rather liked the contrast, the white places surrounded by bronze skin.

Remembering her promise to be quick, she ducked her head under the nozzle. When her hair was soaked, she shampooed it. She rinsed out the suds, then used a soapy washcloth on her face and ears. 'So far so good,' she called.

Hearing no answer, she peered through the glass. Her heart suddenly thumped hard. Her stomach knotted. She tugged open the door. Blinking water from her eyes, she stared through the steam at the vacant seat of the toilet.

'What's wrong?' Tanya asked.

Through the thick drifting steam, she saw her cousin near the closed bathroom door. Naked. Standing on her head.

'What the hell are you doing?'

'Relaxing.'

'Good Christ.'

'It's very pleasant. You should try it sometime.'

Julie laughed. 'Sure thing,' she said, and shut the door. She soaped herself down, rinsed, and turned off the water. As she stepped onto the bathmat, Tanya's legs dropped forward. She landed lightly on the balls of her feet and stood up. Julie reached for her towel. 'Gee, I always knew you were level-headed. I guess that comes from standing on it.'

Tanya came forward feeling the top of her head with both hands. Her body was slim, like Julie's, but her breasts were much larger and swayed slightly as she walked. 'It's not flat,' she said.

'*Level.* Nothing about you is flat.'

'Let me by, smart-ass.'

Julie shuffled sideways to make room, and Tanya knelt by the tub. She turned the faucets on.

'You're gonna take a shower?'

'A bath actually.'

'Gee, I thought you just stripped to show off your boobs.'

'Magnificent, huh?'

'Want to trade?'

Tanya stoppered the drain, then looked over her shoulder. Her eyes settled on Julie's breasts. Julie resisted an urge to hide them behind the towel. 'As a matter of fact, I wouldn't mind. I'd throw all my bras away.'

'Come on, mine aren't *that* bad.'

Tanya laughed. 'What do you want? I *told* you I'd trade.'

'I wear bras.'

'Ah, but that's for decorum, not necessity.'

'I don't know about that.'

'If I had a set like yours, you wouldn't catch me dead in a bra. Especially in summer. And on dates. I tell you, you wouldn't believe the troubles I've had on dates. The thing always gets in the way. Guys get frustrated fooling with the hooks and I have to unfasten it. It takes a Houdini to get out of the shoulder straps without taking off your blouse, which you might not want to do if you're messing around in a drive-in or something, so you end up half the time with the cups in your face. It's a colossal drag.'

Smiling, Julie said, 'I wouldn't know about that.'

'Really? You mean you've never—'

'Never. You're looking at pristine tits.' Except for . . .

She suddenly saw the man on top of her, felt the tight squeeze of his hand. The memory of it made a cold, hard place in her stomach. She realised, vaguely, that Tanya was laughing at her quip.

'Untouched by human hands, huh? Well, a bra can do that for you, if that's what you want.'

'I've just never gone out with a guy I cared enough about.'

'That'll change. Let me tell you.'

'I guess.'

'You can bet on it,' Tanya said, and climbed into the tub.

Still upset by the shock of remembering the attack, Julie quickly finished drying herself. She put on her robe. 'Thanks for, you know, sticking around.'

'Any time. It was a kick. Pristine tits.'

Julie left the hot, steamy bathroom. The corridor felt cool. In her bedroom, she shut the door. She opened her robe. Stepping close to the full-length mirror, she stared at her left breast. The pale skin was stippled with goosebumps; the darker flesh was puckered around the jut of her nipple. It looked little different from her right breast. She stroked them both. The touch of her fingers felt the same on each. She remembered the burning hurt. There might even have been a bruise, though she hadn't noticed one before. Her breast looked fine now.

Hardly pristine, though.

Slightly used.

She shut her robe and glanced at the alarm clock by her bed. Four-thirty-five. 'Gads,' she muttered. Sitting cross-legged on the carpet, she blow-dried and brushed her hair. The lock chopped off an inch short across her brow looked bad. 'Bitch,' she muttered, and got up to find scissors. Her sore legs reminded her of the near miss in the pool. Maybe you've had your run of bad luck for the day. If anything should happen to spoil the date . . . Nick, at least, didn't have the curse on him. The old bitch didn't get his hair or blood. What the hell am I thinking? There is no curse!

Sitting down with the scissors, she did her best to even out the sweep of hair. Try not to poke your eye out, she, thought.

By the time she finished with her hair, the clock showed ten before five. She flung her robe onto the bed, took a pair of fresh, pink panties from her drawer, and stepped into them. She pulled out a bra and started to put it on. *You wouldn't catch me dead ... Guys get frustrated ... It's a colossal drag.* Heart pounding fast, she plucked the bra off and hurried to her closet. Her hands trembled as she removed her blouse from the hanger. She put it on, held it shut, and looked down. Through the shiny, bright yellow fabric, her dark nipples were clearly visible. 'No way,' she said. Not in front of everyone. Even if it were just Nick, she doubted that she would dare.

By five o'clock, she was ready. She gave herself a final check in front of the mirror, approving of the cheery, fresh way she looked in the yellow blouse, the skirt of forest green, and sandals. Her choker of thin gold chain was a nice touch. The bra was the right touch: the lacy pattern of its cups, instead of her nipples, showed through the clinging blouse. 'Decorum,' she said. She grinned at herself and left her room.

Benny was no longer in the den. Through the sliding glass door she saw him outside, sitting with Karen at the table. They were both staring in the same direction, their faces rigid.

Julie tugged the door open and stepped outside. The heat of the afternoon enveloped her. Her father, a few yards away, squirted fuel into the barbecue.

'My God, be careful,' Karen warned him.

'Never fear. I've done this a thousand times.'

'Famous last words,' Julie said.

Dad noticed her, and smiled. 'Say, you look terrific.'

'Thanks.'

He took a book of matches from the pocket of his blue

Aloha shirt. 'If you go up in flames,' Julie said, 'it'll ruin your pretty shirt.'

'Always the wise guy.'

'Let me light it,' Karen said. She started to get up, but Benny reached out and grabbed her hand.

'Don't,' he told her.

'This is ridiculous.' Dad tore a match loose.

Julie walked quickly to his side.

'Stand back, honey.'

'See, you *are* worried.'

'You people are driving me crazy. What are we gonna do, stop eating? If I don't get the fire started before long—'

'I've got an idea,' Julie said. 'Let's wait for Nick.'

'Yeah!' Benny blurted. 'He's okay. Nothing'll go wrong if he lights it.'

'Oh, for Pete's sake.'

'Let's wait for him,' Karen said.

Dad shook his head. Somehow, he looked both dismayed and amused. 'You want us to sit around here like four loonies waiting for the Great Uncursed One to arrive and light the charcoal? Is that the picture?'

'Yep,' Julie said.

Benny nodded.

'We don't have to sit around like loonies,' Karen explained. 'We could sit around like sensible people.'

'I'm not so sure,' Dad said. But he tossed the unlighted match onto the charcoal, and returned with Julie to the table.

Chapter Thirty-three

'We'd better get going,' Julie said. 'It's a twenty-minute drive to the theatre, and there might be a queue.' As she started to get up, Nick pushed back his own chair and stood.

He thanked Julie's father for the dinner.

'Any time,' Scott said. 'I'm glad you could make it. Maybe, if your mother is feeling up to it, you can all come over tomorrow.'

'That'd be great.'

'You can bring your suits. We'll make a day of it.'

'I'll check when I get home.'

'That's all right. I'll give your dad a call tonight.'

Nick made his good-byes to the others. Scott walked alongside him towards the gate. 'You two are sure you wouldn't rather stay here?'

'*Dad.*'

'We've got some spare trunks around, Nick.'

'We can swim all we want tomorrow,' Julie said. 'Tonight we want to go to the movies. You *said* I could.'

'I know. And I won't stand in the way. I was simply offering a suggestion.'

'I wouldn't mind staying,' Nick said.

'We've got a date,' she told him, looking hurt. She frowned at Scott. 'Besides, I'd like to know what's so safe about this place. If you're worried about the curse – which you keep claiming you don't believe in anyway – it can get me here just as easily as somewhere else. This is where I almost drowned you know.'

'I realise that.'

'We'll be very careful,' Nick assured him.

'Besides,' Julie added, 'Nick'll be driving, and he'll be with me the whole time, and he's the Great Uncursed One, as you put it so nicely.'

Scott smiled, but he still looked uneasy.

'I won't let her out of my sight, I promise.'

Scott gave him a pat on the back. 'Okay. What time does the movie let out?'

'It's a double feature,' Julie said. 'The second show's over at about ten-thirty.'

'I'll expect you around eleven, then.'

'Dad!' Julie looked appalled. 'What if we want to go someplace afterwards?'

'I think you'd better come straight home.'

'For God's sake.'

'I mean it, Julie. I don't know what's going on – if it's just been a lot of bad luck or what – but I think we all need to be especially careful until things settle down a bit. So eleven o'clock, or you can stay home. That's final.'

'Thanks,' she muttered.

'I'll have her back by eleven,' Nick said.

'Fine. Well, have a good time, you two.'

'Sure thing,' Julie muttered, and pulled open the gate.

Nick followed her down the walkway alongside the house. 'I'm sorry about all that,' she said, looking back at him.

'It's all right. Your dad's just worried. I guess everyone is. Man, I had no idea all this stuff's been going on. It was bad enough, what happened to Mom and Rose, but Karen and then Benny and then *you* . . .'

'It's looking kind of hairy, isn't it.'

'Maybe we should stay here.'

Julie grinned. 'Scared to be out with me?'

'Naw.' He stepped up beside her as they cut across the front lawn.

Julie spotted the red Mustang at the curb. Her eyebrows raised. 'Not too shabby.'

He opened the passenger door for Julie, then went to the other side and climbed in. The heat inside the closed-up car was stifling. He turned the ignition. As the engine kicked over with a throaty grumble, he pressed switches to lower the windows. It didn't help much until he pulled away from the kerb. Then a mild breeze came in, pushing the hot air out. He glanced at Julie. She was fastening her safety harness, her head turned down, her golden hair blowing lightly.

'You sure look nice,' he said.

The buckle snapped into place. She raised her head and smiled. 'Thank you. So do you. We sort of match.'

'Yeah.' His yellow knit shirt was not as bright as her blouse, his slacks a lighter shade of green than her skirt. His gaze lingered on her knee.

'You'd better watch where you're going,' she said.

'Where *am* I going? You'd better give me directions.'

'You want to make a left at the next stop sign.'

He followed her instructions, but couldn't stop himself from stealing glances as he drove. All through dinner, he'd been astonished by her appearance. Even now, he couldn't get over how different she looked in a skirt. He'd seen her in shorts, he'd seen her in a bikini, but somehow the skirt transformed her, made her seem softer, more mysterious and exciting. The way it draped her thighs. The way it left her knees bare.

'Go right, up here at Ventura,' she said.

Nick made the turn.

Except for giving directions, Julie remained silent. Her hands lay open and motionless on her legs. She seemed a little tense. Nick wished he weren't so nervous himself. Ever since their phone conversation last night, he'd been looking forward to this with a mixture of eagerness and dread.

Our first date.

What if something goes wrong? What if something *doesn't* go wrong?

The way she looked in her skirt was no help at all.

At least he didn't have to worry about taking her someplace after the movies. That was a relief. A disappointment. If only he'd known last night, he might've been saved the fevered tossing and turning in bed as his mind spun images of him and Julie parked on a dark road kissing, embracing, fumbling under clothes for hidden flesh. There would be none of that tonight after all.

Maybe it wouldn't have happened anyway.

At any rate, he should be able to relax and enjoy the evening more, knowing he had no choice but to take her straight home after the movies.

'There it is,' Julie said. 'If you make a left at the next light, there's a big parking lot behind the theatre.'

'Okay.'

She looked at him strangely. 'Are you all right?'

'What do you mean?'

'Is something the matter?'

'No, I'm fine. How about you?'

'I don't feel so hot, as a matter of fact.'

He signalled, and made the turn. 'What's wrong? Should we go back?'

'That wouldn't help.'

'Are you sick?'

She didn't answer. Nick swung into the lot, pulled to a stop in a parking space, and frowned at Julie. 'What's wrong?'

'I asked you first.'

'I'm fine. Well, maybe a little nervous.'

'About the curse?'

He shook his head. He had a tight feeling in his throat. 'No. Just about . . . going out with you. I mean, this is our first time really being together, you know? It feels a little strange.'

'Is that all that's bothering you?'

'I think so.'

'Well.' She unfastened her buckle and pushed the harness aside. 'I'm a little nervous, too. But you know what'll make it all better?' Reaching out, she curled a hand behind his neck and drew him closer. They kissed. Her lips were parted and moist, brushing against his mouth, then pressing firmly. Her other hand rubbed his chest, moved lower, caressed his belly, dropped to his left thigh. She kneaded his leg, squeezed and stroked it as if unaware of the way her wrist sometimes pushed against his groin. Then the hand went away. The lips went away. She stared into his eyes. 'Feel better?' she asked.

'Are you kidding?'

'Not so nervous any more?'

'I feel great.'

'Me, too. Let's see the movie.'

Outside the car, he took Julie's hand. They walked together through the early evening sunlight. The kiss had worked, just as she'd said it would. It had ended the strangeness, made their closeness real again. Nick felt relaxed and fine. Reluctantly, he let go of her hand to buy the tickets. Though the films were R-rated, the girl in the booth didn't question their ages.

'Would you like popcorn?' Nick asked as they entered the air-conditioned lobby.

'Not right now. I'm stuffed.'

'Me, too. Maybe at intermission.'

Julie smiled strangely, as if she knew something he didn't. 'Maybe,' she said.

The theatre wasn't crowded. They chose seats near the centre with no one to block their view. When the lights darkened, Julie leaned closer to Nick. She smiled, and nudged his elbow off the armrest. 'Pushy,' he whispered.

'That's me.'

He stared at the screen. An ad for the *Los Angeles Times* was showing. His arm, pressed by Julie's shoulder, hung down across his leg. It felt awkward and useless. His nervousness came back. He should put the arm around Julie.

Come on, what're you waiting for?

He felt quivery and dry-mouthed.

The title of the feature film, *Getting It*, appeared over a scene of teenaged girls playing basketball in a school gymnasium. As the credits finished, the teacher blasted her whistle and the girls ran for the locker room.

Come on, arm! Now!

He couldn't force himself to lift it.

On the screen, the girls were trotting into the locker room, their shouts and giggles echoing.

'You oughta go for this,' Julie whispered.

Her voice took away the worry. He put his arm across her shoulders. Amazing how easy it was. He let out a trembling breath as she snuggled against him. Why had he even hesitated? Well, it didn't matter now. He caressed her shoulder making the fabric slide over the smoothness of her skin, the narrow band of her bra strap.

Some of the girls were showering now. The camera gave glimpses of their nudity. Then three boys rushed into the shower room, whooping and hollering, wearing only jockstraps. While most of the girls screamed, a slim attractive blonde laughed and attacked. She tackled a chubby guy. His friends fled. Other girls joined in. By the time he made his escape, the main girl was waving his jockstrap like a flag.

The scene changed. She paraded into a classroom wearing the jock on her head. Julie gasped. 'Oh, no!' and the audience roared. The matronly teacher looked aghast. The girl walked up to the chubby boy's desk, plucked the jock from her head, and pulled it down over his face.

The boy's name was Ralph. The girl was Cindy. She was captain of the cheerleading squad, the most popular girl in school, and she wanted nothing to do with Ralph. Ralph wanted 'in her pants.'

As the movie went on, following his antics, Nick continued to caress Julie's shoulder and upper arm. Her blouse was getting damp from his hand. His arm was getting numb. Finally, he lowered it. He rested his hand on his leg. Julie reached down, took hold of it, and squeezed it.

Ralph, in the dark outside Cindy's house, serenaded her, playing 'Lady of Spain' on a sousaphone. She went to her bedroom window and mooned him.

With his free hand, Nick stroked Julie's forearm, barely

touching it, feeling the soft light brush of its hair, the sleek skin.

Though he and Julie laughed at some of the film's raunchy antics, he began to get annoyed. The movie showed sex as a crude joke, not as something beautiful and strange, the way it should be, the way he wanted it to be with Julie. The kids were 'copping feels', trying to 'get it on', to 'lay pipe', to 'fuck their brains out'. There was no tenderness, no caring, no *making love*. Nick began to wish they'd chosen a different movie. At least this one seemed to be nearing an end. The next feature, a spy thriller, should be a real improvement.

Julie lifted their hands over the armrest. She lowered them onto her leg. Nick felt the heat of it through the thin fabric of her skirt.

Though Cindy was doing a striptease for Ralph, the sight of her naked breasts and writhing body seemed not nearly so exciting to Nick as the feel of Julie's leg under his hand. If he inched their locked hands down a bit, he might get past the hem to her bare knee. While he tried to work up the nerve, Julie slid their hands to the very place he wanted. She loosened her grip. As his fingers closed gently over her leg, she stroked the back of his hand. His mouth was parched, his heart racing.

Cindy, done with the striptease, flopped naked onto the bed. Ralph had finally earned a 'toss' with her by dumping a truckload of manure on her unfaithful boyfriend and his new girlfriend while the two were 'scoring' in the backseat of his new convertible. Face flushed, eyes bulged, Ralph tossed off his clothes. 'Come and get it!' Cindy called. With a whoop of delight, Ralph dived at her sprawled body. A freeze-frame caught him in midair. The words 'The End' flashed across his rump.

Nick gave Julie's leg a gentle squeeze as the final credits rolled. Then he took his hand away. When the lights came on, she smiled at him. 'Well,' she said, 'What did you think?'

'The movie? It was all right.'

'A real gross-out, huh?'

'That's for sure.'

'Well, I'm glad poor Ralph finally got his wish. He sure worked hard enough for it.'

The words excited Nick. He wiped his sweaty hands on his pants. 'Are you ready for some popcorn or something?'

Julie got that mysterious look on her face. 'That depends.'

'On what?'

'How badly do you want to see the next movie?'

The question stunned Nick. He stared at her. 'What do you mean?'

'Dad says I have to be home by eleven. It's only eight thirty. If we leave now . . .' She raised her eyebrows. 'What do you think?'

'Are you serious?'

'If you'd rather stay for the movie . . .'

'No. I don't care about that. I . . . uh . . . I don't think we'd win any points with your dad.'

'He doesn't have to know.'

'Jeez, Julie.'

'Are you game?'

He let out an uneasy laugh. 'Yeah, sure, I guess so.'

'Great. Let's get out of here.' She slung her purse strap over her shoulder, and stood up.

They sidestepped towards the aisle. Nick felt tight and jittery. We shouldn't do this, he thought. But he wanted to. He was scared, but he wanted to.

Where'll we go? Park someplace. Oh, my God.

In the lobby, she squeezed his hand. 'Right back,' she said, and pushed through a restroom door.

He remembered his promise not to let her out of his sight. Well, he couldn't follow her into the ladies' room. Ralph might, but not him.

He hurried to the men's room. One of the urinals was vacant. He stepped up to it. The underside of his penis felt wet and slick. Either the movie or Julie had excited him a lot. He didn't think it was the movie.

In the lobby again, he looked for Julie. He didn't see her. Apparently, she was still in the restroom. He waited. Slowly, the line at the refreshment stand dwindled. An usher in a red blazer shut the doors to the auditorium, signalling the start of the second feature.

Nick paced. He stared at the restroom door.

It finally opened, but the girl who came out wasn't Julie.

What was taking her so long?

Had something gone wrong?

The girl behind the refreshment counter was pumping butter flavouring onto a tub of popcorn for the last customer. Maybe, when she finished, Nick would ask her to check on Julie. That could turn out embarrassing.

He'd give Julie a couple more minutes.

He gazed at the second hand of the wall clock behind the counter. It moved quickly, sweeping past the numbers. He watched it make three circuits of the face. Still, he hesitated to interfere.

The restroom door stayed shut.

Come on, Julie! What's wrong?

Chapter Thirty-four

'Can I turn it up?' Rose asked.

'*May* I durn'd up,' Alice corrected, her speech thick from too much wine.

'Go ahead,' Flash said. He could hardly hear himself think, much less hear the television. The helicopter was making another pass low over the house. It had been circling the neighbourhood for the past ten minutes, the whapping noise of its rotors deafening at times, then receding, then growing to a roar as it came back.

He watched Rose crawl to the television, reach up with her bandaged arm, and turn up the volume. She crawled backward to the place where she'd been sitting on the carpet. She crossed her legs.

Alice stared at the ceiling. She looked as if she might cry. 'Why dudn' he go 'way,' she said.

'Must be looking for a prowler. This time, at least, it's not three o'clock in the morning.' That's when the police helicopter usually put in its appearance – seemed like once a month – waking them up, circling for half an hour, sometimes as long as an hour, hovering low over the houses, its searchlight sweeping the lawns and streets. It was a nuisance. A little frightening, too. It reminded him of 'Nam, and it wasn't used for routine patrols. Its presence meant that a suspect was out there. Somewhere close. You always wondered who he was, what he'd done, where he might be lurking.

Alice, beside him on the couch, leaned forward and reached out with her left hand. Her fingertips bumped the wineglass, knocked it over. Chablis sloshed out onto the table.

Heather, in a rocking chair across the room, looked up from her book and frowned.

Alice saw her. '*You* try'n use yer lef' han',' she blurted. Her face was puckered and red.

Flash rubbed the back of Alice's neck. The tense muscles felt like iron. 'It's okay, honey. We all have little accidents. I'll clean it up.'

She nodded. Her lips were pressed together. She stared down at her right arm, wrapped in a cast from fingertips to shoulder, held against her chest by a sling. Her mouth started to tremble.

'I'll get you some more wine, too,' Flash said as he pushed himself off the couch.

Heather put down her book. She followed him to the kitchen and leaned against the stove, watching him take a fresh bottle of wine and a can of Budweiser from the refrigerator. Her pale eyebrows were drawn together.

'Don't let your face freeze that way,' Flash said.

'She's bombed,' Heather said.

'Don't say that.'

'Well, she is.'

'So what,' he snapped.

Heather flinched and blinked. She looked as if she might start bawling.

'I'm sorry,' Flash said. 'It's all this damn *noise*.'

'You shouldn't let her drink so much.'

'If she wants to get plastered out of her skull tonight, that's fine by me. Normally, I'd . . .' He realised he didn't need to talk so loudly; the roar of the chopper had faded a bit. 'Normally, I'd be right with you, honey. It's not good to drink too much. But your mother went through a terrifying experience this morning. She and Rose both.'

'Rose isn't getting bombed.'

'She can if she wants.'

Heather looked as if she thought her father had gone crazy.

'Why don't you wipe off the coffee table for me?'

With a shrug of her delicate shoulders, she limped over to the counter. She tore a yard of paper towels off the roll.

'How's the ankle?'

'It hurts some.' She grinned. 'Can I get bombed?'

'Do you want to?'

'No,' she said. She arched an eyebrow. 'I'll keep my wits about me, thank you.' Then she hobbled out of the kitchen, the towels fluttering behind her like a streamer.

Flash uncorked the wine bottle. He popped the tab of his beer can. As he carried them into the living room, the telephone rang, adding its clamour to the noise of the approaching helicopter.

'The phone,' Alice said.

'I'll get it,' he told her. It rang two more times as he filled her glass.

'Might be Nick,' she said, a look of fear in her eyes.

Taking the beer with him, he rushed back into the kitchen and snatched up the receiver. 'Hello?'

'Hi, Flash, it's Scott.'

'Anything wrong?'

'The kids are . . .' The roar of the helicopter drowned him out.

'What was that? We've got one of those fucking cop choppers raising Cain.'

'I was just saying the kids are off to the movies. How're Alice and Rose doing?'

'Aaah. Who knows? Okay, I guess. Nick fill you in?'

'Yeah. He said the operation went fine.'

'She'll be in a cast for a while. They don't think there'll be any permanent damage, but they aren't making any promises. You know doctors.'

'I sure hope it turns out all right. Look, one reason I called, I was wondering if you'd like to bring the bunch over tomorrow. Nick thought it sounded like a pretty good idea.'

'I bet he did,' Flash said. Chuckling, he took a swig of beer. 'Those two sure hit it off, huh?'

'I'd say so.'

'Well, sounds real good to me. I'll have to check with the general, but if I don't call back, you can expect us. Around what time?'

'If you want to make a day of it, drop in around ten or eleven. Bring your suits.'

'Want us to bring anything else?'

'Just your thirsts and appetites.'

'Real fine, Scott.'

'Have you heard anything from the cops?'

'Their fucking chopper.' He realised that the noise was fading a bit.

'About the situation.'

'Yeah. I know what you mean.' He swallowed some more beer. 'I got a call a couple of hours ago. Some deputies and a ranger went in on horses. Couldn't find the body or the woman. They brought out our tents, though. Said we can pick 'em up at the Black Butte ranger station if we're so inclined.'

'I'm not.'

'Me neither. Not just yet. But anyway, everything's just up in the air, since they didn't get the body. Won't be a inquest or anything.'

'Nick seems to be holding up pretty well.'

'I guess we can thank your daughter for that. How's Karen getting along?'

'She's here now. She's doing pretty well. But that's another thing I wanted to talk to you about. She had an accident last night.' Flash listened, his concern for Karen turning to uneasy confusion when Scott told of the attack on Benny at the library, and Julie's leg cramps in the pool.

'Add in that dog attack on Alice and Rose,' he continued, 'and we've got four incidents in the past twenty-four hours.'

'What do you make of it?' Flash asked.

'I honestly don't know what to think. If it was just Karen falling in the tub and Julie's problem in the pool, I wouldn't be too concerned. I'd say it was just bad luck. But the dog attack . . .'

'Alice insists the thing was dead when it went for 'em.'

'Yeah, Nick mentioned that. And I haven't been able to figure out any logical explanation for what happened to Benny. Both those situations have me pretty worried. You can't just put them down as bad luck. They were actual assaults.'

Flash frowned at the wall. He took a sip of beer.

'Every one of those incidents could've turned out fatal. I'd say we've been damn lucky so far.'

'You thinking it's that old bag's hex?'

'That seems to be the consensus around here. I hate to go along with it, but I'm starting to wonder.'

'What're we gonna do?'

'One thing about it – we're certainly not powerless. In each case, some quick action has saved the day. All I can suggest, for now, is that we keep on our toes and watch out.'

'I guess your kid was right, huh? Benny. We should've grabbed that bitch when we had the chance.'

'I don't know. Maybe. I'm not convinced she has anything to do with all this. If she is behind it, though – I mean, if it's really a curse – apparently you and Nick might be in the clear.'

''Cause she didn't cut us?'

'Right.'

The chopper was returning. Flash set his beer can on the floor.

'She seemed to think she needed blood and hair from her victims to make it work. As far as we know, she didn't get to you or Nick.'

'As far as we know?' Flash asked. He pushed a forefinger into his left ear to muffle the outside noise.

'Well, I've been talking to Benny about this. He thinks you two are probably all right, unless she got something we don't know about. Apparently, it doesn't have to be blood or hair. A piece of your clothing will do. Fingernail parings. Benny was a little embarrassed to mention it, but if she dug around after we left and came up with some faeces . . .'

Flash grimaced. 'A guy can't even take a crap.'

'Did you?'

'As a matter of fact, no. I didn't cut my toenails, either. Does that mean I'm safe?'

'Could be. Assuming we are dealing with a curse. We can't be completely certain in any case. Who the hell knows? None of us are exactly experts on . . .'

In spite of the finger plugging his ear, he couldn't hear Scott's words. The din of the helicopter was too great. 'I can't hear you,' Flash said. 'It's no use. Thanks for calling. And the invitation. See you tomorrow, huh? So long.' He hung up.

The air around him, the house itself, seemed to be shaking. What's that asshole up to? Trying to land on the goddamn roof? He took a step away from the wall, and kicked over his beer can. 'Shit!'

'YOU BEHIND THE TREE,' a voice boomed. 'THROW YOUR WEAPON TO THE GROUND AND STEP INTO THE LIGHT WITH YOUR HANDS ABOVE YOUR HEAD.'

Flash charged into the living room. Alice was pushing herself off the couch, her good arm stretched towards Rose, who was rushing for the front door. 'Stop!' he shouted at the girl.

'I REPEAT, THROW YOUR WEAPON TO THE GROUND AND . . .'

Flash caught Rose by the shoulder as she reached for the doorknob. He yanked her back. 'When I tell you to stop—'

The boom of a gunshot broke through the noise.

Flash threw open the door.

'No!' Alice cried.

He lunged outside and stopped on the lawn. As he'd thought, the copter was hovering low over the house. The white beam of its searchlight was fixed on the trunk of an elm near the street. Behind the elm crouched a man with a revolver. The gun was aimed high. It jumped, blasting another shot at the chopper.

A patrol car, siren blaring, lights spinning red and blue, hurled around the corner at the end of the block.

The man fired again. Flash heard the slug smack into metal.

'You bastard!' he cried out as he raced at the man. The rotor blades threw a hot wind down on him.

In 'Nam, he'd felt the same hot wind as an army gunship descended to pick him up. It meant safety. Survival. In seconds, if a VC bullet didn't chop him down, he'd be airborne after six days of hiding, dodging enemy patrols. No bullets found him, that morning, but a rocket found the gunship as it hovered closer, and it tumbled in flames, shaking the jungle floor as it hit.

If that fucker falls on the house . . .

But the gun wasn't aimed at the chopper any more. It was lowering towards Flash as he ran at the man, as the patrol car skidded to a stop, as the chopper soared over him, no longer threatening the house. It's all right now, he thought. And heard a gunshot.

Chapter Thirty-five

Nick, pacing the theatre lobby, looked jumpy. He seemed to sag, as if worn out, when Julie approached him. His eyes stayed on her face, and she didn't think he'd noticed, yet, what she'd done.

'What's wrong?' she asked.

'I was just . . . You were in there so long.'

'Sorry about that.' She took his hand. 'Did I worry you?'

'I was starting to wonder if . . .' He shrugged.

'Nothing happened,' she said. They crossed the lobby and left the theatre. 'I'm sorry if you were worried. There was only one stall with a door on it. Seemed like everybody was waiting for that one. Me included.'

'Oh. Well. I'm just glad nothing went wrong.'

In spite of the night's warmth, Julie was trembling as they strolled along the sidewalk. She felt excited and daring.

'Where do you want to go?' Nick asked when they reached the car. He sounded very nervous. 'Do you want a sundae or something?'

'Why don't we just drive around for a while?'

'Sure. Okay.'

He started the car and drove out of the parking lot. Julie wished she could scoot over and snuggle against him, but the bucket seats would make it awkward. Deciding to wait, she fastened her safety belt. The pressure of the harness across her breast sent a pleasant tingle through her.

'Any place special?' Nick asked.

'No. I'll know it when I see it. Why don't you make a left up here?'

He turned, leaving behind the traffic of Ventura Boulevard. Except for occasional streetlamps, the road was dark. Lights shone in the windows of houses, but Julie saw nobody wandering about. Dark, empty cars sat in driveways and lined the curbs. At a Y in the road, Julie suggested they go left. The road narrowed as it climbed into the hills. There were fewer streetlights, fewer houses. As headlights appeared on the curve ahead, Nick swung in behind a parked Toyota to make room. A Mercedes eased by, and he pulled out again. He drove forward, slowing at each bend.

Julie spotted a steep lane to the left. 'Why don't we try that one?'

'It's not a through street,' Nick told her.

She nodded as she read the sign. 'That's okay.'

'Hope you don't get us lost.'

'All we've gotta do is point the car downhill.'

'You're the navigator.' He turned, and started up the grade. There were no streetlights. They passed a few driveways on the right, apparently leading to houses nestled unseen on the wooded slopes above the road. To the left, beyond the guardrails, the hillside dropped away. The lights of scattered houses were visible across the ravine.

'This is nice,' Julie said. 'Why don't you park along here someplace so we can enjoy the view?'

'Okay,' he said in a whisper she could barely hear. A few moments later, he eased the car to the right. The right-side tyres crunched over the ground. The branches of a bush on the slope scratched against Julie's window. Nick killed the headlights. He turned off the engine, and a heavy silence filled the car. He stared out the window. 'Not much of a view from here,' he whispered.

'This is fine,' Julie said. Her mouth was dry.

Nick took off his safety harness. He glanced at the side mirror, the rearview mirror.

'Anyone coming?'

He shook his head. 'I wonder if we're off the road far enough.'

'I think it's all right.' She opened her seat belt and pushed it out of the way. 'Besides, there's not a whole lot of traffic.'

'Pretty isolated up here, isn't it?'

'Yeah. Dark, too.' With a smile, she asked, 'You scared?'

'Nah. Are you? We can go someplace else if you want.'

'This is just fine,' Julie said.

Nick turned in his seat. Though light from the half-moon spilled in through the windshield, shadows hid his face. His eyes were patches of darkness, but Julie felt his gaze like a warm caress. She saw him lick his lips. He wiped his hands on his slacks. Then he reached out with one hand and gently stroked her cheek. Turning her head, she kissed his palm. The hand lingered for a moment, then curled around the back of her neck and urged her closer.

She wrapped her arms around Nick. She kissed him. He caressed her face, her hair, her shoulders.

He was too far away from her. They were both turned sideways on the bucket seats, twisted awkwardly and leaning in across the gap. She was uncomfortable and frustrated. Finally, she whispered, 'I wasn't made to bend this way.'

'Oh.' Nick let go of her. 'I'm sorry. Did I hurt you?'

'Don't be silly.' She brushed her lower lip against his mouth. 'Let's get in the backseat.'

'You want to?' Straightening up, he looked up and down the road, as if to make sure the coast was clear. Then he shoved open the door. He muttered, 'Damn it,' as the interior light came on. Julie shielded her eyes against its sudden brightness. Then she crawled over the driver's seat and climbed out after Nick. He thrust forward the seat back. Julie ducked into the car. Nick scooted in beside her and pulled the door shut. As he locked it, Julie snuggled against him, rubbed his chest, kissed the side of his neck.

He cringed. 'Hey, that tickles.'

'Does it?' She nibbled his neck, making him squirm. 'I vahnt your blood,' she intoned in her best Bela Lugosi accent. Then she pulled him down across the seat. Kneeling above him, she probed his ribs, his belly. He giggled and writhed, tried to protect himself, and finally dug wiggling fingers into Julie's armpits. With a squeal, she forced his hands away. She pinned them to the cushion. Then she kissed him. She let go of his hands. They went around her back, caressing.

She was half off the seat, toes on the floor, knees pressed against the cushion's edge. 'I'm coming up,' she whispered. She swung a leg over Nick, pushed with the other, squirmed, and finally found herself on top of him. Her legs were wide apart to make space for his upraised knees. 'Am I mashing you?' she asked.

'No.'

For a long time, they kissed. Julie relaxed a little, savouring the closeness, the intimate joining of their mouths, the feel of him under her body, the touch of his hands. His hands roamed over her shoulders and back, rubbing her through the thin fabric of her blouse. He always stopped at the waistband of her skirt. Though her blouse had come untucked, he never felt beneath it.

Straddling him this way, Julie could barely move. She wanted to hold him, stroke him, not merely lie on him and kiss. 'Maybe if we sit up,' she finally said. She climbed off Nick.

He sat up straight. Facing him, Julie knelt over his lap and lowered herself. Nick leaned forward slightly. They embraced each other tightly. 'This is much better,' Julie whispered.

'Yeah.'

She rubbed his back. He rubbed hers. Heart beating faster, she eased her hands under his shirt. She slid them up his smooth skin. He hesitated for a while, then followed her lead. His hands went under the back of her blouse, and glided up her bare skin. They curved over her shoulders, moved down her sides in a way that made her shiver, then swept in again towards her spine.

Julie leaned away. Nick's hands dropped to her thighs. They rested there, motionless, while Julie raised his knit shirt. She rubbed his bare chest, thumbs pressing his nipples. He was squirming slightly under her, as if uncomfortable.

'Are you all right?' she asked.

He nodded.

'Do you know what I did in the john?'

'I have a pretty good idea.'

'What?'

'I think . . . you took something off.'

'Is that what you think?'

'Yeah.' Nick lifted one hand from her thigh. It was half shut in a loose fist. It moved slowly higher. Julie's heart felt like a sledgehammer as the curled fingers pressed against her blouse just below her left breast. He brushed the underside of her breast, followed the curve upward. She caught her breath as he found her rigid nipple. The hand opened, and held her. Then his other hand closed around her right breast. 'God, Julie,' he whispered.

She clung to his shoulders and arched her back. She quivered as he explored her through the blouse, sliding the fabric over her skin, cupping her, squeezing gently, fingertips tracing her nipples. Finally, he opened the buttons. He spread the front of her blouse. He stared.

'Take a picture,' Julie said. 'It lasts longer.'

Laughing softly, Nick pulled her forward. Her naked breasts pushed against his chest. He covered her face with kisses. His hands went under the back of her blouse, moved up and down as if hungry for the feel of her bare skin.

He went over sideways, holding her, guiding her down. Then she was on her back. One leg hung off the seat and the other was stretched out between Nick's legs. His thigh was a heavy pressure on her groin. She writhed against it, gasping. His chest was on one breast. His hand fondled the other, squeezed it, stroked its swollen nipple. Moaning, squirming with need, Julie thrust Nick's face away from her. She forced his head lower. He kissed her nipple. He licked it. He took it into his mouth. He sucked on it, and Julie whimpered. He tried to raise his head, as if worried, but she forced it down and held it there. He sucked hard. It hurt and it sent shocks of pleasure through her body.

Then it wasn't his thigh against her groin. It was his hand. Outside her skirt, but rubbing. 'No,' she gasped. 'Nick, no.' It didn't go away. She thrust herself against it. 'No. Stop.' She reached down for it, and clutched his wrist, intending to push his hand away. Instead, she pressed it to her. His penis was rigid against her thigh. She shoved at his hip. He raised himself slightly and Julie touched him. He felt hard and hot through his pants. And very big. She wondered how it would feel inside her. The thought of that, the way it felt in her hand, the way Nick was massaging and sucking – all of it was too much. Crying out, she bucked and twisted. She clutched Nick. His penis throbbed against her hand and the agony of Julie's desire broke in a flood of release.

Then they lay beside each other, panting, kissing gently. 'I love you so much,' Nick whispered.

'I love you more.'

'No you don't.'

'Yes I do,' she said. 'And I want to stay here forever. I don't ever want to move.'

'We'll have to move, sooner or later.'

'What time is it?'

He checked his wristwatch. 'About ten till ten.'

'Already?' She sighed. She hugged him tightly. They kissed.

They caressed each other. 'I feel so peaceful and nice,' she said.

'Me, too.' Nick yawned.

'Am I boring you?'

He laughed, his breath warm on her face.

Julie yawned, too. She snuggled against him. 'What if we fall asleep and don't wake up till midnight?'

'Or morning?'

'What time is it?'

'Ten-twenty.'

'Oh, no.'

'Oh, yes.'

'I don't want to leave.'

'We'd better. We don't want your dad to get worried.'

'Yeah, I know.'

They sat up. As Nick straightened his shirt, Julie looked out the windows. Except for patches of moonlight, the street was dark. She saw no one.

Nick turned away from her. The bright ceiling light came on when he opened the door. While he climbed out, Julie took off her blouse. She tossed it onto the front seat.

Nick leaned into the car and stared.

'Something wrong?'

'My God, Julie.'

She scooted across the seat, and climbed out. A warm breeze drifted against her.

'You nuts?' Nick asked.

'Yep.' She raised her arms, and Nick stepped into them. His hands ran up and down her back as he kissed her. Then she eased him away. 'We'd better go,' she said.

'You're so beautiful.'

'But nuts?'

'Yeah.'

With a grin, she turned away. She crawled across the driver's seat, and sat down. Nick climbed in. He left the door slightly ajar to keep the light on while Julie lifted her purse from the floor. She took her bra out.

'Wait,' Nick said. Leaning towards her, he slid a hand over her breast. His fingers curled around it, holding it firmly. Then he let go.

He continued to gaze at Julie while she put on her bra, fastened it, and slipped into her blouse. As she buttoned it, he tugged his door shut. He started the car. He turned on the headlights. He shifted to first gear, and released the emergency brake. The car started to roll forward. Its sluggish motion felt strange to Julie. Nick struggled with the steering wheel. Then he turned off the engine.

'What's wrong?' Julie asked.

'I don't know.' He got out. He crouched by the front tyre, stood up, and stepped around to the other side. He crouched again. Then he stood, and stared through the windshield at Julie.

'Oh, no,' she muttered. A chill, sick feeling spread through her. She scurried across the seat and climbed out the car.

The front tyre was flat.

'This one over here, too,' Nick said. He sounded grim.

'How could it happen?'

He walked slowly towards her, holding out his hand. 'Look.'

She peered at the small, dark object resting on his palm. 'What is it?'

'Part of a valve stem.'

'I don't get it,' she muttered.

'Both front tyres. Somebody cut off the valve stems.'

'Oh, Jesus! While we were . . .'

Nick answered with a nod.

Chapter Thirty-six

Julie's legs went weak. She leaned against the side of the car. She felt crawly with gooseflesh. As she rubbed her arms, her eyes searched the darkness. The narrow, moonlit road looked deserted. There were no streetlights, no parked cars. Bushes along the guardrail looked like silent, watching men.

Nick patted her arm. 'Don't worry.'

'Who's worried?'

Leaning into the car, he shut off the headlights. He came out with the keys, and swung the door shut. Julie followed him to the trunk. 'Can you change the tyres?' she asked.

'I've only got one spare.' He removed the tyre iron.

'Then what's that for?'

'Just in case.' He shut the trunk.

'Oh, man,' Julie muttered.

'Let's go.'

'Where?'

'To a telephone. We've gotta call the auto club.' He took her hand, and they started down the road. They looked over their shoulders as they walked.

'There won't be a public phone,' Julie said, 'till we get to Ventura Boulevard.'

'Probably not.'

'I'm really sorry I got you into this, Nick.'

'It's not your fault.'

'Oh, yeah? It wouldn't have happened if we'd stayed at the movies. Me and my great ideas.'

He squeezed her hand. 'It was a great idea. It was . . . No matter what happens, I'll never regret it.'

'No matter what happens. Oh, wonderful. What are you expecting?'

'I don't know. This is all part of it, though, isn't it?'

'The curse, you mean?'

'I guess that's what I mean.'

'Oh, man.'

Striding around a bend, they came upon a steep, narrow drive. To one side of it, half hidden behind bushes, stood a mailbox. The number on the box was 21; the name, FISH. The lane slanted up the slope, curving, disappearing in the darkness. 'It must be a driveway,' Julie said. 'Should we give it a try?'

'Call from someone's house?'

'If we don't, we've got an awfully long walk ahead of us. What time is it?'

'Ten-thirty-five.'

'We couldn't possibly get to Ventura by eleven. Dad'll start going crazy.'

'Guess we'd better do it then.'

With a final look at the bleak, deserted road behind them, they started up the driveway. Trees blocked out the moonlight. The night was full of familiar sounds: an airliner, the honk of a car, a man's shout, a door slamming. But they all came from far away, as if they belonged to a different world. Only the chirping of crickets came from nearby. And their own noises: the scuff of their shoes on the concrete, their heavy breathing.

'This is one long driveway,' Nick whispered.

'It's almost like we're back in the mountains.'

'No packs, at least.'

Julie looked back. Nobody there. The road they'd left was out of sight, hidden beyond a bend in the driveway.

Nick dropped behind her. He pressed his hand to her back, and pushed as she walked. 'Oh, that's better.'

'Glad to be of service.'

They trudged around a curve in the driveway, and Nick's hand fell away. He stepped up beside her. They stood motionless, breathing hard, staring at the house.

With its rough stone walls and steep tile roof, it looked vaguely foreign to Julie.

'Hansel and Gretel time,' Nick whispered.

She gave his arm a soft jab.

Except for a single post lamp along the walkway to the door, there were no lights. A monstrous, ancient Cadillac was parked near the garage.

'What do you think?' Nick asked.

'We came this far.'

'It doesn't look very . . . inviting.'

'Let's give it a shot, Hansel.'

They walked to the door. There didn't seem to be a bell, just a brass knocker shaped like a fist. Nick lifted it, and rapped three times. Quickly, he propped the tyre iron against the doorframe. Julie wiped her sweaty hands on her skirt. 'Sure hope they have a phone,' she whispered.

They waited. No sounds came from inside the house.

'Should we try again?' Julie asked.

'Maybe they're asleep.'

She lifted the heavy knocker and the door swung open, pulling it from her hand. She flinched. The brass fell with a clamour.

A man looked out at them. He was not old and gnarled, as Julie had somehow expected. He appeared to be about forty. He was bald, and very fat. His blue kimono, sashed at the waist, was shiny in the glow of the foyer lamp. It reached nearly to his knees. His legs were bare. He wore dark socks. He stared, and said nothing. He was frowning slightly, but seemed more curious than angry.

'I'm sorry we disturbed you,' Nick said. 'Our car broke down, and we were wondering if we could use your phone.'

With a nod, he gestured for them to enter. Julie followed Nick over the threshold, and shut the door. The man walked ahead of them, limping slightly. He entered a dark room off the foyer, and turned on a lamp. He waved them in.

The shadowy room looked, to Julie, like a parlour from a century ago. Her eyes took in the Persian rug, the overstuffed, plush sofa and armchairs adorned with doilies, the pedestal tables cluttered with figurines, the shelves of leather-bound books. She saw no telephone.

She breathed through her nose to avoid the room's musty smell.

The man swept a hand towards the purple sofa, as if inviting them to sit down. Julie glanced at Nick. He shrugged. 'Sir,' he said, 'do you have a telephone we might use?'

His bald head nodded. He motioned for them to be seated.

What's going on? Julie thought. The man's odd behaviour and the old-fashioned look of the parlour were making her uneasy. Why doesn't he say something?

She followed Nick to the sofa. She sank into its cushion and sat forward, rigid, gripping her knees.

The man smiled and nodded. Turning away, he bent over to turn on the portable television. The rear of his satin kimono rode up. Julie glimpsed bare rump. She looked at Nick. He shook his head and rolled his eyes upward.

Stepping back, the man stared at the television. It made a loud humming sound. The voices filled the room, and a black and white picture fluttered onto the screen. The man faced Julie. He smiled. 'May I offer you tea?' he asked in a high-pitched voice.

So he *can* talk, she thought.

'We'd rather use your phone, if we may,' Nick said.

His head bobbed.

'I'd better call Dad first,' Julie said. 'Tell him we'll be late.'

The man lowered himself onto a chair near the end of the sofa. He folded his hands on his lap, and stared at her. He seemed very pleased, almost eager about something. He squirmed a bit.

'May I use your phone?' Julie asked.

He pointed at a curtained-off archway across the room, just to the left of the television. 'In there?' Julie asked. He nodded. She pushed herself off the sofa and went to the archway. Sweeping the curtain aside, she peered in. By the dim light from the parlour, she saw a small alcove, apparently a passageway into another room. A curtain hung the other end. Against the wall was a rolltop desk. She spotted the black shape of a telephone on its work top. A floor lamp stood beside the desk.

Reaching under its shade, she switched on a bulb. She let the curtain fall across the entry, took a single step to the desk, and picked up the phone. As she dialled, she heard voices from the parlour television.

Poor Nick, she thought, sitting out there with that weirdo.

The phone rang three times before it was picked up. 'Hello?'

'Hi, Dad. It's me.'

'Julie? Where are you? What's wrong?'

'We had some car trouble. Everything's fine, but we're kind of stuck.'

'What happened?'

'We got a couple of flats.'

'A *couple of flats*?' He sounded shocked.

'Yeah. We're gonna call the auto club, but I thought I'd better let you know we'll be late.'

'*Two flat tyres?* Did somebody let the air out, or what?'

'The valve stems were cut off.'

He was silent for a few moments. 'The auto club won't be able to fix that. They'll have to tow you.'

'I was afraid of that.'

'Look, I'd better come pick you up. The car can wait till morning. Where are you calling from?'

'We're at this guy's house.' She remembered the mailbox at the foot of the driveway. 'His name's Fish. He's up in the hills just south of Ventura Boulevard.'

'What the *hell* are you doing up there!'

'Well . . .'

'Never mind. We'll discuss it later. What's his address?'

'Twenty-one something. Hang on a second, I'll ask.' She set down the receiver, stepped away from the desk, and hooked back the curtain.

The man smiled over the top of Nick's head. He was behind the sofa, leaning over its back, a thick arm squeezing Nick's throat. Nick's face was deep red. He was kicking and struggling.

'No!' Julie cried out. Lurching into the parlour, she glanced from side to side. She needed a weapon. Nothing looked right. With a yell, she flung the television off its stand. It crashed to the floor.

The man's face twisted. He let go of Nick. He stared at the smoking, sizzling remains of the TV as Nick dropped onto the sofa, rolled, and tumbled off. The man's lips moved, but no words came out. His narrow eyes shifted to Julie. Roaring, he threw himself over the sofa.

Julie spun around. She dashed through the curtain, through the alcove, into the dark room beyond.

The man, still roaring, followed.

Scott, clutching the phone to his ear, yanked open the counter drawer. He jerked out a telephone directory.

'*What is it?*' Karen asked.

'I don't . . . quick, look up "Fish." ' He thrust the book at her.

Karen slipped it down on the counter. Her hands shook badly as she raced through the pages.

'"Fish,"' Scott said. 'A man's name.'

She found the *F*'s, flicked the pages until she found *Fi*. She traced the columns with her fingertip. 'God, there's a couple dozen Fishes.'

'It's twenty-one something. The address.'

Half the entries seemed to be for food: Fish Diner, Fish Kitchen, Fish Market. 'Here! Fish, Marvin, Twenty-one Vista Terrace. Tarzana.'

'Gotta be it. Write it down. Tanya!' he yelled.

As Karen scribbled the address on a notepad, Tanya came rushing into the kitchen. Benny was close behind her. They both looked alarmed.

'Julie!' Scott called into the phone. Then he hung up and tugged a Thomas street atlas from the drawer. 'Julie's in trouble,' he told Tanya. 'I want you to call the police. Send them to this address.'

Karen ripped off the note and pressed it into the girls hand.

'Tell them it's an emergency.'

'What's going on?' Benny asked.

'Stay here with Tanya.' He looked at Karen. 'Will you come with me?'

'Of course.'

'Gotta find that street on the map,' he said. He gave her the Thomas guide. 'Meet you at the car,' he said, and dashed from the kitchen.

Karen hurried outside. Her car was parked at the curb, but she figured he would want to take his Cutlass. It was in the driveway. She tried the passenger door. Locked.

Scott came running from the house, a pistol in his hand.

The man whipped the curtain aside and Julie, standing at the wall, swung the chair down as he lunged through the archway. The edge of the seat smacked his head. His legs buckled. His knees hammered the floor. He clutched the top of his head, and ducked. Julie raised the chair high and swung it down with all her strength. The wooden legs slammed across his back. Squealing, he fell facedown. He rolled over as she lifted the chair again. His knees were up, is kimono open.

'Pig!' Julie shrieked, and drove the chair down.

He caught two of its legs, wrenched it from her grip, and hurled it away.

Julie leaped for the curtain. As she shouldered through it, a kick pounded her ankle. Her feet tangled. She fell sprawling into the alcove. She scurried over its floor, thrust herself up, and staggered through the curtain to the parlour. Nick was lying motionless in front of the sofa.

She crouched, grabbed the broken television, and hurled

it as the man's shape bulged the curtain. It struck him at knee level. He cried out. He tore the curtain down and tumbled into the room. In the lamplight, Julie saw that his bald scalp was bleeding badly. His face was a red, dripping mask. As he got to his hands and knees, she kicked. She'd lost her sandal. A shock of pain streaked up her foot, but the man yelped and grabbed his face. He fell on his side and started to roll away from her. He was on his back, whimpering and holding his face. Julie jumped. She brought her knees up high and shot her legs down, driving both feet into his soft bare belly. His breath whooshed out. She windmilled for a moment, then fell, hitting the floor flat on her back. She lay there stunned, fighting for breath, terrified that the man might recover before she could.

Finally, she pushed herself up. The man was still on his back. His knees were up. He was hugging his stomach and wheezing.

Nick was rolling over.

He's alive!

Julie got to her feet. She flung aside the fallen curtain and lifted the television. Staggering towards the man, she raised it high. Her arms trembled as she held it above his face. She stared down at him. 'No,' he gasped. 'Don't. I'm sorry. I couldn't help it.'

Her arm muscles shuddered with the weight.

He pressed his hands to his bloody face, and started to sob.

Twisting sideways, Julie dropped the television. It crashed to the floor just above his head. 'Leave us alone,' she muttered, and went to Nick.

'Here it is,' Karen said. 'Vista Terrace. Go right on Ventura to Avenida del Sol. Then it's a left.'

Scott turned a knob, and the ceiling light went off.

Karen held the atlas on her lap. She grabbed the dashboard with her other hand as the car skidded around a corner.

'They'll be all right,' she said.

'I shouldn't have let them go.'

'You couldn't have known.'

'God*damn* it!'

'Nick's with her. They'll be all right.'

She saw a stop sign ahead. Scott didn't slow down. As he sped towards the intersection, Karen spotted headlights to the right. 'Look out!'

He accelerated, the thrust of the car shoving her against the seat. Light glared through her window. A horn blasted. She hugged her head. Then the brightness was gone, the noise of the horn fading behind them.

'Scott!'

He didn't answer. He was hunched over the steering wheel, speeding up the centre of the deserted road.

Karen tried to keep her voice calm. 'It won't do Julie any good if we get ourselves killed.'

'Fucking curse.'

'*It's on us, too, Scott.*'

Julie flung open the front door. Dropping to a crouch, she snatched up the tyre iron. She rushed into the parlour and gave it to Nick. The man was lying facedown now, holding his head and crying softly. 'If he tries anything, beat the crap out of him.'

She left Nick kneeling beside the man, and hurried into the alcove. The phone was beeping loudly. She pushed its plungers, lifted the handset off the desk, and got a tone. Quickly, she dialled.

It rang once. 'Hello?' Benny's voice.

'It's me.'

'Julie! Are you okay?'

'Is Dad there?'

'No. He's on the way to pick you up. The cops are on the way, too.'

'They know where we are?'

'Yeah.'

'How long ago did Dad leave?'

'I don't know, five minutes? What happened?'

'Some nut tried to kill us.'

'It's the curse.'

'Brilliant deduction, Bonzo.' She hung up.

They sped west on Ventura Boulevard, Scott weaving through the traffic. He accelerated to make it through a yellow light, but was forced to stop at the next main intersection because the cars ahead of him blocked the way. He pounded a fist on the steering wheel. 'Come on, come on, come on,' he muttered.

Tilting the atlas to catch the light from the streetlamps, Karen drew a finger along the thick line of Ventura. 'Avenida del Sol,' she said, 'should be two blocks up.'

'I make a left,' he said.

'Yeah. Then it's a few blocks. We'll come to a Y. You stay to the left. It'll run into Vista Terrace.'

'Which way on Vista?'

'Left again. It doesn't go the other way.'

The traffic began to move. He stayed in the left-hand lane, hissing through clenched teeth, pounding the wheel and muttering about the slowness of the car ahead.

'The police are probably there by now,' Karen said.

'God, I hope so.'

The car sprang out as if escaping, and swung across three lanes of oncoming traffic. The force of the turn shoved Karen against her door. Horns blared. Then they were speeding along Avenida del Sol. The residential road was dark except for a few streetlamps. There were no cars approaching. Scott steered up the centre line.

'Don't let them see the gun,' Karen warned.

'Huh?'

'The cops. If they see you with the gun, they might shoot.'

* * *

461

Julie flinched as a clamour resounded through the house. 'I'll get it,' she said. Pushing against Nick's shoulder, she rose from her knees and rushed out of the parlour.

In the dim foyer, she grabbed the doorknob. She hesitated. 'Who is it?' she called.

'Police officers.'

She opened the door, and let out a sigh of relief at the sight of the two uniformed patrolmen.

'Here's the Y,' Karen said. 'Veer left. We're almost there.'

He slowed down slightly as the road narrowed, and then Karen saw taillights through the thick bushes to the right. Scott hit the brakes and horn before she yelled. He swerved away, but the car speeding down the driveway slammed into them just ahead of Karen with a deafening crunch of metal. The impact threw her against the door.

Their headlights jarred over a hedge across the road. Then they were crashing through the bushes, skidding down a slope. Karen thrust her hands against the ceiling as the car rolled over. The windshield shattered. The roof quavered. She thought it would cave in but it held as the car slid and wobbled to a stop.

She was upside down, the harness cutting into her shoulder and lap.

Just like before.

Only now it was Scott, not Frank, hanging unconscious beside her as smoke started spilling from under the hood.

Part Three

Chapter Thirty-seven

There were four of them.

They came down the trail from Carver Pass at dusk, walking single file.

Ettie, crouched behind an outcropping near her cave, could see only their vague shapes in the distance. But she knew who they were. She knew why they'd come.

They were the survivors.

They'd come to kill her.

She was pleased there were only four.

Chapter Thirty-eight

Karen slipped on the loose earth of the footpath, landed on her rump, and skidded. She dug in the heels of her boots to stop herself. The tingling pain of her scraped buttocks brought tears to her eyes. She wiped them away. Nick and Benny took her by the arms and helped her up.

She followed them to the bottom of the path, with Julie staying behind her. They walked along the lakeshore towards the stand of pine where they'd camped that Monday night, but were still a good distance away when Benny sat on the ground.

Karen stopped beside him. She dropped her pack, and kneeled in front of it. A breeze chilled the back of her sweaty blouse as she unstrapped a side pocket and took out Scott's .45 automatic. She jacked a cartridge into the chamber, switched the safety on, and sat down. She leaned back against her pack, and rested the heavy pistol on the lap of her jeans.

Benny was lying on his back with his knees in the air. Julie was settled against her pack. They were sweaty, gasping for breath. Nick, crouching over his open pack, took out a hatchet. Scott's hatchet. The sheriff still had Nick's. He sat down, and took off its leather sheath.

Karen shut her eyes. Her heart was racing and she felt nauseated. Sweat streamed down her face. She wiped it with her bare forearm, and let the shaking arm fall to her lap. Her wristbone hit the pistol, and she whimpered.

'Let's get moving,' Nick said. His sudden voice made Karen flinch.

'I can't,' Julie said. 'Let's wait.'

'A little while.'

Karen heard movement. Through half-open eyelids, she watched Julie crawl over to Nick and hold him. He stroked her hair. For a moment, he looked as if he might cry.

He'd done some crying in the station wagon today – no, yesterday. It was all so confused in Karen's mind, as if she'd been in a daze ever since pulling Scott's unconscious body from the wreck. That was two nights ago. Last night was Juniper Lake and horrible dreams that kept waking her until Benny crawled into her sleeping bag and they embraced and finally fell asleep in each other's arms.

When she woke up in the morning, Benny was snug against her and snoring. Julie's sleeping bag was empty. She was with Nick. She crawled out naked in the frigid morning air, and Karen saw a smear of dried blood on one thigh. As she knelt beside her sleeping bag, she saw Karen watching. The girl glared as if daring Karen to chastise her. 'Go back to him,' Karen said. 'Stay with him.' The hard look fell away from

Julie's face. Her chin trembled. She nodded, and returned to Nick's sleeping bag.

Later, no one spoke of the incident. But Karen caught Julie staring at her, from time to time, with a curious look on her face.

'How you doing, Benny?' Nick asked.

'I think I'm gonna die,' he said.

Karen winced. Did he have to mention death?

'We're all gonna die,' Nick said. 'But not tonight. It's someone else's turn tonight.'

'Damn right,' Julie said.

'Karen?'

She nodded, and lifted the pistol off her lap.

'Okay,' he said. 'Let's haul ass.'

Haul ass. He sounded just like Flash. Karen's throat tightened, and tears came to her eyes. God, she'd hardly known the man. But he'd seemed like a good fellow. He was Scott's friend and Nick's father, and she supposed the tears were for them and for Alice, for Rose and Heather.

She pushed herself up. Her legs trembled under her weight, and her blistered feet burned. As the others stood up, she untucked her blouse. She lifted it, sucked in her belly, and pushed the pistol barrel down the waistband of her jeans. It was hard and cool against her skin.

'We'll circle this lake,' Nick said. 'Then we'll circle Upper Mesquite.'

'Flashlights,' Karen said.

'Yeah. It'll be dark in a few minutes.'

'And cold,' Benny added.

They searched through their packs. Benny put on his parka. Karen was shivering, and her own parka seemed too bulky. She left it in her pack, but took out her grey sweatshirt. Turning away from the others, she took off her cold, damp blouse. She wadded it. She used it to wipe the sweat off her face, the back of her neck, her sides. Then she tossed it into the pack, and put the sweatshirt on. It felt soft and warm. It made her think of Scott, the night he'd worn it back to his tent.

If only he were here . . .

Benny was gaping at her when she turned around. He looked down quickly at his flashlight, switched it on, and shined it on his face to see that it worked.

Karen took out her own flashlight and tested it.

Nick pointed with his hatchet to the left. 'We'll go that way, head around the back side of the lake till we get to the ridge.'

They started to walk, Nick in the lead with Julie close behind him. Karen let Benny go ahead of her. She didn't want him bringing up the rear; it seemed too vulnerable a position for the boy.

They followed the shoreline back the way they'd come. Where it curved at the northern end, they made their way up the broken granite blocks of the slope until they were thirty or forty feet above the water. Every step was an agony for Karen – for the others as well, she supposed. But nobody protested.

Probably, they could have just waited at the campsite. But they'd discussed it many times on the way in, and agreed to this. Everyone felt it would be better than waiting for the woman to make a first move. Also, there was a chance they might discover her hiding place, come upon her unawares. It was a slim chance, since the deputies hadn't been able to find her, but worth a try anyway. They agreed she must have a hiding place somewhere on the slopes above the lakes. They had enough food for four days. If they didn't find her tonight, if she stayed away from them, they would keep searching until the food ran out.

No one thought it would come to that.

If she was still at the lake, she would try for them. 'She wants me,' Nick had said. 'I'm the one who killed her son. She can't get me with the curse. She doesn't have my blood and stuff.'

'She got your dad,' Julie had reminded him, taking his hand.

'That was an accident. He got in the way of it to save Mom and the girls. He would've been all right, except . . . She has to come for me. That's when we'll nail her.'

'What if the curse doesn't end when she's dead?' Julie asked.

'It has to,' Benny said, and explained that without her psychic power directing it the curse would dissipate.

'What makes you so sure?' Julie asked.

'The book said so.'

'Let's hope the book's right,' Karen said.

'Let's hope she's still at the lake,' Julie said.

'She will be,' Nick assured them. 'She will be. She wants me dead.'

Nick pointed up the slope, stirring Karen from her thoughts. He spoke to Julie. The girl nodded. Sitting on a boulder, she twisted around to watch him climb. Karen followed Benny across the rocks, and joined her.

'Where's he going?' Karen asked.

Julie pointed. Some distance above Nick was a dark crevice in the rocks. 'He wants to check that out. We're supposed to wait here.'

They watched Nick make his way higher, leaping from rock to rock, striding up an angled slab, finally reaching the shadowed gap. He shone his flashlight inside, then turned around and shook his head and started down.

Karen lowered herself onto a rock. It felt cool and lumpy through the seat of her jeans, and the pistol dug into her until she leaned back. She braced herself up on her elbows.

The water below, grey in the dim light, was ruffled by the wind. Directly across the lake was the clearing where they'd left their packs. The fireplace, a distance to the left, was intact and surrounded by the stumps and rocks they'd used for seats. Even a pile of firewood remained – wood they had gathered after swimming. She remembered the good cold feel of the water. Flash whistling at her before she went in. Had the madwoman and her son been watching, spying on them from up here someplace? Maybe if they hadn't gone swimming, if the man hadn't seen her and Julie in their suits . . . Those ifs again. It was pointless to think that way. You can't go back and change anything, so why worry about it?

If they'd just listened to Benny that night and gone after the woman and taken her pouch . . .

Nick leaped down and joined them. 'Just a crack in the rocks,' he said. 'It didn't go anywhere.'

They started walking again. Soon, the last of the evening light faded out. Under the half-moon, the rocks ahead looked grey and bleak, like a dirty snowfield. A snowfield gouged with black shadows. The shadows, all around, made Karen uneasy. She reached under her sweatshirt and pulled out the automatic.

Benny looked back at her. 'What's wrong?'

'Nothing much.'

'Did you see something?'

'It's what I don't see that's got me worried.'

'I wish Dad was here.'

'So do I.'

'Do you think he'll be mad when he finds out?'

'No. I think he'll be very proud. Especially if we do what we came for.'

With a nod, Benny looked forward again. He switched on his flashlight, shone it on Julie's back, then down to the rocks in front of his feet.

Karen turned her own flashlight on, but its brightness seemed to deepen the dark around her. Following close behind Benny, she shot its beam up the slope, swept it over the rocks, probed the black crevices. Her back felt exposed. She twisted around, but the tunnel of light showed only rocks and fluttering shadows behind her. Nobody there, she thought. Nobody creeping up.

'*Yeeeh!*' The sharp outcry came from Benny. She sprang

forward as the boy ducked and covered his head and a coyote leaping from above slammed him over. He tumbled towards the edge. Karen lunged across the boulder. Her jarring beam showed Benny's legs kicking high, flipping backward. She flung the flashlight and pistol from her hands. She stretched for him. Her fingertips brushed a cuff of his jeans, and then he was falling. Karen staggered, her momentum thrusting her towards the edge. She teetered there. Her sweatshirt went taut across her chest, and she was tugged to a stop.

Benny dropped to the rocks ten feet below. He cried out as he hit. With a yelp, the coyote raced away.

Julie let go of Karen's sweatshirt and stepped beside her. 'Benny!'

The boy raised his head.

A crouched figure with a hatchet scurried towards him over the moonlit rocks.

'Look out!' Karen yelled.

'It's just Nick,' Julie said.

As they climbed down, Karen heard Benny whimper, 'My arm, my arm.'

Karen knelt beside him. He was gasping, holding his right forearm.

'I think it might be broken,' Nick said.

Karen stroked the boy's sweaty forehead. 'Where else do you hurt?' she asked.

'Everywhere.'

'You took a pretty good fall.'

'I tried to duck, but it—'

Julie said, 'Is anything else broken or sprained?'

'I don't know,' he said. 'I don't think so.'

He flinched and sobbed as they sat him up. They carefully removed his parka. Julie shone a light on his arm while Nick rolled his right sleeve up above the elbow. The forearm was swollen and discoloured, but the skin wasn't broken. 'We need something to splint it,' Nick said.

'Knives?' Karen suggested.

'Let's give it a try.'

Julie opened her belt and took off her leather-cased knife. From hilt to tip, it was nearly a foot long.

'That'll do for one,' Nick said.

Benny had a similar knife.

Karen held them in place, one on each side of the arm while Nick strapped them tight with Benny's belt. 'I guess that'll have to do until we find something better.'

'Hope we don't need those things,' Julie said.

Nick ruffled Benny's hair. 'Now you're better armed than any of us.'

'*My gun*,' Karen muttered.

She and Julie climbed up the rocks to look for it. With Nick's flashlight, she searched the area where she'd let it fall. Her beam swept the grey surfaces, sought out dark corners, dug into fissures. Julie located the lost flashlight. It was broken. They kept on looking.

'It has to be here someplace,' Julie said.

'You'd think so.'

They went over the same area time and again.

'Maybe it's down there,' Julie said, stepping close to the edge.

'Any luck?' Nick called to her.

'No.'

They climbed down and searched the base of the rock cluster.

Julie glanced at her brother. 'You're not sitting on it, are you?'

'No,' he said.

'I'll try looking,' Nick said.

Julie handed over her flashlight. She stayed below, while Karen led Nick back up the broken rocks to the place where she had dropped the gun. 'Right about here,' she said, standing a yard from the edge.

'Did you throw it, or just let it fall?'

'I just opened my hand so I could grab for Benny.'

'Maybe you kicked it.'

'I might've. If I did, it didn't register.'

She showed him where Julie had found the flashlight. They searched there. They crisscrossed the craggy mound of granite, walking shoulder to shoulder.

'It might've gone down one of these cracks,' Nick finally said.

'Wherever it is,' Karen told him, 'I don't think we're gonna find it. Not tonight anyway. Why don't we come back in the morning when we've got some light on the subject?'

'Morning will be too late,' Nick said.

They climbed down, and spent some time searching the area around Benny and Julie.

'Might as well forget it,' Julie said.

Karen took off her belt and made a sling for Benny's arm. Then they helped the boy to his feet.

'What now?' Julie asked.

'Let's just get back to our packs,' Nick said. 'There's aspirin in my first-aid kit. Maybe that'll help Benny's pain.'

'Build a nice, warm fire,' Julie added.

'And eat,' Benny said. 'I'm starving.'

They were near the south end of the lake. Karen, with one of the flashlights, took the lead. Nick followed, supporting Benny. The boy could walk all right, though he winced with each limping step. Julie, carrying the hatchet and the other working flashlight, brought up the rear.

Karen tried to pick out the easiest route. Her beam probed the darkness ahead, swept the slope to her left. She felt very vulnerable without the gun.

By losing it, she'd put everyone in terrible danger. Nobody had criticized her and she tried not to blame herself, but damn it, she'd thrown away their main defence, the only weapon they had that could reach out and knock someone down at a safe distance. The pocketknife in her jeans was little comfort. The two big knives were belted around Benny's arm. Nick still had a sheath knife at his side, and Julie had the hatchet. A pitiful collection of weapons. Christ, why didn't I hang onto the gun!

Rounding the end of the lake, she came upon the feed stream from Upper Mesquite. Her light shimmered on its rushing surface, followed the water upwards to the low ridge, swept back and forth over both rocky shores. She saw rocks and lurching shadows and flowing water. Nothing more. She crouched. She cupped some cold, fresh water to her mouth. Then she jumped to the other side, and held her light on the stream.

Nick and Benny waded across, the water swirling over their boots, soaking their pants legs almost to the knees.

Julie leaped over the stream. 'Now you two'll come down with pneumonia.'

Nick made a sound resembling a laugh. 'Better than _old_monia.'

Karen crossed the slope, heading downwards, closer to the lake. And then her boot pressed springy earth, not rock. It felt like a cushion. It felt wonderful. The layer of pine needles made soft crunching sounds as she walked.

She took a twisting route to avoid trees and clumps of rock. Then she saw the clearing just ahead. She spotted the fireplace, the stumps and rocks surrounding it like stools, the pile of wood. She was swept by a feeling of pleasure and relief, as if returning home after a long trip.

She staggered forward. She lowered herself onto the flat surface of a stump, stretched out her pulsing legs, and sighed.

'What the shit!' Nick blurted. 'Where'd our packs go?'

Karen shined her flashlight into the darkness. The packs were gone.

Chapter Thirty-nine

Benny felt useless. He sat on a rock shivering, his arm throbbing with pain, while Nick and Julie searched for the backpacks. Karen sat on a stump close to him. She held an open pocketknife. 'You can help them look if you want,' he said.

'That's okay.'

'You don't have to stay and guard me.'

She smiled slightly. 'Sure I do.'

'Boy, I really messed things up.'

'No you didn't. It could've happened to any of us.' She wrapped her arms around herself.

'Are you cold?' Benny asked.

'I'm one giant goosebump.'

'Do you want my parka?'

'No, thanks. It wouldn't fit anyway.'

'You could put it over your back.'

'No. You keep it. Really. You need it more than me. Didn't you know that women have an extra layer of fat?'

'Not you.'

She laughed. 'It's gonna be a rough night if they don't find the packs. We'll freeze our buns.'

'And starve. Like the Donner party.'

'Hardly like the Donner party. We can hike out of here in a day if we have to. We've done it before.'

'We can't leave without . . . We've gotta kill the witch first.'

'At least we know she's here,' Karen said. 'She has to be the one who took our packs. That's something anyway.'

'I knew she would be. She brought us here.'

'What?'

'She brought us here. With her magic.'

'That's a pleasant thought. What makes you think so?'

'We're here, aren't we?'

'We chose to come.'

'Why didn't we have a wreck on the way up? We didn't even have a close call.'

'Nick was driving. As your dad said, he's the Great Uncursed One.'

'Nothing's happened to any of us since Thursday. Nothing happened till we got here. She wanted us here.'

'So she could get Nick?'

'And us. When we're out of the way, she'll go ahead and finish off Dad and Heather and Rose and Mrs Gordon. She can finish them with the curse.'

'We won't let her. Unless we freeze to death.'

'Maybe we should make a fire.'

'With what?'

'I've got matches,' Benny told her.

'*You do?*'

'Sure.' With his left hand, he fumbled open the button of a shirt-pocket flap.

'Oh, you're a life saver. I wish you'd mentioned that five minutes ago.'

'It'll mess up our night vision,' he said, taking out a book of matches.

'Who cares?' She stood and held out a shaky hand. Benny gave he the matches. She rushed towards the trees. Crouching, she gathered pine needles. As she returned, Benny swivelled around to face the fireplace. He remembered building it, collecting the rocks by himself and stacking them to form a low, circular wall, the afternoon they arrived at the lake and everyone was mad at him because it was his fault they had to stay here.

Karen, on her knees, tore off the matchbook cover. She tucked it into a small pile of pine needles, and carefully stacked kindling on top.

'It's all my fault,' he said.

She looked over her shoulder at him. 'What is?'

'Everything. If I hadn't tripped on Heather and hurt her foot, we would've gone to Wilson Lake and none of this stuff would've happened.'

'Bullshit.'

'It's true.'

'You sound just like your dad, you know that? Blaming yourselves. It must run in the family.'

'But it's true.'

'Save the blame for that bitch and her son. We're just victims, Benny. We happened to be at the wrong place at the wrong time. A million things could've changed that. And we would've been just fine, camping here, if that sick maniac hadn't decided to rape me.'

'He . . . he *raped* you?'

Karen hesitated. Then she said, 'Yes.'

Benny felt as if he'd been punched hard in the stomach. He hunched over. The movement sent pain pounding through his arm. He started to cry.

Karen stood up. She stepped close to him and pressed his head gently against her. The sweatshirt was soft. It smelled good. He rubbed his face against it, feeling her belly through the material. It was the sweatshirt she'd worn last night in her sleeping bag when she held him and she was so warm and he could feel her breasts against him and worried so badly that she might notice his hard-on. Then she'd whispered, 'Don't worry about it,' and he'd wanted to die with shame. But just for a minute. After that, it had been fine and peaceful. 'Are you gonna marry Dad?' he'd asked.

'Maybe.'

'I hope so.'

'Why?'

'Because I love you.'

'I love you, too, Benny.'

He'd snuggled against her. He'd never felt so good before in all his life. Thinking about it eased the hurt.

'You okay?' she asked, stroking his hair.

'I . . . I feel so bad he did that to you.'

'He's dead.'

'I wish I'd killed him.'

'No you don't.'

'Oh yes I do.'

She backed away. Crouching, she kissed him lightly on the mouth. 'Let's get this fire going before we freeze.' Turning around, she struck a match and lit the piece of cardboard. Flames curled up. The pine needles smoked and crackled and caught fire, igniting the twigs. Karen added bigger sticks from the nearby pile. The blaze grew high, dancing and throwing out heat. '*Now* we're cooking,' she said.

Nick and Julie came up from behind. They huddled close to the fire.

'No luck?' Karen asked.

'We think she might've thrown them in the lake,' Julie said.

'If she did,' Nick said, 'they'd have to be close to shore. We shouldn't have much trouble finding them.'

'We're gonna take a look,' Julie added. She was bent over the fire, the flashlight clamped between her knees, rubbing her hands together as if washing them in the flames.

'Where'd you find the matches?' Nick asked.

'They're Benny's,' Karen said.

'Good going, Ben.'

'Yeah.' Julie smiled at him. 'You're not a complete waste.'

He smiled back at her. 'No kidding.'

Nick stepped away from the fire. 'Okay, we'll take a look at the lake.'

'Want to go with them?' Karen asked Benny.

'Yeah.'

'It's better that way,' she told the other two. 'It's better if we stay together.'

Benny stood up, wincing as the movement hurt his arm. The rest of his body felt stiff and sore, but he was glad to be included. Karen stayed close to his side as they headed for the lake.

Nick and Julie had the only working flashlights. They walked slowly along the shoreline, sweeping their beams over the water. The lights bent off to new angles where they penetrated. Through shallow water murky with swirling specks, Benny could see the bottom. The rocks down there were mossy. Patches of seaweed swayed with the currents. Farther out, the beams couldn't reach the bottom. They stopped a couple of feet below the surface, as if too weak to drive deeper into the gloom.

'Well,' Nick said, 'I still think they're out there. I'm going in.'

'No, that's crazy,' Julie said.

'Let's wait till morning,' Karen suggested. 'Even if you find them, the sleeping bags'll be soaking.'

'Most of the food should be okay,' Nick said. 'I don't now about you guys, but I'm starved.'

'Nick, you'll freeze.'

'We've got a good fire.' They followed him to the place where they'd left the packs. 'If she threw them in, she probably took them straight over from here.' He sat on the ground, put down the hatchet, and started to untie his boots.

Julie sat down beside him. 'If you're going in, so am I.'

'There's no point in both of us getting wet.'

'I don't care.'

'Julie.' His voice was firm. 'I mean it. You wait here.'

She looked at him. Her mouth opened. Then it shut. Her shoulders slumped a bit. 'Okay,' she muttered. 'If you don't want me to.'

With his boots and socks off, he stood up and took off his flannel shirt. He lowered his jeans and stepped out of them. He left his jockey shorts on, and walked stiffly to the edge of the lake. He rubbed his arms. 'Well' he said, 'here goes.' He charged forward, feet slapping into the water, splashing it high until he was knee-deep. Then he dived, hitting the surface flat out. Karen and Julie kept flashlights on him as he slid along silently below the waves. After a few seconds, he came up. He swung around, and wiped water off his face.

'You standing up?' Julie asked.

'Yeah.' The waves reached his chest.

'How is it?'

He answered with a groan of pain. Then he started walking.

Julie's light stayed on him. Karen aimed hers at the water just ahead of him. They walked slowly along the shore keeping to his pace.

He stopped. His shoulders wobbled slightly. 'What do you know!' he said. Then he ducked below the surface. His back was visible for a moment, pale in the flashlight beam rippling and quivering. Then it sank out of sight. Benny stared at the murky water. He counted silently to ten, and then Nick burst to the surface holding a grey bundle in front of him. He raised it from the water. It was Karen's pack. 'They're all right here,' he said.

'Fantastic,' Julie called.

He lifted the pack overhead, and took a step forward, and just behind him the water seemed to explode. His eyes bulged. His mouth sprang open. The pack fell from hands. It pounded down on his head, driving him under surface.

The flashlights clattered to the rocks. Karen and Julie, side by side, dashed into the lake. One flashlight was out. Benny snatched up the other. He saw Karen dive. She swam out fast, vanished under the surface, and came up pulling Nick by his arm. Julie splashed to his other side, grabbed his other arm. Nick's head came out of the water. They pulled him along between them. He was conscious. He was choking. When they reached shallow water, Benny saw that his legs were working.

'What happened?' Benny asked.

Nobody answered. Supporting Nick, the two women walked him onto dry land and lowered him to his knees. They eased him down flat.

The shiny red handle of a pocketknife jutted from his back.

Chapter Forty

'Oh, my God,' Julie muttered. 'Oh, my God.' She tugged the knife. Nick went rigid and cried out, but the blade, embedded a few inches below his right shoulder, wouldn't come out. She pulled harder. The handle slipped from her wet grip.

'I'll try,' Karen said.

'It must be in the bone,' Julie said. 'It's awfully deep.'

'Keep an eye on the lake, Benny.' Karen rubbed her right hand on her sweatshirt and clutched the knife. She pressed her left hand against Nick's bloody back.

'Aaaah!' He shuddered and dug his fingers into the earth as she yanked on the knife. She worked it back and forth and jerked it free. Nick's muscles unclenched. He lowered his face to the ground. He was gasping and sobbing.

'Let's get over to the fire,' Karen said.

He pushed himself to his hands and knees. Julie and Karen, gripping his arms, lifted him. He staggered between them as if his legs were too weak to support his weight.

When they reached the fire, they sat him down on a stump with his back to the blaze. Julie plucked at the knot of the wet bandanna around her neck. She loosened it, took off the kerchief, and squeezed out the water. Gently, she patted the wound. The gash was less than an inch in length. It bled freely, but the blood wasn't pumping out.

Karen said, 'It doesn't look too bad.'

'It doesn't feel too good,' Nick said. His voice sounded tight and shaky.

Julie folded the bandanna into a thick pad and pressed it firmly against the wound. Nick flinched.

'I'll get his clothes,' Karen said. She hurried away. Benny went with her.

Holding the pad in place, Julie leaned close to him. She pressed her face against his wet hair, kissed the top of his head. Her free hand reached down and rubbed his chest. He was trembling badly.

'I guess I lucked out,' he said.

'Real luck,' Julie muttered.

'She couldn't get the knife out. She blew it.'

'Sure.'

'This time,' he added.

Karen returned, holding Nick's clothes bundled in her arms. Benny had the hatchet.

'You did luck out,' Julie said. 'You've got dry clothes.

'We've gotta rig something to keep the bandage tight,' Karen said. 'Won't be easy. It's in a bad place.' She tugged Nick's belt from its loops. 'You'll have to keep your arm down.' She wrapped the belt around his upper back. Julie pressed it to the bandanna while Karen slipped one end under his left armpit. She pulled the other end over his right arm just below his shoulder, and buckled it tightly at his chest. 'How's that?'

'It's okay if I don't lift my arm.'

'Don't lift your arm.'

'Okay. Unless I have to.'

'I'll get him dressed,' Julie said.

'Fine.' Karen and Benny stepped away.

Karen sat on a rock so close to the fire that steam curled off the wet legs of her jeans. The heat felt very good, but it only warmed her front. The back of her sweatshirt and pants were frigid against her skin.

482

Benny, on the other side of the fire, stared at her through the flashing lenses of his glasses.

'Keep a sharp eye out,' she told him. 'We don't want anyone sneaking up.'

Nodding, he swung his legs sideways and stared towards the lake.

Karen stood up. She turned away from the fire, and peeled off her sweatshirt. She sighed as the warmth sooth her back. Scanning the darkness beyond the fire's glow, she wrung water from her sweatshirt. When she finished, she glanced over her shoulder at Benny. He was watching her. He quickly looked away, and she turned around. She held her sweatshirt over the flames. Steam rolled off it like smoke and was whipped away by the breeze.

Nick, to her left, had his flannel shirt draped over his back. One arm was in its sleeve. He stood up. Julie, crouching in front of him, pulled down his jockey shorts. He held onto her shoulder to steady himself while she pulled the shorts off his feet and helped him into his jeans.

Karen turned her eyes to Benny. He was staring at her. 'No fair peeking,' she warned, and he looked away.

The sweatshirt was still damp when she put it on, but at least it felt warm. For the moment. Sitting on the rock, she took off her boots and socks. She opened her jeans, and drew them down along with her panties.

Julie was putting socks on Nick.

The rock felt cold and gritty under Karen's buttocks, but she stayed seated as she wrung out her panties. She held them close to the fire while Benny continued to scan the shoreline and Julie finished with Nick's socks and boots. Then Karen stood, brushed some grit off her rump, and stepped into her panties. They felt warm and dry.

She turned around to heat up her back, and did her best to twist the water out of her jeans. The stiff material was difficult to work with. Finally, she gave up. She faced the fire and held them over the flames.

Nick swung around towards the fire. With his right arm inside the shirt, Julie hadn't been able to button it.

'How you doing?' Karen asked him.

'A little better. Kind of sick.'

Benny looked over his shoulder. Karen nodded to him, and he brought his legs around. He leaned closer to the fire.

'Guess she's trying to whittle us down,' Nick said.

'Apt phrase, that,' Karen told him.

'I think she's planning to freeze us to death,' Julie said. She stepped to the fire. Karen could see her shaking. 'What the hell,' she said. 'Since I'm freezing anyway, I might as well go ahead and get the packs.'

Nick gaped at her.

'Why not? I'm already soaked.'

'Let's just leave them till morning,' Karen said.

'We don't even know for sure our sleeping bags are wet. They're in stuff bags. They might be fairly dry. Besides, there's the food, the first-aid kit. Especially the first-aid kit. It's got disinfectant. We can put a real bandage on you, Nick. It'd sure be better than keeping you all strapped up.'

'You can't do it,' he said.

'We know right where the packs are.'

'What if *she's* there?' Benny said.

'You think she's gonna stay in the lake all night, just hoping we'll go back in?'

'Maybe she knows. Maybe she's *willing* you.'

'Don't be a dork.'

Karen sighed. 'It's not a smart idea, Julie. She could be waiting.'

'If she is, she hasn't got a knife.'

'We don't know that for sure,' Nick said.

'If she had another one, she would've used it on you.'

'You don't need a knife to kill someone,' Karen said.

'Killing can go both ways,' Julie said. She stepped over Nick and lifted the sheath knife from his lap. He clutched her wrist.

'You can't,' he said.

'We need those packs. Don't tell me no, or I'd just have to go against you.'

'Julie.'

She leaned closer and kissed his mouth. Then she whispered to him. He whispered back, and released her wrist. 'Keep the fire hot for me,' she said. 'I'll need it.'

She moved closer to the flames. She pulled off her belt and slid the sheath onto it. Sitting on a rock beside Benny she took off her boots and socks. She stripped down to her bra and panties. 'You want to heat these up for me?' she asked, offering the wet clothes to Karen.

'I'm going with you.'

'You don't have to.'

Karen smiled. 'Sure I do.'

'We'll all go,' Nick said.

'You and Benny aren't wet.'

'We can stay on shore. At least we'll be close by in case something happens.'

Julie nodded. She strapped the belt around her waist, and slid the knife to her hip. While Nick and Benny got to their feet, she arranged her clothing on rocks near the fire.

Karen spread her jeans over the rock where she'd been sitting.

'Let's get this show on the road,' Julie said.

Julie cringed as she stepped into the water. Earlier, when she'd rushed in to help Nick, she'd been so overwhelmed by the urgency of getting to him that she'd hardly noticed the cold. Now, her whole body trembled as she waded deeper.

'Dive under fast,' Nick suggested.

'Easy for you to say,' she called back.

Karen, just ahead of her and thigh-deep, was pulling up the bottom of her sweatshirt to keep it out of the water. She turned to face Julie. Her small pocketknife was clamped between her teeth. She took it out. 'This good?' she asked. Her voice was pitched higher than usual.

'Fine.'

'It'll be quicker if we both dive for 'em.'

'We'd just get tangled.' Julie moved past Karen. She took a sharp breath when the frigid water lapped her groin. With another step, she was covered to the waist. She sucked in her belly as if to draw it away from the painful touch. '*God*,' she gasped. She turned around. 'I'll pass you three. Take the last one myself.'

'Right,' Karen said.

'Then we'll get our asses over to the fire.'

'I'm for that.'

'Here goes!' she called to the others.

Nick, standing at the edge of the lake, waved his hatchet overhead. Benny, beside him, shone the flashlight in her eyes. The glare hurt. She flinched away from it and muttered, 'Thanks a lot.'

Then she waded out farther. The icy water soaked through her bra, washed over her shoulders. She turned to the right, and began searching. The water buoyed her up so her feet hardly touched the slippery rocks. She took long, slow steps, stroking the water with her arms to propel herself forward.

Then she toed something that wasn't rock. She explored it with her foot. It was a backpack. 'Got one,' she said.

Karen, waiting a couple of yards away in water up to her waist, nodded and clamped the knife between her teeth. Julie took a deep breath. Then she dived. She kept her eyes open, but saw only black as she clutched the sides of the pack, planted her feet on the slick rocks, and lifted. The pack felt nearly weightless.

She surfaced, and filled her lungs with air. Hugging the pack, she took a few slow-motion strides towards Karen. The woman reached out, took it from her, turned away and started wading for shore.

Julie swung around. She swam a few strokes. Lowering her legs, she searched with her feet. As they swept over the rocks, she glanced to the side. Karen was ashore, bending down, lowering the pack.

Her toes caught a strap. She plunged and gripped it with her right hand. It felt like leather. Must be Karen's Bergen. She pulled against it, and felt the pack start to rise as she brought her legs down towards the bottom.

Someone kicked her. The toenails raked her thigh. Ow! What's Karen doing *under* me?

It's not Karen!

A hand clawed her behind the shoulders, pulling her down. Another dug into her back. They held her tight against a bare, twisting body while legs hooked around her. Teeth ripped at her shoulder. Jerking with pain, she grasped long ropes of hair and tugged. The teeth held. They clamped harder. Her shoulder burned with agony. She wanted to cry out, but kept her lips clenched. The teeth released her. She tried to keep the head back, but it darted in, hair sliding through her fingers, and the teeth snapped shut on her collarbone.

She remembered Karen's warning. *You don't need a knife to kill someone.*

Just teeth. Rip out the jugular.

Knife.

The teeth let go.

Now for the throat.

She bent her head sideways and thrust her shoulder towards her ear. The teeth nipped her cheek, tried to get under her jaw. Then a spasm shook the woman as Julie rammed the six-inch blade into her back. Her fingernails pierced Julie's skin. She bucked and squirmed. Julie yanked the knife out and drove it in. She shoved a hand against the woman's face, pushed her away, and thrust the blade into her belly. Feet on the lake bottom, she clutched the knife with both hands and forced it upward.

* * *

Benny shone his flashlight on the water where Julie had gone under. The surface looked more turbulent there. She'd been down for a long time. Longer than it should take to lift up a pack.

Nick was watching, though. He didn't seem worried.

Karen was wading out quickly, but not as if she thought anything was wrong.

Then a head broke the surface. The beam of Benny's light reached to a face that sent a shock through him. The eyes were rolled up so that only the whites showed. The mouth was wide open, lips peeled back in a grimace. Blood spilled down the chin.

A scream filled Benny's throat. She was rising as if about to soar from the lake. Her shoulders burst from the surface. Her arms flapped wildly. Her bare breasts shook.

Then a pair of hands came up, clutching her belly. No, not exactly. But she wasn't about to fly, she was being lifted by those hands and then a head appeared below her.

It had to be Julie.

For just a moment, the woman – the witch – was above Julie's head, out of the water entirely, her naked body writhing and beating the air. Julie bent as she swung the body over her. It hit the water headfirst and threw up a frothy shower.

Chapter Forty-one

Nick stared, frozen with shock, as the body surged up out of the lake. The twisted face was not Julie's. The squirming figure kicked at the sky, and vanished with a huge splash.

Karen lunged forward, knife in her upraised hand.

Rushing in, Nick saw her reach down. Julie was gone. Where? Was she hurt, drowning? He was waist-deep and wading against the heavy push of the water when her head popped to the surface.

Off to Nick's side, Karen's left arm came up. Her hand was wrapped with black hair. She raised the woman's head. Water and blood spilled from the gaping mouth. As the shoulders appeared, she drew back her knife to strike. She hesitated. She lowered the knife. She looked at Nick. 'Dead?'

'Looks that way.'

Julie waded towards them. 'She dead?'

'What happened?' Nick asked.

'Got her with your knife.' As Julie approached, the water level dropped. The flashlight beam found her. She squinted and turned her face away. Nick groaned at the sight of her torn, bloody jaw and shoulder.

'God, Julie.'

'I'm okay. Let's take her ashore.'

'I've got her,' Karen said.

'Good,' 'cause I've got one of the packs.'

Nick waited for them to trudge past, Karen towing the body by its hair. It was facedown in the water, floating along, its back and outstretched legs pale in the moonlight. Nick held the hatchet in his left hand, ready for use, but he saw no sign of life.

Julie was the first to reach the shore. She dropped the pack and returned. She and Karen each took an arm. They dragged the body onto dry land. Benny shone his light on it. Kneeling down, Nick looked at the wounds on its back, two raw pulpy gashes that slowly filled with blood.

'You sure got her,' Benny muttered.

Julie turned the body over, and Nick recoiled at the sight. Benny gasped. Karen turned away, clutching her mouth. Julie muttered, '*Jesus.*'

The torso was split from just above the mons almost to the rib cage. Entrails had spilled from the opening. They looked like a pile of dead snakes.

Julie backed away, shaking her head. Nick went to her. He dropped the hatchet and drew her against him. She put her arms around him. She felt wet and cold. She was shaking badly. 'It's all right,' Nick said.

'I did that,' she muttered.

'You had to.'

'Doesn't make it any better.'

'I know. I've been through it. Remember?'

'Yeah.' She pressed her face to the side of his neck. He felt the brush of her eyelashes. His right hand, still pinned low by the belt, caressed the chilly skin of her flank.

'Let's go to the fire,' he said.

'I want to get the other packs.'

'Are you nuts?'

'Yeah. But you love me anyway, right?'

'I sure do.' He kissed her mouth. She hugged him fiercely, apparently forgetting about his wound until he flinched with pain.

'I'm sorry.'

'That's okay. I hurt *you* last night.'

She smiled up at him. 'You sure did. And don't you forget it.'

'I'll never forget it.'

'Do you still respect me?'

'No.'

She laughed softly.

Nick squeezed her rump through the damp, silky fabric of her panties, and she squirmed against him. He felt a warm surge of pleasure.

'Don't make me feel too good,' she warned. 'I won't want to go back in.'

'I don't want you to go back in.'

'Duty calls.' After a final, brief kiss, she eased herself away.

Karen was crouched near the shore, Benny holding the light for her as she rummaged through one of the packs. She took out a plastic case. 'First-aid kit,' she said. She raised it towards Nick. 'Why don't you take Julie over to the fire and patch her up?'

'I'm all right,' Julie said.

'You're bleeding all over yourself.'

'I'm gonna get the other packs.'

'I'll do that,' Karen told her. 'You and Nick go over and take care of yourselves.'

'Are you sure?'

'Yeah. Go on.'

'Thanks,' Nick said.

He took Julie's hand, and they walked side by side towards the glow of the campfire.

'Maybe you'd better not,' Benny said.

Karen pulled a dripping T-shirt from her pack, and stood up. 'Why's that?' she asked.

'I don't like it.'

'She's dead, Benny. It's over.'

He turned aside and shone his beam on the body. It was still there. It hadn't moved at all.

Karen covered his hand. She pressed his thumb, sliding it back, switching off the light. 'Don't look at it,' she said. 'Why don't you go on over to the fire? I'll be along in a few minutes.'

'I want to stay with you.'

'Okay, but keep the light off.'

'I won't look at her.'

'At me, either?'

'Huh?'

'I don't want my sweatshirt any wetter than it already is,' she said. She wrung out the white T-shirt. Turning away, she pulled off her sweatshirt. Benny swallowed hard. He felt a little breathless as he stared at her moonlit back. The panties looked like a dim shadow across her buttocks. When she raised her arms to pull the T-shirt on, he glimpsed the side of a breast. He felt guilty about looking, but couldn't help himself. Just as he hadn't been able to keep his eyes away when she'd been at the fire.

She pulled the T-shirt down to her waist and turned to him. The way it clung, he wanted to shine the light on her. But he didn't.

'Okay,' she said. 'I'm going in.'

'Hurry.'

He watched her wade out into the lake. She was pale gainst the black water. She looked as if her legs were gone, as if they'd been chopped off just below the surface. The image made him uneasy. He glanced at the body of the witch, only a couple of yards from where he stood, then turned away. He switched on his flashlight, and played it over the ground until he spotted the hatchet where Nick had let it drop. He went to it. He put the flashlight into a pocket of his parka, and bent over. Pain throbbed through his arm, but faded to a dull ache as he straightened up with the hatchet in his left hand.

He stared out at Karen. She was moving slowly to the side, only her head and pale shoulders visible above the black.

Stepping close to the shore, he looked down at her sweatshirt draped over one of the packs. He remembered the soft feel of it when he snuggled with her last night. Then he pictured the way she'd looked in the glow of the firelight when she heated it over the flames and didn't know he was watching. *No fair peeking*, she'd said.

The witch is naked.

She's ugly and she's dead. It'd be perverted to look at her.

But he did. Her breasts, lit by the moon, were grey like stones. The nipples looked almost black.

He glanced towards the campfire. Julie was seated facing the fire. Nick, behind her, was bandaging her shoulder.

He checked the lake. Karen's head ducked under the surface, and she was gone.

With a few quick steps, he was standing over the witch. He pressed the hatchet between his knees. He took the flashlight from his pocket. He shone it down on her. In the pale glow, her breasts looked smooth. They were dingy white. He could see a network of blue veins through the skin. The nipples were very large. Their red-brown flesh had an odd, blue tinge. His heart was thundering. He felt an erection growing. He felt dirty, nauseated. But he couldn't look away.

He had never touched a woman's naked breast. He wondered what one would feel like.

No! She's dead!

Or maybe she isn't dead, and she's willing me.

He switched off the light and took a quick step backward.

The hatchet dropped from between his knees.

He crouched to pick it up, and he was down close to her, gazing at her moonlit breasts. He reached out his trembling left hand.

She grabbed it by the wrist.

Nick slammed against Julie's back, knocking her forward off the stump. She flung up an arm to protect her head. It rammed the fireplace stones, caving them in. The weight left her back. Raising her head, she saw Nick tumble through the fire in a shower of sparks, a filthy naked man clinging to his back. They were only in the flames for an instant before they rolled through the other low wall. Julie shoved herself up. Nick was on his hands and knees, the man straddling his back, choking him with a forearm just as Fish had choked him.

Julie grabbed a rock. It seared her fingers and fell.

Nick rolled onto his side. She glimpsed the face of the man, and gasped as she recognised it. He was the man who had raped Karen, who had tried to rape her. He was the man Nick had killed nearly a week ago.

Behind her, a twig snapped. She spun around. A teenaged girl was lurching towards her. The girl's tangled hair was full of dirt. Soil clung to her grey skin. Bite marks marred her shoulders and breasts.

Julie leaped away from the reaching hands. The girl turned and kept coming. 'Get away!' Julie cried out.

And then she saw a man staggering out of the darkness behind the girl. His head was down, hanging loosely, swaying and wobbling with each step.

She heard herself whimpering as she backed away. Her heel came down on a rock, and she nearly fell. Catching her balance, she crouched and grabbed the rock. It was warm from the fire, heavy, with jagged edges. She hurled it at the girl. It struck her nose and wide-open mouth. Her head was knocked back by the impact, but she didn't cry out or wince or even blink her eyes. The rock bounced off her face. It left her nose torn, her upper lip mashed, her teeth broken. There was no bleeding.

Silently, she bent over and picked up the rock.

The man was at her side.

Julie thrust her hand into the fire. She grabbed a stick by its unburnt end and yanked it out. The other end blazed like a torch. She swung it back and forth in front of the two, but they kept coming as if they didn't care. She backed away. Lurching to the side, she shoved the torch hard against the back of the man on top of Nick. It had no effect. She jabbed his head with it. His tangled hair caught fire. It blazed. But he stayed on Nick's squirming body and kept on choking him.

She flung her burning stick at the others. It missed the man's hanging head as he ducked to pick up a rock. Julie glimpsed the wound at the back of his neck – as if a wedge had been chopped out.

She grabbed a foot of the man on Nick. She wrapped both hands around its cold ankle and pulled, straining backward, dragging him. Nick pried the arm away and shoved the man off him.

Julie yelped as a rock hammered her bandaged shoulder. She dropped the foot and whirled around. The girl swung again. The rock slammed the side of Julie's face. Her head burst with pain. She stumbled backward, stepped on a leg of the man sprawled behind her, and fell on him. His arms latched around her waist. They squeezed her breath out. She felt the heat of his charred scalp against her back.

The girl bent over her with the rock. Julie kicked at her. The man with the drooping head shoved her aside and threw himself onto Julie. She thrust her hands at him, but her arms folded. He smashed down on her, forehead pounding her face. Through her daze, she heard a yell. She felt a crushing weight for a moment. Then it was gone. She opened her eyes. The man was still on her but his head was gone. Nick had it hugged to his chest as he rolled. He flung it away and got to his hands and knees. His terrified eyes met Julie's. Then the girl pounced on his back, driving him down.

'No!' Julie shrieked as the girl swung her rock at Nick's head.

He threw his arms behind his head, and they took the blow.

Something hit Julie's ear. She cried out and held it, and pain erupted in her fingers as the headless man pounded her again with his rock. The arms around her middle let go. With a burst of hope, she thrust at the man's shoulders, forcing him up a bit. He dropped the rock. He clenched her throat with both hands. She gazed at the pulpy stump of his neck as he forced her down.

She felt a tug at her chest. Heard ripping cloth. Felt icy hands.

The corpse under Julie fondled and squeezed her breasts while the one on top strangled her.

The hand snatching Benny's wrist had caught him off balance. Numb with horror, he tried to jerk loose. The fingers held him tight. They yanked, and he fell forward onto the witch. He screamed as his face shoved against a breast. His broken arm burst with pain.

As he lay across her, kneeing the ground, she forced his left arm up behind his back. She grabbed the wrist with her other hand. There was a sudden tug, a thrust at his elbow. He heard a ripping, popping sound as his arm was wrenched out of its shoulder socket. He shrieked and passed out.

Karen was wading backward, chest-deep in the lake, dragging both packs by their straps when she heard an outcry from shore. She swung around. She stared. The straps slid from fingers suddenly gone numb.

She didn't know, couldn't believe what she was seeing.

Silhouettes of tangled bodies squirming on the ground near the scattered campfire.

A moonlit struggle near the shore.

She lunged forward and swam, clawing the water, kicking with all her strength. Her mind reeled as she raced for shore. What the hell was going on? Where had all those people come from? What if she couldn't help? What if she got there only to find the others dead? Oh, God, no. Please!

Her plunging hand raked the rocky bottom. She shoved herself to her feet and dashed, splashing the water high. She lanced towards the fire. What's happening? Then she fixed her gaze on the strange shapes just ahead of her. She felt dry ground under her feet.

It was the woman – the witch – sprawled on her back. Motionless legs stuck out from her side. Benny? The hands were on his head, pushing his face to her torn belly, smothering him.

Karen grabbed Benny by the hips and yanked him back. As she dragged him clear, the woman rolled, snarling, clutched the hatchet, and crawled towards them. Karen leaped over Benny. She stomped the hatchet flat against the round and slammed her other foot into the woman's face. The head snapped backward. Karen grabbed the chin, the base of the skull. She twisted hard. The body flipped onto its back. As the head lifted, she drove her heel down, crashing the head against the rocky earth, smashing the nose. The body went limp.

Grabbing the hatchet, she whirled around. Benny raised his head. 'Hang in there,' she gasped. 'Gotta . . . the others . . . all hell . . .' She started towards the fire.

'Karen!' the boy yelled.

She looked back at him as she ran. He had turned himself onto his back, was sitting up.

'Come back!' he shouted. 'Listen to me! I know!'

Karen raced back to him.

'Kill the witch!' he blurted. 'Quick!'

'She can't—'

'She's not dead!'

If we'd listened to him before . . .

Karen ran, dropped to her knees. The woman below her was mumbling, staring up at the sky.

'Quick!' Benny yelled.

Nick had thrust himself up to his hands and knees, but the girl stayed on his back. The rock pounded his head. He threw himself over, rolled onto her. Her legs encircled his hips. An arm crossed his throat. A hand reached up over his face holding the jagged rock and he knew he couldn't get his arms up in time to block the blow.

Karen swung the hatchet down. It broke through the woman's forehead. The body jumped and twitched. She raise the hatchet, and chopped again.

497

* * *

The rock fell. It bounced off Nick's forehead. The arm at his throat went limp. The legs dropped away from his side.

He flung himself clear of the girl. She was motionless on the ground. He pushed himself to his feet. As he staggered over to her, Julie, pressed between the two naked men, tore the clutching hands of the headless one away from her throat. She was gasping and sobbing. Nick grabbed the man's shoulder and hip, and rolled him off. As the body tumbled aside, a pair of hands slid away from Julie breasts.

She raised her arms to Nick.

He gripped her wrists, and pulled her up.

They stepped away from the bodies. Nick eased her against him. For a long time, they held each other gently and wept.

Chapter Forty-two

Scott heard a soft knocking on the door of his hospital room. 'Come in,' he said. He lay his book aside, and watched the door swing open.

Karen stepped in. She tilted her head to one side, and raised her eyebrows. 'Could you use a little company?'

'Get over here,' he said, trying to sound gruff.

She looked lovely, her hair soft and glowing around her face, brushing her bare shoulders as she approached. Her dress had spaghetti straps. Its silken blue fabric clung to her breasts, was drawn in at the waist by a gold chain belt, floated around her thighs.

At his bedside, she flicked a finger against one of his hoisted casts. 'How you been?'

'Lonely. *Where* you been?'

'On an outing.' She set her purse on the floor, and bent over him. She stroked his cheek.

'Looks like you got some sun,' he said. He fingered a tiny curl of peeling skin on the side of her nose.

'I missed you,' she said.

'I kept waiting for you at visiting hours.'

'I'm sorry.'

'No you. No Julie, no Benny. Tanya came by a few times, but it wasn't quite the same.'

She kissed him. Her lips felt chapped, but they felt very good and he wrapped his arms around her and caressed her. He seemed to sink into her, as if joining with a part of himself that had vanished and left him empty and returned.

Returned from an outing.

He released her.

She sat on the edge of the bed, and held herself steady with a hand on his chest as she drew a leg up beneath her. He stroked her bare thigh. 'This outing,' he said.

'We didn't want you to worry.'

'You went back to the mountains?'

She nodded. 'Julie, Benny, Nick and me.'

'Everyone's all right?'

'We survived. Julie and Benny are waiting in the hall. Julie thought I should see you first.'

'The kid's got style.'

'That she does. You've got a couple of great kids.'

'They have their moments. How's Nick?'

'You know about Flash?'

'Yeah. Tanya told me.' He sighed. He squeezed Karen's knee. 'He was a good guy.'

'Nick's very proud of him. Nick's also madly in love with your daughter.'

'Of course,' Scott said.

She laced her fingers with his.

'O'Tooles are a lovable sort,' he added.

'Don't I know it.'

He stared into her eyes. 'God, I'm glad you're back.'

'Me, too.'

'You shouldn't have gone without me.'

'You would've done us a lot of good. Two broken legs. Old gimpy.'

'How'd it go out there?'

'It got hairy.'

'I assume the good guys won.'

'You assume correctly. The witch is vanquished. The curse went with her.'

'Want to tell me about it?'

'Nope. Benny wants to tell you about it. He's very insistent on that point. If it weren't for him, things might've gone . . . a bit sour.'

'He saved the day, huh?'

'I'd say so.' Karen slipped her hand free. She bent over and lifted her purse from the floor. As she opened it, Scott slid his hand up the smooth bare skin of her thigh. She took a felt-tipped pen from her purse. She didn't try to stop his hand. She caught her breath and arched her back.

'Well now,' he said.

'Take the pen,' she whispered.

'And what should I do with it?'

'Autograph your son's casts.'

'*Casts?*'

'In the plural.'

'Oh, no.'

'Oh, yes.'

He took the pen from her hand. 'Any more surprises?'

'Not at the moment.'

'Then give me another kiss.'

'The kids are waiting.'

'We'll make it brief.'

'But not too brief?'

He drew her down to him and held her and kissed her moist, parted lips, and wanted never to stop.

'Christ, gang!' Julie called from the doorway. 'Break it up!'